Put Me Back
Together
↔

Put Me Back Together

Scars Run Deep 1

Lola Rooney

DEEP DARK PRESS

For You

1

The day I met him was the coldest of the year, and I wanted an ice cream cone. That's why I was out on a Thursday night wearing sweatpants and my ugly glasses—the ones with my old prescription, which I only yanked out when I accidentally sat on the cute ones with my new prescription. It had been a long day. I was also wearing a pair of Uggs, which had survived three winters in Vancouver in pristine condition, but now, after just three months of winter in Kingston, were covered in so many stains from the slush and salt on the roads that they looked like they'd been flushed down the toilet. The wind bit at my ears and cheeks as I trudged down the sidewalk. I pulled up the fur-lined hood of my jacket just as the phone in my pocket buzzed ominously. Okay, not really ominously, because ominous buzzing isn't a thing. But it was still pretty weird. Nobody ever texted me, except...

    Em: Omg, this party is cray-cray. Like, there are no words.
    Me: Give me the highlights.
    Em: Guy just flashed his junk at me. Girl just walked by wearing bottle caps over her nips.

Me: So it's a naked party? Tell me you still have your clothes on.
Em: Most of them.
Me: !!
Em: RELAX! I took my shoes off. But if you're so worried, come and
   join me!
Me: Not that worried.
Em: :(Don't stay home wearing your ugly glasses all night!
Me: Don't pull your pants down for anyone!
Em: No promises. ;)

A part of me hated that my sister, Emily, was out at a party getting drunk and eyeing genitalia while I was on my way to Dairy Queen, but not for the reason you might think. I had no interest in going to some obnoxious party where I wouldn't know anyone—in fact, that was a perfect example of something I would avoid at all costs. What I didn't like was thinking of her there on her own, without me to look after her. I had to remind myself that Emily was never on her own. She'd probably rolled into the place with an entourage. I was the one who found myself alone when Em went out on a Friday night. I was the one who didn't have any friends.

Not that it bothered me. I liked it better that way.

As I reached the corner I looked longingly down Division Street. Division was the fastest way to get to Dairy Queen, the alternative being a twenty-minute detour down University Avenue. If I turned now, I could be back home in twenty minutes, happily riding my sugar high as I defrosted my toes on the radiator. But Division was also home to "party central," a trio of houses rented out to a horde of the most horrifying species of university student: the boozy jock. After a memorable interlude on this block during my first week in Kingston—I stepped in a pile of vomit on the sidewalk, had the drunken vomiter himself ask me if I wanted to take a ride with him (the real meaning of "ride" only made clear to me later when my sister broke it down for me), and then watched him vomit again, this time on my shoes—I'd made a firm rule *never* to go down the block again, especially when there was a party going on, most especially a last-day-of-winter-break party. Already I could feel the thump of the bass in my chest, even from halfway down the street.

Biting my lip, I stared up at the interminable red light, willing it to change. Just being this close to partyland was making me break out in a cold sweat. The idea that this might be the party Emily was at didn't make me feel any better. I felt a hot tightening around my ribs as I imagined her running out to find me and dragging me inside, the suffocating crush of bodies, the seizure-inducing music, the roomful of eyes following me, watching me, and absolutely nowhere to hide…

Giving up on the light, I crossed the street at a gallop and narrowly missed getting hit by a minivan full of old men who shook their fists at me.

Like I said, avoid *at all costs*.

I tried to focus on the ice cream cone I planned on getting—one scoop… no, two scoops… no, at this point it was looking like a sundae, with brownies, and nuts, and extra hot fudge—to keep my mind off my near-death experience and freezing toes. Stupid Uggs. My mother had told me they weren't adequate footwear—they were slippers. I hated when she was right. Then I heard voices in the empty lot coming up on my right, and all thoughts of ice cream vanished.

It was a corner lot, snow-covered and dotted with doggy pee stains. Three big guys were hunched over the bushes by the fence dividing the lot from the sidewalk I was on. They were refugees from the party, I had to assume, judging by their lack of coats, overall drunken demeanor, and the fact that they were laughing at a clump of bushes. Two of them had beer bottles in their hands, which I was sure was totally legal. There was another guy over at the far end of the lot, but I didn't get a really good look at him.

"Here, kitty, kitty!" said Drunk Idiot Number One.

"Pour some beer on its head," said Drunk Idiot Number Two.

"Ow! It scratched me!" That was Drunk Idiot Number One again.

"Oh my God, you're such a baby," said Drunk Idiot Number Three. "Want me to kiss it better?"

I stared through the chain-link fence as One and Three

scuffled with each other. Then Three slipped on the snow and
fell.

"You're such an asshole. I think I broke my ass."

"I'll show you a broken ass!" said Two, launching himself
on top of him.

Interestingly, I wasn't the least bit nervous about being
spotted by these three. It helped that they were morons and
weren't paying me any attention. I would have just walked on,
but something held me back.

"I got it!" said One.

He held a small orange cat up by its scruff as his buddies
scrambled to their feet. They all looked tickled. The cat looked
pissed as hell. When Three leaned in to look at him, he took a
swipe at his nose and missed by millimeters.

"He's a mean little guy," said Three. "Quick, get the
bottle!"

I looked at the three boys, the howling cat, and the bottle,
and that's when I surprised myself.

I stepped into the lot.

"What're you doing to that cat?" I demanded.

They all spun around, Three almost losing his balance
again. Two dropped his bottle. It was possible I'd yelled a little.

"We're gonna get him drunk!" One announced gleefully,
just as the cat wiggled out of his grasp and hightailed it back
into the bushes.

The other two swore and crouched down to find him again.

"Like hell you are!" I said.

Shoving my way past One, I stepped right over Two and
placed my foot into the closest bush, the one that was too
small for the cat to hide in. As soon as I smashed the branches
down, the cat shot out between Three's legs, making him fall
over for real this time. The rest of us chased after the cat, but I
grabbed him first, mainly because they were sloppily drunk and
couldn't run in a straight line to save their lives. I stuck him
inside my jacket, zipping it closed over his fur, and folded my
arms to hold him in there. I could feel him shivering against
me, his heart beating *rat-a-tat-tat*.

"Aww, come on," One whined. "Give him back!"

"There's no way in hell I'm giving him back to you," I said. "He's frozen and terrified. He's too small to be outside in this weather."

"We weren't going to hurt him," Two said, stepping forward, his massive chest exactly level with my eyes.

He was standing a little too close for comfort, and I took a step back.

He said, "Just let me see his little head. I want to pet him."

I didn't like the dark look in his eye, or the way he was towering over me.

"Not on your life," I said.

Out of the corner of my eye I noticed One coming up on my right side. As soon as Three picked himself up out of the snow, they'd have me cornered with my back to the fence. My heartbeat began to quicken as I took them all in. Suddenly they didn't seem quite so harmless or quite so drunk. Moments like this, guys like this, always reminded me of Brandon. Suddenly it was six years ago and I was thirteen again, peering into a boy's face, wondering what kind of violence might explode out of him. As much as I'd tried to change my life, to fix it, to control it, I was still that same girl, perpetually taken by surprise.

Not that I was going to let anything like that happen to me again.

"Listen, you little fuckers—" I began, but I was quickly interrupted by a smooth voice coming out of the darkness to my left.

"Hey, fellas," the voice said. "What's the trouble?"

As he stepped into the light of the streetlamp, I realized it was the guy who'd been standing over at the other end of the lot by himself. I'd forgotten all about him. His tone was calm and friendly, as if trouble wasn't something he expected to find, or, if he did, it wouldn't be anything he couldn't handle. I frowned a little at him. People who felt that comfortable in their own skin made me nervous, though that didn't stop me from taking a small step in his direction. Mr. Calm and

Collected was immensely preferable to the three menacing drunkards.

The reaction of Drunk Idiots One, Two, and Three was fascinating. They each tried to arrange themselves into a casual pose, while at the same time standing up straighter. One even put his hands behind his back, like his military commander had just walked in. They looked like Huey, Dewey, and Louie when Uncle Donald had just caught them red-handed.

Turning back to Mr. Calm and Collected, I felt a flash of recognition. Wasn't he important around campus, something to do with sports? It all started to make sense now. He was like their God.

"Hey, man," said Two. "What's up? Haven't seen you around much lately."

"Yeah, where you been?" said Three. "You missed George's party."

"Did I?" he said, his eyes focused somewhere in the middle distance over their heads. I noticed that, though he was not as alarmingly broad as One, he was taller than him. "I was just waiting for my girl here."

He turned to me and flashed his dimples, which were so pronounced they were almost distracting. I stared at them, still frowning.

Tipping his head toward me, he said in a quiet voice, "You're late, you know."

Suddenly all four of them were looking at me, waiting for a reply. "Well, there was ice cream," I blurted, flustered, "and then there was the cat, and…"

He put his arm around my shoulders and I had to resist the urge to take a big step away from him, reminding myself that he was the nice one. He was helping me out. Warmth flowed through his coat and into my side. I pressed my lips together to stifle a nervous giggle, which came out as a squawky gurgle instead. Basically, I sounded like a drowning seagull. I couldn't remember the last time anyone besides Emily had been this close to me.

"Did he get out again?" he said, concern creasing his forehead.

Then he turned to his moronic disciples. "Thanks for helping her find him, guys," he said. "She loves that kitty. She'd have been heartbroken if he'd been hit by a car or drenched in beer by some heartless thug."

They all nodded in unison.

"No problem, glad to help," Three said as he began to back away.

"I love cattens," said One.

"Don't forget Lori's party tomorrow. Taylor will be there. See you there, man," Two said as he ambled after the others.

Mr. Calm and Collected waved to them as they walked away, waiting until they were out of earshot to mutter, "Not likely."

His arm was still around my shoulder, though he hardly seemed aware of it, unlike me, who felt every inch of him burning into my side like a fiery brand.

I said, "Thanks. You didn't have to do that."

He let go of my shoulder (finally!) but didn't step away from me. Instead he gazed down at me, a smile slipping over his lips. I was practically shaking now, the proximity of this strange guy and all his heat getting the better of me. For a second I thought he was going to reach up and touch my cheek, but instead his fingers snagged on the zipper of my jacket.

"How's he doing?" he said. "My cat back home would flip out if he was trapped outside on a night like this."

Painfully conscious of how close his head was to mine and kind of irritated at the way he continued to invade my personal space, I looked down at the little orange head emerging from the neck of my jacket. "I think he's…"

When he reached forward to smooth the fur on the little cat's head, the tip of his finger dragged lightly across my neck. The feeling was electric and alarmed me so much that I uncrossed my arms and stepped away from him. The cat tumbled down the inside of my jacket and landed at our feet before scampering off again.

We both swore and ran after him, a chase that lasted a lot longer than the first one—the cat seemed to have smartened up—and when he was finally safe inside Mr. Calm and Collected's jacket, we were both out of breath.

"I have to hand it to him," he said. "He's a determined little sucker. We'd better get him home."

I adjusted the glasses on my face, raising my eyebrows at him. "You realize that isn't actually my cat, right?"

"Well, he doesn't have a collar, and he's so skinny. I doubt he's eaten for a while. Seems like he's your cat now."

He grinned at me like this was my lucky day.

"I don't want a cat," I said, shaking my head forcefully. "Why don't you take him?"

"I have two roommates who are an awful lot like *that*." He gestured after the three idiots. "What's the matter, Hero? You don't need a furry friend?"

"No, I don't need friends. I... no, I don't need anything."

I glared at the ground. Had I actually just said that out loud?

He cocked his head and squinted at me, still grinning slightly. God, did this guy ever stop smiling? It was making me hostile.

"I recognize you from somewhere," he said.

"Yeah, I recognize you, too," I said distractedly, freely using my peripheral vision to scout out my escape route. "Aren't you the... you know... goalie... quarterback... captain person?"

He burst out laughing. "What?" he said. "What sport do you think I play?"

"I don't know," I said. "The one with the ball?"

Sports weren't something I made any kind of an effort to keep track of. They lived in a dusty part of my brain along with high school science, French cooking, and other things I never thought about.

Still chuckling, he said, "I guess that rules out hockey."

"I guess," I said, looking pointedly out at the street now. "So I should probably go."

"Great, where to?" he said, falling into step beside me.

"What?" I said sharply.

He looked at me with an expression of mock alarm, which dissolved quickly into a smile.

Again with the smile.

"No," I corrected him. "I'm going home, and you should go to wherever it is you were going."

"I've got your cat in my shirt, Hero," he said. "Wherever you go, I go."

Inside his *shirt?* For some reason I found myself blushing crimson, which really pissed me off.

"Why do you keep calling me that?" I snapped as we made our way up the street. He walked incredibly slowly, like he didn't have a care in the world. People who walked like that in this kind of weather made no sense to me.

"You saved this cat from death-by-beer, didn't you?" he said. "Sounds pretty heroic to me."

"Well, it wasn't," I said. "Besides, you helped. You saved him, too."

"So what are you saying, I'm your hero?" He gave me a warm look, showing off his dimples again.

Oh God, the dimples.

"I'm saying walk faster," I said, powering ahead. "What the hell is wrong with you? It's minus twenty-five out here."

"Whatever you say," he said from behind me.

The wind began to blow and I pulled my hood back up around my head, but I still heard him add, "Hero."

At my apartment door I fiddled frantically with the lock, which had decided to choose this moment to be temperamental. Somehow I'd managed to *not* lose Mr. Calm and Collected on the street, at the door to my building, or on the stairs up to my floor. He was standing next to me right now, still holding the cat inside his clothes—though this was something I'd decided not to think about ever again—and was leaning down to examine my lock in the way of friendly, helpful neighbours. I was now using nearly all of my energy to try to think of a way to get rid of him and the cat.

Finally, the lock clicked open and I backed into my apartment, holding the door tight to my shoulder so he couldn't see inside.

"Thanks for walking me," I said with a lot of head nodding. "You didn't have to. But it was really nice of you, so thanks. Thanks. Thank you."

I'd never thanked someone so many times in my life. It made me feel tired. I liked it better when no one was around to help me, so there was no one to thank but myself.

"I think he's asleep," he whispered to me. I found myself staring at his lips, which were nicely full and pink and soft looking.

Then—and I blinked a lot while this was happening to be sure I wasn't seeing things—he pulled open his jacket and started unbuttoning his shirt. I glimpsed tanned skin and a smooth chest before I looked down, painfully embarrassed. When I looked up again he was holding out a bundle of fur. I gathered the animal into my arms and leaned against the doorframe. My cheeks were throbbing with heat now, which I was sure he could see, and I simply didn't know where to look. I frowned at the hardwood floor.

"I'm Lucas, by the way," he said.

When I glanced up I saw that he was leaning down to peer into my downturned face, his expression curious. At least he wasn't laughing at me.

"Katie," I mumbled.

"Thanks for rescuing me, Katie," he said. "I'll never forget it."

He began walking down the hall, back toward the stairs.

"Rescuing you?" I said. "I didn't—"

"What was that?" he said, cupping his hand around his ear. "I can't hear you, Hero."

"Lucas," I called, leaning out the door. He stopped at the top of the stairs and looked back at me.

I said, "Don't call me Hero." And then I shut the door.

2

"So he gave the cat to you?" Emily said, her voice muffled because her face was pressed into my pillow.

"Yes. No. It was a weird night," I said. "It wasn't his cat."

I set the new litter box on the ground and held up the kitty litter bag. "How much am I supposed to put in?" I said. "Do I fill it up all the way?"

I pushed the curtains farther open so I could read the instructions on the bag. Emily moaned and pulled the pillow over her head.

"No light!" she whined pitifully.

I gave the back of her head a look and yanked the curtains closed a little more.

"I told you to drink two glasses of water before bed."

My sister rolled over grouchily, holding a hand over her eyes. "Sorry, *Mom*," she said, "but since *I* don't have my own apartment like *some* people, I have to *share* a fridge with Manic Melanie, who drinks all the bottled water like she's filling her camel humps. *I* don't have the *luxury* of my own full-sized refrigerator."

Rolling my eyes, I pulled the cat bowls and brush out of my shopping bag. "You could have just gone to the bathroom. Doesn't it have a sink? Or does the school deprive you of the luxury of hand washing, too?"

"It was *so far* away!" Emily cried. "Besides, I didn't feel that bad once I was lying down. The room wasn't even really spinning. This hangover is bullshit."

I shook my head. We had this same conversation almost every weekend. The only difference was that this was a Monday morning and my dear sister had a European history test in about forty minutes.

"I offered to get a bigger apartment so we could be roommates," I said. "And what did you say?"

She pressed the pillow into her face again. "I'm living in Res. Res is where all the fun happens."

"Right!" I said brightly. "And aren't we having so much fun right now?"

Emily moaned again. "I hate you."

When my twin sister had chosen to go to the same university as me, a whopping four thousand kilometers from home, I'd fully expected that we would room together. But Emily wanted to have the full university experience: living in residence on campus, getting a meal plan, Frosh Week, shared bathrooms, and no privacy—all things that horrified me. Just imagining all those people in such close quarters made me break out in hives. I preferred my little apartment on a quiet street close to the Dairy Queen and just a five-minute walk from campus. It had seemed like a good idea to get some separation at first, but the truth was I missed my sister a lot, even if I saw her every day. She had this whole new life filled with all these new people I could barely keep track of. She was discovering the world and putting herself out there. She was opening up to new things, while I, as usual, remained closed up tight, as I had been for the past six years. She'd come all the way here with me; she hadn't left me behind. But it was hard for me not to think of it that way sometimes, and not to envy everything about her life, even her hangovers.

My sister was living her life while I was doing my best to avoid mine.

"So back to the cat," Emily said, "which I still don't believe really exists—"

"I told you, he's under the couch somewhere," I said, although to be honest I had no idea where he was. Last night he'd leaped out of my arms and wiggled his way under the couch, and I hadn't seen him since. I prayed he hadn't clawed anything or thrown up anywhere. Already the idea of what he would deposit in the litter box was grossing me out.

"Why did this guy give him to you, again?"

"His name is Lucas," I said. I ripped open the bag of cat food and poured some into the bowl by my bedside table.

Suddenly, Em sat upright in bed and stared at me. "Lucas who?" she said. "What's his last name?"

"I don't know," I said. "He didn't tell me."

"Was he tall, dark brown hair, golden eyes, rippling muscles?" Her eyes were glued to my face. It reminded me of the time in fifth grade when I'd recounted to her how I'd stolen a pair of Christian Lewis's underwear from his bedroom during Carrie Lewis's sleepover birthday party. That was before *it* happened, back when I was adventurous, back when I chose dare instead of truth every time. Back when my sister had been known as "the quiet twin."

"He was wearing a coat. Well, until he took his shirt off."

Now I had my sister's full, undivided attention. She swiveled toward me, pulling her legs under her.

"Was he so gorgeous he made your knees go weak? Did he smile all the time, the hottest smile ever, with this little twinkle in his eye? Come on, tell the truth."

Yup and yup. "I don't know what you're talking about," I said.

"Did he have dimples?"

I looked up at Em in surprise—how could she know that?—and her face lit up like a Christmas tree.

"Oh my God," she cried. "Lucas Matthews gave you his cat!"

"It wasn't his cat! And who the hell is Lucas Matthews?"

She sighed and gave me an exasperated look, the same look I got every time she dropped the name of anyone who went to our school.

She said, "Lucas Matthews—former basketball star and reigning campus hottie. He's literally the most good-looking guy I've ever seen in real life, and that's saying something."

I nodded. It really was. Em had seen her share of guys. Unlike me.

"He's in his second year," she continued. "He used to be known as a real Lothario. He had a different girl on his arm every week. And believe you me, girls were lining up for the privilege. But then he quit the team last semester, nobody knows why, and since then he's been totally in hiding. He never comes to any parties anymore. There are literally gangs of girls roaming around campus looking for him. He's a ghost. And you spotted him."

Smiling at me gleefully, her hangover apparently forgotten, she clapped her hands. "Go back to the part where he took his shirt off!" she said.

"He didn't take it all the way off," I protested. "He just unbuttoned it. It was no big deal."

I turned away from my sister and moved to the closet, grabbing my purple cardigan and winding a patterned scarf around my neck. All morning I'd been squeezing the events of last night into little boxes labelled "Not Important," "To Be Forgotten," and "Funny Things That Happened To Me On The Way To Get Ice Cream." I hadn't even planned on telling Emily about what had happened, but then she'd shown up at my door and I'd had to explain the bag of stuff from The Cat Emporium. I didn't want this to become a big deal. I'd already been planning out how I would ignore Lucas if I happened to see him on the street. I had no intention of talking to him ever again, that was for sure. He knew where I *lived*. He'd come up to the door of my *apartment*. He already knew way too much about me. Just the thought of it made me feel nauseous. I wanted to pretend like last night had never happened.

And now my sister was looking at me with gossip eyes because apparently he was Mr. Most Wanted on campus. This was going to become a thing.

I closed my eyes and gripped the closet door.

I didn't want to be known as the girl Lucas Matthews gave a cat to. I just wanted to be invisible.

"I have class," I said breezily. I grabbed my bag off the floor and left the room to go find my jacket, Em close on my heels. "And so do you."

She stood in my living room with her arms crossed over her white tank top—actually it was my white tank top. "You like him, don't you?"

I made a sound that was a mix of a snort and a guffaw. "I barely know him. I talked to him for like five minutes. It was nothing."

She perched herself on the couch as I pulled on my boots, not bothering to tie them. It was getaway time.

"Admit you like him. Admit you think he's hot, at least. He's Lucas Matthews. It's not like you'd be the only one!"

I pulled on my mittens and zipped up my jacket. "What's the point of this? I'm never going to see him again."

"I just want you to admit, just once, that you're attracted to someone," she said. "Prove to me you have a pulse. Go on, prove it!"

"What do you want me to say?"

"Say 'Lucas Matthews is a hottie,'" she said, bouncing on the couch cushion. "Say it like you mean it."

I glared at her, adjusting my bag on my shoulder. She was *never* going to let this go. I knew my sister. If I didn't give in, she'd bring it up every time I saw her, in front of other people, even. Appeasing her now would avoid embarrassment later. Well, probably. You never knew with Em.

I sighed. "Lucas Matthews is a hottie," I said, and pulled open the front door. "There, are you happy now?"

"I know I am," said a familiar voice from out in the hall.

My stomach dropped as I heard Em let out high-pitched squeak and I turned slowly to face the doorway.

Hottie Lucas Matthews was standing at my front door.

"You didn't tell me there were two of you," Lucas said as we walked up the street toward campus. I was pushing the pace while he was, once again, casually sauntering. Because he was at least a head taller than my measly five-foot-five frame, he was keeping up with me pretty easily. The bastard.

"Twin sister," I answered curtly. "Gotta get to class."

I'd been flinging these throwaway answers at him ever since we'd left my building, yet somehow he was still walking beside me like we were buddies. For a few minutes I considered turning a corner unexpectedly just to lose him, as if this were a car chase, but then I dismissed it as ridiculous. Besides, a move like that might draw attention, and we were approaching campus. I needed to detach myself from Lucas to avoid attention, not attract more. But he wasn't budging.

"So how's our friend doing?" he asked as we walked up an incredibly long road that passed between the playing fields. "That's why I stopped by. You seemed a little hesitant about taking him in last night."

"Under the couch," I panted as we stepped onto one of the campus paths. I was wheezing like a bloodhound on its last legs as I continued to try to get ahead of him. He'd hardly broken a sweat, of course.

He nodded. "That's what they do when they're in an unfamiliar place. They run for cover," he said.

I know the feeling, I thought to myself.

"I was thinking we should probably make up some flyers. He didn't have a collar, but he might still belong to someone."

"Already done," I replied. "I have it on a flash drive. I'm going to print them out after class."

He gave me an appreciative look, his eyes lingering on my face. His gaze made me feel hot inside my clothes even though it was ten below outside. I averted my eyes, irritated.

"Well done, Hero," he said. "I'll help you put them up around town."

My eyes snapped back to his face. I said, "Don't call me—"

"Hey, man! Where've you been?" I had been interrupted by a guy with longish blond hair sticking out from under a blue-striped tuque. He was riding a bicycle and had stopped beside us to chat with Lucas. I wanted to ask him what the hell he was doing riding a bike on the icy roads—did he have a death wish?—but realized a better idea would be to take my chance to escape while Lucas was distracted.

I edged away from them both and made it about ten feet up the path before I heard Lucas calling to me.

"Katie, hold up a sec," he said. I stopped in my tracks as he finished up his conversation with Death Wish Guy. I don't know why I did. I could have just ignored him and walked on. There was something about the way he said my name...

I took a few steps back toward them as I waited. Looking around, I became aware of the fact that people were looking at me, or more specifically at us, or even more specifically at Lucas. A couple of girls who were walking by grinned widely as they passed him, then began whispering furiously to each other. I saw a guy at the door to the building point in our direction. Another guy ran over and started talking to Lucas animatedly as Death Wish Guy rode off. Then I saw a gaggle of girls looking me over—with little interest, I was glad to see—before honing in on Lucas. It made me nervous, but more than that it was a little bewildering. It was as though Lucas were some kind of campus celebrity. Was that even a thing? How could this many people possibly know him, enough to stare and point and whisper, enough to gather around him waiting for their turn to bask in his glow? It was kind of creepy. Who the hell was this guy?

I didn't want to hang around to find out.

I turned back toward the building, but this time I didn't even make it one step. Lucas and his friend were suddenly right beside me, walking with me up the path.

"Our next game is tomorrow night. You should really come," the guy said. He seemed to be waiting for an answer.

I glanced up at Lucas, and for the first time I saw him look uneasy. He didn't seem angry, but there was something closed off about his face. I realized he wasn't smiling.

"I'll try," Lucas said, but I recognized the tone. It was one I used all the time with Emily when she was trying to convince me to attend some social event. The lying tone.

"You said that last time, man," the guy went on, but suddenly I wasn't listening because another sound had met my ears. It was coming out of the ear buds hanging around the guy's neck. He had been listening to the radio and must have had the volume up loud because I could clearly hear the news anchor's voice.

"...six years ago, shocking a nation by the sheer brutality of the crime. But his time's up and in just a month—that's four weeks away—he'll be out in the community, serving out the rest of his sentence under supervision. Not surprisingly, parents' groups are up in arms and have been petitioning the court..."

I felt my whole body tense and heard the rushing of blood in my ears, which luckily blocked out the sound of the news report. My breath caught in my throat and I found myself backing away from Lucas and his friend quickly, my feet tripping over themselves. When I turned to run—because I really was planning to run away, at top speed, preferably—I smacked right into a girl carrying an enormous cello case and fell hard on my back, knocking that caught breath right out of my lungs.

I moaned, just as Em had this morning, though I was pretty sure I felt a lot worse right now.

Cello Girl and a few of her friends were leaning over me, asking if I was okay. One of them held out a hand to help me up and I was about to take it, my cheeks already reddening at the spectacle I'd made, when I felt a strong pair of arms pulling me up from behind. All of a sudden Cello Girl and her girlfriends were all smiles.

I felt warm breath by my ear, sending delicious shivers down my spine. "If you wanted to get away from me that bad, you could have just said so," he whispered.

I spun around to find Lucas looking down at me with some concern. He had a hold of me by both arms, but my legs were still a little weak from my fall and I faltered, pressing both my hands into his chest for balance. Even through his coat I could feel the firmness of his muscles and my mind drifted suddenly to the view of his chest I'd gotten the night before. I was still short of breath, but all of a sudden it was for a completely different reason.

He leaned toward me and I found myself staring once again at his lips and his strong jaw and his warm eyes and his lips...

"You okay?" he said to me. I had the feeling he'd said it a few times already.

Shaking myself out of my reverie, I did a little pain check. Nothing major—no broken bones at least, though my back was still throbbing. I glanced around to find every eye within a twenty-foot radius staring in my direction as I stood in the middle of campus swooning in Lucas Matthews's arms. They might not have been all that interested in me before, but they sure as hell were now.

Perfect.

"I'm fine," I said, brushing the snow off of my bag and jacket, trying my damnedest not to meet anyone's gaze, especially Lucas's. "I'm going to be late for class."

He let go of my arms but moved a hand to my shoulder. He was still standing incredibly close to me. I was going to have to talk to him about personal space, I really was. Except, for some reason, I didn't really mind him invading my space the way I did with everybody else. I didn't really mind it at all.

It made me want to punch him in the face.

Pulling away from him, I stalked up to the door and yanked it open, wincing as I felt a muscle in my back twinge. Not surprisingly, the door stayed open because Lucas was right behind me holding it open.

"You have snow in your hair," he said and I felt him tugging at the bottom of my dark curls, his hand lingering on my back. All my senses suddenly zeroed in on that hand.

I swatted it away.

"Look, Lucas," I said, "I don't want to be mean or anything. I don't want to give you the wrong impression—"

"Like when you called me a hottie?" he asked. "Like that impression?"

He was smirking at me. I narrowed my eyes.

"I just really need to focus on my work. I'm not looking to make any new friends right now. Especially not right now."

"Why? What's so special about right now?"

"Don't change the subject," I said. We'd reached the door to the art studio and I stopped there, crossing my arms. "I think it would be better if you just left me alone. I'll take care of the thing with the cat. I really just want you to go away. Okay? Just go."

"Sure, Katie," he said. "If you want me to leave you alone, that's what I'll do."

My eyes strayed to his face. He didn't seem the least bit perturbed that I was basically giving him the brush off. He'd taken off his coat and I could feel the heat coming off of him, right through his shirt. Why did guys always give off heat like they were a furnace? All of a sudden I was sweltering.

He added, "Although it might be a little difficult, considering—"

"Considering what? There's nothing to consider. Just go to your class and I'll go to mine," I said, scowling at him. Why wouldn't he just go already?

He leaned against the locker beside me, watching me with curious eyes. His expression was soft, like a caress, and I felt my resolve beginning to buckle.

Then I thought of the news report and squared my shoulders, purposely trying to bring out the pain in my back. Pain was good. Pain was a reminder.

He wasn't budging, so I decided to move instead. For some reason my hand was trembling as I pulled open the classroom door.

"Goodbye, Lucas," I said without turning around.

"Goodbye, Katie," he replied with a mysterious smile on his lips.

Breathing a sigh of relief—although it sort of felt a little bit like regret at the same time—I made my way around the studio to my easel in the corner. Most of the other students were already present and Professor Wilkins walked in just as I put my bag down. This was good. This was my favourite class. This would help me refocus, forget about the news report, forget about campus hotties and cats and the date that loomed on my calendar, the one that was distracting me more and more these days.

As I was setting up my canvas, a guy stepped up to the easel next to mine. I glanced up, ready to tell him that spot was normally taken by a girl named Naomi, when my mouth fell open. The guy standing next to me looked very familiar, and by the way he was handling the paints and brushes I could tell he'd been in the class all semester. I watched him adjusting the height of his easel. Then he looked over at me and grinned in a self-satisfied way, putting his dimples on full display.

Lucas Matthews was in my class.

3

I woke up with a start and sat up in bed, breathing hard. My entire body was covered in a thin sheen of sweat, even though it was a chilly winter morning. I kicked the covers to the foot of the bed and lay back down, covering my face with my hands. I'd been having a dream about Lucas. And not just any dream. A sexy dream. An incredibly hot and sexy dream that had left my body aching and entirely frustrated. I groaned and buried my face in my pillow. Only I could manage to be embarrassed even when nobody else was watching. I was actually blushing over a dream, in my empty bedroom, with windows so frosted over no one could see in.

I was hopeless.

Staring at the delicate patterns of frost swirling over my windowpane, I debated the matter. So I was attracted to Lucas. It wasn't a big deal. I was nineteen years old, after all. These feelings were totally natural. Like Em had said, it wasn't like I was the only one. He was a gorgeous guy and I was just having a normal reaction, that was all. No problem.

Except it was a huge problem.

I'd been attracted to guys before, obviously: celebrities, handsome strangers, unattainable classmates I'd never actually spoken to. But my attraction had never reached this kind of intensity—how could it when I barely knew the guys? I'd only ever felt like this once before, and the memories that came flowing in when I thought about *that* time, *that* guy, were ones I wanted to forget. Because that time my feelings had led me so far astray I'd barely found my way back. In fact, I wasn't entirely sure I had, though I'd been trying to for six years.

Brandon Tomko. The boy who'd ruined my life and the lives of so many others. The boy I hadn't seen face-to-face in years. The boy I was trying so hard not to think about, especially now as the date came creeping steadily closer. My eyes drifted to the calendar hanging on my wall. I hadn't circled the date but it still jumped out at me as though it was in 3D. March twentieth. Just a little less than a month away.

Now was the time for keeping a low profile, slipping under the radar, staying safe. Now was the time for survival. Now was not the time for Lucas Matthews.

I sat up and swung my feet over the edge of the bed, feeling irritated with myself. I'd spent years making sure I didn't find myself in this exact situation, and yet here I was, and at the worst possible time. I kept to myself for a reason. I avoided making friends for a reason. And boyfriends? Not on your life. I knew what I could handle and what I couldn't. I knew what I was good at and what I'd failed at so miserably that I should never try it again. Ever.

Tying my thick hair up into a bun, I walked into the bathroom and turned on the shower. Steam filled up the room, fogging up the mirror so I couldn't make out my own face. I stared at my wobbly, indistinct reflection. Who was I kidding, anyway? This was Lucas Matthews I was talking about. The guy every girl on campus was mooning over and dreaming of. The basketball player. The Lothario of Queen's University. What made me think he didn't already have a girlfriend? Of course he did. With dimples like that, how could he not?

As I climbed into the shower and began soaping up my

skin—a little more roughly than usual—I realized how I'd been completely blowing this situation out of proportion. Just because I was having sexy dreams about Lucas did not mean he was having sexy dreams about me. Just looking down at my body confirmed this. I was no model, that was for sure. Emily was the stereotypical image of perfection, the prom queen type, the hot one. I was the one who ate ice cream for dinner three times a week and whose face was round like the moon. Okay, my boobs weren't terrible, and everybody always complimented my light caramel skin tone—being mixed race had its perks—but my black hair was always frizzing and flying every which way, my thighs I didn't even want to talk about, and then there were the glasses that made my already big brown eyes look frighteningly enormous. I wore contacts whenever I could, but they irritated my eyes.

Getting out of the shower, I stepped back into my room, towel in hand, and stood in front of the full-length mirror.

Was this the girl Lucas Matthews fantasized about?

I didn't think so.

Then I thought about the disastrous outfit I'd been wearing the night I met him.

I didn't have a chance in hell.

It was funny—and a little depressing—how much this cheered me up.

I resolved to put Lucas out of my mind and to concentrate on doing my work and getting through the winter. I didn't think it would be that hard. I'd been avoiding him pretty successfully for the last week—avoiding eye contact in class, making a beeline for the door as soon as the lesson was over, and staying off campus as much as possible. It wasn't really that different from my usual routine. Forgetting about Lucas was going to be a snap.

After wolfing down a quick breakfast of leftover pepperoni pizza and trying unsuccessfully to coax the cat out from under my dresser—he'd abandoned the couch for this better hiding place a couple of days ago—I got ready to face the frosty day. I didn't have a class until modern American lit at eleven thirty, but I was eager to get to the studio and do some painting. A little more than eager, maybe. More like desperate. Nothing calmed me the way painting did, and I was in dire need of some calming down. I glanced up at the canvases covering my living room wall.

I favoured landscapes, darkness, and obscured faces. Every painting was a variation of the same theme, the same subject. All grouped together like this, my paintings could be overwhelming and a little disturbing—that was why I didn't like to let anyone into my apartment—but I didn't see them that way. These paintings were me. I poured myself onto the canvas every time. I knew the feeling that had caused every single brush stroke and I was glad to have them out of me. Better on the canvas than inside my heart.

I was pulling my door closed while rifling through my bag to find my keys when I heard my name and reluctantly turned around. My neighbor, Mariella, stood at her own front door carrying a Thomas the Train backpack, a yellow toy truck, a purse, and some kind of animal costume. She was also eating an apple and texting on her phone.

"Hey, girl!" she said in that enthusiastic way she had, as though you were the most interesting person she'd ever known. "I'm so late, you have no idea. And did you see the snow coming down? I'm never going to get him to school on time. Ethan, come *on*!"

From inside her apartment I heard a little voice cry out, "I found one boot but I can't find the other one!"

"*The Wizard of Oz*," Mariella said, shaking the costume at me with a gag-me expression on her face. "Since when do they have them doing plays before they know how to read? It's like they want to punish me! Ethan, I swear to God!" She gave out an exaggerated sigh. "So how's it going? I haven't seen you in weeks." She looked at me expectantly as she took another bite of her apple.

I bit my lip and tried to give her my most genuine smile. "I've been good," I said. "Just busy with school, you know." Without actually looking, I thought longingly of the stairs that

31

would lead me outside and away from this conversation.

Mariella was one of the nicest people I'd ever met. She was only three years older than me and had a five-year-old son, whom she was raising on her own because his father was a "douchecanoe." Ever since I'd moved in, she'd been on a mission to make me her best friend—inviting me over for dinner and movie nights, offering to quiz me for tests, complimenting my outfits. She'd even forced homemade lasagna on me during finals week last year when she knew I'd been subsisting entirely on microwave meals and Kraft Dinner. Considering how much she had going on—she worked two jobs and was caring for another human being—I should have been grateful and flattered by her attention. Instead I was always trying to avoid her. I couldn't help but feel uneasy around her, and as I stood in the hallway trying to think of an excuse to run away, the reason for my uneasiness walked out of her apartment.

"Mummy, there's a knot in the lace," Ethan said, hopping on one foot so he could hold the other up to his mother.

"Katie," Mariella said as she dumped everything in her arms onto the floor and bent down to deal with Ethan's bootlace, "when you have kids, don't ever get them lace-up boots. Go Velcro all the way. I don't know what I was thinking!"

Ethan grinned up at me with his adorable two-teeth-missing smile. He was a beautiful boy, half-Jamaican—that was Mariella—half-Caucasian—that was the douchecanoe—with skin just a little darker than mine and astounding blue eyes with lashes so thick you could brush them.

Looking into those eyes only reminded me that I had no intention of ever having kids. But I didn't say this to Mariella.

"Well, I'd better get to class," I said as I tried to edge past Mariella's enormous pile of stuff.

"Not so fast!" she said, pointing an accusing finger my way. "You're not going anywhere until you explain the beautiful man I saw leaving your apartment the other night. Don't even try to deny it."

I gaped at her. How did she always know everything?

"I saw him coming down the stairs," she continued, giving me a knowing look. "I want all the details. That man was far too delectable for you to leave out any details."

"How do you know he was coming from my place?" I protested. "It could have been—"

"We're on the top floor, ours are the only two apartments up here, and he was coming down our staircase," Ethan piped up.

I looked from Ethan to Mariella, who shrugged.

"Who else do I have to talk to?" she said.

"Nothing happened. I barely know him," I said as I began to back away. "I really have to go."

"Don't you dare think this conversation is over. I know where you live!" Mariella cried as I finally made it to the stairs and began to bound down them like a jackrabbit on speed.

Once I reached the street I let out a long breath and slowed my pace. I couldn't be friends with Mariella, no matter how much she wanted to be, not when just looking at her son broke my heart.

There was only so much a person could stand.

As I approached the third floor art studio, the smell of oil paint greeted me like an old friend. The studio, which also served as a classroom for my daily art course, was only about a quarter full of students working intently on their projects. Still, it was pretty loud, as usual, as people fought over what music to play and commented on each other's work. I walked inside and made straight for the back corner, speaking to no one, which was surprisingly acceptable. I loved that about the art studio. With so many artistic types crammed into one space, no one batted an eye if you concentrated on your painting silently for six hours straight; they just assumed you were lost in your artistic genius. It really should have been printed on the art school brochures: "Want to be ignored? Art school is the place for you!" This room was the only one on campus I felt completely comfortable in, even when it was filled with people.

It was a lovely thing to ignore and be ignored.

I approached my easel, smiling contentedly, until my gaze fell on the guy standing at the back of the room by the windows. Suddenly, all the comforting feelings that had been percolating inside me vanished and I swore under my breath.

So much for putting Lucas out of my mind.

The sunlight streaming through the window was falling directly onto his shoulders, lighting him up like a beacon. There might as well have been a huge arrow above his head, pointing him out to me. And, of course, my easel was just beside his.

Great.

As I approached his side, I couldn't help but take in his tousled dark hair and the worn plaid shirt he wore open over a grey t-shirt that fit him snugly across the chest. He was frowning, his honey-coloured eyes searching the canvas as though they might find some precious secret hidden there. Even frowning he was drop-dead gorgeous. I silently cursed myself for thinking this. His concentration was so complete that he didn't notice me at all, even when I was almost directly behind him. Looking over his shoulder, I saw that his canvas was completely blank.

I understood the intimidation of the blank canvas—I think every artist does. A part of me wanted to give him some tips to get through it, but another part of me warned vehemently against it. This was exactly what I'd vowed not to do less than an hour ago. In the end, my clumsiness made the decision for me when I knocked over a jar full of brushes, sending them scattering across the floor, including right under Lucas's easel.

"Oh, sorry!" I mumbled as I fell to my knees and began frantically collecting the brushes. I heard Lucas chuckle and then he crouched down beside me to give me a hand.

"I was just thinking about you," Lucas said as he handed me a bunch of brushes smiling broadly. His fingers grazed mine as I took the brushes from him, causing me to yank my hand away and nearly drop them all over again.

"I hope that's not true, considering how hard you were

frowning at your canvas," I said shakily.

We both stood up and I busied myself with shoving all the brushes back into the jar as he looked over at his canvas again.

Calm down, I told myself. *He was probably just thinking about what a crazy spaz you are.*

"I was just thinking how easy the assignments must be for you, with all your talent."

I gave him a puzzled—and maybe a little resentful—look, feeling my hackles rising. I really wasn't good with compliments.

"I've been in the class since the beginning of the semester, Katie," he said gently. "You're an amazing artist. I've always thought so."

"Did you realize we were in the same class when we met last week?" I demanded, crossing my arms. I might have been overreacting, mainly because I felt bad. He'd noticed before last week, but I hadn't noticed him at all.

"It took me a few minutes to place you," he said. "But I figured it out. Your paint-spattered fingers reminded me."

I glanced down at my hands, rubbing at the red paint on my index finger. Emily was always chiding me about it. When I looked up at Lucas, his eyes were also focused on my hands. He took his time raising them back to my face, his gaze leaving a slow trail of heat up my body. I shivered involuntarily.

Now my hackles were up for real.

"What are you doing taking introductory fine art, anyway?" I said, my words taking on the tone of an interrogation. "You're not an art student, are you?"

Surprisingly, Lucas didn't seem the least offended. He shrugged lightly. "I convinced them to make an exception for me," he said. "I wanted to try something new."

I couldn't exactly fault him for that. I cast around for some other way to chastise him, but couldn't come up with anything, especially not while he was watching me so closely, the beginnings of a smirk at the corner of his lips.

"So what's the problem with the assignment?" I said instead, pointing at his canvas, drawing his gaze away. We were restricted to using a limited colour palette, and, as always, we had to paint from a photo. The painting itself could be of anything

"I just can't decide what to paint. I've been going through my photos for over an hour but...I can't settle on one," he said, and there was disappointment in his voice. He sighed as he looked down at the photographs in his hands. For some reason this block was really bothering him.

"That happens to me sometimes," I admitted. "Usually when there's something on my mind, something I could paint but I don't want to."

The look he gave me was full of recognition before it drifted back to the canvas in front of him.

I wondered what it was he was trying to avoid.

Settling myself in front of the easel next to his, I said, "You'll get better at getting past blocks like this as you paint more. Just keep telling yourself to pick the photo that matters to you, the one that makes you feel something."

"You mean I should paint what I love?" he asked, and was I imagining it, or did his eyes linger on my lips as he said it?

I cleared my throat. "I mean paint from the gut," I said. "The best artists always do."

"Is that what you do?" he asked.

This time I avoided his eyes. "No," I said. "I paint the past."

Then I put in my ear buds, turned on my iPod, and tuned him out. It was easier than I'd expected. Within moments I'd slipped into what I liked to call my "artist trance," losing myself in the act of painting and letting the rest of the world just fade away. Sometimes when I did this the painting sitting on the easel when I was done looked entirely foreign to me and I had no memory of creating it at all. Those paintings were often the most abstract, full of dark, angry strokes and spatters of paint. I never showed them in class or hung them on my wall. Truthfully, they frightened me.

A little more than an hour later I turned my music off. My painting was by no means finished, but I'd made a good start. I wasn't working from a photograph, which I knew would get me into trouble, but I didn't have much choice. Even if I could go back to that place and take a picture, I knew I never would. Luckily, I didn't need a photograph to paint the scene. It was seared into my brain.

Today I'd worked on the sky, which didn't pose much of a challenge for me. I'd become an expert at painting the fading light of day, the lingering blue, the peeking stars. I'd painted that sky a hundred times. No matter what I did, even if I painted a daytime scene, there was always that sky hanging over it, scattered with darkening clouds.

I could never escape that sky.

Looking around, I noticed Lucas wasn't at his easel. Instead, he was leaning against the counter behind me. As I turned around, I caught him looking at my painting and a wave of panic shot through me. How long had he been watching? Had he seen me in my artist trance? I had no idea what I looked like when I was in that state—probably like I was high or a little mad. To cover my embarrassment, I jumped from my seat.

"Let's see yours!" I said, stepping over to his easel.

"It's not finished," Lucas said hesitantly, and he was right; it wasn't. The right-hand side of the painting was mostly blank. But he'd recreated the trees in his photo with surprising skill. I was impressed by the way he'd managed to make it seem as though the sun was shining through the branches. His style was more realistic than mine, but far more advanced than I'd expected. I couldn't quite believe it.

I turned to him and he raised his eyebrows at me. He actually looked anxious to hear what I thought. I'd never seen him look anything but relaxed before.

"It's really good," I said with a genuine smile and he seemed to let out a breath he was holding. "I love your use of light here." I pointed at the branches. "I can't wait to see it when it's finished. I had no idea…" I shook my head.

"No idea what?" he asked.

"You surprise me," I said simply.

My certainty that the attraction I was feeling was entirely one-sided crumbled in an instant as Lucas stared into my eyes, making my stomach flip. He looked at me like he'd never seen anything like me before, like I was the only girl in the world, like I was the most beautiful thing he'd ever seen.

Nobody had ever looked at me that way in my entire life.

"Go out for coffee with me," Lucas said, his eyes locked to mine.

I didn't even take a second to think about it.

"Okay," I said.

4

I convinced Lucas to go to a local coffee shop I knew of on a side street off campus. I told him it would be less crowded, when really I just didn't want to be whispered about for the rest of the day for having a coffee date with Lothario Lucas. If he had any idea I was lying, he didn't let on, which left me feeling a little buzzed with relief. I didn't bother asking myself why it mattered so much to me if Lucas thought I was a liar.

We passed one of our cat flyers stapled to a telephone pole, flapping depressingly in the wind. In the end Lucas had insisted we put his number on the bottom, just in case some kook ended up calling, but he said he hadn't gotten any calls.

As we walked through the door to the coffee place, my cell buzzed in my hand.

Em: Econ is sooooo boring. Make me laugh. Now. Go.

I considered telling my sister I was about to sit down for coffee with "Lucas Matthews is a hottie," but decided against it. Knowing Em, she'd probably scream right there in class and hold it against me later. Better to make her wait.

Me: But how? I'm so boring, too.
Em: True. Sighhhhh.
Me: Might have a story for you later, tho.
Em: What what?
Me: Maybe something about a certain hottie...
Em: WHAT!
Me: Oh, sorry, gotta go.
Em: Evil tease!
Me: TTYL :)

As much as everything to do with Lucas felt completely ill advised to me, it was fun to have something to gossip with my sister about, even if I was pretending—it was just coffee; I was pretty sure there wouldn't be much of a story to tell. She was usually the one coming to me with juicy tales of heartbreak and outrage and adventure. I liked the idea of being able to deliver something back.

It was almost like I had a life.

Lucas had been waiting behind me in line, respectfully not asking whom I was texting with. When it was my turn to order, I got a giant hot chocolate with extra whipped cream and covered it with chocolate and cinnamon shavings. I liked my beverages to be as much like dessert as possible. I collected my drink and grabbed a seat at a table by the window, wondering only after I'd sat down if that was the socially correct thing to do. Should I have waited with him while they made his drink? Should I have paid for his drink? (In actuality, he'd paid for mine, even though he was behind me in line. Was that normal?) I eyed him nervously as he stood with his coat under his arm, chatting with the guy behind the counter. I could say I didn't check out his ass from across the room, but that would be another lie.

His coffee in hand—he got it black and in the smallest size, like he was trying to make me look like the biggest pig in the world—he walked over to where I sat, and a dozen female eyes followed him.

"Is this how you live?" I asked, fixing him with a horrified look.

"What? Did I spill?" he said checking the front of his shirt for stains, as I glanced back around the room with lowered lids. Now those same female eyes were looking at me instead. Middle-aged ladies and teenage girls and soccer moms. A skinny girl with long brown hair stared daggers at me. Apparently it didn't really matter if we were on campus or off. Lucas caused a stir everywhere he went.

I took a breath, detesting the feeling of being stared at. I remembered that feeling. Like everyone knew something about you. All of them pitying you. And then, later, like everyone was wondering what the hell was wrong with you.

I felt rather than saw Lucas leaning toward me over the table, my eyes glued to the wooden surface.

"They wouldn't be staring if you weren't so beautiful," he whispered.

What?

I gulped my drink, burning my tongue and getting whipped cream all over my nose and upper lip, which I wiped off with amazing speed, though I was pretty sure he'd seen it. I couldn't be certain, because I still hadn't looked him in the eye.

"Uh," I muttered as I squeezed my napkin into a ball in my fist. "That's just so...completely not...whatever."

He kept quiet—though I was pretty sure he was laughing at me under his breath—until I calmed down enough to look up at him. In what seemed to be his typical fashion, he was sitting back in his chair, completely at ease.

"How can you be so okay with all of...this?" I blurted, gesturing at the room at large. "How can you stand being stared at and talked about and stalked by random girls? Don't you ever get sick of being Lucas Matthews?"

I bit my lips hard, realizing I'd probably way overstepped my bounds. As Em would have said, *You really should have backed the truck up there, Katie.* I'd basically implied I would hate myself if I were him. And just ten seconds after he'd called me beautiful.

Nice.

But Lucas didn't look particularly insulted. Instead, he was looking thoughtfully out the window.

"Do I ever get sick of being Lucas Matthews?" he said to his own reflection. Then he looked at me again, his expression melancholic. "All the time," he said.

Never in a million years would I have thought that Lucas and I would have a single thing in common, let alone two things in one day. Maybe I would have something to tell Em when I got home after all.

Shaking away the gloom, Lucas set his elbows on the table and crossed his arms like he meant business.

"So, Katie," he said. "Your turn. Tell me something about you."

I busied myself with taking another abnormally long sip of my drink. Uh-oh. He wanted to do the whole 'getting to know you' thing. I heard mayday cries blaring in my ears. Luckily, I'd spent years learning evasive tactics for just this situation.

"I really love this drink!" I said happily, holding it up for him to see.

He nodded at me as if agreeing and then his nodding turned to head shaking. "Really?" he said with some amusement. "That's all you're going to give me? You love chocolate?"

"But I really do," I said seriously.

A mischievous grin spread over his face as the girl who'd taken our drink orders came over to us with a plate in her hand. She set it down on the table and batted her eyelashes at Lucas as he thanked her. I tried not to roll my eyes in return, but did not succeed.

On the plate now sitting between us was a warm and delicious looking brownie so thick and glistening with chocolaty goodness that my mouth started watering just looking at it. Then Lucas took his fork and cut it in half and the thick, fudgy insides began to flow out onto the plate, like some kind of volcanic eruption of chocolate delight.

I looked up at Lucas, my mouth still hanging partly open.

"I want that," I said.

Lucas smiled even wider, holding the fork out of my reach. "Well I was going to just share it with you," he said, "but now I have a better idea. Let's call this our official Getting To Know Katie brownie. For every bite you take you have to answer a question about yourself. No answers, no brownie."

"Every bite!" I said, gazing hopelessly at the treat and trying to count the number of bites with my eyes. There were ten bites there at least, unless I made them really big, which I imagined he wouldn't let me.

Ten questions. I could do that...couldn't I?

"What do you say?" Lucas said.

"Fine," I said crossly, snatching the fork out of his hand. He didn't put up much of a fight. "But I get the first bite for free. I need to make sure it's worth it."

Lucas nodded in agreement, his eyes twinkling. He said, "What the lady wants, the lady gets."

Pulling the plate toward me, I cut the brownie into ten equal bites, letting the molten insides ooze out everywhere.

"You're making a mess," Lucas commented.

"Hush, you!" I said.

I dragged my fork through the chocolate sauce, then scooped up the first bite of brownie and brought it to my lips, inhaling that freshly baked smell before putting it into my mouth. It tasted so good I had to close my eyes as I chewed. I liked to worship my desserts in private.

When I looked up at Lucas again his eyes were so dilated they looked black.

"Forget the questions," he said. "I just want to watch you eat it."

I froze with the fork still in my mouth and there was a pregnant pause as we stared at each other. Then I set the fork down and looked away. A part of me liked this, just a little, while another part of me was seriously freaking the hell out. I wasn't sure which part was winning.

Lucas sat back in his chair, as though he thought it would be better if there were a full table-length between us. He shook his head a few times like it was an Etch-A-Sketch and he was trying to clear it.

I just want to watch you eat it.

I couldn't deny that when he'd said those words I'd wanted nothing more than to let him watch me eat it.

Oh God, what was happening to me?

"First question," Lucas said, rubbing his hands together. "What's your last name?"

Okay, not too bad. Easy does it. "Archer," I said, claiming my second bite.

"That's British, isn't it?" he said. "Like the author, Jeffrey Archer."

I breathed in, readying to make my speech. "My mother is Indian and my father is Danish, but his father was English, hence the last name Archer. My mother is actually from Australia, she was born and grew up there, but her parents emigrated there from India and then eventually to Canada, so here we are."

I readied myself for the typical remarks Em and I had gotten all our lives. Exclamations of, "Danish and Indian. What an interesting combination!" and, "You're so lucky. I'm just plain old Canadian." They were all basically conversation killers. What exactly was there to say about your diverse ethnic background? Thanks for finding my racial mix fascinating? (Emily had once told a man in a checkout line that he had her to thank for keeping his world diverse. "You're welcome," she'd said to him, perfectly seriously. He'd tipped his hat to her.)

Lucas just looked at me and said, "I'm one-eighth French-Canadian."

"Oh, I totally win," I said, spearing two bites of brownie on my fork at once and shoving them both in my mouth.

"Cheater!" Lucas cried, picking up the plate and holding it to his chest. "Now you have to answer two questions in a row."

"Fine," I said, holding up my hands to prove my innocence.

He narrowed his eyes at me but placed the plate back down

between us.

"Where are you from?" he said, his voice still laced with suspicion.

"Vancouver," I answered honestly. Good. A nice big, anonymous city. Nothing to see here, move along. "And where are you from?"

He raised his eyebrows at me, but didn't protest my table-turning move.

"A little town called Christie," he said.

I shook my head slowly to show I didn't know it.

"It's a tiny place about an hour northwest of here. Blink on the highway and you'll miss it," he said. "There's nothing much there, just a lake and a four-street square downtown, a rundown movie theatre, and a girl's boarding school, but it's home to me."

I'd noticed that students who came from small towns were often apologetic about it, as though they thought their homes were too boring to mention. But not Lucas. I liked that about him. I liked that he wasn't embarrassed to come from some small town nobody had ever heard of, like his past was nothing to be ashamed of.

I wished I could say the same.

"So your parents still live there?" I asked, claiming another bite while he wasn't looking. A muscle clenched in his jaw and he scratched at the back of his head. When he smiled at me this time, I could see the strain. This wasn't a question he wanted to answer.

"I thought I was the one asking the questions," he said.

But he didn't. I drew designs in the fudge with the tines of the fork and he watched me do it. It was the first time in a long time that I'd been able to stand being quiet with someone. Usually I would obsess about what they were thinking of me or how to get away or what to say next, because God knew I wasn't exactly a stellar conversationalist. I didn't know why I wasn't feeling that way now, but I didn't question it.

"Sometimes I miss living at home," Lucas said. "That town was the world to me in high school. Everything was so much simpler then."

"I bet you were the king of the school," I said with a smirk. "You had a hundred close friends and you were class president." His sheepish look told me I was on the right track. "I bet everyone knew your name, just like here."

"What? Didn't the kids all know your name at your school?" he said.

I winced internally. I'd walked right into that one.

"Oh, they knew my name, all right," I said. They hadn't printed my name in the papers, but every kid in my high school had still known exactly who I was even before I'd set foot on school grounds.

"Were you one of those popular girls?" he said with laughter in his voice. "Did you walk down the hall, swinging your ponytail around and making snarky remarks to your underlings?"

I had to laugh along. "No!" I said. "That was Emily." I had another bite of brownie.

"But I'm sure you had boyfriends," he continued, he tone light and teasing while my stomach dropped like a stone. "How many were there? Dozens, I bet."

Nope, just one.

In my lap I began twisting my fingers, an anxious and painful habit I'd developed during the trial. I would twist my digits until the skin puffed red and the bones cracked, gripping so hard it felt as though my fingers would actually break. My hands would throb for nearly an hour afterwards as I went over in my head everything the prosecutors had said, and every look the Wesleys had given me, and every lie I'd told. Especially the lies.

I released my fingers and jerked my head up, startling the worried look right off of Lucas's face.

"Why'd you quit basketball?" I blurted out, which was a pretty rude question to ask out of the clear blue, I realized, but I wasn't too concerned about it. Anything to change the subject. Besides, Lucas was as unflappable as ever, as he cocked his head to the side slightly, considering his answer.

"Sometimes things have to end," he said.

Now that was a bullshit answer if I'd ever heard one.

I said, "Yesterday when that guy asked you to come to the game, you lied to him."

Lucas raised his chin at me. "How do you know I was lying?" he asked.

"It's a talent of mine," I answered. "But I'm right, aren't I? You aren't going to any game."

His glance slipped to the window again and for the first time I suspected I'd made him uncomfortable.

That was the downside of evasive maneuvers. Sometimes in trying to deflect attention you ended up drawing unwanted attention somewhere else. For someone who'd spent her life hoping nobody would find out her secrets, I sure loved ferreting out other people's. It was a sick habit.

"Sports are overrated, anyway," I announced as I got to my feet and started gathering my things.

Lucas chuckled, shaking his head. "Where do you think you're going?" he said. "There are still a few bites left here." He taunted me by spearing a bite and eating it himself, smearing chocolate sauce across his bottom lip. As he wiped it away with a napkin I had to stop myself from leaning forward and capturing the last drop he'd missed with my finger, or better yet, my lips.

Dear God, did I just think that?

I was still staring at Lucas's lips and as I glanced up at his eyes I realized he was staring right back at me.

"I think that's enough questions for today, Mr. Inquisitor," I said briskly. "Besides, I have class in twenty minutes."

"I feel like I've been gypped," he said sadly as he followed me out the door. "You used me for my baked goods and gave me nothing in return."

If he thought that was nothing, he clearly hadn't been paying attention. I'd told him a novel-length saga compared to what I normally shared with people, which was nothing.

"You'll recover," I said. "I'm sure some blonde beauty in your next class will be more than happy to fill you in on every detail of her life."

"Yeah, well, Blondie doesn't hold my interest," he said, walking backwards in front of me. "Too much gum popping."

He stopped in his tracks all of a sudden, causing me to plow right into him. "Besides," he said into my hair, "I've always been partial to dark-haired beauties."

His hands were at my waist, gripping my jacket at the hips, and somehow I'd looped one of my arms over his. Our feet were tangled together and I could feel his warm breath tickling my ear, his chest pressing against mine, almost as though we were embracing. For a brief moment I felt faint.

"Lucas," I said, and he looked down at me, his lips tantalizingly close to mine. Resisting the urge to reach up and touch them with my own suddenly became an epic battle.

What the hell was happening to me?

I said, "You're going to make me late."

"God, I hope so," he said.

I smacked him playfully on the shoulder and stepped away, filling my air with lungs as though I'd been holding my breath for an hour.

But Lucas wasn't quite done with me.

"Give me your number, Katie Archer," he said, holding his phone out to me.

It might have sounded like a command, but the expression on his face was hopeful, as though he thought I might say no, which wasn't too far off. I held my arm tightly at my side, eyeing his phone doubtfully. Give him my number? I never gave out my number. In fact, I was always forgetting my own number for just that reason. Nobody had it except Emily, my parents, Mariella—she'd finagled it out of me on the same day she'd insisted we exchange keys, in case of emergency—and an aggressive girl named Lara I'd sort of been friends with for a few weeks first semester. She'd never called me.

Giving out my number to a guy was something I did not do. It broke every one of my rules. It was the sort of thing Emily did, the sort of thing normal girls did. I didn't want to start pretending I was a girl like that, a girl guys called on the phone and invited over, a girl who deserved that kind of attention. I didn't want to give him my number and be heartbroken when he never used it.

This wasn't wise. This wasn't safe. This wasn't the Katie Archer I knew.

But then again, the Katie Archer I knew would never have been asked for her number by a guy like Lucas.

I'm pretty sure I imagined Lucas's sigh of relief as I finally took the phone from his hand and typed in my name and number, but I know I didn't imagine the gigantic grin that covered his face as I handed it back.

Having no idea what to do next, I turned and walked to the corner and crossed the street without checking to see if he was following me. When I reached the other curb, I looked back. He was still on the other side of the street, looking down at his phone.

"Hey, Lucas," I called. He looked up. "Thanks for the brownie."

He smiled and continued typing on his phone. My cell vibrated in my hand and I turned it on.

Lucas: Thanks for today. :)

By the time I finished my classes for the day and was on my way back to my apartment, my mind was a jumble of contradictory thoughts. I remembered my conviction as I'd left for school that morning that I would forget about Lucas altogether. Obviously I'd failed at that completely, but instead of feeling afraid and guilty about it, I could only feel warm and excited. All through my English class I'd kept turning on my phone to check his text—yes, I'd devolved to this kind of high school behaviour—and each time a giddy feeling swept through my body and I had to stop myself from giggling. Then, of course, had come art class, three long hours of me sneaking looks at Lucas only to find that, more often than not, he was looking back. There was still a scolding voice that ran on a continual loop in the back of my head, listing all the reasons why being friends with this boy—and I couldn't really think of us as anything more than friends without feeling like I might pass out—was the very worst idea, a monumentally stupid idea, the most idiotic idea I'd ever had. For once, that voice sounded muted and hardly worth listening to.

I trudged into my room and threw myself down on my bed, startling the cat, who'd been sleeping on my pillow. Before I could reach out and pet him he'd hightailed it back under the dresser. On another day I might have felt dismayed at the cat's rejection—he'd yet to show even the slightest interest in me—but right now I could only sit, still gripping my phone, wondering what this carefree feeling was.

Then I realized: I was happy.

My cell made a dinging sound that meant I had a new email waiting.

I clicked on my phone, opened my mailbox, and waited for the message to load, expecting it to be from Em. Probably some ridiculous video of people dancing in the rain wearing fake goat heads or something. She loved it when people wore animal heads for some unknowable reason.

But the email wasn't from Emily. It was notification telling me someone had sent me a Facebook message.

This was a little odd. I barely used my Facebook page and had only created it in the first place because my little cousin, Harriet, who was nine, had insisted I try it once, just to see if I liked it, then immediately friended me. My profile picture was still blank. The whole concept of social media confounded me. Why would anyone care that I'd had a really great sandwich at Earl's Kitchen, or that I'd stubbed my toe on the corner of the coffee table and it hurt like hellllll? Harriet and Emily were my only friends on there and neither of them had ever sent me a message before.

None of this really occurred to me as I opened the email, however. My thoughts were elsewhere—on the good day I'd had. On Lucas and the fact that he'd called me beautiful and asked for my number. On the fact that I was happy.

When I glanced down at the message, my face froze in its

happy, grinning state, as though it was trying to keep those feelings for as long as possible, as though my face knew before I did that I would never be able to keep my happiness. Happiness wasn't meant for me.

You'd better watch yourself, Katie Kat.
I remember everything.

5

"Why does your closet think you're Amish?" Emily cried.

I was sitting crossed-legged on my bed, calmly eating chocolate chips out of the package by the handful as my sister rifled through my clothes, her entire upper body out of sight inside my closet. As I watched, she began throwing my shoes over her shoulder, one "disturbing" sandal at a time.

"Where's the top I gave you for your birthday?" she demanded.

"That bright pink thing with the sequins?" I asked. "I cleverly hid that abomination away."

"Don't talk to me about abominations!" Em said, disentangling her head from one of my dresses, her cheeks rosy red with annoyance. "Your wardrobe is the abomination. What did you and Mom buy when you went clothes shopping for school last fall, anyway?"

"Those shoes," I said, pointing to a pair of brown ballet flats Emily had rejected only moments ago, "and those jeans."

She was holding the jeans up in front of her; they were my most comfortable, baggy jeans. The legs were twice the width of her body. She looked up at me in horror as I spoke.

Depositing them on the ground with her fingers as though she thought they might infect her with bad fashion sense, she flopped down on the bed next to me and gave an exaggerated sigh.

"I knew I should have brought some clothes for you to wear. We're never going to get there at this rate," she whined.

That didn't sound too bad to me. In fact, it sounded great. After three straight days of obsessing over that Facebook message nonstop, I was exhausted. The first night I hadn't slept at all. It had taken me a full hour to get the pounding of my heart under control, and another hour to convince myself to stop checking the chain lock and bolt on my apartment door every five seconds. I'd never thought two sentences could make me feel so unsafe, but they had. As the long hours had stretched toward morning, I couldn't stop staring at those last two words printed boldly across the screen. It wasn't that some stranger was threatening me—that wasn't what had me so freaked. I knew exactly who the message was from.

Only one person called me Katie Kat.

But how? I knew Brandon couldn't have sent it—I'd looked up the rules on internet access for youth offenders in custody somewhere around two o'clock in the morning—though I figured it was possible he'd snuck onto a computer somehow and sent the message from the account he'd created with the name "Somebody You Know." I didn't even want to think about the alternative, that he had help, a buddy out here in the world, a friend willing to do his bidding. A friend free to go anywhere, do anything, without the restriction of the bars that held Brandon in. A friend whose face I wouldn't recognize if I passed him on the street. A friend who could be anyone: the guy, or girl, sitting next to me in class, the guy having a cigarette outside my apartment building, my mailman, my professor, Mariella.

You'd better watch yourself, Katie Kat.

I hadn't left the apartment in three days.

Logically I knew there probably wasn't anything to worry

about. Brandon was locked away; he couldn't hurt me. The message was just an empty threat. It was incredibly unlikely that he had a friend on the outside loyal enough to travel across the country just to find me. But then, there were a lot of things about my relationship with Brandon that were unlikely. The truth was, I had no idea what Brandon was capable of these days. I had absolutely nothing to go on, and nothing, unlike something, left room for my imagination to come up with a thousand different possibilities, each one more terrifying than the last. I'd always had an active imagination. It was what fueled my art. I'd never thought of it as a curse until now.

So I'd hidden away in my apartment, painting and skipping class and eating every single thing in my fridge, including a Tupperware container full of pasta I was pretty sure was two weeks old, a shriveled peach, and the healthy cereal I'd bought after I'd watched the documentary about how fast food was killing us all and had never opened.

I'd forgotten that I'd agreed to go out with Em and her friends—it was someone's birthday; I couldn't remember whose—until she'd texted me saying she was on her way over. I'd only just managed to change out of my pajama uniform when she'd knocked on the door.

"You know, I think I might be coming down with something," I said, giving what I hoped sounded like a pathetic cough.

Emily was texting and didn't even notice.

"It's okay," she said with audible relief. "Sally says she can bring you something to wear."

Oh, wonderful. I'd seen the type of outfits Slutty Sally normally wore. (To give you a hint, she'd given herself that nickname.) We'd once had to force her to go back to her room and change when she'd come outside wearing underwear instead of shorts. They were boy-short undies, but still. I'd also once seen her nipple in a disastrous cleavage incident.

"Please tell me you're kidding," I said to Em.

"What?" she said, oblivious to my discomfort, still busily texting on her phone.

Close as we were, Emily had never been great at sensing how I was feeling. Maybe because I hid my true feelings from her, as I did everyone else. But even if I'd been in full-blown panic attack mode, I wasn't sure she would have really understood. Dark feelings didn't really exist in my sister's world; I'd worked hard enough to keep it that way. Emily had never been depressed, sick to her stomach with fear, or even lonely as far as I could tell. How could she possibly understand the tremulous emotions that coursed through my body on a regular basis? Which was why I was pretty shocked at the words that came out of her mouth next.

"Are you okay?" she asked, glancing up from the glowing screen of her cell phone. "You just seem a little off today. Is anything the matter?"

"I'm fine," I lied, digging farther into my package of chocolate chips. It was almost empty, which meant I'd eaten the entire bag in one sitting—gah!

"Mom wanted me to ask," she said. "She's always asking me about you. Have you been avoiding her calls? Because you know that only makes her manic."

Well, that explained it. This was all my mother's doing.

"I guess I must have missed them," I said, throwing the empty wrapper in the garbage. A part of me wanted Em to call me on my crap. (How could you miss a call and not realize it when your cell phone yelled this information at you whenever you turned it on?) A part of me wanted Em to realize why Mom was calling constantly to check on me. A part of me wanted my sister to remember the date on the calendar and realize what it meant.

But Emily was Emily, and I knew deep down that I wouldn't have wanted her to be any other way.

"They're here!" she cried, bouncing off the bed and down the hall, our conversation forgotten.

I heard her yank the door open and the racket of a gaggle of girls crowding into the small space of my living room.

I lay back on my bed and enjoyed my last ten seconds of quiet. Maybe this night would be good for me. I'd be surrounded by people I knew the entire time. I wouldn't be alone. I could pretend I was someone else for a night, pretend I was my sister and had no problems, no demons, no worries. I could escape the funky smell in my apartment. I could get away from myself.

Then Sally burst into my room, the other girls on her heels, holding up a sheer black top with a plunging neckline and a pair of knee-high leather boots.

"It's time for a makeover, girlfriend!" she cried, her blonde curls bouncing.

Out of the corner of my eye I spotted the cat easing out from under the dresser and stealthily slipping out of the room. I'd never wished I were a cat so much in my entire life.

I plastered a smile on my face as Anita kneeled on the bed behind me, gathering my hair in her hands. "Should we do her hair up or down?" she asked the room at large.

"Oh, fake eyelashes!" Emily cried as she pawed through Sally's makeup case. "I also brought those new coloured contacts I ordered. They're sapphire blue. You're going to look so hot you won't even recognize yourself!"

I groaned inwardly as they crowded around me, holding up various garments like I was a mannequin.

"Are you wearing a thong?" a girl named Melissa asked me quietly in my ear.

It was going to be a long night.

The Limo was a club on the edge of town that I'd never been to before. It had three floors, four DJs, and apparently no parking. We'd been circling, trying to find a space, for ten minutes. It was a little too far from campus to attract the university crowd, which, Sally informed me, was the whole point.

"I want to meet older guys," she said as she flawlessly applied another layer of Hot Mama red lipstick without a mirror. It was kind of impressive. "Guys our age have no money. I want a sugar daddy!"

"I thought Alex was your sugar daddy," Emily said as she jerked the wheel to the right, finally slipping into what appeared to be the last available spot on the block.

"Alex lives off his trust fund," Sally said with distaste. "I want a guy with his own cash, preferably lots of it, which he'll have no problem showering all over me. Maybe even while I'm naked, 'cause that's super hot."

"Way to dream big, Sally," Anita said.

I liked Anita. Not only was she wearing normal clothes instead of the overly revealing apparel her friends favoured, but she seemed to find Sally as ridiculous as I did. I even forgave her for wearing a tiara on her head tonight. It was her birthday, after all.

"Is Alex aware of this rich man desire of yours?" I inquired as we all piled out of the car.

"What would I tell him for?" Sally said with a puzzled look on her face.

We took off our coats and left them on the backseat to avoid paying for coat check. I linked arms with Emily as we crossed the street and joined the line outside the club, shivering in our seasonally inappropriate outfits. Barely a minute had passed before Sally was nuzzling up to the beefed-up guy standing in front of us in line, shamelessly whining that her boobs were cold and would he mind warming them up for her? He looked happy to oblige.

I took a step out of line to check how far we were from the front. The line was moving pretty quickly. We probably only had about five more minutes to wait.

"Who are you looking for, Katie?" Emily said as I came back to her side. I just saw the tip of a flask as she shoved it back into her blue sparkly clutch. That explained why they were all so giggly already. I hoped nobody would throw up before we made it inside. "Oh, I know who you're looking for. You're on the lookout for Lucas, your secret beau!"

"Emily!" I cried, giving her a look of death as her friends all gushed at once: "Oh, Lucas!" They drew out his name until it had about five syllables, all high-pitched and mortifying.

Clearly they already knew about Lucas and me, though there wasn't much to tell. I didn't even want to think about how completely Em must have exaggerated the little I'd told her about my encounters with him. She probably had the two of us doing it like bunnies in his room. There were probably already rumours of our sex tape circulating campus.

"Shut up, you guys," I said, trying to get control of the tipsy, giggling horde. "Lucas and I are just friends. Don't you dare go telling anybody anything different."

"Wait, didn't he buy you a kitten?" Melissa said.

"And hand it to you half-naked?" Anita said.

"And covered in chocolate?" Em chimed in.

I groaned in the back of my throat as they veered off into a discussion of Lucas's abs, the abs of the whole basketball team, and how many jocks Sally had slept with last semester—they were in disagreement whether it was eleven or twelve. I gratefully tuned out.

The subject of Lucas had left me feeling guilty and out of sorts. During my three-day hibernation, he'd texted me a few times. Once to ask why I'd skipped class, and another time during class to inform me that Naomi had taken the easel next to him and that he wished it was me instead. Because she smelled like cheese. I'd wanted to text him back to say she *always* smelled like cheese, but I didn't think it was a good enough reply. Texting was all about being clever and hilarious. It was a lot of pressure, especially when your brain was turning to mush from watching six hours straight of daytime TV. Then, just a few hours ago, he'd sent me this text:

Lucas: Hey, disappearing act. Where'd you go?

I hadn't replied to that one, either.

A really stupid part of me had started examining my life in the context of the creepy Facebook message late last night. Other than March twentieth, the only new thing in my life was Lucas. And—here was the really dumb part—I sort of felt like I was being punished for letting him into my life. Yeah, it was pretty crooked logic, but that's how it felt. I'd broken my rules. I'd let him get to know me, even if only a little. I had a cat under my bed. I'd lost the tight control I usually kept on my life, and look at what had happened.

Brandon had never contacted me before, not once, not in six years.

I felt like I'd been caught with my hand in the cookie jar.

And as gorgeous as the cookie jar was, I was furious with myself. What had I been thinking? That I could break my rules with no consequences? That six years ago had never happened? That I could be just like everybody else? That was a laugh.

Just before I'd fallen asleep I'd made myself a promise. No more Lucas.

If for no other reason than because I was pretty sure he would probably break my heart and I was already broken in so many other ways. I needed to keep my heart intact.

Lucas was bad news. He was out of my league. He was one hundred percent trouble.

We finally made it to the front of the line and I followed Emily into the pounding beat of the club. The girls made a beeline for the standing tables clustered in front of the bar at the back of the first floor, and Em and I took drink orders. As we pushed our way through the crowd to the bar, I was about to comment to Em that Sally would be disappointed—I didn't see a single guy anywhere, only girls—when she grabbed my arm so tightly I jumped.

"Katie, look who it is!" she said gleefully into my ear. "Why don't I let you order the drinks?"

I craned my neck to catch a glimpse of who she was pointing at—why was I always stuck behind people who were so much taller than me? Through the crowd I spotted broad shoulders under a black t-shirt, dark hair, those honey-coloured eyes focused downward on the drink he was mixing, and, as he handed the drink over the bar, those dangerous dimples.

Our bartender was none other than bad-news-out-of-my-league-one-hundred-percent-trouble Lucas.

6

I turned back to my sister to tell her she could make the drink order while I went and hid in the bathroom—okay, I wasn't going to tell her that part—but she was nowhere to be found.

Great.

I considered going to one of the other bars, but I didn't know exactly where they were. Besides, it was a Friday night and the place was packed. It would take me an hour to get back to our table with all the drinks, by which time the girls would have probably disappeared onto the dance floor.

I glanced hopefully up and down the bar, checking if there was another bartender on duty on a night as busy as this, but no such luck. All I saw was Lucas and his crowd of adoring fans. Accepting my fate with a sigh, I half-heartedly placed my elbow on the bar, waiting my turn. My face felt heavy with all the makeup those evil harpies had painted on me and the contacts were making my eyes burn. I desperately wanted to yank them out of my eyes, but how would I even get in there with all the mascara in the way? (I'd drawn the line at the fake eyelashes.) I closed my eyes to try to ease the burning, and when I opened them again Lucas was standing in front of me.

Considering what I looked like, I was a little surprised at his reaction. He smiled warmly and asked how I was, then leaned forward so I could hear him better.

"Is your sister here with you?" he asked.

I gave him a confused look. Lucas had barely shown any interest in Emily before. "Yeah," I said. "She's over there somewhere." I gestured over my shoulder, nearly hitting the girl standing behind me in the eye. She seemed pretty irritated, not because I'd almost blinded her, but because I was taking up so much of Lucas's time. I mumbled an apology and she raised her voice as she called out her drink order to him for the third time. He ignored her.

"I don't see her," he said as he peered into the dark, trying to locate our table.

When he looked back at me again, he said, "I like your hair," and I looked down at my dark locks hanging over my shoulder, super-straight tonight because of the magic flat iron Melissa had provided.

It suddenly dawned on me why Lucas was asking about Emily.

"Lucas, it's me," I said. "It's Katie."

The grin slipped off his face. His eyes widened with surprise and then darkened with something else as they moved from my eyes to my lips and then downward to the insanely tight black top I was wearing. Sally had wanted me to wear nothing but a black bra underneath the see-through material, but I'd insisted on wearing a camisole. She'd produced the laciest one I'd ever seen from her bag of tricks and pulled it over my head. I noticed Lucas's gaze lingering on that lace stretched across my chest and the generous amount of cleavage just above it. More cleavage than I'd ever shown in my life, that was for sure. I felt my neck flushing, the redness creeping up to my cheeks. As much as being stared at made me want to break something, I had to admit the guy sure knew how to make a girl feel seen.

"Katie?" Lucas said. His voice was thick and at least two octaves lower than it had been a minute ago.

"You know, you might recognize me a little better if you looked at my face," I snapped.

"Oh, I…right," he said. Now his eyes were planted firmly on the bar in front of him. "You're not wearing your glasses."

"Emily made me put on these ridiculous blue contacts," I replied. "She says brown eyes are boring."

"She doesn't know what she's talking about," Lucas muttered so low I wasn't sure if I'd heard him correctly. He cleared his throat and suddenly he was all business. "What'll you have?" he said, picking up a cocktail glass.

I recited the list of drinks and he didn't even bat an eyelash, just began setting out the glasses in a row. I wondered if he thought Em and I were drinking them all ourselves and I was going to clarify that there were five of us in all, but I didn't get the chance. The show going on in front of me was far too distracting.

First he dropped the glass in his hand twice then nearly dropped a full bottle of vodka when he set it down too close to the edge of the counter. I placed my chin in my palm, frowning at him. As I watched, he put double the amount of rum in Anita's rum and Coke and then accidentally threw a lime wedge into the glass when I was pretty sure it was supposed to go on the rim. Then he asked me to repeat the names of the other drinks because he'd forgotten them. While all this was going on he didn't look at me once.

"What the hell is wrong with you?" I asked with some amusement as he dropped yet another glass. They just seemed to be slipping right through his fingers tonight.

"What? Nothing!" he said as he finished the last drink—a vodka cranberry, for me. He'd put three cherries in it, which I was pretty sure also wasn't right, but I didn't mention it. I was just glad he hadn't made it a triple by accident—I wasn't much of a drinker.

As I handed him the cash for the drinks he glanced down at the floor and shook his head, as though he couldn't believe the mess around his feet. I couldn't, either. Was he drinking on the job? Was that allowed? In movies bartenders were always doing shots with the patrons, but I was pretty sure in real life it was a no-no.

When I thanked him for the drinks he finally managed to look me in the face again. He held my gaze there, his eyes darting between mine, his chest heaving as though he'd run a mile. When he broke the gaze to look down at the drinks in front of me, I felt a physical loss and cursed myself for it.

Bad news, out of my league, one hundred percent trouble, I repeated silently to myself.

"That's too many for you to carry," Lucas said, and before I could say a thing he was calling over one of the waitresses, a tattooed girl with severe eye makeup and bleached blonde pigtails. "Brit, can you help her carry these back to her table?"

Brit started collecting the drinks onto her tray.

"Try not to hurt anybody, okay?" I said to Lucas as we walked away, and I thought I saw him heave a sigh of relief as he smiled at me.

"Wow," Brit said. She was expertly carrying the five drinks on a tray balanced on her palm. "I've never seen Lucas like that before."

"Do you think he's drunk?" I said to her as we maneuvered through the crowd. If that was the case, I was going to ask her to get him some coffee. I didn't want him to lose his job.

Brit gave me a funny look. "No, hon," she said. "I'm pretty sure it was the sight of you that had him tripping over his own feet."

"What?" I said with a laugh. "Don't be ridiculous!"

The girls grinned as Brit set the tray down on the table and they all reached forward to grab their drinks. Brit leaned in to talk into my ear while they were distracted.

"Girls shove their boobs in his face all the time and he doesn't even react," she said. "Trust me, I've been working with him three nights a week for months. Lucas has the hots for you, sweetie. You'd better watch yourself." She winked at me as she picked up her tray and made her way back to the bar.

"What's wrong, Katie?" Anita said. "I mean, besides the fact that these drinks are crazy strong!"

I let my eyes travel back to the bar where Lucas was pouring a line of shots. Lucas had the hots for me? Lucas was dropping glasses and acting like an idiot because of me? It was beyond comprehension. Guys didn't fall all over themselves for me. They did that for Em, for Sally, for the flirts of the world, not me. Still, my stomach was doing all kinds of ecstatic cartwheels at the idea. I wished I could settle into that feeling, just for a minute or two, snatch back some of that happiness from two nights ago. But Brit's last words—*You'd better watch yourself*—reminded me why I couldn't. No matter how he felt about me, all I could do was stare at him from across the room and wish and dream and yearn. The dream of Lucas—that's all I could ever have.

Except, that wasn't quite true. I could also have the drink he'd made me.

"Cheers!" I said and downed more than half my cocktail in one gulp as the other girls stared at me, goggle-eyed.

"Oh yeah!" Sally cried, putting her arm around my shoulder. "Let's get smashed!"

Oh, hell yes.

An hour later I was out on the dance floor with Sally, my head all kinds of fuzzy, Emily and the others girls nowhere in sight, and grabby male hands coming at me from every direction. If I'd had to write out the definition of a situation that was way out of my comfort zone, this would probably be it to the letter. As I watched Sally grinding up against the same beefy guy she'd met in the line, her skirt hitched up so high I could literally see half her ass, I felt another pair of hands gripping me by the hips and flung them off.

What it all came down to was bad decision making. My first bad decision had been agreeing to come out for Anita's birthday in the first place, although I now seemed to recall that

I'd given a noncommittal maybe and it was Em who had transformed my answer into a yes. My second bad decision had been imagining that actually coming tonight was in the realm of a good idea, that Em and her friends would create a little cocoon of safety around me, allowing me to avoid actually speaking to anybody but them, that I could actually let loose and get away from myself. And the third bad decision was the most obvious one. That decision was sloshing around in my stomach and making me lightheaded and would soon be showing itself to the entire dance floor if I didn't get out of there really soon.

As the crowd thrashed around me, I tried to remember where Emily had said she was going before she'd disappeared through the press of bodies. To get more drinks? To the bathroom? I couldn't remember how long it had been since she'd left. I didn't even know what time it was. The evil harpies had made me take off my watch. My head began to feel very heavy as the crowd shifted around me and I lost sight of Sally altogether. Suddenly I felt the seeds of panic beginning to germinate in my gut and I turned around, scanning the faces on every side, trying to spot Sally's red lips and blonde curls. The threat of the Facebook message loomed large in my mind, the words echoing in my brain, louder than the music— although it occurred to me that the music in here was so loud no one would be able to hear me scream. If a hand came out and grabbed me, dragging me down, nobody would even notice.

Just as this thought entered my brain an arm reached out and looped itself around my waist, the fingers spreading across my stomach, and I felt my panic spike up into real terror. Without looking around to see who it was, I tried to scramble away, but we were packed in so tightly there was really nowhere to scramble to. Feeling my movement, the hand tightened slightly and something inside of me snapped. I took hold of the fingers gripping me just above my bellybutton and bent them backwards as fast and as hard as I could. I heard a shriek of pain—which, as I predicted, went unnoticed by the rest of the dancing crowd—and then I lunged forward and roughly shoved my way through the bodies, adrenaline pumping like jet fuel through my veins. I focused on the edge of the dance floor and nothing else until I reached it and slammed headfirst into something sturdy and warm and tall.

Something or someone.

This time I actually screamed and pushed out hard with my forearms, flinging myself backwards. I heard someone calling my name but I ignored it, so intent was I on getting away, although it didn't really seem like that was going to happen. Not when I was wearing four-inch borrowed heels and I was losing my balance, my arms pin wheeling as I careened toward the floor. I squeezed my eyes shut, preparing myself for the horrifying crunch of my bones breaking, when a pair of arms reached out and caught me at the critical last second.

My eyes flew open as I found myself once again on my feet, my hands locked onto those arms like vises, not only to brace myself, but also out of fear of who was attached to them.

"Katie, it's me," a voice said. "It's Lucas."

They were the same words I'd said to him earlier when he'd mistaken me for Emily. I guess it was a night for mistaken identities.

"Lucas," I breathed, loosening my grip on his arms. I felt one of his hands slide down to the small of my back, holding me steady, his eyes focused on my face, full of concern. "Get me away from here."

Taking me by the hand, he led me up one staircase and then another to a lounge at the very top of the club. There were couches and armchairs scattered around the area and it was mostly empty, just one couple making out and two girls who seemed to be sleeping, their heads resting one on top of the other. Lucas and I sat down on a couch in the corner. It was a loveseat, meant for two people in theory, though in this case I had to assume two twelve-year-old girls—it was that narrow. I was practically sitting in his lap. I tried to wiggle over, but there was no couch left next to me, and he kept leaning toward me and touching me with his warm hands and murmuring softly to me, which was so calming, almost like a lullaby, except liking his lullaby was *so* totally against the promise I'd made myself. The more he tried to calm me, the more agitated I became, until I felt his hands cupping my face, holding it still.

"Breathe, Katie," he said. "Breathe."

With his words, and the steady breaths that followed, I felt the adrenaline leeching out of my body being replaced by a none-too-subtle pounding in my head. Drawing my legs up onto the couch, I wrapped my arms around them and pressed my cheek into my kneecaps, closing my eyes. I felt his palm, warm against my back as he rubbed it and smoothed my long hair, something I'd done countless times for Emily when she was hungover, though having it done to me was quite a different thing. If the music in the club hadn't been so incredibly loud, I might have actually drifted off.

When I finally opened my eyes again and sat up, Lucas was still right there beside me with a sweet smile. I tried to smile back but I was too embarrassed, remembering the perfect fool I'd made of myself downstairs. Luckily, Lucas didn't ask for an explanation. Instead he handed me a bowl of pretzels.

"Here, eat this," he said. "Sorry, it's all we have to snack on. And drink this."

He handed me a glass full of clear liquid, which I eyed warily.

"It's water," he added.

Looking down at the food in my hands, I gave him a puzzled look. "When did you get this?" I said. Had he left me alone on the couch while my eyes were closed? I hadn't felt him move. And if he had gone, whose hand had I felt on my back? I felt my heart begin to pound again.

"I texted Brit to bring this stuff up," he said, his voice full of reassurance. "I'm actually hiding up here with you. Brit's covering for me."

"You should go back to work," I said. "I don't want you to get into trouble because of me."

"No trouble," Lucas said easily. "I covered for her last month while she spent four hours behind the club having a screaming fight with her boyfriend. She owes me. This won't even cover it."

I nodded feebly, nibbling on a pretzel, wishing heartily that they were the dipped-in-chocolate kind.

"Are you feeling better?" Lucas said tentatively.

I took a gulp of water so I could have time to think of what to say. "I'm really fine," I said. "I just don't usually come out to places like this. All the people. And I lost Emily. I was just overwhelmed and a little freaked and I'm going to strangle Sally later."

Lucas raised his eyebrows. "And who's this Sally?"

"One of Em's friends," I said.

"And that's all it was?" he asked. "You just got overwhelmed? There wasn't anything…"

He left the sentence hanging, waiting for me to fill in the blank. I could tell he sensed I was leaving something out, but I wasn't about to explain.

"I'm never going clubbing again," I said.

"It's really not that bad once you get used to it," Lucas said. "Although I guess I had to get used to it, since I work here. And I get to enjoy it all without the help of alcohol, which is quite a treat."

"You never mentioned that you worked here," I said. I was actually a little surprised. I'd naively thought Lucas was living on his daddy's dime, another rich kid like Sally's Alex, like me—although in our family it was my mom who made the big bucks. I didn't have to work during the school year, but it looked like Lucas did.

He shrugged. "There's a reason I work so far away from campus. I don't want the party to follow me here. I just want to get the work done. So I don't really mention it to anyone."

"Yeah, there's not much of a party going on down there," I said teasingly.

"But it's not my party," Lucas pointed out, and I nodded in agreement, though I didn't really get it. Wasn't Lucas supposedly the life of the party? What exactly was he hiding from?

"And what about you, princess? Since when did you become such a party girl?" Lucas asked.

He pointed at my head and I reached up to find I had on Anita's tiara. I vaguely recalled her placing it on my head earlier. Had I been wearing it this entire time?

I snatched it off my head.

"That's just an inside joke," I said lamely, trying to discreetly drop it into the seam of the couch behind me, but Lucas snaked his arm behind my back and grabbed it.

"Oh, no," he said with a wicked grin. "You have to keep it on. It goes so well with your ensemble." He tried to place it back on my head, but I twisted away with a laugh, wrestling with his outstretched arms until I looked up and he was hovering over me, one knee next to my thigh on the couch, his other leg planted on the ground on the other side of me, his face just inches from mine. I stopped struggling and he placed the tiara back on my head, then eased slowly back into his seat, letting his eyes trail down my body as he did so, ending at my boots.

"Did I mention how much I'm enjoying these?" he said with a slow grin, placing a light hand on my left calf.

"They're not mine," I said, painfully aware of every finger pressing into the leather.

"And this?" he said, tugging at the bottom of my top, his fingertips grazing against the skin of my stomach.

I sucked in a breath, sharply. "It doesn't really fit me," I said. It really didn't. Sally was two sizes smaller than I was.

"Oh, it fits you," Lucas said. "Trust me."

My body flushed again and this time the flush didn't fade as his eyes moved to my face.

"And this makeup," he said, his gaze darting from my eyes to my lips to my cheeks to my lips again. "It's certainly interesting. But you don't need it. Same with the contacts. It's covering up the real you."

"It's all covering up the real me," I said. "That's what I like about it."

I blinked. The alcohol seemed to have loosened my tongue

along with making the room spin, though I noticed it had pretty much stopped spinning now.

I said, "I mean, we all want to pretend to be someone else sometimes, don't we? We all want to hide."

Suddenly, he got to his feet and pulled me up with him. I gazed around dizzily.

"Come with me," he said. "There's something I want to show you."

We descended the same stairs we'd taken to come up and found ourselves on the second floor dance floor. There weren't nearly as many people dancing as there had been earlier and I hardly had any trouble getting across the floor. I was nearly to the second staircase when Lucas tugged on my hand, pulling me back. When I saw that he wanted me to join him in the middle of the dance floor, I shook my head firmly. Was this what he had in mind? Dancing? If so, his mind was about to change very quickly, because I had no intention of going out there again. Ever.

I let go of his hand and folded my arms around my middle. He came to join me by the wall.

"Let me guess," he said. "Aggressive guys? Grabby hands? I work here, you know. I know what some guys are like on the dance floor."

"It wasn't just that," I protested, though I was surprised at how much he had guessed. "I just don't like being on display, like... I'm not really a good dancer. I'm just not comfortable and it's so... I'm not... I just..."

I clamped my mouth shut, sick of listening to my own stuttering.

"You want to lose yourself?" he said and my eyes snapped to his face. "I do it all the time, right out there." He pointed at the people dancing in front of us. "It's easy. I can show you how if you'll let me."

Straight ahead of me a girl in a strapless sparkly top threw her head back, shaking her hair, a luminous smile on her face. I wanted to be like that, to be free. But I didn't want to feel that panic creeping in again, not tonight. I looked up at Lucas.

When he was around, I never felt afraid, probably because he was always so at ease—well, except during the glass-dropping intro to the night. A little dancing with Lucas couldn't hurt, could it?

"If you embarrass me I'll punch you in the junk," I said as I put my hand in his.

He gave me an affirmative nod. "Got it, Hero," he said.

Taking both my hands in his, he towed me into the middle of the fray. The song that was playing was one I knew and liked with an added house beat and synthesizer. Standing still in the middle of the dancing crowd I immediately felt self-conscious and my eyes kept darting to the people around us, watching to see if they were watching me. Lucas put his hands on my shoulders, drawing my eyes to his face.

"Don't worry about them," he said. "They don't care what you're doing. All they care about is looking hot."

I smirked and his smile joined mine.

"Just look at me. Keep your eyes on mine," he said. "Don't look away."

I nodded yes, but I didn't think I'd be able to do it. I was terrible at keeping eye contact. Even when I was having a conversation with someone I would find myself staring at the wall behind their head. I didn't like the feeling of being looked at, examined. It always made me feel as though the person looking was trying to figure me out. Then again, I didn't seem to mind when Lucas looked at me. And looking at Lucas, well, that wasn't what I would call hard. Actually, it was pretty damn easy.

As I stared into those big golden eyes of his, I felt Lucas place his hands on my waist. Instinctively, I felt my body tense and I was surprised that he didn't say anything about it. He just left his hands there and kept his eyes on mine until I slowly felt my muscles relax.

"Now, I want you to move like I move," he said. "Put your hands here."

He placed my hands on his hips so we were mirroring each other. I nearly laughed. This felt very much like an elementary school dance. Then he started to move his hips and I felt his fingers digging into mine, encouraging me to do the same, and suddenly all thoughts of elementary school were gone.

I could feel the taut muscles of his stomach through his shirt. I wanted so much to look down at his body, to touch his chest, but that would mean breaking eye contact. My hips began to mimic his movements, moving much slower than the music, and he smiled at me, showing off his dimples, as our rhythm fell into sync. He ran one hand up my back and then back down again, sending a shiver down my spine, and then I felt the gentle pressure of his palm, pushing me forward until we were hip to hip. I forgot about keeping eye contact at that point—I sort of forgot about everything—and pressed my cheek into his shoulder, looping my arms around his neck.

"Close your eyes," he whispered into my ear.

And I did.

The music throbbed around us, keeping our hips in motion and wiping out almost everything else except the feeling of his chest against mine and his hands holding me. I didn't have a thought in my head. I certainly didn't know and didn't care if anyone was watching us. I didn't know anything except that I loved this feeling of oblivion, of disappearing into the music, of being here with him. I felt one of his hands cupping the back of my head, his fingers moving through my hair. I clung to him and danced.

We were both sweaty when we finally pulled apart. His hand was still in my hair.

"How'd you do that?" I said to him. He was staring down at me so intently I wasn't sure he would answer.

"Do what?" he finally said.

"Make the world disappear."

He grinned, letting his hand slip out of my locks and down to my back. "And just think, you can do it any time you want. The wonderful land of the dance floor is always here for you."

"Not just any time," I said, and he gave me a questioning look, his eyes returning to my face. "I only feel like this when I'm with you."

What did I just say?

I was still tangled in his arms and he looked like he had every intention of keeping me there, his eyes riveted to mine as though we were still dancing, but I pulled free and this time I was the one to guide him down the stairs, holding his hand, leading the way. This was good. Moving was good. Talking on the other hand, clearly not so good.

Back on the first floor I was swarmed by Emily and her friends. I caught Lucas's eye and saw him wink and wave at me, then disappear into the dark leading toward the bar.

"We've been looking for you everywhere!" Anita said, then took a sip of her drinks, one in each hand.

"Sally's in the bathroom throwing up," Melissa announced.

"We didn't abandon her there," Emily explained, as though worried I would disapprove. "She always insists on throwing up alone. She's psychotic about it. She bit me. Are you okay?"

This last question she directed right into my ear, then looked at me worriedly as Anita and Melissa danced a circle around us. Em couldn't always read my moods, but she sure as hell knew I didn't like facing a nightclub alone, especially when she'd been the one to drag me there.

"Where *were* you?" I asked with more venom that I'd meant to, only now realizing how angry I still was at the way she'd left me alone. I watched her take a step away from me and lower her eyes to the floor.

Right away I regretted my outburst. How could I blame Em for not babysitting me the entire night? She was entitled to have her own fun. But before I could tell her this, Anita interrupted us.

"Did I see you holding hands with Lucas?" Apparently Anita's reaction time was on a drunken five-minute delay.

"Oh my God!" Melissa cried. "Did he rescue you?"

"Did he dance with you?"

"Did you guys make out? Tell me you made out. You totally did. You made out, right?"

I didn't answer any of their questions. I could still feel his fingers in my hair.

We left about an hour later. Sally was so drunk both Melissa and Anita had to help her to the car, her arms around their shoulders as she shouted obscenities at the beefy guy and his whole group of friends. None of the other girls seemed to know what had gone down between them, and I, for one, didn't want to know. It seemed that Sally was a fun drunk right up until she got really loaded. Then she became a scratch-your-eyes-out-for-no-reason drunk.

"I'm gonna rip your head off and feed it to my snake!" she yelled as Melissa stuffed her into the passenger's seat.

The beefy guy made a rude gesture back.

"Does she even have a snake?" I asked as Anita leaned on the car door to close it. We were all reluctant to get into the car with Sally.

"You think she has the ability to take care of a snake?" Anita asked.

"Don't be mean," Emily said. "Just because she goes a little nuts when she's drunk doesn't make her an idiot. She's planning on going to law school after she's done—"

At this moment Sally rolled down the window and threw up onto the street right beside my sister's shoes.

"Puking," Em finished.

We all piled into the car and Melissa eased us out into the non-existent traffic. I was impressed to find out she'd volunteered to be the designated driver and had stopped drinking two hours ago. Point one to Melissa. Sally was currently at point negative forty-two.

Emily put her head on my shoulder. She was always the most affectionate when she knew I was pissed at her. "So what really happened with Lucas?" she asked.

"Um," I said, hoping Sally would scream out something else and I wouldn't have to answer.

I couldn't tell her the truth, of course. How could I when I hardly knew what the truth was? He'd rescued me from a panic attack and taught me to dance? I thought of his honey-coloured eyes. I'd stared at them for so long now I could picture perfectly how they were rimmed with dark gold and the exact way they'd stared into mine when I'd told him I could only feel that way with him.

My secret made me smile so wide I had to turn my face toward the window.

Melissa stopped the car at a light and that's when I saw Lucas sitting on a bench by the curb with a girl. They weren't touching, but they were sitting very close together. She had long blonde hair that stuck out of the hood of her winter coat. They were turned toward each other and she was talking animatedly with her hands. I couldn't hear what she was saying, but as the moments passed I could tell she'd started yelling. Lucas looked distraught. He covered his face with his hands. And then he looked up at her and reached a hand out to touch her face, brushing his thumb across her cheek. He seemed to be about to speak when the light turned green and we drove on.

Emily repeated her question.

"Nothing," I said, turning away from the window. "Lucas and I are nothing to each other, and we'll never be anything more. End of story."

She stopped asking after that.

Just then my phone buzzed in my pocket with a text message. I dug into my jeans to pull it loose, hoping against hope it would be Lucas and that somehow he'd intuited that I'd seen what I had and he'd explain it and everything would be fine.

But it wasn't Lucas, and nothing was fine.

There were three messages from an unknown number.

Unknown: You'll never get away with it.
Unknown: You're about to get what you deserve.
Unknown: I'm coming for you.

7

If there was one thing I was good at, it was pretending. Actually, that's not true. If there was one thing I was good at, it was complete avoidance and denial—which counted as one thing in my mind because I never did one without the other—but pretending definitely came in a close second. For the next few days I put all my years of practice at pretending to very good use. As I walked to class I pretended that it didn't matter that Brandon had tracked down my cell phone number, which was unlisted, and that he was somehow sending me texts when I was fairly certain he didn't have access to a cell phone. I pretended it didn't bother me that his texts had gone from subtle to aggressive threats. I pretended I wasn't concerned by all the evidence that someone out in the world was helping him harass me, and that I wasn't at all worried that this someone might come after me for real. By the time it occurred to me to change my number—the pretending was really slowing down my brain—I'd already received enough threatening texts to last a lifetime. Though Emily accepted my "lost phone" story without question, I was pretty sure the message I'd left on my parents machine would elicit a string of questions all leading back to Brandon.

Not that it bothered me.

The girl with the blonde hair was another thing that wasn't bothering me. Nope, not in the slightest. I certainly wasn't thinking of her as I sat through class on Monday, avoiding looking in Lucas's direction—which wasn't exactly easy, seeing as he was sitting directly next to me. And I certainly wasn't thinking about how close together they were sitting on that bench or the emotions her words had brought out in him, or the intimate way he'd touched her face. Nuh-uh, I wasn't thinking about that at all, just like I wasn't thinking about how, an hour before, that same hand had been caught up in my hair.

Most of all I was pretending that whole night at The Limo hadn't even happened.

While all this pretending was going on I was also on a healthy-eating kick, which was really my biggest delusion of all. Those three days of refrigerator-emptying madness were the last straw, or so I sternly told myself, and it was time to get smart about my diet. On a snowy Wednesday evening I went to the store and stocked up on veggies, fruit, whole-wheat pasta, and quinoa and bookmarked all kinds of good-for-you recipes on my laptop. I bought a soup pot; I bought beets; I bought another box of healthy cereal.

All this lasted for about a day and a half when I realized I had a fridge full of ingredients and no idea how to cook them. The recipes all required abilities I hadn't yet mastered and cooking implements I didn't own. (A cheese grater? A wok? A working oven?) Also, whole-wheat pasta tasted like cardboard. In an unprecedented moment of solidarity, the cat was completely rejecting the more expensive, vet-approved, healthy cat food I'd bought him. The stony eyed glare he gave me every time I opened the bag exactly matched the look I gave all the food in my fridge whenever I opened the door.

Which is why on Friday, after my economics class, I was at a diner around the corner from campus eating a cheeseburger with extra bacon and curly fries when Mariella sat down in the seat across from me.

"That's right," she said, fixing me with a try-and-stop-me look, "I'm rudely interrupting your lonely lunch by sitting down in your booth. I'm one of those people who can't eat alone, so sue me." She set her plate of food down in front of herself and began to unfold her napkin.

"Oh, hi!" I said, trying to sound simultaneously unalarmed and delighted to see her—*pretend, pretend, pretend*—while also quickly glancing around for a stray child. "Where's Ethan?"

"Ethan is at school, and then he's staying with his grandparents," Mariella explained as she dipped her fries in my ketchup. "Thank God! I mean, I love the kid to death, but I feel like I haven't sat down in about four years. He's wreaking havoc on my figure! Look at how much weight I've lost in the last month because I'm running after that little munchkin all day!" She pulled her sweater away from her sizeable stomach and gave me a horrified look.

Oh, Mariella. Why do you have to be so awesome?

I could feel myself giving in to her undeniable charm and for once I didn't feel like pretending I didn't love her. Emily was in a three-hour film class, and I was in desperate need of some conversation. And if there was one thing I could count on Mariella for, it was conversation.

"Don't you have work?" I asked as I picked up my burger with both hands and took an enormous bite.

Mariella nodded appreciatively and clinked my burgers with hers.

"Hell, no," she said. "By some miracle I have the day off, and you've caught me during my free half-hour in between doing groceries, cleaning the entire apartment, going to the dentist, baking cupcakes for the bake sale, and folding all the laundry I did this morning. Aren't you lucky?"

I was definitely feeling pretty lucky after hearing that list.

Mariella grinned. "So I've got all the time in the world to ask you which boy did what to put that sad look on your face. Did he run over your kitty with his car? Or was it just your heart?"

"Nobody ran over anything," I said, though the strain of all this pretending kind of made me feel like I had been. "I'm just worried…about an assignment…for my art history class."

She gave me a look. "Well, that was pathetic," she commented. "Art history class? That's the best lie you could come up with? Make up a fight you had with your sister or something at least. Put some effort in."

"I am in a fight with Emily, actually," I said. Truthfully, she was acting like there was nothing wrong and I was letting her do it, our spat over her abandoning me at The Limo disappearing as though it had never occurred, like always.

"What's his name?" Mariella said, taking a bite out of a fry with each word. "You're crying over a guy, so just tell me his name."

"I am not crying!" I protested.

Mariella gave me that same look again, her jaw working as she chewed. I knew she'd wait me out all day if she had to, even if it meant missing her dental appointment.

"His name is…Lucas," I said reluctantly, giving her a sour look. "And by the way, still not crying over here."

"Lucas!" she cried, a little louder than I would have liked. "Oh yeah, Lucas. I like it. It's a good name. It's very…white boy. But that's okay. That's all right. We all have our weaknesses, myself included, obviously. So what'd white boy Lucas do to you?"

"He didn't *do* anything," I said, setting my burger back down and wiping my mouth. "We just danced and there was… He thought I was Emily and then he gave me that look… And brownies and texting and putting his hand in my hair—"

"Oh, hand in the hair," Mariella said knowingly.

"And there was a moment on that loveseat," I added.

"Oh, loveseats are trouble," she agreed.

"And calling me Hero and giving me a cat and then he goes and touches that blonde girl's face!" I cried, slamming my hands down on the table.

Mariella frowned as I stared at her grumpily, my chest heaving with aggravation. "Wait, so what did he do?" she asked.

"I just told you!" I answered so loudly the people at the next table glanced over, which had literally never happened to me before in my life.

As amazing as I was at pretending and denying and avoiding, it also tended to turn me into kind of a basket case.

"There was this other girl…" I added more quietly.

"So now he's with this other girl instead of you?" Mariella asked as she pushed her plate to the side.

"Well, I'm not really sure, he—"

"But you saw him with this other girl after he said he liked you?"

"He didn't exactly say he liked me. And I'm not exactly sure what I saw, because—"

"What did he say when you asked him about it?"

"You see, I haven't actually asked—"

Mariella shook her head so vehemently that I couldn't go on. "No, girl, no," she said. "I will not have you falling apart over something you don't even know is real. You've just got to ask him straight up what the deal is. Does he like you or does he like her? I don't want to hear another stuttering excuse about it."

I stared down at my plate. "But what if I don't like the answer? I want him to like me best," I said miserably, and the words, as I heard them coming out of my mouth, stunned me to the core. I wanted Lucas. I wanted him to be mine. No, I needed him to be mine.

Oh God, I was so screwed.

Mariella put her hand on my arm. "He will," she said. "You just have to give him a chance to get there."

"Or maybe he's just playing me, like Jeremy did you," I said. (This was Jeremy of the canoe of douches.)

"Well, that's no problem," Mariella said with a sly grin. "Because in that case you know you've got your trusty friend Mariella to help you whoop his lily-white ass!"

We cackled so loudly the entire diner was looking, and I

didn't even care.

Later that day I was coming down the stairs outside the library after spending two exhausting hours researching my art history paper on Gauguin when I spotted Lucas leaning against the building. I hovered on the stairs, my arms laden with books, wondering what I should do. He was facing the other way and so hadn't spotted me yet, his back against the bare ivy that snaked over the bricks. I could slip away unnoticed. I could escape. A week and a half ago that was exactly what I would have done. I'd made an art form of avoiding students I knew peripherally from class, or professors, or even people I knew better like Melissa or Anita. I'd once run out of a building to avoid Sally. A week and a half ago my life had been orderly and predictable, all of my actions fitting a mold I'd made myself years ago.

And then Lucas had come along.

The feelings I'd expressed to Mariella came back to me as I looked at him gazing forlornly down the road, his hands deep in his coat pockets. There was no point in trying to pretend anymore, or trying to force myself to give him up. I'd already failed at that twice. If a part of me tried to avoid him, there would always be another part of me looking for him everywhere I went, trying to find him, trying to keep him. As furious as it made me, both with him and with myself, Lucas was in my life now. I guessed I might as well get used to it.

As I walked toward him across the snow, I considered asking him Mariella's question. I pictured myself demanding to know who it was going to be, the blonde or me, while Lucas stared at me in surprise. Even in my imagination the scene disintegrated before it was fully formed. How could I possibly ask him a question I already knew the answer to? Lucas was a flirt and he'd flirted with me just as he did every other girl. It didn't mean anything. I had to stop giving it meaning. Silently, I gave myself the same kind of pep talk I had given to Emily in the tenth grade when she was lovestruck over Brad the Cad.

He doesn't like you like that. You need to stop liking him like that, too. You need to try to be friends. And if you get the urge to kiss him, you need to resist. Resist!

Emily hadn't been able to follow that last piece of advice. She'd kissed Brad at the end-of-year dance, in front of the whole school, in front of his girlfriend.

As I called out to Lucas and he turned to me, his face lighting up, I finally understood why Emily had done that. Because *goddamn*, it was hard to think about anything but kissing when he looked at me like that.

"Damn!" Lucas said as he took in my pile of books. "You know you can photocopy the pages you need, right? You don't have to check out all the books in the library."

I didn't want to explain that photocopying meant spending even more hours in the library looking up all the appropriate passages in the books, and then standing at the photocopier for an interminable amount of time while other students stood behind you sighing and urging you to hurry. I preferred to do my research in the safety of my apartment. I would live my entire life inside my apartment if I could.

"Well, what are you doing skulking beside the library, anyway?" I said with an obvious note of irritation in my voice. "You know you have to read the books to learn something. You can't just suck up the knowledge through the walls."

I knew something was wrong when that didn't get a chuckle out of him.

He pointed down University Avenue. "This is the route I used to take to the gym. I used to walk this way every day when I was on the team."

We both looked down the street, almost as though we expected to see the Lucas of the past walking by, his gym bag over his shoulder.

"When's the last time you went in there?" I asked quietly. I didn't know why Lucas had quit basketball, but I knew a thing or two about avoiding things and places and people. I knew what it felt like to be afraid of going back.

He shook his head, and his small smile didn't reach his

eyes. He was trying to make light of it. "A long time. Months. It doesn't matter."

"We should go there, together. We should go to a game," I said, startling myself as the words left my mouth.

We should what?

"That's the kind of thing friends do, isn't it? Friends go to games together. Sporting events are very friendly." I clamped my mouth shut and bit my cheeks to keep it closed.

Lucas raised his eyebrows, not capable of holding back his laugh this time. "Sporting events are friendly?" he repeated carefully.

"Well..." Having no explanation for that nonsensical string of sentences, I decided to start over again. "Isn't there a game tonight? A basketball game?" This was a wild guess. I had no idea if there was a game tonight.

"Actually, there is," Lucas said. "They're playing against Carleton tonight. But I'm not going. I'd love to go out with you, Katie..."

Resist!

"But I can't go to a game," he finished. "I can't sit there and watch them play. I just...I can't." He wasn't even looking at me anymore, just looking out at the snow and the street. He looked so melancholy. I just couldn't leave it at that.

"What if you didn't have to watch?" I said. He frowned at me, but I could see the hope in his eyes. The desire to believe that I could find some way to get him into that gym again, that he could leave his fear behind.

"What've you got up your sleeve, Hero?" he said, that reliable grin hovering at the edges of his lips again. I should have known. A guy like Lucas could never resist a little mystery.

"Take me to the game tonight and find out," I said.

8

He picked me up at seven thirty after I'd spent a humiliating amount of time picking out what to wear. I'd settled finally on the sweater and jeans I'd been wearing all day because lord knew what a person was supposed to wear to a sports game, anyway. Besides, I didn't have to look nice. This wasn't a date after all.

I repeated this to myself a lot, both in my head and out loud to the cat as he lay purring on my pile of discarded clothes.

This. Isn't. A. Date.

Although it did kind of feel like one when he rang the buzzer and I met him at the door. His hair was slightly wet, as though he'd just washed it, and I could smell his cologne as he held the door open. His blue pea coat, which made him look a little like a sailor, was smartly buttoned. He'd shaved. He looked like a shiny new penny, while I looked like that crumpled five-dollar bill you found in the bottom of your pocket after it had gone through the wash.

Great.

I wondered if he could tell that no guy had ever come to pick me up before, that no one ever buzzed my apartment, not even Emily, who had her own key. I wondered if he could tell how incredibly nervous I was, and then I realized that he probably could, since I was still standing on the upper step near the door, staring at him, without having said a word. Although it's also worth pointing out that he was standing two steps below me staring back, and he hadn't said a word, either.

It was as though we were both in some kind of dream state where time moved more slowly and all social conventions, like conversation, were suspended.

His eyes swept over my face languidly and then moved upward to my hair, which I'd shoved into a messy bun on top of my head.

"I like your hair like that," he said, and actually reached out as though he wanted to touch it, but I caught his fingers just as they reached the level of my face and gently pushed them away.

No. This was not a dream I wanted to have.

"Are we late?" I said, jogging down the stairs ahead of him and heading for the street, effectively breaking our joint daydream.

He easily caught up with me and took my arm, placing it over his. And I let him, because it was cold, and...well, because it felt nice. But that was okay, because it was the type of thing friends did, wasn't it? I suddenly realized I had no idea what guys and girls who were friends did.

"Well, are you ready to attend a friendly game of basketball, Hero?" he asked, steering us down the sidewalk toward his car. "Because this is a friendly night, the type of night I would only share with a friend. And I want you to know I can only ever be your friend. I think it's important that we both understand that. Don't you think so, friend?"

So apparently he'd heard my whole "friend" tirade loud and clear.

I glared up at him as we reached his car, a battered red Civic with a big dent in the passenger's side door.

"I definitely think so," I said with more confidence than I was actually feeling as he let go of my arm and stepped toward me, causing me to lean back against the door.

I saw a twinkle in his eyes as he moved forward, placing his hands against the car window on either side of my body. I felt my breath catch in my throat and a thrill rise up from my belly as the front of our coats brushed against each other and he leaned in.

"That's good," he said into my ear, my cheek growing warm just from the knowledge that his was centimeters away. I could hear the smile in his voice. "Because I wouldn't want there to be any confusion."

He pulled his face back and looked me in the eye. Our faces were lined up perfectly for a kiss, and I felt my body betraying me, my face moving toward his without my permission, my senses awakening with something new.

Desire.

My lips trembled, though I tried to still them. As much as I wanted him, I was also terribly afraid. This wouldn't be just any kiss. It would be my first.

I held my breath, waiting, as his eyes dipped to my lips and then his face changed, his eyes zipping back up to mine with a question in them that I couldn't read. Suddenly he was all business and movement. He pulled me toward him—more like a jerk, really—and yanked the car door open, then ran his hands roughly up and down my arms, as one would a child who had stayed out too long playing in the snow.

"Cold, isn't it?" he said with forced enthusiasm, and gestured for me to get in as he ran around to the driver's side.

"Sure is," I replied as I climbed in and buckled my seat belt. I was still in a little bit of shock, all my emotions jumbled and jumping and disorderly.

As he drove us toward the Athletics Centre, keeping his eyes firmly glued to the road, I tried to console myself with the fact that I'd been right. Lucas and I were just friends. Because when he'd had his chance, he'd come this close and changed his mind. It was a good thing I'd put the kibosh on the whole boyfriend idea that morning. It was smart of me, really. Wasn't I so clever? Wasn't it so wonderful to be right?

Except that it wasn't.

Being right had never felt so awful.

The gym was crowded and bright and loud. Having never been to a game, any game, before, I hadn't known what to expect, but the noise was the biggest surprise. I wondered how the players could stand it. I thought to ask Lucas, but I didn't much feel like talking to him right then, and he didn't look like he was up for a discussion, either. In fact, he looked downright ill.

"Hold on a minute," he said as we walked through the gym doors. They were the first words he'd spoken since our moment by the car.

He'd stopped in his tracks just inside the doorway, and as I walked back toward him I saw him swallowing hard, as though he was trying to get down a particularly large pill.

"You're *not* going to throw up, do you hear me?" I said as I pulled him toward the bleachers. In the short ten minutes it had taken us to drive here and walk into the building, the awful feeling inside me had morphed into a simmering rage that I didn't question or examine in any way. I was certainly in no mood to rub his back as he hurled.

It seemed like we were a little late after all, because the game had already started and the bleachers were full. Lucas held back, keeping himself out of sight of the crowd as I scanned the stands for two seats together, finally spotting them on the left side near the top. Looking over at Lucas again, I found him staring intently at the floor. He seemed to be doing everything he could not to glance at the game itself.

"Snap out of it," I said, clapping my hands in front of his face. "You're fine. It's fine. Come on, let's go." I grabbed him none too gently by the sleeve.

Apparently rage turned me into the type of person who barked orders and was obeyed, because he didn't resist. Or maybe he was just so out of it that following me was all he could handle. Whatever the reason, we were about halfway up the bleachers and I was still towing him by the arm when I realized everybody around us was looking our way. I faltered on the stairs, jarred by all those eyes, but Lucas didn't skip a beat. He swiftly passed me, his head bowed and hands plunged into his pockets, and reached the seats I'd been aiming for a full minute before I got there.

I let out a slow sigh as most of the heads turned back to the game, though I did notice a few girls still staring.

We might not actually be on a date, but every person within a twenty-foot radius definitely thought we were.

Just perfect.

To distract myself from the realization that my first friendly activity with Lucas had been such a colossally bad choice, I fiddled with my bag, pulling out what we would need to get through the game. Then I turned to Lucas, still chock full of fury—because, of course, all of this was entirely *his* fault—until I took in what was happening to him.

He was sitting in his seat with his back straight as a board and his eyes closed, his hands curled into fists on his thighs, his mouth clenched closed so tightly that I could see the muscles in his jaw bulging. He was breathing hard through his nose—too hard. He looked like he was about to explode.

"I can't be here," he hissed through his teeth. "I have to get out of here. I have to go, now."

I would have agreed, except going right then would have meant getting him down the stairs in this state with a couple of hundred people watching. He was in no condition to weigh in on the matter, but I was pretty sure making his panic attack public knowledge wasn't something Lucas would want. Lucky for him, I was pretty much an expert on panic attacks, having had one at least once a week for as long as I could remember.

Grabbing his left fist, I quickly opened up his hand and placed it on my chest, just below my collarbone. His eyes flew open and I nearly smiled despite myself. At least I had his attention.

"It's okay, Lucas," I said in my most soothing voice, focusing my eyes on his frantic ones. I placed my hand over his. "You're going to breathe like me. Nice and slow, okay? Close your eyes and breathe."

His chest continued to shudder at first and I worried that it wasn't working. My next best idea was to put his head between his knees, but considering how tall he was he would have probably ended up knocking skulls with the guy sitting in front of us. Worriedly, I reached up with my free hand and cupped his cheek, rubbing my thumb gently over that clenched jaw muscle until I finally felt it ease. I continued to whisper to him as his breathing slowly returned to normal, not even really hearing what I was saying. I knew I'd always found it comforting when my father had done this for me. I'd just never done it for someone else before. It was sort of nice, being the strong one for a change.

As the attack subsided, I let go of his cheek, but he didn't move his hand. I was keenly aware all of a sudden of how close his palm was to my breasts and of the fact that only a few moments ago a number of girls had been avidly watching us. Were they still watching now? I nearly turned to check, but then Lucas opened his eyes.

"Almost lost you there," I teased. He blinked at me as though he was coming out of a long sleep. Then I watched his eyes lower to where his hand was still pressed to my chest. A grin pulled at his lips.

"If I'd known this was the reward I would get, I might have come to more games," he joked and I threw his hand back at him, swatting him hard on the arm while I was at it.

"Do you still want to go?" I asked as I watched him glance down at the game still going on below us. Somebody had just scored and the crowd around us cheered.

"After all that?" Lucas said, taking a deep breath. "Hell, no."

"Good," I said, handing him one of the sketch pads from my lap and two pencils. "Let's get started."

"What's this?" he asked, giving the pad a quizzical look.

"I told you, we aren't here to watch the game," I said. "We're here to sketch."

This was something I did all the time when I found myself stuck in a social situation I couldn't handle. Art was my passion, but it was also a really great smokescreen. When you were drawing, people thought twice about bothering you or even talking to you. The trick was to look really absorbed and focused. I took a sketchpad with me everywhere I went, just in case. You never knew when you might need to disappear.

"This is speed sketching," I informed him, "so don't waste time trying to make it perfect. The idea is to get at least twenty solid sketches in by the end of the night. You've got to just pick something and start drawing. And we'll be moving around to get different angles."

I'd expected a little bit of push back, but Lucas surprised me. He flipped open the pad and set it on his knees, his pencil poised, and when I said, "Go," he went right to it, sketching a player running for the hoop. I guessed it was the challenge that piqued his interest. He was an athlete after all. He was used to playing to win.

Even though sports bored me to tears, there was plenty to draw in the gym. I got in a really good sketch of two girls gossiping while their boyfriends watched the game, and another of a player sitting in the front row with his head bowed, a towel over his neck. Then it was time to move. I'd thought this part might be tricky, everybody's attention drawn back to us again as we blocked their view, but after the first few moves it seemed to be working in our favour. The crowd had lost interest in keeping track of us and nobody was looking our way.

At my elbow, Lucas sketched diligently. Since he was taking Introductory Fine Art II, I knew drawing couldn't be entirely foreign to him—they never would have let him take the class otherwise. He frowned as he drew and chewed on his lip. It was adorable, and I couldn't help but picture the little boy he had been once, with that same look on his face as he built a sand castle or aimed for the basket. When he looked up at me, surprised to find me watching him, I realized it was time to move again and I hadn't drawn a single sketch.

"Maybe we should split up this time," I said, my cheeks reddening. "I don't see any two seats together."

Big, fat lie.

"Whatever you say, Hero," Lucas said with undeniable amusement.

But before I could squeeze past Lucas to get to the stairs, I found my route blocked by a pair of long, thin legs ending in spike-heeled boots. They looked like the kind of heels you would use to stab someone through the skull. Looking up, I realized that description was right on the money, because from the look she was giving me, I was pretty sure she would have stabbed me if she could.

"Hey, Lucas," Stabber Girl said in a sickly sweet voice. "Who's your *friend*?"

I would have gladly scurried away at that moment, but Lucas took my hand and gently pulled me back into my seat, and there was something about the feeling of his fingers in mine—and the fact that he wasn't letting go—that kept me there. Besides, Stabber Girl was still standing in my way.

"Hi, Monica," Lucas said blandly, his attention mostly remaining with his drawing. "This is Katie." I plastered a smile on my face as I looked up at her, but she barely glanced at me now. She only had eyes for Lucas.

"When did you start coming to the games again?" Monica said, twirling a finger around a strand of her auburn hair. "You should have told me. I would have saved you a seat."

From the way she said the word "seat," I was pretty sure she wanted to find hers in Lucas's lap. I was wondering how familiar this girl was with Lucas and his lap, when all of a sudden she fell forward and landed directly in it, her short skirt fanning out around her thighs and her arms looping around his neck.

"Oops," she said perkily as she pressed her ample breasts against his chest. I had to reach up and snap my mouth closed. This girl's moves put Sally's to shame, and that was saying something. "I guess I tripped."

"I guess you did," Lucas said.

He let go of my hand then, and I couldn't even blame him. What guy wouldn't with those long legs and that cleavage and all that hair right in front of him? But I did notice that he didn't put his arms around her. He was gripping the edge of his seat as she wiggled around in front of him, trying to keep his balance.

"Are you sure you don't want to come over and sit with Taylor and Danny and me?" Monica said as she smoothed the front of his shirt with her fingers, each of which ended in a perfectly polished nail. "You can share my nachos."

Share my nachos? That had to be code for something dirty.

"We're fine right here, Mon," Lucas said, moving his head to the left so he could see around her pouting face. "Thanks for offering, though."

I heard the tone of dismissal in Lucas's voice, but apparently Monica did not. She lingered for a few more minutes, licking her glossy lips and nuzzling Lucas's neck until she seemed to realize she wasn't going to get the reaction she wanted. With a *hmph*, she hauled herself to her feet and folded her arms over her chest.

"Well," she said before she turned away, "you have my number. Remember you can call me any time you want, day or night. I'm always available." She gave Lucas one more suggestive look before walking slowly down the stairs on her precarious heels.

I looked over at Lucas as he tore off the crumpled page Monica had sat on and started on a new sketch without missing a beat. I hoped he didn't think we were just going to go on as if *that* hadn't just happened, because, frankly, I wasn't that mature.

"Old friend?" I inquired, my tone innocent.

Lucas looked away from the court, his eyes following Monica as she moved through the crowd. "No," he said. "Monica and I were never friends, that's for sure."

I guessed it served me right for asking. All of a sudden I

was the one who felt like vomiting. The only thing that stopped me was the entirely disinterested look on Lucas's face as he watched Monica walk away and the memory of his hand in mine.

A few minutes later we both got up to move. I watched Lucas move down three rows and take a seat on the stairs, and then picked a random seat for myself, trying to shake the image of Monica in Lucas's lap out of my mind.

I was already folding my pad open to a fresh page when I heard the person next to me squeak, "Katie?"

Emily was sitting in the seat beside mine with an enormous soda in her hand, the straw in her mouth. A guy with light brown hair and nice blue eyes sat next to her, looking from my sister to me with a stunned expression I'd seen a hundred times before. Twin sisters tended to attract attention. "What is happening right now?" Emily said, her expression a cross between surprise and suspicion. "Is this a class assignment or something?"

I leaned over my sister and proffered my hand to her date. "Twin sister, Katie," I said by way of explanation.

"This is Marty," Em said dismissively, gesturing at him without looking his way.

"Matt," he corrected, and Em shrugged. I groaned inwardly. It was typical Emily behaviour to get a guy to take her to some event, buy her ticket and snacks, and drive her there and back only for her to forget him before the sun rose the next day. If she had already forgotten his name, Matt here was a definite goner, and here he was looking all starry-eyed. Poor bastard.

"I'm just doing some sketches, for practice," I explained, holding up my pad. I hoped Em wouldn't notice Lucas in the crowd, but just then he stood up and moved down a few more stairs. He looked over and gave me a wink before sitting back down. My sister's eyes widened with delight.

Oh, crap on a stick.

"You're here on a date with Lucas?" she whispered excitedly into my ear, loud enough that Matt and the entire row of people behind us could hear.

"Wait, Lucas Matthews?" Matt said, giving me a suddenly far more appreciative look.

"Great, Em," I said. "Thanks so much."

"I can't believe you didn't tell me," she said. "Is he a good kisser? Does he have a long tongue? Tall guys often do, you know."

Though I didn't look, I could feel the row of people behind us leaning forward to hear my answer.

"Lucas and I are *not* on a date," I said forcefully. "Remember, I told you, we're nothing to each other. Well, not nothing. We're friends. That's it." Em nodded at me her nod that said, *I don't believe a word of this.*

"Weren't you the one that told me he was the school Lothario?" I demanded.

"What's your point?" she asked. "I saw the way he looked at you at The Limo. Every Lothario has his downfall. "

"Well, let's just say I'm not it," I said and Em's expression suddenly turned serious. "Lucas has a girl in every class, in every Res, in every club." And apparently in every gym, too. "You really want me to go for a guy like that? You should be warning me away from him, not pushing me into his arms."

I wasn't really angry with her, it was my irritation with that whole Monica moment that was doing the talking, but Em took my words completely seriously.

"You're right," she said with a firm nod. "If he doesn't want you, then screw him! In fact, I'm going to give him a piece of my mind."

Both Matt and I caught her before she flung herself out of her seat.

"No, no," I said. "Lucas and I are friends. It's okay. We don't want to kill him right now." I thought of how different my response might have been if I'd run into her an hour before and had to bite back a grin. "I'll let you know if that changes, though." I nudged her with my arm and she gave me a reluctant smile of agreement, but I could still see her frowning in Lucas's direction.

The crowd cheered again as the yellow team—that was us, right?—got another basket. Going by the clock on the wall, it looked like the game was about to end. Matt had stopped listening to our conversation and was watching the court like the outcome would decide the rest of his life.

Sports were so weird.

Lucas stood again and caught my eye, gesturing toward the door. I got the impression he wanted to leave before the game ended and his old teammates could spot him, although it seemed like they'd be hearing about it either way. I could see Monica whispering to her friends at that very moment.

As I stood to follow him, Em said, "Be careful, Katie. You might want to be just friends, but you'd better make sure that's what he wants, too. Lucas isn't really the friends-with-girls type of guy, if you know what I mean."

Did I ever.

I was still thinking about what Emily had said as Lucas drove me home, and when I looked up we were sitting in front of my apartment building. I hadn't said a single word to him on the drive back. I wanted to ask him about Monica and whether he was dating her or had dated her or still wanted to date her, but it all seemed very un-friend-like, and I couldn't get the words out. Even though I told him he didn't have to, he insisted on walking me to my door.

"Where's your Res, anyway?" I asked. "You never told me."

"Why?" Lucas said. "Are you going to sneak into my room later tonight? I can tell you which window is mine and leave it open just a crack—"

"You're sure of yourself, aren't you?" I said, gracing him with a big eye roll as I unlocked the door to the building.

"Not all the time," he said. I had to remind myself what a big night it had been for Lucas and that I should give him a break.

"Anyway, I live in Victoria Hall," he said as we walked up the stairs. I noticed that his legs were so long he took the steps two at a time and sometimes three.

"I should have just met you there," I said, feeling guilty. "The gym is barely a five-minute walk from here. Instead you had to drive all the way over here in your car just to get me."

"Actually, it's my roommate Danny's car," Lucas confessed. "He drives like a maniac. I think he dented the door slamming into a mailbox. He was drunk."

"Sounds like a stand-up guy," I muttered.

"But I would never have asked you to come meet me," Lucas said as we reached my door. "I wanted to come pick you up."

"Why's that?" I said, feeling bold. I think a part of me was just sick of these little games we were playing. He had to learn that he couldn't flirt with me mercilessly if he didn't really want me. I had to draw a line.

"Don't you know?" Lucas said.

This time my back was already against my apartment door and I had time to think, to see him coming. He stepped toward me gradually, inch by painful inch, and instead of pinning me there with his hands on either side of me, I felt them running down my arms to find my hands. The heat rose between us in a slow boil, and this time I didn't tremble. This time I was able to meet his eyes and anticipate, and wish, and yearn.

It didn't stop my heart from pounding though.

"Know w-what?" I stuttered as he pressed his forehead against mine, our breath mixing.

Even up close he was completely exquisite, perfect skin, dark and thick eyelashes, and those gorgeous eyes. I couldn't stop staring into them—which was exactly the kind of thing friends did, right?

"Oh, Katie," he said, bringing his hands up to my cheeks and holding them in his palms. I couldn't believe how incredible it felt to have him hold my face in his hands. My eyes nearly rolled back in my head. "If I tell you now, I don't think you'll believe me. You'll probably punch me in the stomach or something, and my body's taken enough of a beating today."

"I'm not violent!" I said, insulted. My hand came up automatically to smack him for what he'd said, but I wouldn't let it. That's how non-violent I was.

Chuckling, Lucas let go of my face—I almost groaned out loud—and leaned down to pull something out of my bag.

"Maybe I'll just let the art do the talking," he said, pressing his sketchpad into my arms. "That's what the cool guys do, isn't it? I'd write you a song, but I'm not much of a writer."

"You don't have to write me a song, Lucas," I said, shaking my head at him.

"But I would," he said, pressing his forehead against mine one last time before backing away toward the stairs.

"Don't you want to keep your sketches?" I said, holding up the pad.

"No," he answered, showing me his dimples. "They're for you, Hero."

"Don't call me—" I said, but he'd already started down the stairs.

I unlocked the door to my apartment and dumped my bag on the couch before making straight for the cupboard. I knew what to do at a time like this. I pulled out a jar of Nutella. I had a spoonful in my mouth when I flipped Lucas's sketchpad open.

The first few sketches were of the game: a jersey in motion, a player doing a layup, the ball going through the hoop.

Then I flipped to the next page and sucked in a quick breath.

There were ten more sketches in his pad. They were all of me.

9

When I woke up the next morning there were three texts waiting on my phone, and this time they didn't make me scowl or flinch or make my stomach drop. These texts only made me smile.

> **Lucas: Thanks for getting me back to the game, even if I wasn't in the game.**
> **Lucas: You really are my hero. :)**
> **Lucas: Did you like the sketches?**

Lying in bed with my cell gripped in both hands, I debated whether or not I should text him back. Our texting relationship had been very one-sided so far. The only text I'd ever sent him was to let him know I'd gotten a new number. I was actually impressed with Lucas for not giving up. I bet all the other girls couldn't wait to reply to him.

The thought of all the other girls gave me pause as my fingers hovered over the letters on the screen. Then I pushed them out of my mind. Not even the blonde girl could ruin my memories of last night. I'd spent at least an hour—and the rest of the jar of Nutella—poring over his sketches, turning the pages so many times that a couple of them started to fray and I figured I'd better put them away. If he wanted the pad back, I didn't want him to know how long and hard I'd stared at them. His drawing technique wasn't the best; he often left much of the scene as a vague outline and then focused in extreme detail in one place, leaving the sketch uneven. If this had been an assignment, the professor would have chastised him for it, but I couldn't. Not when his point of focus was always my face.

Biting my lip to stop from giggling, I typed out my first text to Lucas.

Me: Sketches? What sketches?

I threw my phone down on my pillow and went down the hall to make some toast. I figured he'd reply to my text when he woke up, which would be God knew when. It was eight o'clock on a Saturday morning. Emily never replied to a weekend text from me before three. But as I pushed the button down on the toaster, I was surprised to hear the three-toned sound of a text coming in. I flew back down the hall and flung myself onto the bed, snatching up the phone.

Lucas: Don't tell me you didn't even look at them. You break my heart, Hero.
Me: I ain't your hero, buddy.
Me: And of course I looked at the sketches. They're lovely.
Lucas: You're lovely.

My heart was already racing a tiny bit from my mad dash down the hall, but now it revved itself up to triathlon pounding level.

Lucas: Oh no, now she's blushing.
Me: Am not!
Lucas: The lady doth protest...and we all know what that means.
Me: That was some brilliant quoting right there. Well done.
Lucas: Don't change the subject. I bet you're still blushing right now.

Goddamn him.

Me: You have no proof. This would never hold up in a court of law.
Lucas: Well, maybe I should come over and get my proof. Want to
go out for lunch with me?

I stared at the screen and thought of all the reasons I should say no, not the least of which being our utterly confounding friend-not-friend-not-boyfriend relationship. I thought of what Mariella would tell me to say, and what Emily would tell me to say, and what Katie of a week and a half ago would tell me to say, and then I thought of how I wanted to answer and everything suddenly seemed so simple.

Me: Yes.

Lucas seemed about as stunned as I felt, immediately replying that he'd come by my place at noon, which would give me a luxurious four-hour period to obsess over what to wear and what to say and what to do with my hair. As I stood in front of my closet, frowning over the possibilities, my phone rang and I picked it up with a smile on my face without checking to see whom it was, figuring it would probably be Em and wouldn't she love to hear about my morning.

But it wasn't Em.

It was my mother.

"Well, I'm glad to know you can still pick up a phone," she said as I sat down at my desk, turning to face my books. I knew this was where my mother wanted me to be on a Saturday morning, and somehow, even though she couldn't see me over the phone, it was always where I put myself when she called.

"Hi, Mom," I said, trying to sound chipper. Luckily for her I was already in a pretty good mood, so chipper wasn't too much of a stretch. I almost sounded believable.

"Honey, I've been trying to get a hold of you for weeks, which is more than enough time for you to come up with a valid excuse for dodging my calls. So let's hear it."

There was a television on in the background and the news was on, naturally. My parents only ever turned on the TV to watch the news or the History Channel. Dad had a bizarre interest in the American Civil War that bordered on obsession. It helped that he was a history professor and could chalk it all up to "research." I recognized the Vancouver local news anchor Leslie Wong's voice and knew exactly what she would be reporting on. That damn station hadn't changed news anchors in six years. I detested the sound of her voice. I still heard it in my dreams…

"The babysitter, whose name also can't be revealed due to her age, testified today that she had never met the boy before that afternoon, and had no idea why he had targeted the Wesley family…"

There was nothing like hearing your lies repeated over and over, broadcast to the world, printed in every newspaper.

It was almost enough to make you commit cold-blooded murder.

"Can you go into another room, please?" I replied tensely.

My mother sighed and I could hear her walking up the stairs, the jingle of her gold bangles as she moved. It was such a familiar sound—a childhood sound—that it almost made me wish I was at home. Almost.

"There, is that far enough?" my mother said. "Really, Katie, you'd think after all these years—"

"It's not so bad anymore," I lied. "It's just lately, because of all the coverage."

"But the coverage isn't even about you," my mother went on. "It's about Brandon and his punishment. I know we all feel the sentence was too light and it's frightening to think of him—"

"I'm not frightened," I said.

"All right, Katie, you're not frightened. Then what is it, hmm? Your sister says you've met a boy and you—"

"She said what?" I cried, slapping my hand down on my desk so hard the cat sprang out of his hiding place in the hamper and scampered for the door. God, Emily had such a big mouth sometimes. I was sure she'd brought up Lucas to avoid questions about *her* love life. Some sister, throwing me to the wolves.

"Katie, really, calm down. Emily just mentioned it in passing. I'm glad you've made a new friend."

Oh lord. What was it about talking with my mother about guys that made me feel like I was eleven years old again? Just the way she said the word "friend" made me want to cover my ears and yell at her to leave me alone.

And she wasn't done. "I just worry about you getting into a relationship at this delicate time."

"How did we go from friend to relationship? That's quite a leap," I protested.

"Well, do you want to have a relationship with him?"

I wasn't about to walk into that trap. I wisely kept quiet.

"I know you must be feeling very emotional right now. I've seen it so many times with clients, even years later, some news item surfaces and it all comes rushing back—"

"Well, that's not happening to me," I said, looking over at the clock radio I'd permanently unplugged from the wall, and my TV, which I'd never hooked up to cable, so I could only watch DVDs and never accidentally stumble onto the news.

"Katie, you don't have to pretend with me. Your father and I are here to support you. Dr. Lepore said—"

"You've been talking to Dr. Lepore?" This time I tried to keep the outrage out of my voice. I don't think I was really successful. "God, Mom. He isn't even my therapist anymore."

"Still, we wanted to consult him. Just so we'd be ready to address the emotional impact. So we could help you get through this."

I pulled off my glasses and rubbed at my eyes.

"Emotional impact, Mom? Really?" It was the way she said the words that got to me, as though she was reading from a script.

"You know this blasé attitude isn't exactly reassuring, Katie. In fact, it's exactly what Dr. Lepore—"

"Listen, Mom," I interrupted, because if she mentioned Dr.

Lepore one more time I was going to scream obscenities. "I know you're worried about me. And that's sweet, it really is. I know you think I'm hiding some deep, dark hurt, and that the trauma of what happened is going to take me down as soon as March twentieth hits, but I'm telling you, I'm really fine. I'm doing well here at school. Kingston is a beautiful town. And Emily's here to look after me." I think I heard my mother actually snort when I said this. "I'm doing great. And I'm going to keep doing great. So you can stop worrying about me. Honest."

I sucked in a deep breath, trying not to drown in my own bullshit.

"All right," Mom said in that defeated voice she used when she knew she had to agree even though she didn't want to. "All right, Katie. If you say so, then I believe you. You're fine."

"I'm fine!" I repeated, and this time I almost believed myself.

"How's art class going?" she asked.

"Which one?" I replied, a purposeful dig just to punish her. I was taking two art classes—one studio, one history—and of course she didn't know the name of either one.

"Should I guess the name of the course?" my mother replied.

"It's going well," I said grudgingly. "We're on to painting right now, so I'm in my element."

"Good. I think it's good that you're keeping busy."

I wanted to ask if Dr. Lepore had suggested "keeping busy" as a good way to mitigate the "emotional impact," but I didn't think the conversation could handle that many air quotes.

"So how's the case going?" I asked, eager to change the subject to anything other than my life.

"Which one?" my mother said. I could just picture the 'gotcha' expression plastered all over her face.

"The one you almost settled, but then they took back their offer at the last minute," I replied.

Really the description could have fit any one of her cases. I could have just as easily said the one where the little girl got cancer and you swooped in to help her family, or the one where the evil corporation tried to swindle a whole town out of their land, or the one where you worked for the good of humanity while your daughter sat back painting pictures, having only ever brought evil into this world. Yup, being my mother's daughter was really the best.

She said, "We're working on them."

"How's Dad?" I asked.

"Your father is your father," she replied. This is what she always said about him. It reminded me of the phrase from that movie, "Stupid is as stupid does," which I'd never really understood.

"So back to this boy—"

"Oh, Mother," I muttered.

"This Lucas," she went on. Oh terrific, Em had told her his name. "Is he your boyfriend?"

My eyes darted to the hallway, paranoid that he would be standing there eavesdropping, even though there was no way he could have gotten into the apartment. I closed the door anyway. The Lucas-Matthews-is-a-hottie incident had really done a number on me.

"It's a possibility," I replied, the first honest answer I'd given her.

"Is that a yes or a no?"

"It's an 'I don't know,' I guess," I said, rolling my eyes to the ceiling.

"You don't know or you don't want to say?" she persisted.

"Overruled, Mom! Stop lawyering. I don't want to talk about Lucas Matthews anymore."

"Oh, is that his last name?" she said with barely concealed triumph.

Point to Mom.

"Mom," I said tiredly, "can I get back to my Saturday now? I haven't even had breakfast yet."

Or coffee. This whole conversation would have been a lot easier to deal with if I'd had just one tiny cup of coffee first.

"Okay, darling," she said, and I heard the disappointment

in her voice, the wish that this talk had been something entirely different. "Your father sends his love, and so do I. I hope you know that…"

This time I didn't interrupt her. She just never finished her sentence, and it hung there between us until I said goodbye and hung up.

There was no question in my mind that lying to my mother was the right thing to do. The alternative—telling her the truth about what had happened six years ago—was completely out of the question. Just the thought of it made my entire body clench as though tensing for an explosion. Because that's what it would be like, my entire life exploding before my eyes. But there were levels of deception, and when she pleaded with me to share my feelings with her, to open up to her, sometimes I wondered if it would be so bad, so wrong, to confide some of my pain to her. I wouldn't have to tell her everything. I could just unload one of the rocks on my back, or maybe two. I could lighten my load a little.

Then I remembered what my life had been like in high school, back before I'd learned to lie as well as I did now, back when I used to lay on the couch and stare into nothing for hours, when I stopped making or keeping friends, when I wore my self-hatred like a cape and nearly drowned in its folds on a daily basis.

My mother hadn't been quite so eager to hear about my every worry then. In fact, she'd essentially ignored my distress for months until my father insisted they take me to see Dr. Lepore. As much as she said she wanted me to be honest with her, I knew my mother. She didn't want to be the parent of a troubled girl again, to have to comfort me as I wept, to have to stop herself from screaming at me to get it together. She wanted a daughter she could understand, even if I had to study art instead of law, even if she could tell that all I fed her were lies. A daughter who lied about being fine was trying. That was far preferable to a miserable daughter who wasn't trying at all.

Still, all that lying took its toll.

I placed my cell down on my desk and crawled onto my

bed, lying down on my stomach with my arm under my cheek.

I'm fine, I repeated silently to myself. *Fine, fine, fine.*

But I didn't feel fine. I couldn't remember the last time I'd spoken out loud about everything that had happened, even peripherally. It made me feel out of control. Like I was in a car about to drive off a bridge and though I was in the driver's seat, there was nothing I could do to stop it. She'd even said Brandon's name! I never let myself do that, never let myself think about Dr. Lepore, the trial, or, God forbid, that horrible day itself. If my mind drifted there, if I found myself picturing it—Tommy Wesley's face, stained with tears, the last time I saw him alive. Brandon's insistent voice, *"I'm doing this for you"*. The officer with his face in his hands when they found the body, so little, so bloody. My own hands shaking uncontrollably as they asked me what I'd seen. *"Did you see what happened? Did you see who it was?"*—I always, always yanked my mind away.

Those memories weren't safe. Those memories were against the rules, out of bounds, completely off-limits. If I got lost in those memories, I might never find my way back out again. That's why I didn't watch the news or listen to the radio. That's why I didn't read the articles. Not because I didn't want to know what happened. Because I knew too much. Because I knew so much that had never been told. Because I could drown in all the things I knew and couldn't tell.

When the doorbell rang, I still hadn't gotten dressed or put in my contacts. I drifted into the living room, pulling on a sweater to mask the fact that I wasn't wearing a bra under my pajama top, and opened the door.

Lucas stood in the hall carrying two pizza boxes, a Styrofoam take-out container, a paper bag, and a pretty adorable goofy grin.

"One of your neighbours let me in," he explained. I took the pizza boxes out of his arms and moved aside so he could come inside. "I didn't know what you'd want, so I got pizza, Cantonese chow mein, a hamburger, fries, and chicken nuggets."

"And a turkey dinner?" I said, eyeing all the food laid out on my coffee table.

"Nope," he said. "That'll have to wait for next time."

Next time. I wanted those words to make me giddy with happiness, but they barely made an impression.

I sat down on the couch while Lucas busied himself getting plates and cutlery out of the kitchen, another first. I actually didn't think I'd ever had a guy inside my apartment before, except the super that time the radiator had stopped working. One nice side effect of my current mood was that I also couldn't feel the insane discomfort Lucas's presence so close to my dirty hamper and unflattering photos would usually have created.

"I thought we were going out," I said as he handed me my napkin and plate.

"I thought I'd surprise you," Lucas replied as he sat down next to me.

When he'd piled his own plate high with food and I still hadn't served myself—I think I'd also missed a couple of questions he'd asked me—Lucas put down his plate and turned to face me on the couch. He had such kind eyes. That was what you noticed when you were teetering on the edge of the bridge, about to go over—the people who looked on you with kindness and the ones who turned away.

Lucas brushed a strand of hair off of my cheek. I wondered idly if I'd even brushed my hair that day.

"Hey," he said. "You okay?"

"I'm fine," I said, and forced myself to sit up straight, to pick something to eat, to speak and move and live.

It was a quiet meal, but not a strained one. Lucas seemed to sense that I wasn't in the mood for our usual repartee and didn't question it, which meant more to me than I could say. My most talkative moment came when the cat popped out from under the couch and rubbed himself against Lucas's legs, and I told Lucas I'd decided to name the cat Turner after my favourite artist, Joseph Turner.

"I guess he's really yours, if nobody's claimed him by now,"

Lucas said.

"He's yours, too," I insisted. "You helped rescue him."

"Well, then, I guess I'll have to come over all the time," Lucas said with a grin, "to visit him."

I almost managed a smile back.

Lucas chatted a little about his roommate Eric's awful girlfriend—she'd stolen his credit card and maxed it out, twice—and his classes, keeping the topics to things I didn't have to respond to with much more than a laugh or a "Really?" He made it easy for me.

When we finished eating, he put in a movie so I wouldn't have to talk at all. We both leaned back on the couch under the same blanket and I put my head on his shoulder.

And that was easy, too.

10

"Maybe it's not too late to call him and cancel," Anita said. Even I could hear the desperation in her voice, and I wasn't even really listening. I was gripping my head so hard I thought my skull might cave in from the pressure—it made listening a lesser concern.

"Chicks don't cancel on Lucas," a male voice said. "That shit just doesn't happen."

"Shut up, Matt!" Emily cried. "You are not helping. Why are you even here?"

"You invited me over," Matt said.

"Maybe she should lie down," Anita suggested.

"Don't let her lie down," Em said. "What if she swallows her tongue?"

"Oh shit, for real?" Matt said.

Anita said, "She's not having a seizure!"

Was I having a seizure? I didn't think so, but then what did I know? Maybe intense nausea, a pounding headache, and the desire to weep and scream at the same time were what a seizure felt like. Or maybe it was just what being a big, fat, terrified baby felt like. It was an either/or situation.

I was sitting on my sister's bed in her room, flanked by Anita—it was her room, too—and Emily, with my head in my hands and my eyes squeezed shut. Earlier I had been screaming into a pillow, which had sparked Anita's alarm. She'd never seen me like this before. Honestly, nobody had ever really seen me like this before. I'd only come to Emily's room because I was seriously freaking the hell out and also I needed help with my hair and she had all the good hair products. And because I needed my sister.

"Why did you say you'd go with him if you didn't really want to?" Anita asked as she rubbed my back.

"I want to go," I replied miserably without opening my eyes. "This is me wanting to go."

I heard Matt laugh. "Damn, girl," he said. "You've got problems."

"Get *out!*" Em cried, and I felt the bed shift beneath me as she got up and wrestled Matt toward the door.

"Hey," he protested. "*You* invited *me* over."

"And now this is me kicking you the hell out!" Em cried, slamming the door, presumably in his face.

I heard a girl's voice outside the door say, "Dude, that's harsh!" and some laughter. Poor Matt would probably be hearing about this for a while.

"God," Em muttered. "I hate it when they keep coming back like that."

"You invited him over, you idiot," Anita said in an irritated whisper. "If you don't want them to get clingy, then don't be such a tease!"

"How dare you ignore my sister's pain to chastise me," Em replied haughtily, also in a whisper. "This is about Katie. Let's take care of Katie."

"Maybe Katie's freaking out because her sister's a dirty little skank," Anita shot back. I heard a *thump*, which I was pretty sure was Anita being hit by a pillow.

"I'm a skank?" Em cried. "Who slept with Greg Ranski twice after he got back together with his girlfriend?"

Thump, thump.

I had to open my eyes for that one. "Oh my God, Anita," I said to her.

"That doesn't make me a skank!" Anita protested, socking Em another time with the pillow from her bed. "That just makes me guilty of…bad decision making. Besides, that was first semester. We agreed that anything that happened first semester doesn't count!"

"Oh yeah? Well, count this!" Em said, brandishing a cushion from the armchair.

A few minutes later, after a furious pillow battle that I think we all ultimately lost, we found ourselves lying on the floor in a row with our feet up on Manic Melanie's bed, staring at the ceiling. I had a pink bunny slipper under my head.

"It's a party," I said. "You know I'm no good at parties."

"That's not true," Anita said. "You're good at everything." I had no idea what she was basing this on, but it was reassuring, nonetheless.

"What if I can't think of anything to say?" I said.

"Just think of what the coolest person you know would say in that exact situation and say that," Em replied. "It works for me all the time. By the way, the coolest person you know is me."

That one was a little less reassuring. If I were going to be Em at this party, I'd have to do some serious drugs to get through the night.

"What if they try to force me to play beer pong or quarters or do that thing where they make you drink beer out of a tube that kind of seems like waterboarding?"

"Then tell them to fuck off!" Anita and Em both said at the same time, and we all cracked up.

"What if they try to make me dance on a table?" I said.

"Nobody ever makes someone dance on a table," Anita explained. "It's kind of a voluntary thing. And I think we can all agree you won't be volunteering."

"Hell, no!" I said.

"I've got the perfect solution for all your worries," Emily

said. "Here it is: Drink as much as you can as fast as you can. Tada! No more worries."

I expected Anita to dismiss Em's solution as quickly as I did, but instead I heard her agreeing.

"Seems like a wise plan," she said.

"Guys, the only thing worse than going to this party with Lucas would be going to this party and getting plastered and throwing up all over Lucas," I said. Considering how quickly I'd gotten drunk at The Limo, that was a real possibility. "I reject your solution!"

"Seems like a wise choice," Anita agreed in a bout of fickleness.

"Okay, then, let's talk about Lucas. He'll be with you the whole time, right?" Em said. "Just stay with him. I'm sure he'll take care of you." I ignored her unspoken question: *Because this is a date, right?*

"Except Lucas is a man-whore who can't be trusted," I reminded her. "You're the one who told me that, remember?"

"I once saw him go into a room with a girl at a party—I'm guessing to sleep with her—and then later go into another room with another girl—I'm guessing to sleep with her, too," Anita piped up. "Then he went home with my friend Gretchen's sister, but they didn't sleep together. They just made out."

"*What?*" I cried.

Emily half-sat up and glared at Anita. "Do you want to get the pillow again?" she threatened.

"What?" Anita answered, not the least bit intimidated. "He *is* a man-whore. Everyone's heard the stories about Lucas. He's done half the girls on campus, and probably most of the townies, too. Girls fall at his feet wherever he goes, and they always come back for more. That insane brawl in the cafeteria last year where one girl got a hunk of her hair pulled out and the other lost a tooth? That fight was over Lucas. Katie should know what she's up against."

I seriously felt like I was going to be sick.

"What if he tries to take me into a room?" I said. The idea

was simultaneously enthralling and horrifying.

"Then you only go in if you want to," Emily replied.

"What if he doesn't try to take me into a room?" I said.

"Then you call me from the bathroom, where you'll be hiding," Emily said. Though I resented it, this was an accurate statement.

"What if he goes into a room with another girl?" I said.

"He invited you, Katie, didn't he?" Anita said. "That means something. Even if he *used* to be a slut, he has good taste now. Maybe he's changed."

"Maybe he'll surprise you," Emily agreed.

"What if he leaves me alone?" I said, turning my head to the side so I was staring at the side of my sister's face, a face that looked so much like my own and yet, not at all.

I saw Em stiffen. She knew what I was referring to. When she turned to face me, her expression was more serious than it had been all evening.

She said, "I'll make sure he doesn't."

An hour later I was sitting on a bench outside Ban Righ Hall waiting for Lucas, feeling a little less like I was going to throw up and a little more like I might live through the night, though I wasn't positive about it. It was a mild night for early March, and I didn't really need the gloves I was wearing but I kept them on anyway. They stopped me from twisting my fingers, which I desperately wanted to do right then. In the end the girls had said the clothes I was wearing were unacceptable, and after a near-fight with Emily over her insistence that I wear her red halter, I'd settled on a cute teal-coloured dress of Anita's, a pair of patterned tights, and Em's calf-length suede boots, proffered to me in a moment of real sisterly selflessness—which was only slightly ruined by her telling me that if I stained them she would stab me to death with one of my paint brushes. They'd piled my hair on top of my head and secured it there with a pair of black lacquered chopsticks. I'd even let them put a little makeup on me.

I looked good and that made me feel strong. What I liked even more about it was that I looked just slightly like someone other than myself, which made me feel like someone other than myself, which was a good thing. Maybe this other me could get through a university party in one piece. She was the one who'd gotten us into this mess in the first place, clearly, since I hadn't been the one to agree to go to this party with Lucas. That was all her.

Lucas and I had gotten into a nice routine lately almost without my being aware of it. The Monday after our stay-in lunch he'd asked me if I wanted to grab some food after art class and I'd agreed, mostly because I was hungry and I'd come to realize that Lucas knew all the best cheap places to eat. We'd gotten poutine at Earl's Kitchen and then he'd walked me back to my apartment. And then we'd done the same the next day after working in the studio, and then again on Thursday.

He didn't mention the sketches or the moment we'd had outside my apartment, though several times it seemed like he wanted to. He seemed to be waiting for some kind of cue from me. But I was happy just to leave things as they were, the two of us buddies—although I had to admit he seemed to take every opportunity to touch me that he possibly could—our banter light even if our gazes were heavy. Don't get me wrong, it wasn't exactly easy to sit across from him watching him eat a taco in the messiest possible way and not lunge over the table and kiss him. Actually, it was pretty much agony. But nothing had changed. He was still a player. I still didn't need a boyfriend, or a hookup, or a whatever. Having Lucas as my friend was a big enough change for now. It was a bigger change than I'd ever thought I would make—that was for sure. I didn't need more right now. I needed strong and stable, and that was Lucas. I needed comfortable, and somehow that was him, too. I was getting used to him.

So when he asked me if I wanted to go with him to a party Friday night, I heard myself giving the comfortable answer, the answer I'd been giving him all week. I heard the casual, "Sure, sounds good," flowing off my tongue, and I wondered who the heck I had become.

Who was this new Katie, friends with Lucas Matthews, going to games with him, and sharing fries with him and letting him take her to parties?

I understood the old Katie. I knew her limits. But what were the new Katie's limits? What could the new Katie handle? And if the new Katie suddenly disappeared, leaving the old Katie in her place, what the hell was I supposed to do then?

My great look armor had basically started to disintegrate and I was about two seconds from running for my life when Lucas appeared on the path to my left. Slutty man-whore Lothario Lucas. But he didn't seem slutty to me. Seeing him was a breath of fresh air and as I got to my feet I found myself drinking in the sight of him, every beautiful well-sculpted inch. It was weird the way just looking at him and knowing he was near made me feel strong. Maybe that was how the new Katie handled it all. She didn't handle it alone. She had Lucas by her side.

"What are you doing out here in the cold?" Lucas said. "You should have waited inside for me."

Reaching out, he ran his hand up and down the back of my coat, which only pressed me closer to him. I got the impression that was kind of the point.

"It's not that cold; I'm wearing gloves, and it's not even below zero. Why are we going to this party?" I said in one big rush, forcing out the question I didn't even realize I'd been holding in. The validity of the question didn't stop me from staring at the ground in embarrassment as Lucas barked out a laugh.

"I mean," I continued—wow, the cement really was fascinating!—"I know you haven't been going to a lot of parties…"

"You know that?" Lucas said. I could just picture the glint in his eye as he said it. "And how do you know that?"

"Well, you know, Em mentioned…"

This time I could see him bending down to get a better look at my face. "So you've been talking to your sister about me?" His warm, minty breath against my face made me shiver.

"Oh, shut up!" I said, looking up at last, narrowing my eyes at him. "Emily knows you and I are friends."

Lucas stood tall again as we started walking down the path. "There's that word again," he said as he put his arm around my shoulder. "*Friends.*"

I chose to ignore this, even though being snug in the crook of his arm, my side pressed into his, was making my heart skip every second beat.

"But really," I persisted, "what changed your mind? I thought you wanted to stay away from the party scene. What made you want to go to this one all of a sudden?"

"You mean besides the terrible free beer and awful conversation and, oh God, those friends of mine? They really are a miserable bunch," he said. His tone was light and sarcastic, but I suddenly felt as though I'd stepped in something. Did he sense that I had no interest in meeting his friends or drinking their beer or talking to them? Was old Katie rearing her ugly head?

"I mean, no," I said frantically. "What I mean is… I didn't mean—"

He stopped and took me by the shoulders. "Katie," he said softly, but firmly. "I was just kidding."

I felt my whole body sag with relief. Jesus, we hadn't even made it off campus and I was already exhausted.

"And to answer your question," he went on, pushing a stray curl behind my ear, "I couldn't think of a good reason to go to those other parties. That's why I didn't go."

I nodded, eager to be agreeable, though I still didn't really feel like I understood.

Then he took my chin in his hand and tilted my face up toward his. Unconsciously, I found myself leaning in. It was incredible, like he was the flame and I was the moth. I just couldn't stop gravitating toward his touch.

He said, "I guess I was just looking for a good excuse."

"So what's your excuse?" I breathed.

"The chance to show you off," he replied

And just like that going to a party with Lucas didn't seem like such a bad idea after all.

We left campus, going north. I lived east of campus, but I knew the area—we were close to the Dairy Queen. (I mapped out all locations in Kingston by their distance to the Dairy Queen.) Though Lucas had told me the party was on Frontenac, I'd had no idea it would be so close by. We'd only been walking for about five minutes when we began to notice parked cars crowding both sides of the street. It was pretty clear which house we were aiming for. As we approached on the sidewalk, the three-story grey house on the other side of the street stood out not only because the porch was crowded with people, but also because the Christmas lights that lined the roof and wound up the porch columns were all lit. The booming music was also a pretty good indicator.

My footsteps started to slow as we came closer and I was surprised to see that Lucas's did, too. By the time we were standing directly across from the house, we were at a standstill.

A guy on the porch spotted Lucas and called out his name. I examined his face for a reaction, but saw nothing. It had taken on that closed-off quality again.

He swallowed. "I guess it's too late to change our minds," he said, and my heart did a little pitter-patter at the idea that getting out of the party was still a possibility. I began to think of all the other things we could do with the evening: go to the movies, or out to eat, or to the studio, or maybe…

Another voice, a girl's voice this time, joined the first guy in calling Lucas's name, and then suddenly the whole porch was chanting, "Lucas! Lucas! Lucas!"

Wow. Yeah, there was no turning back now.

"Another thing Em told me about you is that you used to be a slut," I said. I suppose I should have felt bad for being so blunt about it, but there was a porch full of girls chanting his name. Blunt was sort of unavoidable.

"Did she?" Lucas said. We were both still watching the house instead of each other. "She's right, I used to be. But I'm not anymore." He took my hand and squeezed it and when I glanced at him he gave me a friendly smile, dropping the stoic mask he'd been wearing.

He could easily have been bullshitting me. That was what players did, wasn't it? My distrustful nature should have been telling me to run, but it wasn't. The old Katie and the new Katie, both our brains and both our hearts were telling me that what he said was true. Who was I to argue?

"Let's go in already," I said. "It's colder out here than I thought."

We crossed the street and joined the party.

Entering a party—my first party—with Lucas was your basic terrifying experience. If I'd come in alone I would have been pretty much ignored, and could have slunk to the back and hid, clutching my red cup of beer. But I'd come in on the arm of Lucas Matthews, which meant all eyes were on us.

The house was pretty big, the entrance opening up onto a staircase leading upwards with rooms on either side, all of which were filled with partygoers in varying states of drunken splendor. There were people sitting and standing on the stairs, lining the hallway that led back to the kitchen, sprawled over the rug and on the couches and around the dining room table, where they seemed to be playing strip poker. One guy wasn't wearing any pants, and another appeared to be down to his socks and underwear. It satisfied me to see that the two girls at the table were fully clothed. The scene matched perfectly the American college party sketch I'd drawn in my head with details I'd gleaned from various movies and TV shows and stories Em had told me, though I was glad no girls were wearing bottle caps as pasties. Although the night was still young.

Moving through the crowd was slow going, because everyone seemed to know Lucas and wanted to greet him. I couldn't really blame them for wanting to be close to him. There was no chance in hell I was leaving his side—that was for sure. But dear lord, we'd barely moved an inch from the entranceway. At this rate we'd never make it to the keg, which I'd caught sight of sitting next to the fireplace, and which was looking pretty tempting right about now. And I didn't even like the taste of beer. I'd already been introduced to so many people whose names I'd already forgotten and had gotten the evil eye from at least three girls, one of who actually tried to have a conversation with me—she'd asked me why I was wearing my hair "like that," and made a face.

I was still watching her walk away when a big bear of a guy with a full beard came barreling toward us, his arms open wide.

"That's Oleg," Lucas explained moments before he was engulfed in his friend's arms and lifted off the ground.

It was Oleg's party.

"Lucas, my good friend," Oleg boomed. "How wonderful of you to join us on this joyous March evening. Where's your drink and who's your friend? I think Taylor is looking for you, and she's—"

The name "Taylor" triggered a memory that wouldn't quite surface. I knew I'd heard her name before, but I couldn't place where.

Lucas leaned forward and spoke quietly in Oleg's ear, and then Oleg's big brown eyes landed on me with a wide, merry grin. He looked a lot like a younger version of Santa.

"My lady," Oleg said, taking my hand and placing a chaste kiss on my knuckles. I gave Lucas a puzzled look. What exactly had he whispered in Oleg's ear? "You know, you look like one of my kin. Are you a fellow Jew? Maybe Moroccan?"

I sighed quietly while giving Oleg a warm smile. "Nope," I answered. "I'm half-Danish, half-Indian."

"Well that's an interesting combination!" Oleg said.

Then Oleg looped an arm over each of our shoulders and began to guide us down the hall, his considerable girth creating a kind of battering ram effect in which people were either mowed down ahead of us or forced to get out of the way.

"Let's get the two of you a drink!" he said, depositing us in the kitchen, at which point he was instantly distracted by a game of quarters taking place on the stove—it really was just like the movies!—and abandoned us.

I pressed my stomach into the edge of the kitchen counter as yet another friend came over to greet Lucas. We were in the very centre of the party now, surrounded on all sides, and with no jolly Oleg at my side and Lucas distracted, I really started to feel claustrophobic. I tried to remind myself to breathe. But it wasn't easy. It was sort of like being at The Limo again, that panicked feeling of being packed in a room with so many people, that feeling of being so incredibly out of place. I'd never felt safe in a crowd, not in six years. I'd always thought it was because it reminded me of school before and during and after the trial, all those kids watching me, wondering when I would break, their eyes judging or pitying—it didn't really matter which—and watching, always watching, as I disintegrated in front of them. But now, as yet another girl walked by and gave me a puzzled once-over, I realized it wasn't a flashback to high school misery I was having. It was the trial itself I was remembering, that very particular feeling of being in a fishbowl, those moments when I'd taken the stand and I'd known I wasn't just imagining all their looks; it was really happening. All eyes had been on me. All ears had been directed at that microphone as I'd opened my mouth and spewed one lie after another after another.

That's what this crowd was doing to me.

It was making me relive my shame.

Covering my burning cheeks with my hands I cast around desperately for a place to hide. I was going down for real this time. I was going to collapse. I needed to get out of here, not in a minute, not in a second, *right now.*

I didn't even notice Lucas talking into my ear or feel his arms go around me until suddenly I was being lifted into the air. My arms shot forward, grabbing hold of his shoulders. He set me down on the kitchen counter and, keeping his arms around me, moved forward, gently ungluing my knees with the pressure of his body so he could stand between them. Even then, with Lucas literally between my legs, I wasn't really paying him that much attention—although now that I was sitting on the counter, we were exactly the same height, his eyes perfectly level with mine. Only when he leaned in and pressed his forehead to mine—this seemed to be his signature move—did I find myself focusing on his face, and specifically the details of it. The little scar above his right eyebrow that sort of looked like an arrow, his longish nose, and those remarkable dimples that were so deep they were like caves.

Without realizing it, I found myself reaching up and placing my thumbs into each perfect dimple, my fingers splayed over his neck.

"Katie," Lucas said, "are you poking my dimples?"

"Mmmhmm," I answered dazedly, until all of a sudden his words rang a bell in my head and I realized that I was doing something that seemed incredibly intimate in *a room full of people* while Lucas was standing *between my legs*.

For a second I actually stopped breathing.

"Okay, okay, okay," Lucas said quickly, his hands holding me firmly around the waist as I tried to wiggle free and escape this horrifying moment. "Just pretend we're alone. It's just you and me alone in a room. There's nobody else here. Just imagine it."

Guided visualization had never really worked for me before—it was something Dr. Lepore and I had tried—but this time, in Lucas's arms, it sort of did. With his forehead resting against mine, the rest of the room kind of disappeared and it was as though it was just the two of us in our own little bubble.

"That's better, isn't it?" he whispered.

I nodded. "Better," I said.

"Now, instead of trying to run away, why don't you tell me what the problem is?" he said kindly. "Are you disappointed to be at this party with me now that you've seen all the other dreamy guys in the room? Is that what it is?"

What other guys? I wondered.

"It's just..." I squirmed under his hands, trying to get the words out. "It's just that everyone is looking at me, at us. I just...don't like to be looked at."

He jerked his head back, breaking our little forehead teepee and filling me with alarm, but he didn't go far. He seemed to have pulled back just to stare at me.

"You don't like being looked at," he repeated, saying it as a statement, not a question. "You don't want all these people looking at you."

"I just don't like feeling like—" Lucas interrupted me before I could finish, which was a good thing, since I had no idea where I'd been going with that.

He brought his hands up to cup my face, so delicately, making sure I couldn't look away. "Katie," he began, "I'm going to tell you something now that will probably shock you, but I need you to believe me. Can you promise me that?"

"I guess," I said. I really had no idea where he was going, and the way his fingers were brushing against the skin of my face so gently was getting a little—no, a lot—distracting.

"You are beautiful, Katie," he said.

I rolled my eyes and tried to turn my face away, but he held me in place with the slight pressure of his fingers.

"No," he said. "You promised you'd believe me. You need to know this. You need to know how beautiful you are. Everybody else does."

"Oh, give me a break!" I said. "I think you're mistaking me for my sister."

"Your twin sister," Lucas said. "Your sister who has the exact same face as you. If you can admit she's beautiful, then why can't you admit that you are?"

I gave him an exasperated look, though I wasn't sure he could see it, given how close his face was to mine. "Emily knows how to do it," I explained, as if it weren't obvious. "She has charisma and she knows how to dress and she has so much personality it's impossible to ignore her. I'm…not like that."

"I hate to tell you this, Katie, but you're more beautiful than your sister," Lucas said, and this time I was the one to pull away just to scowl at him. "I'm not saying Emily isn't a knockout; she is. But you're beautiful without even trying, without even realizing it. You're the most fucking gorgeous girl in this room, and everybody knows it."

The way he said it, swearing like that—and Lucas really wasn't one to swear—somehow got the message through to me. I didn't believe everyone in the room thought I was gorgeous—that was ridiculous. But I believed that Lucas did.

Lucas thought I was the most fucking gorgeous girl in the room.

I nearly swooned.

"I said this to you once before, but I'll say it again," Lucas said, his words uttered so close to my mouth that it was like he was breathing them into me. "They're only staring at you because you're so beautiful. Got it?"

"Got it," I said weakly.

And then he leaned in and kissed me on the cheek.

My hands were trembling as I slipped off the counter, my cheek stinging in the exact spot where he'd placed his lips. I glanced around quickly to see if anyone had noticed the mind-altering moment we'd just shared but nobody was looking at us. The party had gone on around us while we'd been in our little teepee and nobody seemed to care about what Lucas had been saying to me. It seemed incredible.

Lucas's cell buzzed and he slipped it out of his pocket to check the text. He shook his head as he placed it back in his pocket.

"One more thing," he said, slinging an arm around my shoulder.

"Anything," I said. Wow, I'd really drunk the Lucas Kool-Aid.

"Can you ask your sister to stop threatening to cut off my balls if I don't treat you right?"

"What?" I cried out in alarm, grabbing for the phone in the front pocket of his shirt. He covered it with his fingers. "Did she really write that? I don't even know how she got your number. Oh my God!"

"It's okay, I understand," Lucas said. "It's natural for her to be overprotective when her sister's out on her first date ever."

I literally felt all the blood drain out of my face. "She said *what?*" I said, though I wasn't sure it even came out. I might have just been silently mouthing it like a goldfish that had been flung out of its bowl, its little fishy lips opening and closing as it died. Because that was exactly what this felt like. Slow and painful death.

Lucas's eyes were full of mirth as I worked overtime to salvage my dignity.

"Emily is deranged, okay? She says these things just to mess with me and you, because you're a guy, and she likes to tell lies and create chaos where guys are involved," I prattled. "I've been on plenty of dates. Lots of dates. I just can't say no. It's a real problem. Just because I don't post pics of my bad dates on Facebook doesn't mean they didn't happen. I can't even tell you the number of times I—"

"Katie!" Lucas said all of a sudden, jarring me out of my monologue. "I'm pretty sure she just meant your first date with me."

"Oh, right," I said, biting at my bottom lip, hoping he'd ignore the heap of lies I'd just emptied on his head. "Wait, so…does that mean…I mean…did you want this to be…"

I looked at him hopelessly. Was he really going to make me ask if we were on a date?

"Let's avoid labels for the time being. I don't want you to hurt yourself," he said diplomatically, steering me toward the keg.

I couldn't help but feel a little let down. Not that I wanted this to be a date. Except that I kind of did.

As we stood waiting for our turn, Lucas standing behind me, he put his chin on my shoulder and whispered into my ear, "But for the record, if it was up to me, this night would have the label of 'date' all over it. I have one of those label makers. It's very high-tech. I'd make a label that says 'Lucas and Katie's first date' and make us both wear them as nametags. I just wanted to make sure we were clear on that."

I beamed as I drank down my cup of mostly warm beer. I'd never tasted anything better in my whole life.

For the next half hour, Lucas and I crept around the periphery of the party. His hand remained planted on my lower back and he was very attentive, always grabbing me a seat and giving me most of his attention, which didn't seem to be entirely for my benefit. Though coming to the party had been his idea, he didn't seem ready to participate in it fully, happy to chat with me about our final assignment for art class instead of playing beer pong. A dance floor erupted in the middle of the living room and I was glad to find he didn't want to drag me onto it. He didn't even really seem to want to talk to anyone. I noticed him trying to end every conversation as soon as it began, even one with his roommate Eric, who I wouldn't have minded chatting with a little longer; he looked a little like Ryan Gosling.

We were talking about maybe cutting out of the party early and getting some ice cream—be still, my beating heart—when a familiar girl came up and nudged Lucas with her hip. I couldn't help but stare as Lucas smiled widely at the sight of her, set down his beer, and picked her up in an Oleg-style bear hug.

"I'm so glad to see you," Lucas said, and I could tell he genuinely was. His eyes brightened when he looked at her in a way they hadn't all night.

As he set the girl back down on her feet, she giggled and tossed her long hair over her shoulder.

It was the girl with the blonde hair, the one I'd seen sitting on the bench with Lucas, the one who'd been so angry with him and whose cheek he'd touched.

My stomach sunk like a rock-filled rowboat.

I didn't know exactly where to look. Watching Lucas's absorption in this girl was like pushing razors into my eyes, but at the same time I couldn't look away. A part of me seemed to feel that I deserved this punishment for thinking I could judge a guy's character, that I could trust a word Lothario Lucas said to me. I'd always been a terrible judge of character, that's what had gotten me into all that trouble when I was younger. Guys were always liars, and I was always so eager to believe them— that was my weakness, that was why it was so much better to be alone. At least I didn't come out looking like I'd been duped. At least alone I still had my pride.

I was just about ready to disappear out the back door without a word—I could just see it out of the corner of my eye, over beside the fridge—when I accidentally bumped into Lucas's elbow and he turned and blinked at me as though he'd forgotten I was there.

Most gorgeous girl in the room, my ass.

"Oh, Katie," he said breathlessly. "I want to introduce you to—" but before he could finish, there was a tap on his shoulder and another girl was waiting to talk to him.

"Jennifer," the blonde girl finished, holding out her hand for me to shake. "I'm so happy to meet you. Lucas talks about you all the time. You're exactly like he described you, except maybe even prettier." She smiled sweetly at me as I tried not to look like a deer in the headlights. Had she just called me pretty? And it didn't even seem like she was being sarcastic. But why would one of Lucas's girls be so happy to meet me and so eager to give me a compliment?

"Oh, thanks," I managed to get out before Jennifer barreled on.

"What nationality are you? Italian? I wish I had your skin tone instead of my pasty pink cheeks. My friend Sandra is Italian and she tans so dark in the summer. I burn red as a lobster after, like, five seconds in the sun. Or are you Middle Eastern?"

"I'm half-Danish, half-Indian," I parroted.

"Wow! That's so diverse. And you're an artist, aren't you? Lucas says you have so much talent. I always wanted to take up the piano, but my mother always said, 'Jenny, stick to what you're good at,' which is child rearing, of course. I'm majoring in education, but I was thinking of taking an art class next year. Do you think…"

Her mouth never stopped moving. It was remarkable. As she continued to chatter I stared at her heart-shaped face, her barely-there blonde eyelashes, and innocent, wide-eyed gaze. She seemed like a genuinely friendly girl, if a little sheltered. I was trying to puzzle out how exactly she and Lucas knew each other and would have loved some help from Lucas himself, but he'd been completely waylaid by the other girl. Her head was blocked from my view by Jennifer's. As I edged a little to the side, trying to get a better look at her, I heard Jennifer's monologue dwindle to a stop.

"Oh yeah, that girl's trouble," I heard Jennifer whisper in my ear, showing more animosity than I would have thought her capable of. She moved over to my side, giving me an open view of the girl who currently had Lucas's attention.

If before my stomach had sunk like a broken rowboat, now it fell like the *Titanic*.

At first I thought it was Monica, the girl we'd met at the game, but a moment later I realized I was wrong. This girl was on another level altogether.

She was a vixen if I'd ever seen one. She had on a red dress so skin-tight I could see the outline of her thong. Her chestnut hair was thick and fell over her shoulders in perfectly sculpted waves. She was stick-thin, with flawless skin and eyebrows arched high like a supermodel's. She was currently pouting her ruby-red lips at Lucas, who stood facing her with his arms folded, probably trying to hold in the urge to throw his perfect body at hers. It would be like two Barbie dolls making love— they were both that perfect. Seeing them next to each other, I couldn't help but think they should be together. Who would ever want to be a single piece of perfection when you could be a part of a matching set?

"That's Taylor," Jennifer said into my ear. "She's been after Lucas forever. She scared off his last girlfriend, the little witch with a 'b.'"

I couldn't help but chuckle at Jennifer's inability to swear, and the fact that if there were teams we were suddenly on the same side, when five minutes ago I'd thought she was the enemy. But my good humour was fleeting. Watching Taylor and Lucas together—now she was pawing at his chest, pressing her perfect body against him—was infinitely worse than watching him with Jennifer. This time I found myself turning away for fear of tearing up. Already I could feel the telltale prickle behind my eyes.

"Not that I think she has any kind of a chance with him," Jennifer said, looking at me worriedly. "She's totally not his type."

"Well, it's none of my business, anyway," I said as I backed away, not really even looking where I was going. The back door escape plan was a no-go now. It would mean circling around them. I'd have to find another way.

"Oh, but I thought—" Jennifer began.

"I really have to go to the bathroom," I announced, and, turning abruptly, edged my way through the crowd and out of sight.

Finding an adequate hiding place in a strange house on short notice when you think you might be about to burst into tears is a high order. The first door I tried ended up being locked and the second led me into a small den. The room wasn't empty, but it was dimly lit and I was able to stand in the corner leaning against a bookcase for a few minutes without being disturbed, which was exactly what I'd been looking for. During those few minutes I decided three things. One, coming to this party had been a stupid idea. Two, leaving the party as soon as possible would be the best way to counteract my original stupid idea. And three, it was about time I got it into my head that Lucas Matthews wasn't for me, for real this time.

I was moving back toward the door, wrapping my arms around my stomach as I always did when I felt sick, when the flickering TV caught my eye. There were a couple of armchairs pulled up around it and some guys were watching the screen. The sports segment on the local news was playing, but that wasn't what they were talking about. I froze when I heard Tommy's name.

"...cut him to pieces," one guy said. "I read an article about it once that went into all kinds of detail. And the kid was only, what, five? Shit was fucked up."

"I don't get it," another guy said. I recognized him as Tim, one of the friends Lucas had introduced me to earlier. "Why's it on the news now?"

The first guy finished swallowing a gulp of beer before replying. "Who the hell knows? The media's gone ape shit over the case from the beginning. Probably some tiny little piece of evidence came to light, like a hair follicle or something. Who cares? What I want to know is the guy's name. They never released it because he was a minor when he killed that kid. But I bet you anything the second he gets out somebody will leak it. Can you imagine being the one who has that information? The media would pay a pretty penny for his name."

I leaned back against the bookcase wanting dearly to leave the room and yet unable to move my feet.

"Wasn't there a chick, too? Some babysitter?" This voice came from the floor in front of the TV. I froze again, this time with my hand on the doorknob. Suddenly it felt as though my entire arm had turned to ice and I couldn't move my wrist.

"Oh yeah, I always had a theory about her." This was the first guy talking again. His voice sounded vaguely familiar to me.

"Oh, do tell, Sherlock," somebody said.

"Well, you know how women are," first guy went on. "Always nagging, badgering, bitching. 'Get me a soda. Hand me the remote. Come pick me up.'"

The whole room laughed. I didn't see how they could. There didn't seem to be enough air in the room to breathe, let alone laugh.

"Babysitter chick always claimed she was knocked out, didn't know a thing, didn't see nothing. Total dead-end investigation-wise, right? Or maybe perfect alibi?"

"Wasn't she, like, thirteen years old?" said the dude on the floor.

"So what? So was he. The way I figure it, the whole thing was her idea. She was the mastermind behind the whole murder. You know how chicks never want to get their hands dirty, so, yeah, he did the actual cutting. But she was right there next to him, egging him on, whispering in his ear, 'Do it, you loser. Don't be a pussy! Do it and you can have me right here on his bloody little corp—'"

"Shut your mouth!" I yelled.

Somebody flicked on the overhead light. Though I didn't remember deciding to do it, I had launched myself off the bookcase and taken the four steps across the room, shoving the guy who'd been talking back in his chair with both my hands planted on his shoulders. When I'd yelled out, I'd done it right into his face. Now I stepped back, panting, as the guy looked up at me with a mildly freaked expression on his face. I recognized him as his face was illuminated by the muted television set. It was one of the guys from the night I'd first met Lucas. It was Two.

"Whoa," Tim said.

Looking around the room at the other guys, I began to twist my fingers.

"Easy, girl," Two said, very slowly, as though I was a skittish horse who had just kicked him. "What the fuck was that about?"

"Well," I said, my self-righteousness fading quickly under the lights, "I guess I overreacted a little. But I just don't think you should be making up stories—"

"How do you know it was made up? Maybe it's the truth. You don't know," said the guy still sitting on the floor

I felt my anger rising again, and a steady whistle growing louder in my ears. "That girl is a real person who went through a terrible trauma—"

"She isn't the one who got cut up. All she did was stand by while that kid got murdered." The guy on the ground was really starting to piss me off. He was eating a licorice whip, and as he spoke I could see little bits of red stuck between his teeth.

Then Two spoke up. "I think we're getting away from the matter at hand," he said, "which is that you owe me an apology."

There was a hard look in his eye that I remembered from the night with the cat.

"In your dreams," I said as fiercely as I could while also backing toward the door. As I took another step I bumped into something. Only when I turned to find my route to the door blocked by the guy wearing a football jersey did I realize my real mistake in taking my eyes off of Two. In that second of diverted attention he'd clamped his hands on both of my wrists.

Behind me I heard the door to the room open and close, but it hardly registered.

"Let me go," I said angrily, struggling against his hands as they pinched at my skin.

"You don't think I remember you, do you?" Two said, leaning in toward me. He wasn't a bad looking guy. He had a boyish look about him and light eyes that I might have found attractive if we'd met at some other time when I didn't want to scratch them out.

He breathed in my face. His breath smelled sour, as though the beer he was drinking was rotting in his stomach. "I remember you," he said.

A shiver ran down my spine at his words. It took me a moment to realize he was talking about the night with the cat and not any events much further in the past.

"Dude, just let her go already," said the guy at my back, who seemed to be reconsidering his position. Two wasn't quite so changeable.

He yanked hard on my arms, pulling me even closer. My thighs pressed into the side of the armchair as he brought his ear closer to my lips. "What was that, honey?" he said. "Did you say, 'I'm sorry, Buck?'"

I swallowed hard as he tugged on my arms again and the whistling in my ears reached a fever pitch. All of a sudden I wasn't at a party anymore. I was in the woods, with the cold seeping through my clothes and another boy was tugging on my hands and telling me to hurry it up.

"You heard him, Katie Kat. You'd better hurry now. If I get there first who knows what might happen."

"Let me go!" I screamed directly into Buck's ear, and to my

surprise he did let go of my hands and I fell backwards, landing hard on my ass, my hair falling over my face.

Only when I looked up again did I realize he hadn't let go of me of his own volition.

Behind the armchair, which must have fallen over during the scuffle, Lucas had Buck trapped on the ground, his forearm jammed under his chin, and his fist raised in the air, ready to smash his face in.

I scrambled over to his side. The room was alive with noise as Buck's friends yelled at Lucas to let him go—though I noticed nobody made a move to help him. Buck's bulldog face was an angry shade of red as he strained against Lucas's arm.

"Let go of him, Lucas," I said calmly.

Breathing hard, his eyes glued to Buck's, Lucas didn't look like he had any intention of letting go. His face was screwed up in a look of intense revulsion I'd never seen on him before.

"Not a chance," he said gruffly.

"I'm fine," I said. "Look at me. I'm totally fine. You can let go."

"See?" Buck choked. "She forgives me. She wants you to let me go."

"Shut up!" Lucas growled.

Without loosening his grip, Lucas turned his head to look at me. When his eyes met mine they were blazing with fury, but they gradually cooled and I saw the tension in his arm begin to ease.

"That's right," I said, nodding. "It's okay. I'm fine. You can let him go."

Releasing Buck from his grasp, Lucas sat back on his haunches, massaging his hands. I saw the muscles in Lucas's jaw flexing as Buck sat up and looked at us both. "Are you guys crazy, or what?" he said.

That was when I punched him in the face.

11

I ran. I ran out of the room, past all the gaping faces, through the living room and right out the front door. I ran down the driveway and onto the sidewalk, and that was when I really picked up speed. The cold air pouring into my lungs felt amazing, like ingesting a gallon of ice cream in one go after spending a sweltering day in the sun. I gulped it down as I ran, my thighs burning, my whole body working in a way it wasn't used to, though I was finding that I kind of liked it. Car horns honked behind me, but I ignored them. It was such a glorious thing just to run, and run and run and run, and never think of what I was running away from.

"Katie!"

I reached an intersection I didn't recognize, but that didn't slow me down. I turned right and kept on running. The honking was louder now and continual, like music to accompany the pounding of my feet on the frozen pavement. Wind blasted my skin, freezing my cheeks and making my eyes water. I tipped my head up and watched the streetlights as I passed under them. I started counting them. Seven lights to the next intersection, and then ten after that. I wondered if I could reach the end of the street. Could I run that far? Could I run all the way through town? I didn't know. But I knew I wanted to try.

"Katie!"

I had run like this only once before in my life. I remembered now that it had been just like this, running without thought, a weightless, mindless moment. But different, too, because my head had been bleeding and I couldn't stop crying, my mouth hanging open and a strange bawling sound coming out of it as I had run along the tracks. I'd fallen several times because I'd kept getting dizzy. And they wouldn't let me run as far as I'd wanted to. They'd stopped me. But I could have kept running. If they'd let me I would have.

I would have run forever.

"Katie, stop!"

Lucas pulled me out of the road, gripping my body with both his arms, holding me from behind. I wanted to keep running, but he was holding me too tightly. At first I struggled against him even as he held me back, murmuring into my hair, but within a few moments I went limp. My legs were burning anyway, and my eyesight was blurring. I stared at him blankly as he put my jacket on me, helping my arms through the holes and zipping it up the front. I was surprised. I'd thought I was already wearing it.

When he was done Lucas bent over, placing his hands on his knees, panting hard. "Where did you think you were going?" he asked.

Looking around at the unfamiliar houses on the road, I shrugged. "I was just running," I said.

"Down the middle of the street?" he asked.

Not wanting to give away the fact that I had no idea I'd been running down the middle of the street, I shrugged again. "Which way is my apartment?" I asked.

Pulling on his own coat, which he'd been holding under his arm, Lucas gave me an exhausted look before pointing back the way we'd come.

I put my hood up against the bracing cold and walked past him without looking at him.

I wondered when it had started snowing.

"Are you okay?" Lucas said. Apparently he'd decided to follow me, even though I was walking squarely down the middle of the sidewalk—a sure sign that a girl doesn't want company. "Katie, are you okay?" My silence didn't seem to be getting through to him, either.

"Lucas, leave me alone," I said. I would have picked up my pace, but I was beginning to realize that my run in my sister's very un-sneaker-like boots had possible destroyed my feet. I felt at least four blisters. Going faster wasn't an option.

"Is your hand okay?" Lucas persisted, reaching for my arm, which I yanked away.

"Why wouldn't it be?" I snapped. The snow was really coming down now, making it harder to see, which only added to my mounting irritation. I also still didn't quite know where I was going.

"Because you just punched a guy in the face, that's why," Lucas said.

We came to a side street and I paused, trying to get a look at the street sign, and Lucas took his opportunity to scoop up my right hand.

"Hey!" I cried. I wanted to pull my arm away again, but he had it in a firm grip and I didn't want to hurt my hand worse by yanking it free. Not that I minded the pain. I barely felt it. The throbbing was similar to the way my hands had felt after a full day of the trial, when I'd been twisting my fingers for hours on end. There was something sickeningly comforting about that kind of pain.

We always welcome the hurt we think we deserve.

"Doesn't look like you broke anything," Lucas said, after turning my hand over a bunch of times and bending all the fingers. Loosening his hold, he let me slip from his grasp, but his eyes lingered on my face, full of concern.

I couldn't stand that look.

"Thanks a bunch, doc," I said coldly, then turned away and

crossed the street. I thought he might leave me then, but I sensed him jogging beside me. When I reached the curb he was already there.

Damn his athlete's body.

He walked backwards ahead of me, so he could keep me in his line of sight. "Katie, what the hell happened back there?" he said. "How did you get into a fight with Buck Mullard?"

"He's an asshole," I responded, pulling the cords on my hood so my face was nearly obscured.

"I'm aware of that," Lucas said, "but what were you doing in that room in the first place? I turned around and you were gone. Jen said you went to the bathroom, and the next thing I knew Tim was dragging me over, telling me my girl was about to beat up four guys at once."

I stopped in my tracks. Lucas kept going a few steps, putting some space between us. "I'm *not* your girl," I said angrily.

"What?" Lucas said, shaking his head in confusion. "I was just repeating—"

I found myself panting hard, though I didn't know why. We weren't running anymore. "I don't need you to rescue me, Lucas," I said. "I can fight my own battles."

"Clearly," he said.

"I'm not some damsel in distress who needs your help. I'm not some stupid—"

"I know you're not," he said in a low voice.

But that wasn't helping. All of his compassion, his caring, his kind eyes, and his concerned looks were making me crazy. I didn't want his worry. I didn't want his pity. Not now, not ever.

Balling my hands into fists—even the wounded one—I faced him like a prizefighter. "Stop it," I said. "I don't need this. I don't need you. I just want to be left alone. I can take care of myself." Ignoring his bewildered expression, I turned on my heel and kept walking.

I'd gone about ten steps when he called after me. "You're still going the wrong way," he said.

He was right. I'd missed the turn that would take me south toward my building. Grudgingly, I turned back. And as I passed him the stupid boy started talking. Again.

"I'm not trying to baby you," he said. "I'm not here because I think you need me. That's not why I went into that room. That's not why I threw Buck Mullard on the floor."

I looked him right in the face for the first time since we'd left the party, and I made myself hold his gaze, just for a moment, just to be sure. Then I felt my lips begin to tremble, because it was just as I'd feared. When I looked at him I didn't see Lucas. I saw eyes of stone, that expression of revulsion on his face, that desire to tear someone apart. I saw the animal. I saw the rage. And nothing else.

"Why, then, Lucas?" I said. "Tell me why you did it."

He threw his arms up, and for a second I thought he might lunge forward and strangle me.

"Jesus Christ, Katie, why do you think?" he said, giving me an exasperated look.

My body shook at the sound of his raised voice, and I felt tears in the corners of my eyes, threatening to fall.

Not now. I couldn't cry now. Not in front of him.

Then he stepped toward me and I braced myself for whatever was coming.

"All right, if you don't know why, then I'll just have to show you," he said, and then his lips met mine.

At first I didn't understand what was happening. I felt his lips, soft against my own, and the delicate pressure of his hands against my cheeks. For a second there was no movement, it was as though we'd become a statue sculpted of ice, our faces frozen together. But then his mouth opened, just a little, and I felt him suck at my bottom lip, and suddenly I found myself melting. His lips moved against mine, hot like embers, warming me to the core as he pushed his fingers into my hair. He explored my mouth with the accomplished movements of a seasoned lover while my face followed his clumsily, my lips betraying my inexperience. It occurred to me that only a moment ago I had been about to cry, but I pushed this thought away as an ache began to build in me, beginning just below my bellybutton and spreading through my stomach.

My hood fell off my head and I felt Lucas's hands leave my face, his arms encircling my body as the snow kissed our cheeks and melted instantly.

Is this what I want? I asked myself, though my body seemed to have no reservations, my mouth opening to his and letting his tongue slide against my own. I heard myself moan, which only seemed to embolden him, his lips becoming more insistent, his kisses delving deeper. My knees went weak and I nearly sagged against him.

Are you what I want? I asked myself, and though I was still kissing Lucas, suddenly I was imagining a different place and a different boy who I'd wanted to kiss just like this and who had made me melt just like this, whose words had been sweet and looks tender right up until his eyes turned black and the heart that had beat only for me turned hard, and the boy who had made me feel so whole turned into a monster.

I pulled out of Lucas's arms, breaking the kiss, my heart pounding for a new reason now. We stood facing each other, breathless, and I could feel him trying to lean toward me, to press his forehead against mine, to block out the world, but there was no blocking this out. This was inside of me.

"So, Hero, now do you understand why…" Lucas began, but right away his words began to falter as though he knew what I was going to say before I even said it. As though he could see the fear in my eyes.

"Stay away from me, Lucas," I said, backing away. "I'm no good for you."

"No good for me?" he said, uncomprehending, reaching for me, but this time I didn't fall into his arms. This time I leaped away from his touch and he stared at me in disbelief.

Good, I thought to myself as I turned and walked carefully away through the snow.

I was glad he couldn't believe this was happening. I couldn't believe this was happening. Lucas Matthews wanted me and I was walking away from him. It was probably the first time in history that such a thing had ever happened.

My cell phone buzzed before I reached the corner and I hesitated before taking it out. If it was a text from Lucas, I wasn't sure I'd be strong enough not to turn around and run back to him. When I glanced down at the screen, I was almost relieved.

Brandon had found my new number.

Unknown: Get ready, you little bitch. It won't be long now.

It was the message I needed to hear, a reminder not to make the same mistake again.

That was when I knew I'd done the right thing.

12

"What did he do?" Em asked for the tenth time, giving me her most intense you-will-spill-all-your-secrets stare.

I gripped the straps of my backpack as a crowd of students passed us in the hall, my eyes frantically darting from one face to the next to see if Lucas was among them. A sigh of relief escaped my lips when I saw that he wasn't.

Turning back to my sister, I saw that she was still staring me down, her eyes open so wide I could see the white all around her irises.

"I hate it when you do that," I said. "It makes you look creepy."

"Whatever! It always works on Sally," she said. "I'm the only one she told that she actually did make out with Alex's brother while they were still together, and that she thinks he's the love of her life."

"Who's the love of her life, Alex?" I said as we reached the door to the studio. "I thought Sally didn't believe in soul mates and lifelong love. I thought she was after the sugar daddies of the world."

"She's had a change of heart. Love has changed her," Em said. "And it's not Alex that made her change her ways. It's his brother."

"Brother doesn't have a name?" I said, discreetly glancing down the hallway. No Lucas in sight.

"Oh, I'm sure he does," Em said flippantly. "I just can't be bothered to keep track of Sally's guys. Hell, I can hardly keep track of my own."

Sadly, this wasn't true about my love life, on which she was keeping vigilant tabs at the moment.

"So just tell me what Lucas did to make you hate him," she said, circling back, as I knew she would. She'd been on this track for a few days now. I was getting to know all the stops. "Seriously, I need to know if I have to cut off his balls or just maim him. Poking out one of his eyes is also a possibility."

"Don't poke out Lucas's eyes," I said, mildly alarmed. My sister had once shaved a guy's head in his sleep. I knew what she was capable of when enraged. And it wasn't pretty.

"Not both eyes, just one. He'll still have the other one. He can wear a patch."

"Well, that's a relief," I replied.

I watched as the last of the students from the previous class trickled out of the studio, more evidence that I was ridiculously early. Today was critique day, the day we had to display the painting we'd been working on for the last few weeks and have it assessed by the other students and the professor—otherwise known as Katie's monthly breakdown day—although this month had been so fraught with breakdowns I was thinking I'd have to change the name to something else.

I hated letting anyone see my work, let alone give me their opinion on it. Letting the professor see it was bad enough. I'd already been through a few critiques during the sculpture module earlier in the semester and knew that most of the students were nice enough—nobody wanted to be too harsh, knowing their head would soon be on the chopping block— but that was sculpture. I knew from catching glimpses in the studio that almost all the students in the class had gone for photorealism for their paintings. Our assignment didn't require any particular style of painting; the idea was to learn how to paint distance and incorporate two figures from one photo into the landscape of another, keeping the light source and palate of hues consistent. I'd done that; I knew I had. I'd just taken a more impressionistic approach, which would make my painting stand out from the others.

Which was exactly what I didn't need right now.

"Look, can I be blunt?" Emily said then plowed on without waiting for my answer. "Did Lucas try something Saturday night? Is that what has you so freaked?"

"I'm freaked because it's crit day," I corrected her, gazing through the window next to us at the pouring rain. Em was going to get soaked when she crossed campus to get to her own class. "And what do you mean 'tried something?' Tried what?"

He tried to kiss me, that's all, was what I didn't say. *He tried to love me. He just didn't realize I was unlovable.*

Not that a single kiss meant he loved me. I didn't think that. Though it might have made me fall in love with him just a little. A lot of good that was going to do me.

"What I mean is," Em said carefully, putting on her thinking face, "did he try to...touch you?"

Still gazing out the window, I thought about Lucas's touch, his fingers gently caressing my cheeks, the feeling of his tongue slipping into my mouth, and I felt my entire body flush. I'd replayed those few short moments over in my head so many times in the past two days, and every time I had my body had reacted the exact same way: the ache pulsing to life again in my belly, my every nerve tingling. It was mortifying and thrilling at the same time, and it was happening to me right now.

Luckily, I had only to think about how the moment had ended to make the fantasy come crashing to a stop.

"Katie!" Em cried, shaking me by the shoulder.

"Huh? What? Yes!" I said, focusing on my sister's face as Lucas's disappeared into the snow.

"Yes?" she said, her voice rising. "You mean he *did* try to have sex with you?"

Several students from my class turned our way as they filed through the door across from us. I saw Naomi trying not to laugh.

"Shut up!" I said, smacking Em on the arm. "What the hell are you talking about? Lucas didn't try to have sex with me! We barely even kissed."

"You kissed!" Em said, her face lighting up, then falling back into a frown. "Oh, wait, so it was a bad kiss? I don't really see how that's possible, since this is Lucas we're talking about, but—"

"It wasn't bad," I said, looking down at my shoes. "It was really nice."

Understatement of the year.

"Then what the hell happened?" Em demanded, rounding on me and forcing me to look her in the face. "I'm your sister. You can tell me. I'm an amazing secret keeper. By the way, forget everything I just told you about Sally and Alex's brother."

"I should really go in," I said. "Class is about to start."

Em's face fell and she pursed her lips. "Fine," she said in that clipped tone she took when nothing was fine at all.

I winced internally. There was no way I could tell her the truth, not about this, but that didn't make lying to my sister any easier.

"I can't tell you what happened," I said to the side of her face, because she was refusing to look at me, "but I can say that Lucas didn't do anything wrong. So don't be mean to him. It wasn't his fault."

She frowned, letting her eyes creep back over to my face. "Whose fault was it?" she asked.

I smiled weakly. "Nobody's," I said as I walked toward the door instead of saying what I really felt—that the fault was mine, as usual, as predicted. The fault was always mine.

"Hey, sis," Em called in a whisper as I reached the classroom door. "Your first kiss and it's with Lucas—that's still pretty exciting, isn't it?"

I nodded and tried to look thrilled for her sake, my sweet sister who thought I'd never looked at a boy before, who thought her twin was the last nineteen-year-old bastion of purity. My sister who'd kissed dozens of boys, each peck as simple and uncomplicated as the next. My sister who had no idea that though Lucas had been my first kiss, he hadn't been the first boy I'd wanted to kiss.

If only Lucas had been my first in every way, I thought to myself as I stepped into class. *Then maybe I could have kept him.*

I walked into the studio and added my painting to the others at the front, feeling the hairs rise on the back of my neck as I stood there with my back turned. And it wasn't because of my painting. Sure enough, as I made my way to my stool I saw more than a few eyes following me. A girl who always spoke really slowly when she asked questions in class whispered to the skinny guy who sat next to her. He nodded as I walked by. My right hook to Buck's nose and my dramatic exit from the party certainly hadn't gone unnoticed. I'd had the same experience walking into my art history class yesterday. I'd become a person that got noticed, the exact thing I'd been trying to avoid all along, and this time I couldn't blame it on any boy. This time it was all me—hitting this guy and kissing that one and destroying everything around me.

I had nobody to blame but myself.

A feeling of incredible defeat fell over me as Professor Wilkins entered the room and we began the critique. Though we were all meant to participate, I didn't say a word, shrinking into myself instead like Alice after taking a sip from the "Drink Me" bottle, wanting desperately to become so small that I could be lost among the folds of my clothes. I had spent years feeling this way, living this way, years wasted wanting to be nothing, wanting not to exist at all. And here I was thinking I'd been making such strides, that I'd been changing my fate, changing my life, that I was getting better at living. It turned out I was exactly where I'd started: scared and alone and lying about everything and hating myself for it. I really hadn't changed a bit.

The other students' paintings paraded before my eyes, but I barely saw them. Later, I could only recall one out of the bunch, the work of a girl named Paula who always wore her curly hair in two braids. The painting featured two children at the beach, one a little black boy with a coy expression on his face, and the other a little white girl in a blue bathing suit and pigtails. The little boy's face took up a third of the canvas, almost as though he'd run up and presented himself to be painted up close, while the little girl was farther away and had turned her back. The class agreed that it was somewhat over-painted and there wasn't enough flow, but I found it enchanting, as I often did pictures of childhood. It was the one part of my life I could look back on without having to worry about feeling ashamed. Before I turned thirteen I had nothing to be ashamed of.

When my turn came around I nearly got up and fled the room. I only stayed in my seat because I knew a scene like that would just make them whisper about me more. I'd never felt less inclined to be evaluated as I reluctantly raised my head and prepared to face the onslaught.

"Who would like to begin?" Professor Wilkins said. She raised her eyebrows, her gaze flitting over my face. She was greeted by an avalanche of silence. Normally there were a few students who spoke first, eager to get in their comments before somebody else had the same idea and they had to come up with something new. Not for my painting, apparently. As the seconds passed, all I heard were crickets.

I was really beginning to feel like I might drown in my own misery when a pompous guy I'd never liked spoke up.

"It's too dark," he said. "The brightness of the sky distracts the eye and I can't even make out the figures in front of the trees. I feel like it's muddled."

Gee, thanks for breaking my heart, Pompous Guy.

Unfortunately, he seemed to have triggered a reaction in the rest of the class.

"I agree," said a girl named Haylie. "Is that a woman in the bottom right corner? Or a man? It's hard to tell."

"The brush strokes are distinct," somebody threw in.

"Yes, but what does that matter if you can barely see them?"

"I think it just comes down to poor subject choice. A photograph with less disparity in colour and brightness would have made a much stronger painting. Of course, it would be easier to judge if we actually had the photograph to compare it to."

I wasn't about to mention that I hadn't painted from a photograph.

Professor Wilkins blinked silently for a few moments as the riot of flagellation came to an end. "Does anyone else have a comment to make about Katie's painting?" she asked politely. Professor Wilkins was always so polite and proper, possibly the most well-groomed artist ever to exist in the world. She didn't seem to know how to address the communal condemnation of my painting, except to send out the request one more time for the right answer. I wished she wouldn't bother. I didn't want some pity comment about the way I'd mixed my colours so well. I just wanted it to be over.

But it wasn't.

"I like it," I heard a voice say.

He was sitting off to my left, blocked from my view by several bodies and easels, yet I still leaned back when he spoke, as if that would better hide me from him. I'd thought he'd skipped class because the spot next to me was empty, but apparently he'd been there all the time.

Lucas.

Just the sound of his voice made my hands tremble. I hadn't seen him since our kiss, though he'd texted me multiple times and I was pretty sure he'd come by my apartment on Sunday night and waited for a while at the door of the building when I hadn't buzzed him in. Mariella had called to tell me a good-looking guy had asked if he could come in, that he was a friend of mine, but she'd told him that he should wait for me to let him in. I'd thanked her for that. (She wisely had not asked anything more, but I knew that wouldn't last long.) I wished I was stronger than this, but the truth was I couldn't bear to face him.

And now we were stuck in a very small classroom together.

"The way she painted the sky is incredible," Lucas went on. "Both the texture and the range of colour she used. The figures are indistinct, yes, but I think that makes them more compelling. The stroke of red paint here, over the head of this figure, draws the eye, and the darkness of the trees closing in gives the impression of being trapped. Overall, I find it haunting. And beautiful."

Professor Wilkins thanked him for his contribution then gave the painting her own evaluation, which I hardly listened to. Lucas's words had stirred up a storm of conflicting emotions in me that I could hardly make sense of, and anyway I didn't have the time. Class was ending and I had to get the hell out of there. I didn't have anywhere to be. But I sure as hell didn't want to find myself alone in the room with Lucas.

Grabbing my backpack, I gunned it for the classroom door without looking around to see where he was. I figured if I rushed, I'd certainly get ahead of him. Lucas never rushed anywhere. But I was wrong. I was the second student to burst out of the classroom doors and there he was, leaning against the lockers across the hall, waiting for me.

I didn't want to catch his eye. I wanted to brush past him as if I hadn't even seen him. I wanted to run like hell. But those honey-coloured eyes held me in place and I knew that running from him would be no use. He would only follow me.

He was standing in almost the exact same spot Emily had stood in earlier, so I walked forward and took my place beside the window. I was next to him now, no longer in his line of vision, but he didn't turn his head. He just looked down at the floor, his hands in the pockets of his jeans. He was wearing a close-fitting white shirt and his hair was wet—from the rain, I had to assume. He looked so beautiful I had to look away. I'd always found it painful to look with longing at the things I couldn't have. Instead, I looked out the window at the brown, waterlogged grass surrounding the building. It had shocked me that morning to find the first spring rain melting the snow Lucas and I had walked through. It was almost as though the entire night had never happened. Except that I couldn't stop thinking about it.

"Thank you," I said quietly.

I felt his eyes flick to my face, felt the heat of his gaze like rays of sunlight against my skin. Until he looked away.

"I was just telling the truth," he said. "It's a beautiful painting."

"That's not what I'm thanking you for," I said, and as soon as the words were out of my mouth I knew they were the wrong ones. Because they made him turn to me, his eyes falling on me for real this time. I'd only wanted to express, that the kiss, his kiss, had meant the world to me. I'd meant it as a goodbye. But instead he was reaching for me, one hand grazing my cheek while the other nudged my hip, pulling me toward him. My hands pressed against his chest, stopping him from pulling me in any farther, but it didn't matter. I was already in his arms.

His scent surrounded me, a mixture of laundry detergent and the woodsy smell of his cologne and something else that was just him. I breathed it in greedily, as though it was my oxygen, as though I knew that the second I turned away from him I would be unable to breathe. I had to store him up for later. I hate to take in as much of him as I could just to survive.

"Katie..." he murmured, sending a thrill through my body.

He tried to coax me to raise my eyes to his by tugging lightly at my cheek, but I wouldn't. Instead I stared at his lips, those lovely, soft lips. I felt wobbly all of a sudden just looking at them, and a second later I realized why. I was going to cry.

"Katie, what happened?" Lucas asked me as I retreated from him, pulling my body away from his. It felt like wrenching off one of my own limbs. "Just tell me. Talk to me."

But what could I say? How could I explain? There was no way he would ever understand that the girl he thought he knew didn't exist. The Katie Archer he knew wasn't real. There was just me, and I was far more trouble than he could handle.

His fingers were still caught in the ends of my hair, his body still just a hand's breadth away. He still thought I was with him, but I was already gone.

"I'm sorry," I said, grabbing my things and pulling away for real. My eyes were wet but the tears hadn't yet started to fall as I looked at him one last time. Then I walked quickly down the hall away from him.

13

When the day finally came, I felt nothing.

I'd taken to sleeping on the couch, not only because I'd been staying up watching movies later and later into the night in an effort to make the days last longer, to stop tomorrow from coming, but because it was like an island in the middle of my apartment. From the vantage point of the couch, I had a good view of the two biggest windows so I could watch for intruders with ease. And since it was only five feet from the door, I could more quickly make an escape if I needed to. But I wasn't paranoid or anything.

It had been days since I'd gotten a text from the unknown number, which didn't fool me one bit. There was always a calm before the storm. But it had been a nice little break. A girl could only be called a "motherfuckinglyingbitchwhore" so many times before she developed a complex. And I was already sporting a pretty big complex of my own. I didn't need any extras.

Now, as I sat up on the couch on the day of days, I gently palmed my cell from the coffee table and took a breath before turning it on. Nothing.

Phew.

Well, no threats from the unknown number anyway. There were three calls from my mother and a call and two texts from Emily, all of which I ignored.

Lying back on the cushions, I gazed out the window across from the couch at the grey day outside and marveled at my own calm. I felt numb, really. I felt nothing. It reminded me of an article I'd read once about a Japanese man from Osaka who'd been the only person to survive the bombing of his neighbourhood during World War Two. He'd described how he'd walked aimlessly through the rubble afterwards, all alone, and that for many hours that day he'd believed that he had died while everyone else had survived. He'd thought he was a ghost.

That's how I felt when I woke up that day. As though I wasn't real. As though I hadn't survived, although I had. As though I was nothing.

I walked to school through a drizzle that left my hair in a frazzled mess. I'd left my phone at home for the day, marveling that I'd never thought of this solution before. Let Mom and Em worry about me if they wanted to—I was going incognito. To someone passing me on the street I'm sure I looked like any other person rushing to get out of the rain, going about their errands and daily life, as if the day had no meaning at all, which was amazing to me. The only difference in myself I could really feel was a trembling, not of my limbs, but deep inside me. I felt as though a strong wind could bowl me right over.

All the rules were in place today. This was, after all, the day they were made for. I avoided my coffee shop, knowing it might have the radio playing, wore my biggest noise-cutting earphones just in case, and inside the school buildings I kept my eyes averted from every TV screen. I spoke to no one, took copious engrossing notes in class, and tried to emulate my morning self as much as possible: say nothing, feel nothing, be nothing. Before I knew it, my school day was over and I was on my way home.

My only mistake was stopping at the newsagent at the edge of campus to buy a Snickers bar—my reward for not staying home all day hiding under the covers. The daily papers were all stacked neatly on the counter, ready to be taken away to wherever unpurchased newspapers went at the end of the day, and as I struggled to fit my change into my wallet I happened to glance down at them. The headlines jumped out at me, all reporting the same thing, all in bold, block type. Because this was the biggest news story of the year. And it was right there in front of me.

Evil Gets Cut Loose

Killer Walks Free

Kid Killer Comes Home

The coins fell through my fingers and scattered on the pavement.

"Are you all right, miss?" the old man behind the counter asked, glancing down at the change that I hadn't bothered to pick up.

My inner tremor threatened to take over my entire body as the awful memories pulled at me, trying to drag me back there—Brandon's dirty fingernails as he gripped the knife. Tommy's high-pitched scream ringing in my ears. My dirty running shoes pounding on the forest path as I ran and ran and ran—but I resisted with all my strength. I didn't want to go back there ever again. I wouldn't.

"I'm great!" I said with forced enthusiasm, jamming a bite of chocolate into my mouth and chewing as though my life depended on it. Then I turned away and left the headlines and the memories behind me, where they belonged.

As I pulled open the door to my building I noticed the sun was going down. I'd made it through the day in one piece. Nobody had attacked me. Nobody had found me out. I'd survived this day just as I'd survived every day leading up to it, and I was going to keep surviving. The day had just been one long boring bout of nothing.

In a sick way, it was kind of a letdown.

In the doorway I quickly checked my mail slot, spying a manila envelope waiting for me through the little holes in the metal door. My name was printed in small, neat writing on the front, and there was no stamp, which meant that whoever had left this for me had been inside the building. I set the envelope down on the table in the lobby, staring at my pale face in the mirror hanging above it.

Evil Gets Cut Loose.

Maybe Brandon hadn't sent me a text today because he'd planned to leave this for me instead? I knew logically that this wasn't possible. It would mean his travelling all the way from Vancouver to Kingston in just a few hours. He'd only been let out this afternoon, and I was pretty sure the terms of his release barred him from leaving the province. My nagging worry that he had an accomplice made my fingers shake as I picked up the envelope again. I knew I was being silly. What danger could an envelope possibly pose? It was light enough that I felt nearly certain it contained nothing other than paper. So no bomb to blow me to bits, then. Another empty threat, maybe, written out by hand this time? I'd never know unless I opened it, and yet I couldn't seem to convince my fingers to tear the seal.

As I approached the stairs, dragging my feet now, all my earlier excitement doused in anxiety, I squinted down at my own name. The handwriting seemed familiar to me, which meant it couldn't be Brandon's. I'd never seen him write anything down. I puzzled over this for a moment until the photo of Turner I'd taken on my phone flashed through my mind and I suddenly knew whom the envelope was from. All that extra anxiety lifted from my shoulders and floated away. I knew his handwriting because I'd watched him writing out his name on the missing cat flyers we'd plastered all over town. The envelope was from Lucas.

It had been nearly two weeks since the moment Lucas and I

had shared in the hall outside of class. Since then we hadn't spoken once, and he hadn't called or texted me, either. I was back to my old tricks, avoiding any places on campus where I thought he might be and keeping my head down in class so as to not catch his eye. But this time I noticed he was doing the same. He'd even skipped class last Friday. And earlier this week when we'd had our closest call, somehow managing to end up at the door to the art studio at the same moment—keeping your eyes down all the time did have its drawbacks—I'd stepped back, murmuring an apology, my eyes drifting up to his face, but he'd kept his averted. His demeanour had been one of annoyance, as though I'd been holding him up. His face has been stonily blank as I'd walked passed him through the door, just inches from his chest. The gravity that always pulled me toward him had screamed at me to throw myself into his arms, but I'd held back. Gut-wrenching as it had been to have Lucas look at me like I was a stranger, it would've been like an actual knife in the stomach to have had him peel me off his body, that same stony expression telling me he wasn't interested, he never had been.

When his coldness came back to me, freezing my heart solid, I had to remind myself that I was the one who'd told Lucas to stay away from me. He was just doing as I asked. And when I was out grabbing a bite Sunday night with Em and her friends and spotted him across the room with that redheaded vixen Taylor plastered to his side, I had to remind myself again. And again and again and again. This was what I'd wanted. This was what I'd asked for. He was moving on. He was doing just what I'd told him to.

"That Taylor's so full of herself," Melissa offered, pushing her basket of fries my way. "I'm sure he doesn't want her around."

"She throws herself at everyone," Sally agreed. Then, in a moment of real clarity, she added, "I should know, so do I."

"I know he misses you," Em said.

But it really didn't seem like it. Later that night Anita accidentally mentioned that she'd seen him at a couple of parties, hanging out with Eric and Oleg. He was out with his old friends, whatever had been holding him back apparently no longer an issue. It occurred to me that maybe what had been keeping him from his other friends was me. Now that I was out of the picture he was free to go back to his real life, the life he fit into just right, the life that had been waiting for him.

I thought bitterly, *He's probably glad to be rid of me.*

So then what the heck was in this envelope, and why had he sent it to me?

I still hadn't opened it when I reached the top of the stairs and found Mariella and Ethan at my door.

"Oh thank God, Katie!" Mariella said as she looked up from her phone. "I've been texting you like crazy. Stefano's totally going to fire me. I'm already thirty minutes late and you know how he gets." I did know. Mariella was always going on about her Nazi boss at the spa where she worked as a masseuse. She was sure he had it out for her.

"What is it? What's wrong?" I said, glancing nervously at Ethan, who looked back at me with a blank expression of extreme boredom. Count on a five year old to find his mother's hysteria totally uninteresting.

Mariella hefted her enormous purse back onto her shoulder. I was always wondering what the heck she kept in there to make it so heavy.

"I know it's a total imposition," she said, "but my mama's sick and my stupid brother, Ray, took off on a road trip to the Maritimes—like winter's the best time to go sightseeing—and if I don't make it to my shift, Stefano's going to fire me for sure and give all my shifts to that skinny biatch Cecily. So I'm begging you."

She looked at me pleadingly as I tried not to show the rising panic I was feeling inside. She hadn't actually said the words yet but I could see where it was going. I felt my windpipe closing up, my ability to breathe dwindling as I gripped Lucas's envelope in my fingers, crinkling the paper. Today had been going so well. I might have even called it a raging success. I'd planned on spending the evening sketching and eating cookie batter and maybe, if I felt up to it, calling my mother back. My grand plans shattered at my feet as I looked into Mariella's pinched and worried face.

Please don't do this to me.

"Save my life?" she said with a grateful smile as Ethan stepped forward and took my hand. He stuck his tongue through the hole a missing tooth had left in his smile and wiggled it at me as his mother put a bag of toys down at my feet.

His hand felt like a grenade in mine. My palm was so sweaty against his that I was sure his fingers would slip right out of my grip and we'd both be blown to bits.

"I'll be back at nine thirty, ten o'clock at the latest," Mariella said, slapping a Post-It on Ethan's forehead that had her work number on it. "He'll eat anything you put in front of him and his bedtime's at eight. Just leave him on your couch or whatever. I can just come and grab him when I get home."

Before I had fully processed what was happening, she was already going down the stairs, waving goodbye.

"Wait, Mariella," I cried. "I don't know if I can—"

I heard the door in the lobby closing behind her with a click and just like that Ethan and I were standing in the hallway, alone. Nine thirty…that was *four and a half hours* from now.

I swallowed hard and stared at my front door, because it was better than staring at Ethan. Just looking at him made me feel as though I might pass out.

"Did you forget your keys?" Ethan asked, pulling his hand from my grip and reaching for the zipper of my purse. "My mom always finds hers hiding right at the bottom in the same old place, but she swears a lot before she remembers to look there."

"Right, keys," I whispered, shakily pawing through my purse until I found them.

I swung the door open and Ethan ran inside with his bag of toys, bouncing onto the couch and turning on the TV. "Do you have Treehouse? Do you have Nickelodeon?" he asked, already clicking the remote, though the screen remained blank.

He gave me a horrified look. *No TV?*

I grabbed a DVD off my bookcase, thanking Jesus that I had a childish taste in movies, and threw it into his hands. "Here, watch this," I said as I practically jogged down the hall away from him. "I just have to make a phone call, okay?"

"Okay," Ethan called back. I heard the opening music to *Toy Story* drifting down the hallway to my room just before I shoved the door shut.

Throwing my purse onto the bed—where it promptly exploded because I hadn't zipped it shut—I started pacing with my hands over my face. From his perch on my desk chair, Turner's eyes followed me around the room. The tips of my fingers were tingling and my stomach was churning, a sure sign I was about to have a panic attack. Though I desperately wanted to keep moving, I shooed the cat off my chair and sat down, putting my head between my knees.

Think, I urged myself, *think. Who can I call?*

I didn't even consider the alternative. I couldn't be here alone with Ethan. That was out of the question. I hadn't babysat a child, not in six years. And there was a very, very good reason for that. I clutched my thighs, squeezing them so hard I left bruises. This was not happening, not again. I couldn't let it happen. I needed somebody to come and take care of this kid *right now*, but who?

Emily.

Burrowing through the pile of purse crap on my bed, I finally located my phone and dialed Em's number, trying to think of where she might be at that moment. What day was it? Wednesday? Didn't she have yoga at dinnertime on Wednesdays? But sometimes she skipped. A lot of the time, actually. She and Anita sometimes went out for burgers instead. But apparently not today. I left several incredibly frantic and probably alarming messages on both of their phones and then started pacing the room again, tapping my cell against my stomach. As I passed the door I pressed my ear up against it, but I could only hear the movie playing from the other room. Good, good. He was fine. Unless he'd already choked to death.

Who else could I call?

I didn't have Melissa's number. Sally would probably set the place on fire herself. My parents were too far away. I shook my fist in the air, cursing myself for insisting on running four thousand kilometers from my past. Wouldn't thirty have been enough? Then they could have been here in half an hour. I couldn't remember the last time I'd wanted my mommy this much. I thumbed through the measly list of contacts on my phone. There was only one name left.

I stared down at his number then pressed my forehead into the windowpane, gazing out at the dark street below. He was my only option. I could either call him or spend the evening with Ethan by myself. Just the thought of it made my breath hitch in my throat and I had to spend five minutes with my head between my legs again.

I didn't consider what he would think when he saw my number on his phone. I didn't think about how pathetic it was that I was calling him now, or how pathetic he would think I was, or how pathetic I thought I was. I didn't think about anything at all. I just closed my eyes, pressed my thumb down on his number, and listened to it ring.

"Hello?" Lucas said, speaking loudly due to the background noise. Just the sound of his voice made tears spring to my eyes.

"Lucas?" I squeaked, holding the phone with both hands. "Lucas, I'm sorry to be calling. I—"

"Katie?" he said, and the noise around him receded. I wondered if he'd stepped into a closet or something.

Silence spread between us as I tried to think of the right words to say that would make him come. How could I explain this? I'd sound like a lunatic. He had no reason to care about my problems now, after I'd left him standing on the street alone in a storm and then ignored him for two weeks straight. What could I possibly say to fix all of that and express my desperation at the same time? There weren't words enough in the English language.

"Lucas," I repeated, my voice breaking, "I need you. Please

come."

There was a pause. I held my breath, waiting for his reply.

"I'll be there in ten minutes," he said, and then hung up.

They were the longest ten minutes of my entire life. I spent them pacing around the kitchen eating marshmallows and peeking over the back of the couch at Ethan playing with his dinosaurs on the coffee table. Every time the toy dinosaur came on the screen, he cheered and held up his Tyrannosaurus rex and I ate another marshmallow. The only time we interacted was when he asked me if he could have some marshmallows, too, and I gave him ten. His eyes lit up like it was his birthday, and he'd been quietly stuffing his face ever since.

Finally the front door buzzer went off and I rushed over to press the button. Standing in the living room, I noticed all my dark paintings hanging on the wall in an alarming cluster and quickly pulled them off the wall, leaving them in a pile by the couch. That done, I swung open the door and stood with one foot in the hall and one in my apartment. I didn't really start breathing freely until I saw him hurrying down the hall toward me. I'd never seen him hurry anywhere before. At the sight of him, my chest started heaving as though I was the one who'd just run up the stairs.

He stopped in front of me, his eyes full of questions, and before I realized what I'd done, I was pressing my cheek into his chest and breathing in his Lucas smell.

Oh my God, I was throwing myself at him, just like I'd said I wouldn't do. And now he was going to push me away.

But, surprisingly, he didn't. His strong arms came around me, the fingers of his right hand running down my back, his chin resting on the top of my head. I noticed he wasn't wearing a jacket, and it was barely five degrees outside. His arms were cool, but they heated up quickly as I stood inside them. I heard him make a *hmm* noise, kind of like a sigh, and it had an amazing calming effect on me. Barely a minute had passed, but a minute in Lucas's arms was like a lifetime in anyone else's. They were magic healing arms.

"What's wrong, Katie?" Lucas said into my hair, and I shook myself back into the present moment, remembering there was a five year old in the room with us.

Pulling out of Lucas's arms, I pointed at Ethan, who, thank God, didn't seem to have been paying us any attention.

"Th-this this is Ethan," I stuttered, and Lucas glanced at the kid, who waved a dinosaur, then back at me. "He belongs to Mariella." Had I ever mentioned Mariella to Lucas? "She's my neighbour and she had to work and I'm watching him until nine thirty or maybe ten and these are his dinosaurs," I finished in a rush.

Lucas looked back and forth between me and Ethan a few more times, then his eyes settled on my face and I stared at him, shaking my head because I knew none of this made any sense to him. Wordlessly I begged him just to put up with my craziness one last time and he'd never have to do it again. He gazed at me a few minutes more, blinking thoughtfully, then nodded once and turned and closed the door.

"Can I be the stegosaurus?" he asked Ethan as he sat down beside him on the rug.

The little boy nodded and handed over the toy, then started to telling him the names of all the characters in the movie, pointing at the screen.

I closed my eyes and let out a long sigh of relief.

Somehow we made it through the night. Like a real trooper, Lucas sat with Ethan and played dinosaurs and built a fort and harassed Turner while I made us a dinner of chocolate chip cookies—I had the dough, after all—French toast, and apple slices, using up all the fresh ingredients I had in my fridge. We watched the rest of *Toy Story* and made it halfway through *A Bug's Life* without Ethan bursting into tears, which he finally did only because I reminded him that it was already ten minutes past his bedtime. Though the sight of those tears nearly sent me over the edge again, Lucas dealt with them like a pro. He got the kid to stop crying and brush his teeth and put on his pyjamas, all for the promise of being able to go to sleep inside the fort.

When it came time to go to sleep, Lucas lay down on the floor next to Ethan's cushion fort and they whispered secrets into each other's ears while I watched from my perch on a kitchen stool. I hadn't really known if my rescuer would be good with kids when I'd called him in a panic, but he really was. It was really precious to watch, and kind of a turn on in a weird way, although I tried to ignore that. He would make a great dad one day.

We retreated to my pillowless bedroom once Ethan was asleep so as to not wake him up. I collapsed facedown onto the mattress, nearly delirious with happiness that the nightmare was finally over. Then I felt the mattress sag next to me as Lucas sat down on my bed and I scrambled into a sitting position, all of a sudden very aware that there was a guy in my room. I'd never had a guy in my room before, or on my bed, or leaning back on my headboard watching me with his legs splayed. Or grinning at me because I'd been staring at him, speechless, for five minutes.

"Thanks for coming," I said. "I guess I just got a little…" Upset? Overwhelmed? Maniacally hysterical? There didn't seem to be any adequate word to finish the sentence.

"Are you going to thank me from over there," Lucas said, gesturing at my perch on the corner of the bed, "or over here?" He patted the bedspread beside him.

Uh-oh.

"Uhhh…" I stalled, glancing around the room for something to distract him, but there was nothing but art supplies and books. Why the hell was my room so boring? Then I felt two hands grab me by the waist and suddenly I was sprawling, my butt on one side of his legs and my feet on the other, not quite sitting in his lap, but pretty close.

"Over here—that's what you said, right?" Lucas said, pulling at my hip so my side was pressed up against his chest. "That's what I thought." He rested his arm around my shoulder, coaxing my head onto his chest. I resisted at first, but it was the scent of him and the all-encompassing warmth of his arms—they were intoxicating. I let my head fall against him,

161

just for a minute, I promised myself.

"Are you going to tell me what tonight was all about?" he asked.

A band of anxiety wrapped itself around my chest, but I forced it loose. "Maybe another time," I said, hoping that would be enough.

"Mmmhmm," Lucas said. He was rubbing his hand up and down my arm in a way that was incredibly distracting. Then his other hand, which I'd lost track of, brushed against my cheek and I felt the beating of my heart begin to speed up.

His fingers reached farther, grazing against the skin of my neck and easing into my hair. I let my eyes fall closed at the tantalizing feeling.

"I missed you," I murmured into his shirt, and suddenly I felt the beating of Lucas's heart pick up, as well, the pounding precisely even with my own.

He removed his arm from my shoulders and I felt him guiding me backwards until I was lying flat on the bed and there he was next to me, propped up on his side. Our bodies weren't exactly touching. His hand was braced against the mattress beside my hip, his chin in the palm of his other hand as he gazed down at me.

I swallowed and tried to catch my breath as my heart went completely crazy, beating a mile a minute. *Whoa*, I said in my head, and a second later I realized I'd also said it out loud.

"Katie Archer," Lucas said, and I couldn't believe how much I loved hearing him say my name, "you are driving me crazy."

I wanted to protest, but then his lips were on my neck and all possibility of thought was lost. From somewhere in the back of my brain where I was still aware of what was going on, I heard myself breathing hard as I let my head fall back, baring more of my neck to his insistent lips. Then I twisted to face him, feeling the tight curve of his waist through his shirt as my hands pressed against his body. When he found the sweet spot where my neck met my shoulder, I felt something blossom to life inside me and pressed my hips against his. He reacted by making a sound like a growl deep in his throat.

How had this happened? A minute ago I was just sitting beside him on the bed and now suddenly his hand was caressing my hip and I was wishing he would let it move higher up. He leaned over me, feathering kisses across my jaw as he moved to the other side of my neck, and I felt him against my leg, warm and hard. All the fuzziness cleared from my head in an instant as my eyes flew wide open.

"Wait," I said, gently pushing him away. His eyes, which had been clouded over, cleared just a little as they focused on my face.

He leaned back so we were essentially lying down facing each other, our faces just inches apart.

"Wait?" he said, his hand cupping the side of my face as his thumb slid over my bottom lip. I felt my eyes begin to roll back in my head.

"Stop it!" I snapped, swatting his hand away, and he let it rest on my waist instead, which wasn't exactly better, but at least I could mostly think clearly.

"Am I stopping for a reason?" he asked, and I saw his dimples make their first appearance of the night. My God, it had been a while since I'd seen them, and they were looking good.

I tried to articulate my thoughts, but the emotions that were rushing around in my body had me all turned around. Why exactly had I asked him to stop? Did I even know?

"What about Taylor?" I asked abruptly, and watched Lucas's eyes narrow as though he were trying to place her name."

"Don't act like you don't know who she is," I said with irritation. "Redhead, perfect body, big red lips planted on your cheek whenever she gets the chance."

"Right, Taylor," Lucas said, looking amused. "Sounds like you don't like Taylor's lips touching me, Hero."

My temper flaring, I grabbed his arms and wrestled him back until he was pressed against the headboard. "Stop. Calling. Me. Hero," I said though gritted teeth. He held up his hands in a gesture of innocence. "I promise," he said seriously. "I will never call you Hero again…unless I want you to press your whole body up against me like that. 'Cause that was kind of great."

"Ugh!" I pummeled his arms with my fists and he fended me off until we were both lying on our backs, spent.

"So what's all this about Taylor?" Lucas said.

"Well, you two are obviously—"

"Obviously?" Lucas said with interest, rising up on his side again.

I sighed, looking up at the ceiling. "I know you said you're not like that anymore, but I also know your reputation, Lucas," I said. "You've got Taylor and Monica and Jenny and God knows how many other girls waiting in line."

Lucas made a strange sound and my eyes snapped to his face. Was he actually laughing at me? I stared at him, as he struggled to get himself under control.

"First of all," he began, his face still red with laughter, "I don't *have* Jenny. She's an old family friend. We grew up together, but there's absolutely nothing going on there. I'm just really fond of the kid."

"She's not a kid, she's the same age as me," I said, frowning at him.

"Jenny will always be a kid to me," Lucas said, pressing his finger into the frown line between my eyebrows, trying to smooth it away. "I will never have feelings like that for her, trust me."

I wanted to bring up the moment I'd seen on the bench, but I didn't want to invade his privacy or embarrass him. I was willing to concede that maybe I'd misconstrued what I'd seen, though I still didn't see how. Did Lucas really go around caressing the cheeks of his childhood friends? Then I remembered that she'd been yelling at him that night and for the first time it occurred to me to wonder what she'd been yelling about.

"Monica is in the past, and I mean the distant past," Lucas went on, "and Taylor…Taylor is the type of girl who's used to getting what she wants. That's all I can really say about her."

"And what she wants is you," I said, realizing after the words were out of my mouth how pouty they sounded.

"Just because she wants me doesn't mean she gets me," Lucas said gently. "I have to want her, too, don't I?"

"I saw the two of you out together last weekend."

"Keeping tabs on me, are you?" Lucas said, raising his eyebrows.

I narrowed my eyes at him. "By coincidence we happened to be in the same restaurant Sunday night. And don't dodge the question."

"My roommates dragged me out for dinner and Taylor and her friends joined us," he said. "I admit she was coming on pretty strong that night. She's not used to hearing the word no, like I said. But I didn't encourage her and I didn't go home with her. I didn't want to."

"Didn't you?" I challenged. Taylor was every guy's fantasy—gorgeous, experienced, and a little naughty. She was everything I knew I could *never* be.

Lucas groaned loudly and then his body was on the move. He braced his body over mine, putting his weight on his forearms, both his hands cupping my face.

Oh, wow.

"What do I have to do to convince you how crazy I am about you, Katie?" he said. His eyes were drawn to my lips and I thought for sure he was going to kiss me, but he held back. I suppressed a whine of disapproval.

My God, he was so beautiful. Looking at him just never got old. A few locks of his hair hung down over his forehead and I pushed them back with my fingers. He hadn't shaved in a few days and there was a little bit of scruff across his cheeks, which only made him look deliciously disheveled, as if he'd just rolled out of bed, still warm from sleep, and naked, of course—because when I imagined Lucas in bed, and this wasn't the first time, he was always naked. The very idea made me flush. And he wanted to know why I couldn't believe he was interested in *me*?

He was still looking at me expectantly, waiting for an answer. "I'm just going to stay here until you're convinced," he said, settling in with a smile. Was this supposed to get me talking? If it were up to me, he could stay here all day.

"It's just..." I picked at the sleeve of his shirt, avoiding his eyes. "These last couple of weeks you've been acting like... When we ran into each other in the art studio, you looked at me like... I thought you were sick of me."

"You rejected me, Katie, in case you forgot," Lucas reminded me. "What was making me sick was running into you all the time, seeing you in class and knowing I could never have you. Though, I'm beginning to think that's not exactly true..."

"It's not true," I said quickly, a little too quickly.

Real smooth, Archer.

Liking this answer, Lucas eased himself higher until his face was level with mine, but I couldn't let myself be distracted. I clamped my eyes shut and said, "But why would you want to be with me when you could have any girl you wanted?" I cringed inwardly. This was so humiliating. "You need to make it make sense. Because it doesn't make sense to me."

Lucas paused before answering. I sensed that something I'd said was bothering him, but he didn't want to say what.

"I want to be with you instead of all the other girls because you're not like all the other girls," he said.

Thanks. Way to be vague.

"Yeah," I agreed. "I'm way less outgoing, way less adventurous, way less—"

"If you say beautiful, we're going to have words, Archer," Lucas warned.

"Fine," I said uncomfortably, squirming a little under his body. "So what do you mean, then? How am I different?"

He thought about this for a minute, letting his eyes roam over me. "You don't expect anything of me," he answered finally. "And you don't play games. You're just you, and when I'm with you, I guess I feel like I can just be me."

It was a nice thing to say, and flattering, but something still clenched inside me at his words. He thought I was just being myself when I was with him, that I wasn't playing any games, wearing any masks. But my whole life was a mask. The girl he thought he knew wasn't me at all. I was glad the Lucas I knew was the real him, that he felt he could be himself with me, but what would he do when he saw the real Katie Archer? Would he still call her Hero? Would he still want to kiss her?

And even if he did, who would he become with her?

What would happen to the grinning, playful Lucas? What would I make him into?

Lowering my eyes, I rolled out from under him and lay on my side with my back to him. Gradually I felt him cuddle up behind me, curling his arm around me so my back was pressed into his front.

"Don't push me away, Katie," he whispered. "I want to be with you, only you. I haven't been with any other girls since last semester."

"Really?" I said, surprised by how desperately I wanted to believe him. He found my hand and laced my fingers with his.

"When exactly do you think I've had the time to chase after other girls? All I do is go to class and work and hang out with you!"

"I don't know, in class? At work?"

"I'm not as good at multi-tasking as you might think," he said, and I snickered.

Hugging me closer to him, he pressed his face into my hair and breathed deeply, just as I breathed him in whenever I saw him. It felt strange to be on the other end of it, like we'd suddenly switched lives. I wondered what life as Lucas Matthews would be like. As I thought about certain body parts that I'd definitely like to get a better look at, I was glad my back was turned, because I was suddenly blushing furiously.

"I want to take you out on a date," Lucas announced, and I half-spun around, a protest ready on my lips. He pressed a finger against them before I could speak. "If I don't take you out properly, how will you ever believe that I'm serious about you?"

"I believe you, Lucas," I said lamely. "I'm just not sure…"

I'm not sure I won't break you into pieces. I'm not sure I deserve you. I'm not sure I won't ruin your life forever.

"Katie," Lucas said, pulling at my arm until I turned to face him again, "there's nothing you could ever tell me that would make me stop wanting you."

My eyes rose to his as he said this. How did he know that was what I'd been thinking? And how could I tell him that it wasn't only that I was afraid he would stop wanting me? I was afraid that eventually, when I was done with him, I wouldn't want him, either.

"What if you're wrong?" I said sadly.

"I'm not," he replied simply. "Want me to show you how I know?"

He pushed his face forward, letting his lips come dangerously close to mine. He hadn't kissed me yet tonight and my body had clearly been yearning for it, because it was as though he'd flipped a switch. Every nerve ending in me flared to life as I felt his bottom lip pressing against mine and I leaned forward to meet him. Then there was a loud knocking on the door and we both froze in place.

"Oh no, it's Mom!" Lucas whispered. I let out a combination of a laugh and a groan as inwardly I cursed Mariella's punctuality. Lucas gave me a quick and thoroughly unsatisfying peck on the lips before he launched himself off the bed and helped me up, too.

Looking back at the wrinkled sheets on the mattress, I realized we'd been lying right next to the pile of junk from my purse. Lucas reached forward and pulled his envelope out of the pile. "Didn't you open this yet?" he asked.

"I didn't have the chance," I admitted, my curiosity piqued now. I tried to grab it out of his hands, but he held it out of my reach.

Mariella knocked on the door again.

"Better not keep Mom waiting," Lucas warned, and we both went down the hall to answer the door.

Mariella was all smiles and thanks as we gathered Ethan's toys and she carried him back to her apartment. Before she closed her door she gave me a big-eyed look that told me I'd better spill tomorrow, and I shrugged my shoulders at her like I had no idea what she meant.

When I came back to my own apartment, Lucas was clearing the dirty dishes off the coffee table, which was basically the hottest thing I'd ever seen a man do with dishes.

Then he walked over to the door and my heart gave a dispirited *thud* as I realized he was leaving.

"Why didn't you wear a jacket?" I asked. "It's freezing out."

Lucas shrugged. "I guess I forgot it," he said. "The minute I heard your voice I ran out the door." He patted his jeans pockets. "I don't even have my wallet on me."

I tried not to show how much his words warmed my heart.

"So tomorrow," he said.

"Tomorrow?" I replied.

"Date night," he explained. "Say you'll go with me and I'll let you have this." He held up the envelope.

"You already gave it to me; now you're using it as blackmail?" I protested.

"Wow, I've never heard a girl call a date with me blackmail before," Lucas mused as I tried in vain to snatch at the envelope.

Finally I gave up. "All right, Lucas," I said. "I will go out with you, just once."

"Just once with a chance of more?" he asked, lowering the envelope.

"A very small chance," I said wickedly, grabbing it out of his hands. "And no guarantees!"

Lucas smiled the big smile all guys reserve for the moment when they know they've won. He leaned in and whispered in my ear, "You know how I love a challenge, Hero."

Then he kissed me, pressing me backwards until I was against the door, his tongue probing my mouth with delicious intensity. He kissed me until I felt thoroughly kissed, until I felt breathless. He kissed the breath right out of me.

I followed him out to the stairs and watched him cross the lobby and go out the door before I opened the envelope.

It was a sketch, a view of what I assumed had to be his apartment window. He'd drawn the bare trees and the building across the street. There was a shaggy dog framed in one window looking totally forlorn. Beneath the drawing he'd written, "Without You."

I hugged the sketch to my chest, a grin spreading across my lips as I followed the hallway back to my door. I'd dreaded this day for so long. It stunned me to realize how differently it had turned out than how I'd feared it would.

Or maybe no differently at all.

My door had drifted partly shut, and I noticed a paper tacked to the outside of it, a paper that hadn't been there when Ethan and I had come in five hours earlier.

My eyes ran over the two words as my body broke out in a cold sweat.

FOUND YOU

14

Em: Is it happening now?
Me: We're in the car going to the restaurant.
Em: Don't put out on the first date. He'll never buy the cow if he can motorboat your boobs for free.
Me: Omg, stop now.
Em: Make sure you show him that bra, though, it's my best one!
Me: I'm turning my phone OFF now.
Em: No glove, no love!

"What's so funny?" Lucas asked, giving me a quizzical look as he stopped at a red light.

I quickly hid my phone in my purse before more of Em's X-rated texts could come through. "Just sister stuff," I answered.

"You're not telling her to call you in an hour with an emergency so you can get out of this date, are you?" Lucas said suspiciously. "Because you gotta give a guy a chance."

"No, I told her to save her gaping head wound for the two-hour mark," I replied. "The whole point is to get a free meal out of you first, obviously."

"That's my girl," Lucas said with a grin.

My girl. I recalled how on the night of Oleg's party those same words had filled me with rage. Now I felt my chest fill with anticipation and bubbly excitement. I was surprised at how little nervousness I was feeling, actually. Though Lucas might not know it, this was my first date—ever. I should have been white-knuckling it, but instead I felt giddy. Lucas, on the other hand, seemed pretty cool on the outside, but I had the feeling he was a little apprehensive about tonight.

When we first got into the car, he'd accidentally put it into reverse instead of drive, and he kept turning on the windshield wipers by mistake, even though it wasn't raining. He blamed in on the fact that it wasn't his car—and thank God, because this one was worse than the last one. One door was a different colour than the rest of the car, and my seat was stuck in a leaned-back position—but I remembered what Brit had said that night at The Limo; that it was my presence that made Lucas lose his cool.

Feeling mischievous, I decided to test out Brit's theory. Sitting up in my seat as we sat at an intersection waiting to make a left turn, I leaned toward Lucas and brushed my fingers through his hair. His golden eyes darted to my face as I gave him a sly smile.

"What're you doing?" he said uneasily.

Edging over even farther, I placed my lips beside his ear and whispered, "Am I making you nervous, Lucas?"

I heard him beginning to respond when I opened my lips and slid my tongue across his earlobe. Lucas sucked in a breath and the car swerved suddenly to the left, then back again. Luckily I'd checked that there was no traffic around the car before making my move.

"Jesus, Katie!" Lucas said as he completed his turn, breathing hard, his eyes wide and his hands gripping the wheel for dear life.

I fell back into my seat, giggling. "I got you, I got you!" I sang until he was laughing along with me. "You're such a sucker! I would have seen that one coming from a mile away."

"I told you I wasn't any good at multi-tasking," he said, still shaking his head. "But you just wait, I'll get you back."

I didn't have to wait long. At the next stop he swiftly put the car into park, undid his seatbelt, and pulled me toward him, kissing me so firmly and deeply that for a moment I forgot entirely that we were in a car on a busy street with people walking by. When a car behind us honked, he broke the kiss and gave me mocking frown. "That's for using your siren ways against me," he said, shaking his finger at me as he took the wheel again.

"Well, if that's my punishment, I think I might just have to do it again," I answered with a coy grin, and he groaned like I was hurting him.

I didn't know who this flirty, brazen girl was that had taken my place tonight, but I hoped she stuck around. She was already a hit, both with Lucas and with me.

We turned into the parking lot of a sketchy looking strip mall and I began to hope this wasn't actually where we were eating. Maybe there was a super-secret entrance to a swanky restaurant hidden between the dingy dry cleaner's and the seventies decor family eatery? But I didn't want to seem judgmental, so I kept my hopes to myself.

Lucas got out of the car then ran around to my side to open the door for me. I stepped out gingerly due to the heels Em had insisted I wear and took the arm Lucas held out.

"What a gentleman," I said appreciatively, and saw that his eyes were still riveted to the four-inch strappy sandals on my feet. (I was stunned Emily had let me have them considering the state her boots had been in after my daring run through the snow, but she'd said they were her first date good-luck shoes and I had to wear them. "For the sake of the date," she'd said dramatically, handing them over.)

I felt the palm of Lucas's hand run down to the small of my back, then press me closer to him so he could speak into my ear. "You wouldn't think I was such a gentleman if you knew what was going through my mind after seeing those shoes," he said, his voice thick, his lips grazing my ear. It was the same move I'd pulled on him in the car. I was surprised he'd only swerved. I would probably have crashed right into the curb.

In my heels I was much closer to his height, and I didn't have to stretch that far to whisper back. "Well, get ready, because under this coat I'm wearing a dress to match."

Lucas gave me a burning look and I literally had to take him by the hand and lead him toward the sidewalk to get him to move.

As I'd feared, we stopped in front of the rundown-looking restaurant. I wasn't wrong about it being a family eatery. Its name was actually Mama's Table. Glancing through the window I saw lots of parents and kids, booster chairs, and booths with cracked vinyl seats. I remembered Lucas's long hours at the club and his borrowed car. He obviously didn't have a lot of cash. Maybe this was the best place he could afford.

"Looks great!" I said amiably as I waited for him to open the door for me.

He gave me a funny look and kissed me on the forehead. "Thanks for faking that for me," he said. "This *is* going to be great, though, I promise. I just need you to wait here for a sec." He waited for my nod, confused as it was, then went through the restaurant doors.

Only when Lucas was out of sight did I feel the heaviness descend upon my shoulders. Leaning against the brick wall beside the door, I quickly scanned the half-empty parking lot and began twisting my fingers. My hands were already puffy and startlingly red because I'd been doing it all day, almost nonstop except for the car ride. Without Lucas to distract me, my mind was drawn immediately to the note.

After placing it on the coffee table I'd been irrationally afraid to touch it, and had sat huddled on the couch for most of the night, staring at it as though it was a poisonous snake and might uncoil and strike me at any moment. I had not slept at all, and when morning came I'd gone straight over to Em's under the pretense of date prep. She'd done my nails and taken me out for lunch, chatting almost nonstop about Lucas and the date and how sure she'd been that we'd patch things up, and

I'd been more bright and cheerful than I'd ever been. (Em had actually asked me several times if I was feeling all right.)

Suddenly, my own defence mechanism revealed itself to me like a jack-in-the-box and I saw that the flirty girl in the car was just another version of that persona, a gay and giggly mask to cover the quivering girl inside. When I was laughing and happy, even as a pretense, the fear couldn't touch me. It was an opposite method to the one I'd been using for years to battle my fear—namely lonerdom and a surly disposition—but then, I realized, I'd never been this afraid before, not in six long years.

I couldn't be sure that Brandon himself had been in my building. But somebody he knew had been there. Somebody he was in contact with knew my phone number and where I lived. How hard could it be for this person to pick my lock and break right in? I'd held my baseball bat—the one my father had bought for me when he'd found out I would be getting my own apartment—clutched in my sweaty palms all night with that very thought in mind. I had no idea where I would be sleeping tonight, but I knew I couldn't go back there, not alone. I couldn't face the two words on that piece of paper again.

This date with Lucas felt like a last meal of sorts, a tantalizing treat before the nightmare set in. I could have rescheduled, made up some excuse. In truth, a part of me had gravitated to this response, a knee-jerk reaction from years of hiding, of avoiding, of lying. But I didn't want to lie to Lucas, and I didn't want to be held hostage by my fear anymore. I wanted to go on my first date with a guy I thought might just be able to survive me. I wanted to disappear into his embrace and forget about what was waiting for me at home: a terror so big, so strong, I was sure it would tear me away from my moorings and I would never see Lucas again. I didn't want to let it have me. I didn't want to see what it had in store. So, instead, I swallowed it whole, hiding it deep inside so I could have this one night for me. For Lucas and me. For us.

Just in case it was our only chance.

I was still staring into the dark when Lucas pushed the door open and poked his head out.

"Ready to have the best meal of your life?" he said with a smile.

Was I ever.

Taking my hand, he led me through the brightly lit restaurant. I imagined maybe he'd had a special table laid out for us at the back, but that wasn't the case. Once we reached the back wall of the restaurant, we kept going down the hallway that I assumed led to the bathrooms and the back door.

"Uh, Lucas?" I said. "Are we going to eat out by the dumpsters, or...?"

"I knew I should have blindfolded you," he answered. "We're almost there, so don't get your panties in a bunch. Or, actually, whatever you want to do with your panties is fine with me." He grinned widely over his shoulder at me.

"Shut up about my panties!" I said. "Or you'll never get to see them."

This seemed to sober him somewhat, and as we reached a pair of swinging doors he held them open for me, the perfect gentleman once more.

We were in the back of the kitchen. There were metal sinks and stacks of pots and a mop and bucket leaning against the wall. I was just about to ask Lucas what the hell was going on—had I worn these awful heels for dish duty?—when a guy in a white apron and chef's hat appeared from around a corner. He had chubby cheeks and incredibly long sideburns.

"Mario, I'd like you to meet Katie," Lucas said formally, and I shook Mario's extended hand.

Then he took me by the arm and started leading me through the kitchen as Lucas followed behind. "You're in for a special treat tonight," Mario said. "An exclusive table has been set especially for you so that you might be one of the first to experience the delectable..." He paused in mid-sentence, his eyes darting around.

"Genius," Lucas whispered, and I had to bite back a laugh.

"...genius of Chef Mario." Mario patted himself on the chest. "In a quiet and exclusive..."

"You already said exclusive," Lucas whispered.

"Well, whatever, man!" Mario said frowning. "I'm a chef, not a great orator. You made the lines too long anyway!"

Lucas chucked as we reached our table and Mario pulled out my chair then stalked off, grumbling. The table was out of the way of the bustle of the kitchen, next to an alcove where the employees kept their coats and bags. Unlike the tables in the main restaurant, it was nicely set with a white tablecloth, shining cutlery, and some sweet-smelling pink flowers in a vase. I leaned over to smell the flowers, and when I turned back to Lucas my mouth went dry. He'd taken off his coat and I saw that he was wearing a grey suit jacket over a crisp blue shirt, the dressiest clothes I'd ever seen him wear, even if he had matched them with dark blue jeans. He'd shined his shoes, as well. Looking at him, I couldn't believe he was for me. He looked so gorgeous it left me speechless.

"Mario works part-time at the club," Lucas explained as he helped me off with my coat. "He's a culinary student, and this is his other job. The owners let him practice recipes on his days off or after hours. He brought these lobster puffs in to work once and they were so delicious Brit almost cried when she saw I'd eaten the last one. He made a special menu for us tonight. I hope you like pork chops with fudge sauce."

I paused halfway through unfolding my napkin in my lap. "Did you say fudge sauce?" I asked, finding my voice again.

"Yup," Lucas said with a self-satisfied smile.

I looked around the room. "I think I'm really going to like this place," I said.

"I think I really like you," Lucas said, his gaze intense, and I bowed my head as a blush spread across my cheeks. "And that dress," he went on. "Did I mention yet how much I'm liking it?"

"You didn't," I said.

Reaching out, he ran the back of two of his fingers down my arm, causing a throb to take up inside me.

He said, "I like it so much it's making me forget what we're doing here."

"Now, now, Lucas," I said sternly as I saw Mario approaching with the first course. "Don't get distracted."

"With you around?" he said. "Impossible."

Our eyes met as Mario set our salads in front of us and lifted their covers. "*Bon appetit!*" he said.

The meal was like one long dessert, with each course seemingly impossible to top until the next course did. We began with a salad of romaine lettuce, cucumbers, and berries with pecans and dark chocolate flakes. This was followed by a potato soup with bacon and chocolate chunks, braised pork chops, mashed potatoes, and green beans with fudge sauce, and a cheese and milk chocolate plate. By the time Mario was serving us our Nutella-filled churros I was basically having an orgasm at the table with every bite.

"Do I have chocolate all over my face?" I asked Lucas as I cleaned my plate. I'd basically been gobbling everything in front of me like a starving orphan. I wouldn't have been surprised if my entire face was covered in chocolate by now.

"Nope," Lucas answered. "Oh, but wait. You just have a little bit here…" He leaned forward and placed his lips a little to the right of my own, and I felt his tongue slowly lick at the corner of my mouth. His lips were warm and so tantalizingly close. I had only to turn my head a little to capture his mouth entirely, but before I could he pulled away. I had to suppress a whimper.

"No second dessert until we're alone," he warned.

"And when will that be?" I said, eyeing his lips, not caring if I sounded desperate. At that moment I *was* desperate to feel his lips on mine again.

"As soon as humanly possible," Lucas said, and I saw him catch Mario's eye and make a gesture with his hand that I presumed indicated he wanted to wrap things up. Now.

There was no cheque to pay, since we weren't official

customers. I assumed from the way Mario and he shook hands that they'd organized some alternate form of payment. I hoped Lucas didn't have to take too many of Mario's shifts at the club to cover the evening.

"She loved it, man," I overheard Lucas saying as he patted Mario on the back. "I owe you big."

"You're a chocolate God and I would marry you if I could," I said to Mario as I slipped on my coat.

He smiled widely as I said this and kept hold of my hand even once we'd stopped shaking.

"All right, enough of that," Lucas said, taking back my hand and gripping it firmly. He didn't seem to like the way Mario was looking at me at all, which amused me to no end.

As we went out the doors, I looked back at Mario and whispered, just loud enough for Lucas to hear, "Call me!"

Lucas growled and playfully grabbed me by the waist as we walked through the restaurant. "He can't have you, you're mine," he murmured into my ear.

Yes I am, I thought but didn't say.

When we reached the car, I snatched the keys out of his hand and opened the driver's side door. "Maybe I should drive, since you had so much trouble with it earlier," I teased, and though Lucas grinned, his mood seemed to have shifted.

It was snowing very lightly, insubstantial flakes that melted as soon as they hit the ground. The temperature was meant to go even higher tomorrow, so I knew that even if a light layer fell overnight, it would be gone by midday, snow that wasn't meant to last. Lucas held out his hand to catch some flakes and we both watched as they melted in his palm.

Then he approached me and took my face in his hands. I yearned for him to kiss me again, and I was sure he would, but he spoke instead.

"The night of the party—why'd you run away?" he said.

The fear I'd been holding at bay crept into my body, gurgling in my stomach. I exhaled and looked down at the ground, trying to avoid his gaze. "You really want to talk about this now?" I said. "While I'm wearing this dress?" I wanted to distract him, to arouse him, anything to not have to answer this question, but he wasn't letting it go.

"I want to know everything about you, Katie," he said, running his hands over my hair and lightly pulling the strands all the way to their tips. "I want to understand you inside and out. I want to know your every thought, even if you're thinking there's something about me you don't like."

Something about him, or something about me? He had no idea what he was asking.

"What if I don't want to tell you everything?" I said, trying to sound defiant, but ending up sounding like a whiny child instead.

"Then I'll keep asking until you're ready to tell," he answered.

Gazing into Lucas's honey-coloured eyes, I felt something click into place. I believed him. I believed he would wait for me to be ready to tell him all my secrets, and I thought I might just trust him enough to tell him one. Just one to start. A baby step secret. One piece of the whole giant puzzle, which, I was pretty sure, I'd never let him see. Not completely. That would probably kill me. But one secret wouldn't hurt too badly, I thought. A first secret for a first date.

"When you...knocked down that...guy," I began haltingly.

"Buck?" Lucas said.

I nodded, staring at his chin. "Your face changed. You were furious with him. You looked like you wanted to tear him apart."

"I did," Lucas said simply. "He was hurting you."

I lowered my eyes farther still. "I didn't like it," I said.

"Most girls like it if you come to their defence," Lucas said. "You know, knight in shining armour and all that." He seemed truly confused, which only made it harder to go on.

"Not me," I said. "I don't like that side of guys, that violent side."

"You're the one who punched him!" Lucas said.

I met his eyes with a serious look. "I shouldn't have," I said. "I scared myself. And you scared me."

Lucas seemed to consider this. "I didn't mean to scare you. I never want you to be afraid of me. But you can't expect me to stand back and let someone hurt you. When I stepped into that room and saw you screaming at him to let you go, saw his hands pressing into your arms, I just…" A muscle flexed in his jaw and he couldn't seem to go on.

"You lost your head," I finished for him. This was something I understood. This was something I had experience with. "Most people would say it was a natural reaction and just brush it off. But I'm not most people. I can't have that kind of…behaviour around me. I can't have you hitting people for me, not ever. I need you to promise."

His eyes were almost fearful as they looked at me now. He drew his arms around me, holding me lightly by the waist, as if he thought putting too much pressure on my body might break me into pieces. "God, Katie," he whispered, searching my eyes, "what did he do to you?"

I turned my head and looked out at the snowflakes. I was *not* going to explain. I was not going to address the "he" Lucas had referred to. He might want to know everything about me, but that didn't mean I was willing to tell him everything, or even that he'd like what he found out. Telling him about Brandon and the reason aggressive guys made me run for the hills wasn't a first date secret. It was a last date secret.

"Promise me," I repeated.

Letting my eyes creep back to his face, I saw the muscles in his jaw working overtime as though he was picturing Buck Mullard with his hands gripping my wrists again. "I can't say I won't get furious if someone tries to hurt you again," he said carefully. "But I can say that I'll try to control myself. How does that sound?"

I nodded, but my trust was waning. I knew I was the one who'd asked for his promise, but now that I had it, it didn't seem like enough.

"I'm not a violent guy, Katie," Lucas persisted. "You know that, don't you?"

They never are, I thought. *Until they are.*

"I want you to stay like this," I said, sadly stroking his cheek. "I don't want you to change." I think a part of me had forgotten I was saying any of this out loud. My sorrow at the idea that I'd have to give Lucas up had taken control of my mouth. Even though I'd known it would probably turn out that way all along, it devastated me. I was like a little girl holding a puppy that wasn't hers.

I wanted to keep him forever.

"I won't change," Lucas said. "I don't know why you think I will, but I won't. I'm not pretending, Katie. When I said yesterday that I'm the real me with you, I really meant it."

He looked so sure of himself, so harmless with his soft hands and his beautiful face. I so wanted it to be true.

"Can you do one more thing for me, Lucas?" I said.

"Anything," he replied.

I sat down in the driver's seat and looked up at him.

"Kiss me," I said.

He followed me into the car as I moved backwards over the gearshift and into the passenger's seat. He grinned and his face looked nothing like the animal I'd seen in him that night. He was just himself, the guy who was stealing my heart.

"Oh yeah, I can do that," he said as his lips met mine.

15

"Mmm," Lucas said, "you taste like chocolate." I smiled against his mouth because so did he, and the glorious taste had me kissing him more hungrily than I ever had before.

One of his hands grasped the back of my neck as he lavished his appreciation on my mouth while he placed the other lightly on my knee. Within two minutes of being in the car our coats had come off, though I had no real memory of taking them off. His bulky suit jacket was a barrier to my hands, which were itching to explore his chest, but I was too shy to ask him to take it off, as well, or worse yet, to undo the buttons myself. I worried over this for a moment as Lucas's mouth traveled down my neck, but when he delved farther, feathering kisses over the bare skin of my upper chest, I pushed both my hands into his hair and concentrated instead on the heat of his lips and the explosion of feeling wherever he placed them. Both his hands moved to my waist as he pressed his mouth into my neck just below my ear. I felt almost delirious with heat, as though I were actually losing my senses. I was wishing his tentative fingers would move higher when, as if at my command, they did. The moment his right hand brushed ever so lightly over my breast I moaned into Lucas's ear, my fingers digging into his arms.

We fell back against the seat, which was still in its leaned-back position. I wasn't exactly sure how Lucas had maneuvered his body over the gearshift, but he didn't seem particularly bothered about it.

"When you make that noise, it makes me lose my mind," he whispered, and I responded by lightly biting his bottom lip, too overwhelmed to form words of my own.

Then two things happened at once. Lucas placed his hand on my bare thigh, and pretty high up on my thigh, since the skirt of my dress was pooled around my waist—and to be honest I had no real idea of where, or how much of my legs were actually showing—and I turned my head to the side and saw a middle-aged Chinese woman glancing at us through the window of the car as she walked by.

"Oh my God," I cried, turning my back to the window, which coincidentally brought my hips exactly in line with Lucas's—a fact he seemed to be a big fan of.

Lucas was still busily ravaging my neck, his kisses moving back up toward my mouth, his hands wandering every which way as I struggled to rearrange my dress.

"Lucas," I said, trying in vain to gently detach his face from mine—and a little amused by his obliviousness.

"Hmm?" he said, finally breaking his kiss to look at me.

"I think we just gave a soccer mom the shock of her life," I said, gesturing toward the windows and the strangely large number of people in the parking lot at that very minute, all of who could clearly see into the car. The windows hadn't even had a chance to fog up completely.

His arms still around me, Lucas popped his head up and glanced around, then burrowed his face in my neck to stifle a laugh. "I feel like I'm fifteen again," he said sheepishly. I was too busy laughing along with him to bother mentioning that nothing like this had ever happened to me at fifteen.

Grabbing our coats, Lucas placed them on top of me as I

continued to try to wiggle the tiny black dress Anita had lent me into its proper place on my body.

"You don't think anyone really saw anything, do you?" I said as he pulled the car out into traffic and started driving at least twenty kilometers per hour over the speed limit. Mortification was really starting to set in as I thought about exactly what we'd been doing, and how I'd been feeling, just moments before.

"Whatever they saw, I'm pretty sure it was totally hot, so you have nothing to be embarrassed about," he answered. "I'm not. I don't care who sees us together."

Pulling on my beige trench coat, I buttoned it up all the way to the neck, trying in vain to button away my earlier half-nakedness. "Oh really?" I said. "Even if all your friends had walked by? Even if it was Taylor?" I knew we'd covered the Taylor issue the day before, but I didn't really feel like he'd explained it away to my satisfaction. It was hard to understand how he could be so uninterested in a girl who matched him so perfectly and choose me instead.

Lucas gave me a look before turning his eyes back to the road. He barely braked the car as he took a turn, making the tires squeal. "Do you think I'm driving this fast because I'd rather be with Taylor right now?"

"Maybe," I said meekly, the beginnings of a grin pulling at my lips.

"Just for that, I'm going to take my time unbuttoning all those buttons," he said, pointing a warning finger at me. "It's going to be torture for you."

"Torture" suddenly took on a whole new meaning.

He brought the car to a sudden halt, yanking up the parking brake, and I realized we were in front of my building. Anxiety prickled at my skin at the sight of it. I'd thought maybe we were going to his room in Victoria Hall, which I'd never seen, but then he did have three roommates and he knew I lived all alone. It made sense that he would bring me here, to the place where just yesterday we'd made out on my bed. He didn't have any idea that my apartment had become tainted to me. I'd had him pick me up on a random street corner earlier, making up an excuse that I'd been at a friend's place picking up some notes I'd lent her, both the friend and the notes figments of my imagination. That white lie weighed on me as Lucas opened my door and pressed another kiss to my lips. How many other little lies would I be telling tonight to the boy I didn't want to lie to, I wondered.

I was still lost in these thoughts as we entered the building and I placed my key into the second lobby door. Lucas was watching me expectantly.

"Are you inviting me in, Katie?" he said, nuzzling my neck, his fingers already unbuttoning the top button of my jacket to give him better access.

All of a sudden the building didn't seem quite so menacing, and I found the particular worries I'd been harboring fizzling to nothing under Lucas's touch. What was I so worried about, anyway? What could happen? Lucas was with me.

"Yes," I murmured into his ear. This was followed by more yeses as he pressed me against the glass door until it opened under our weight and we literally fell into the lobby, nearly landing in a heap.

Grabbing my keys out of the door, Lucas dangled them from his finger. "Race you to the top!" he said then ran for the stairs.

I swallowed once before following him, his words echoing painfully in my mind.

"Race you to the tracks, Katie!"

"You heard him, Katie Kat. You'd better hurry now. If I get there first, who knows what might happen."

"You call that racing?" Lucas called down to me in a whisper, and I looked up at him. The memory dissolved when I saw his face and that dimpled grin waiting for me.

"I'm coming," I called, the same words I'd spoken years before, but I put it out of my mind, because looking back was doing me no good. I wanted to look forward. So I cleared a path through the memories and ran after Lucas, hoping maybe, just maybe, we could look forward together.

This was by far the most interesting thing that had ever happened on my couch.

The moment we walked in the door of my apartment Lucas pulled me down onto it, seating me on his lap. I only had a second to think about the fact that I was literally sitting on top of him, every cake and ice cream-loving pound of me, when his mouth found mine. His hand ran up my thigh as though he wanted to start exactly where we'd left off in the car, and all thinking went right out the window.

"Finally alone," Lucas said, the hand he'd placed on my thigh making a soft circular motion on my skin, making me feel very much as though I were a wind-up toy. With each turn of the circle, he was turning me on. "It was very forward thinking of you not to have any roommates," he went on as he kissed across my jaw and over my chin, then downward, toward the low V-neck of my dress. "Thank you for orchestrating this moment."

"Well, I aim to please," I breathed as his mouth found the base of my cleavage, that place where my breasts intersected, and I felt his warm tongue lick me in that perfect spot, his hands griping my hips. The heat that had been rising between us sparked into a fire and I parted my lips and began to pant, afraid that if I didn't I might burn right up.

This time he'd taken off his suit jacket along with his coat, and as my hands pressed into his shirt I could feel the muscles of his chest pressing back. What did a chest that felt like that look like, I wondered dizzily, and before I could stop myself I'd reached forward and unbuttoned the two top buttons of his shirt. My hands stilled and so did Lucas's as we both realized what I'd just done.

"Are you undressing me, Miss Archer?" Lucas said, and though he was trying to tease his voice had suddenly gone hoarse.

"No," I said quickly and perhaps not too convincingly, since I couldn't pry my eyes away from the expanse of smooth, muscled chest I'd revealed. In a sudden fit of daring I leaned forward and placed a kiss in the exact spot he'd just kissed me, eliciting a tortured noise from deep in Lucas's throat that I dearly wanted to hear again. And again. And again.

Leaning forward, I let my lips slide against Lucas's cheek until I reached his ear. "When you make that noise, it makes me lose my mind," I said. Then I leaned back again, letting my eyes meet his only to find they weren't gold at all anymore. They were so dilated they were black as night.

Placing his hands under my arms, I felt Lucas lifting me slightly off of his lap and then back down again, this time with one leg on either side of his so I was straddling him. My breath caught in my throat at this sudden, more intimate position and I gripped his biceps hard as he slipped his hands up both my thighs this time, not stopping where he had before, but reaching farther, until his hands were cupping my ass under my dress.

It was at this moment that it occurred to me that maybe I should tell Lucas I was a virgin.

It wasn't like I'd been keeping it from him. I just hadn't thought the night would go like this. All our wrestling on the bed the night before had seemed like a distant dream after a night of no sleep, and by the time morning came I'd chalked it up to male hormones. My own hormones were a whole other matter. But never in a million years had I imaged that tonight I'd be straddling him on my couch, telling him he was making me lose my mind. Things like this just didn't happen in my life. For good reason.

As his lips made their journey down my cleavage again, his mouth so incredibly close to my breasts that I thought I might go mad if he didn't kiss them, my nervousness made me pant even harder.

Where did Lucas think this was going? I was pretty sure I knew where he wanted it to go, if the way his hands were gripping my ass was any indication. But every make-out session didn't have to end in sex, did it? Or did it? What did I know? All I had to go on were Emily's stories, and I could hear her voice in my head right now telling me this was Lucas

Matthews. If Lucas knew one thing, it was how to screw, and girls all over campus wiggled right out of their panties at his very first kiss. Well, I hadn't taken my panties off—although I realized I had mentioned that he might get to see them earlier—but I had started undressing him.

Oh God, I thought, *is that some kind of a signal?*

Was I leading him on? Was I a tease?

Did I want to have sex with Lucas tonight? Was I going to have sex with Lucas tonight?

I heard him sigh and bring his face up to meet mine, kissing me lightly on the mouth. "I'm getting the feeling I don't have your full attention," he said, pushing a lock of my hair behind my ear before returning his hand to my butt. He really seemed to like it down there.

"No, you do," I lied. I wondered what I should do to make him stop looking at me with that questioning expression. Maybe kiss his chest again?

"Katie," Lucas said softly. "I don't know if you realize this, but your body is very responsive."

I don't think I'd ever turned beet red before. With my skin colour I didn't even think it was possible. After that moment I didn't have to wonder anymore. It was possible. My cheeks had never burned so hot in my life. I had to cover my face with my hands to block out my mortification. "Oh my God, shut up!" I cried.

"I'm not saying it to embarrass you," Lucas said, pulling at my hands, though I kept them clamped over my eyes. "All I'm saying is considering what I was just doing to you, it was easy to tell your mind was elsewhere. You were barely paying attention. What's going on in that head of yours?"

I could hear my heart pounding in my ears, louder than any drum. I gazed into his kind eyes, afraid to speak. Would it matter to him? Would it turn him off? Would it make him walk away?

And if he did, could I stand it?

"Are you—" Lucas began until I interrupted him, graceless to the last.

"I'm a virgin," I blurted.

Lucas clamped his mouth shut but didn't break our gaze. I couldn't read the expression on his face, but I did feel him take his hands off my ass and smooth my dress down over it.

"I'm sorry, that was stupid," I said, frowning.

"What's stupid? Being a virgin is stupid, or telling me about it?" Lucas said, rubbing my arms lightly. "You don't have to be embarrassed."

Peering at his face, it began to dawn on me that he didn't seem particularly perturbed. In fact, he didn't even seem all that surprised.

"You already knew, didn't you?" I said, and the fact that he didn't deny it right away gave me my answer. "Oh, just kill me now," I moaned, pressing my forehead into his shoulder. I tried to scramble off his lap, but he held me in place by my legs.

"Katie," he murmured into my ear. "Don't hide from me."

"This is mortifying!" I said still refusing to raise my head. "Here I thought I was being all hot and seductive, and all this time you knew I had no idea what I was doing!"

"Who really knows what they're doing, anyway?" Lucas said flippantly. "And for the record, I think you were doing a pretty good job at seducing me. For your first try, I'd say that was an expert-level performance. Two thumbs up."

I punched him on the arm. "Stop trying to make me laugh, I'm too embarrassed."

"What's so embarrassing about being inexperienced?" he said, running his fingers up and down my spine, sending fluttering waves through my body.

This time I did look up at him. "Think about how old you were when you first had sex." I could see his mind going back to that day. "Right, now subtract that number by how old I am right now, and maybe you'll get why this is so embarrassing. I bet you were having sex when you were fourteen."

Lucas pursed his lips and looked up at the ceiling.

"Oh my God!" I cried. "You really were fourteen! You must think I'm a freak."

His hand reached up and covered my mouth. "Don't say things like that about yourself," he said, which quieted me. Nobody had ever interrupted the hateful dialogue in my head before, probably because I never said it out loud in front of anyone. I didn't quite know how to react. "You know what I thought when I figured it out? I thought, how could this stunning girl have possibly managed to escape the notice of every guy she's ever met in her nineteen years on Earth? Because if I'd been there…well, let's just say your high school memories would be a little more X-rated."

This made me feel a little better, though not completely. "How'd you figure it out, anyway? Am I that bad of a kisser?"

"I don't know, let's check," Lucas said, leaning in and placing his lips on mine, teasing my mouth open with his. He smiled against my lips. "Seems pretty great to me."

"How, then?"

"Remember the day when we went to the basketball game, when I leaned you up against the car?" he said.

Did I remember? It was pretty much seared in my brain—the first time I'd really realized how much I wanted him.

"I was just playing with you, trying to make you admit you liked it, even though you kept insisting you wanted to be 'just friends.' But then I saw your lips trembling and I could tell I was moving a little too fast. I put two and two together and I just knew."

"And it doesn't make you want me less?" I asked him, wishing my voice didn't sound so weak and small.

"I really don't think it's a question of how much I want you," Lucas said. Placing his hands on the small of my back, he very gently pressed me forward until I was right up against him, my panties pressing right against his crotch, and I could feel how hard he was right through his jeans. The slight pressure in that oh-so-sensitive place made my body flush all over again.

"Even now, while we're talking? We aren't even kissing," I said, my voice very low. It seemed wrong to be talking about this in anything other than a whisper.

He wrapped his arms around me, somehow pulling me even closer, and the whole room seemed to shake as we rubbed together, the sensations that had been coursing through my body all redirecting their energy to that one little place. "Whenever you're around me," he said, his lips against my cheek. "In the car, at dinner, even in class." He moved his hips and I let out a gasp. "This is what you do to me."

Throwing my arms around his neck, I pushed my mouth against his, my every reservation disintegrating as my whole body throbbed.

"Take me to the bedroom," I breathed into his ear, and I heard him take just one ragged breath in response before he stood up, my legs still wrapped around him, and carried me down the hall.

I had the sudden urge to scream out "Yippee!" but thankfully I was able to hold it in.

He paused as he reached the closed door, pressing me back against it. His lips met mine, but his kisses weren't quite as frenzied as they'd been earlier.

"Katie, I'm going to take you into this room," he said seriously. "And I'm going to do things to you that will make you scream."

I giggled. Oh boy, I was really going crazy with desire if I was giggling.

"But," Lucas went on, "I don't think we should have sex tonight."

"What do you mean?" I whined. All the right parts were still pressed together in this position. I could barely see straight, let alone control myself, or my mouth.

"Don't get me wrong, I want to," he said. "I think that's pretty obvious. But I don't want your first time to be on our first date, do you? Your first time should be wonderful. I want to make it wonderful for you. And I want to be sure that you're ready."

"Oh, I'm ready," I said. The searing heat between my legs told me so.

"Just trust me on this one, okay?" Lucas said, and his

expression was so pleading that I couldn't help but agree.

"I'm still going to scream, though, right?" I said playfully as he leaned down to open my bedroom door, which, come to think of it, I didn't remember closing that morning. My own words echoed in my ears as the door swung open and Lucas tensed, tightening his grip on me and trying to back out of the room again, but I was too fast. I slithered out of his grasp, taking in the confusion and panic in his eyes before I swung around.

I'm still going to scream, though, right?

But I didn't scream right away. I didn't scream as I took in my paintings, the ones I'd taken off the wall to hide from Lucas, strewn across my bed, torn to pieces. I didn't scream when I saw the paper with its two haunting words, the paper I hadn't noticed was missing from my coffee table, sitting now on my pillow, stabbed through with a knife. And I didn't scream when I saw the four-letter word written across the wall above my bed in a red substance that might have been blood.

LIAR

Lucas put a hand on my arm and said, "Katie, what—"

That was when I started screaming.

"Get out!" I cried, shoving him backwards as hard as I could, ignoring the look of utter shock on his face. "Get out of here!"

I'd caught him off guard and he stumbled backwards, though he had thirty pounds on me at least. But he didn't have the weight of my horror bearing down on him. He didn't have the strength of my barreling dread, or the fear I'd been holding inside of me for what seemed like forever. Fear of this moment. Fear of what was happening right now.

"Katie, let me help," he said. He'd regained his balance and turned back to the door, but I was too quick for him. "No, stay out!" I shouted, terrified more than anything that he might come back in and see it all again.

I slammed the door in his face and swiftly turned the lock

as he called my name and shook the door handle.

That was when the tears came, blurring my vision and pouring down my cheeks. I slid down the door, which vibrated against my skin as he pounded on it. I slid all the way to the floor, and wept.

16

I slept right there on the floor, my cheek pressed into the hardwood, shivering long into the night in my flimsy dress. I didn't even consider moving to the bed, and not only because it was a god-awful mess and my pillow—which I would be throwing out later—had a knife cut right through it. Not only because I didn't want to lie down under those four letters, dripping with malice. The real reason I didn't at least pull a blanket off the mattress to cover myself was that I didn't think I deserved it.

My past had finally, completely caught up with me. My shame had nowhere to hide.

The sun woke me up the next morning, an errant ray of light falling through the window I'd failed to cover the night before to pierce my eyelids. I dragged myself off the floor and Turner did the same, uncurling himself from his position beside me on the floor. It was the first time he'd ever slept beside me.

Great. I'm so pathetic even my cat feels sorry for me.

Grabbing my glasses from my dresser, I stood in the middle

of my room facing my reflection in the mirror. My face was a disaster, my eyes raw and red, my skin a wan yellow, my cheek inflamed from spending the night shoved into the uneven wooden floor. I'd forgotten to take out my contacts the night before, but it didn't matter; I'd cried them out. My bedraggled hair fell over my shoulders in knots I knew it would take me hours to brush out. Anita's dress, now so wrinkled I doubted it would ever be the same, hung on me weirdly, making me look about fifty years old. I realized it was because I was stooping, as though fifty years of sorrow were piled on my back. Overall, I looked like a homeless widow, or a mad feral girl. What was most frightening was that I recognized myself in these figures.

That's me, I thought. *That horror is me.*

I didn't know where Lucas had gotten to. For a long time, far longer than I would have expected, he'd stayed by the door, pleading with me to let him in. After a while I could tell he'd sat down with his back against it, because his voice had seemed to be calling right into my ear. As I sat there, still crying, I could almost feel the heat of him through the door, just a thin plank of wood separating his back from mine. Eventually I cried myself to sleep.

Peeling off the dress, I yanked on a pair of yoga pants and a Queen's sweatshirt and pulled my nightmare hair into a ponytail, all the while peering at the crack at the bottom of the door to try to discern a shadow. But there wasn't one. I assumed he'd gone home. Maybe he'd left a note.

My glance moved to the bed.

Or maybe not.

I didn't touch the bed. I didn't go anywhere near the bed. I stepped close enough to see that the red letters were not painted in blood, but in red paint, the paintbrush and tube pilfered from my supplies on the floor by my desk. Having seen this, I turned and left the room.

When I walked into the living room I saw some movement out of the corner of my eye and started, ready to scream, but it was only Lucas getting up from the couch. We stared at each other for a moment. His hair was sort of sticking up and his clothes were rumpled, but he was still the most beautiful thing I'd ever seen. Even if his expression was unreadable. The emotions that bubbled up in me at the sight of him were so strong they were almost frightening, mainly because I didn't feel as though I had the right to them anymore. I'd never really felt like I had a right to be with Lucas. It figured that I was about to lose him.

"I didn't think you'd stay," I said. It was the only thought in my head.

Lucas practically gaped at me. "You thought I would leave you here alone after seeing *that*?" He gestured in the direction of my bedroom. "Katie, what the hell is going on?"

He stared at me as I tried to avoid his gaze. He hadn't exactly raised his voice, but he was as worked up as I'd ever seen him, his every muscle tense as if he expected some nameless enemy to come crashing out of my room at any moment.

"Nothing, it's fine," I answered, though since my voice was shaking when I said it I think it was pretty unconvincing. Out of the corner of my eye I saw Lucas flexing his fingers as though he was considering strangling me.

But he's not going to strangle me, I reminded myself. *Lucas is not Brandon.*

Still, when he moved toward me I took a step back automatically. It seemed important to keep some space between us. I felt shaky and easily startled, like a wounded animal that has to be trained to trust again. I wasn't ready to be touched. I didn't mean to upset him, but the look of hurt that passed over his face said it all.

"Tell me you're okay," he said tensely.

"I'm really fine," I answered, remembering how I'd said the same thing to my mother just a few weeks ago. It was as much a lie now as it had been then. "I just...overreacted a little about...something, but I'm really fine. Everything's fine."

"You're fine," he repeated, his tone fully implying how little he believed me. He picked up his cell phone from the coffee table. "Are we calling the cops?" he said. His thumb was poised over the call button and I could see that the numbers 9-1-1 had already been entered. I wondered how long he'd been sitting on the couch staring at those numbers.

"No," I practically yelled, lunging forward and taking the phone out of his hands. He let me do it. "No cops."

He stared at me.

"I'll make some coffee," I said, trying to sound normal, chipper, but I suspected I came off as mildly deranged instead. "Do you want eggs?"

I heard him make an exasperated noise, and when I stepped toward him to get to the kitchen, steadily avoiding his eyes, he took my arm and pulled me down onto the couch. He wasn't forceful about it, but the way his hand was clamped on my arm definitely indicated he wasn't about to let me go anywhere.

"Katie, you just spent about ten straight hours crying while I listened to you through the door, basically losing my mind with worry. You say you're fine? You are about as far from fine as you could possibly be, and I'm not feeling exactly ship-shape myself. We are not going to sit down and have breakfast like everything is normal right now, okay? That is not going to happen."

I could feel him peering down to get a look at my face as he'd done to me so many times before, but I'd tucked my chin in so tightly there was no way he was getting a glimpse. Taking a different tack, he leaned forward and placed one hand on the armrest and one on the cushion behind my back, forcing me to lean back and raise my head.

"There she is," he said as my eyes met his at last. His gaze was steady and unflinching and it hurt like hell. I didn't want him to see me now, like this. I didn't want him to know the girl who'd spent the night lying on the floor. I wanted to get away, to hide, but he had me pinned. Ducking under his arm and scurrying back to my room was a little too pathetic even for me, but that didn't mean I didn't consider it.

He reached for my face and I had to grit my teeth to stop myself from turning away. Ever so gently he removed my glasses then smoothed his thumb over my throbbing eye. His palm cupped my cheek and a current of warmth flowed through it and into my body; it felt so good, so safe and comforting that I felt tears welling under my eyelashes. I clamped my eyes shut, trying desperately to keep those tears from falling, but one escaped anyway. Lucas's thumb brushed across my cheek and smoothed it away.

Then I was in his arms, though I wasn't sure exactly how I'd gotten there. His body finally seemed to relax, the strain in his muscles disappearing as I buried my face in his shirt and his hand smoothed my hair. I heard him let out a long sigh. Though no more tears came, I felt an aching deep inside, as though I was still weeping. A desperate need I'd been ignoring for such a long time was rearing its head at last—the need to be held, to be known, to be loved.

Tucking my head under his chin, Lucas said, "Do you know how hard it was for me to sit outside your door and listen to you crying for hours," he said, "when all I wanted to do was hold you like this?"

I wanted to tell him that he could hold me forever if he wanted to, but the words stuck in my throat. I could only stare up at him mutely as he pressed his lips to my eyelids and my forehead and my cheeks, and when more tears began to fall, this time without my even realizing it, he kissed those away, as well.

"I know you don't need a protector. You don't need me to take care of you. But I need you to promise never to do that to me again." He looked down at me, his eyes so full of pain I would have agreed to anything. "If you're hurting, I need to be with you. I need to hold you. Last night...it almost drove me mad. I would have kicked the door down except I was pretty sure you were leaning against it."

"I was," I admitted.

"I don't ever want to feel that way again," Lucas went on. "You have to promise me you won't lock me out again. Can you do that for me?"

Could I? Could Katie Archer, the girl who kept everyone out, the girl who prided herself on not needing anyone, ever, the girl who wore her solitude like a protective cloak, could she promise to let someone in? His request was so much larger than he knew, but I felt too spent to resist it. I wanted to give this to him. I wanted to let myself need him and be needed in return.

I wanted to let Lucas in.

"I'll try," I croaked. It was the most honest thing I'd ever said to him.

I worried that it wouldn't be enough, but it earned me a small smile and the whisper of a kiss on my lips, so I guessed it was good enough for him, for now, anyway.

"Did you touch anything in there?" Lucas asked as I got up to finally make us that pot of coffee.

I shook my head once. Funnily enough, I'd almost forgotten about the mess in my room and what it meant. Remembering wasn't pleasant.

"Good," he said. "I'm going to make a call, and then I'm going to take you somewhere. You don't have any plans today, do you?"

"No," I replied as he walked toward the front door to go make his call in the hall.

"Just to be with you," I whispered once he was out of earshot. "My only plan is to be with you."

The words thrilled me as they came out of my mouth. It was like the first time I said a dirty word—so exciting, and yet still a little bit scary. Forbidden.

And most thrilling of all, I knew they were true.

A spring breeze blew through the car window, ruffling my hair, as we drove out of town. The snow had mostly melted away and brown grass stretched away from the highway to meet bare trees, their branches swaying. Coming from Vancouver, this year I'd experienced my first real winter—with snowstorms and freezing rain and icy streets, as promised—and I could already tell spring was becoming my favourite season in this part of the country. The wonderful release of being able to go outdoors without bundling up, to roll down the window, to wear shoes again, was intoxicating. If the world could start anew—leaves growing, plants waking up from their slumber, crocuses blooming—then maybe I could, too.

I looked over at Lucas as he stared out at the road. He'd been oddly quiet since we'd gotten into the car, which should have worried me, but it didn't. A really determined part of me insisted I couldn't doubt him every time he frowned, that I take my newfound trust in him seriously. He'd caught a glimpse of my demons and he hadn't run away. It was more than I'd ever hoped for from him, from anyone. Of course, he still didn't know the whole story, but I was trying to put that out of my mind.

"Who'd you call?" I asked as we passed the empty fields of a farm.

"Eric," Lucas answered. "I had to ask him if I could keep his car for the day…and tell him I never returned it last night."

"Did he ask why?" I said as I gazed out at the barren landscape. Though I trusted Lucas not to judge me for spending the night weeping, I didn't trust anyone else. I wondered what he'd told his roommate about last night. The idea than anyone else might know about the chaos in my bedroom made my stomach knot.

"Why I stayed over last night?" Lucas said. "He didn't have to ask. Eric knows how I feel about you."

"He does?" There was something exciting about knowing that Lucas liked me so much he'd even told his friends about it, but at the same time I couldn't picture that scene. Had he admitted his feelings for me during a gossip session over margaritas at the local bar? Or had he whispered it across the room when they were all lying in their beds, confiding secrets under cover of dark? I realized I had no idea how guys interacted with one another when they were alone.

Then it occurred to me what "staying over" usually meant.

I said, "So he probably thinks we…" Though we'd been headed in the general direction of sex the night before, I still didn't have the nerve to finish the sentence.

"Eric doesn't think much," Lucas reassured me, "so I wouldn't worry about it." Seeing the frown of worry on my face he took his hand off the wheel and pulled a lock of my hair playfully. "You should stop thinking, too! Besides, we're almost there."

I hadn't asked him where we were going and I didn't ask now. Instead, I took his advice and let my mind go blank for the rest of the ride, staring out the window, watching spring come rolling in. Eventually, we took an exit and entered a small town, though I didn't see the "Welcome To" sign, so I wasn't sure where we were. I only clued in when Lucas slowed the car to a stop on a residential street in front of a neat bungalow.

"That's my parents' house," he said, looking past me out the window.

"Oh, are we going in?" I said, taking off my seatbelt and immediately worrying about my choice of clothes. If I'd known I was going to meet his parents, I would never have worn yoga pants, my glasses, or this puffy face.

"Not today," Lucas replied, and there was a heaviness in his voice that implied this statement was non-negotiable. Not that I was about to fight him on it.

We sat a little longer looking at the house with its brown-shingled roof and flower boxes that were empty now but would be filled with cheerful blooms in a month's time, I was sure. There was a great climbing tree in the front yard. I wondered if little Lucas had ever sat in those branches. Through the front window's sheer curtains I saw someone moving around inside, probably his mother. When I turned to Lucas again, he was putting the car back into drive.

"That's Jenny's house," he said, pointing, as we passed a similar bungalow with a red door on our way down the street.

So Jenny was literally the girl next door. Yeah, that didn't make me jealous. Not at all.

Lucas pulled the car into a lot beside a large park about two blocks from his house. We walked across the dead grass to an empty basketball court dotted with puddles from newly melted snow. I thought maybe we'd sit down on one of the benches that ran along the sides of the court, but Lucas passed those and sat down right on the centre circle on a patch of dry cement. I sat down beside him.

He was quiet for a while, thoughtful, and it began to dawn on me that this trip might not be about last night at all. There was something else making Lucas so serious and melancholy, something that I suspected had nothing to do with me. Not wanting to question him in this moment, I looked out at the little wood overlooking the court and felt a spark of recognition. These were the trees Lucas had painted when I'd told him to paint from the gut. He must have taken the photograph from the exact spot I was standing in. This was the place Lucas loved.

"I used to play ball here almost every day after school," Lucas said finally. "Sometimes my dad and I would come by on the weekends and play together. He was better than me. He almost made it to the pros, but then…"

"But then?" I prompted gently.

"But then I came along," he finished. There was so much sadness in his eyes as he gazed out at his beloved playground. I wanted so much to wipe that pain away, to make it better, even if I didn't understand it. I wondered if this was how Lucas had felt all last night while I'd been alone in my room crying myself out, and I felt a hard tug of guilt in my chest. This was agony.

I took one of his hands in mine and kissed it, holding it tight.

When Lucas spoke again, he wasn't looking at me. He was looking out at those trees. "Katie, I wish you would tell me what happened yesterday, who broke into your place, who this person is that you're so afraid of that you don't even want to call the police. I'm guessing it's the same person you were referring to when you got so upset that I nearly beat up Buck Mullard."

He glanced at me for confirmation, I could feel it, but I could only stare at my feet.

"But I also know it's not fair of me to expect you to tell me all your secrets when I'm keeping so many myself," he went on.

"You don't have to tell me anything, Lucas," I said, running my fingers over his hand. "You don't owe me anything."

"But I want to," he said. "No, I have to. I need you to know this. I need to get it out of me."

I looked up at him and nodded. I knew what it felt like to keep something inside of you for too long, to want desperately to tell someone, to be rid of it. I'd just never tried.

Lucas was braver than me.

"It was the end of last summer when my dad got sick, just a few weeks before the start of classes," he began. "Stomach cancer, stage four. It came on all of a sudden. One day he was fine and the next he was confined to his bed, crippled by this disease he didn't understand. He was so outraged about it. He kept working for a little while, but pretty soon he had to stay home. The money for my tuition had to go to pay for the drugs that weren't covered by insurance, and to pay the mortgage because my mother had gone down to part-time so she could take care of him."

"So that's why you had to quit the team," I said, thinking out loud. "So you could get a job to pay for your tuition."

Lucas nodded. "But it wasn't just that," he said. "I didn't really want to play anymore. It was like the love I had for the game just left me when he got sick. He was the one who'd wanted me to play in the first place. Basketball was the thing he loved, and I came to love it, too, but without him calling me to ask me how practice went and coming to all the games...there didn't seem to be much point in playing anymore."

I tried to think of giving up painting, of losing interest in it, but I couldn't. My art was what got me through. Before Lucas, and especially in high school, I often felt like it was the only thing I had. I couldn't imagine what it would feel like if this thing I was so good at, the only thing I had to hold on to, were suddenly taken from me.

"I offered to take a year off from school, get a job to pay for the bills, but they wouldn't hear of it. They didn't even want me to quit the team, but there was no way I could keep up with practice, work, and my schoolwork. So I came back to school in the fall, and the truth is, I was relieved to get the hell out of there. Being in that house with my dying father was destroying me. I just wanted to get back to my carefree life of girls and partying and forget any of it was happening."

He spat out those last words, looking completely disgusted with himself.

I touched his arm. "It's natural to want to escape something like that, to deny it. There are some things the mind just isn't equipped to handle." I hoped he couldn't tell I was speaking from personal experience.

"But he needed me," he said, his weary eyes searching mine like he was trying to find in them the solace he couldn't give his father. He looked so forlorn I couldn't bear to be separated from him, so I leaned into him, wrapping my arms around his chest, and he locked a grateful arm around me.

"I didn't go home to visit all semester," Lucas said. "I avoided his calls, but the guilt weighed on me. I stopped partying. I hooked up with a few girls, just out of habit, I guess, but..."

I could feel his hesitation. He didn't want to talk about other girls with me. "It's okay," I said quietly.

He cleared his throat. "Afterward I realized I couldn't even remember their names. I was just going through the motions, and although the sex was great..." He paused here again. "It wasn't making me feel any better, so I just stopped dating altogether. I guess I got a little depressed. Nothing really seemed to matter—not my classes, not my friends. The only thing that mattered what happening somewhere else, and I couldn't go there."

I ran my hand up and down his back, thinking of the two of us last semester, both locked in our own secret miseries. "I wish I'd been there," I said sadly. "I wish I could have helped you."

"You're helping me now," he said, planting a kiss on the top of my head. I reached up and kissed his stubbly cheek before he went on.

"By the time Christmas break came along, I was dreading going back home, sure they'd both be furious with me. But they weren't. I think my dad was just glad he could see me at all before... The cancer had spread into his lungs and his pancreas. He didn't even look like himself anymore. The strong, healthy, barrel-chested father I remembered was gone forever, and then..."

I placed a hand on Lucas's chest, right over his heart. If I could have, I would have reached into his chest and held his heart in my hands, held it together. Because I was pretty sure it was about to break.

"He died just after New Year's," Lucas said, his voice cracking on those last words. Beneath my hand, his lungs stuttered as they expanded and collapsed. He was trying to hold in his tears.

Getting onto my knees, I took his face in my hands as he'd done mine this morning, and though there were no tears to wipe away, there were cheeks to kiss, and eyelids and lips. I covered his face with kisses as he held my arms tight. "I'm so sorry, Lucas," I whispered. "I'm so, so sorry."

"Me, too," he said, then pulled me right into his lap and wrapped both his arms around me, placing his chin on my shoulder so his cheek was right next to mine. "You're the only one I've told."

"You didn't tell your friends, your roommates, Oleg, Tim?" I asked.

He shook his head. "At first I didn't want them to know. I didn't want to talk about it with anyone. And then...I knew what they wanted of me. They want me to be the same old Lucas, always ready to party, easygoing and fun. The basketball star. The stud. They wouldn't have understood."

"You never gave them the chance," I said, trying my best to be delicate. "They might have surprised you. I bet they would have wanted to be there for you."

I frowned, realizing how hypocritical it was of me to preach openness when I'd been lying about my pain to the people closest to me for much longer than a couple of months. Try six years.

"I'm not so sure," Lucas replied, oblivious to my inner turmoil. "But that's why I was so glad when I met you."

"What do you mean?" I said as I interwove my fingers with his.

"You didn't know me before," he answered. "You don't expect anything of me. I can be quiet with you, or even sad, and you don't question it. You don't need me to be the old Lucas. When I'm with you it's like I can breathe again."

I pulled my hands away from his. "So that's why you like me? Because I didn't know you before this?" I said, his words stirring up something I didn't like in my stomach. "Then I could be anyone, any girl you happened to stumble upon. It's not really me that you want."

I shifted in his lap, trying to dislodge his arms, but he wouldn't let me go. "You're not just any girl," Lucas said steadily, his lips warm against my ear. "You're the girl who didn't even know what sport I used to play, who never noticed me in class, who doesn't care about the next big party. You're the girl who almost got into a fight with three guys twice her size to save a cat, who punched Buck Mullard in the face, who got me through a panic attack and then handed me, a jock, a sketchbook and expected me to draw. You're the girl who would never even think of chasing me, who doesn't care what I look like." I wasn't so sure about that one. "You're the girl who told me she just wanted to be friends. Do you know the last time a girl said something like that to me?"

"A while?" I said timidly.

He squeezed me tight. "Try *never*," he said. "And as much as I loved it, I don't want to be your friend, Hero. I want to be with you. Only you. The girl wearing glasses and sweatpants with wild hair flying everywhere and a cat inside her jacket. The girl I can't stop myself from wanting to kiss and hold in my arms and do everything else with. The girl who makes me feel like I might get through this if she's there next to me. That's the girl I want."

Suddenly I was the one whose chest was heaving with unshed tears, whose heart felt like it might burst. I only had to turn my head slightly to find his lips waiting for me, those sweet, soft lips and that moan-inducing tongue. Before long we were lying back on the cement and neither of us felt much like crying anymore. Breaking our kiss before things got too out of hand—we were in the middle of a *playground*, after all—I lay my head on his shoulder and we both looked up at the cloudy sky.

"So I'm the only one who knows?" I said.

"Well, family, too," Lucas said. "And there's Jenny. She came to the funeral with her family. They've lived next door since I was six."

"I'm glad you have her," I said, and it was the honest truth. "It must be comforting to have somebody from home so close by."

"She'd actually pretty pissed at me most of the time," Lucas admitted. "I haven't come back here to see Mom since the semester began. It's just…too painful. But Jenny comes every few weeks and she checks in on my mom. She thinks I'm neglecting her. She keeps telling me how much she needs me now, how she's all alone. She yells at me a lot."

The scene on the bench suddenly made a lot more sense and I wanted to kick myself for reading it so incorrectly. I'd thought they were having a lovers' quarrel and really she'd been scolding him for not visiting his grieving mother.

"You'll go see her when you're ready," I said.

"I will," he said. "Soon. Just not today. Maybe I'll call her tonight instead. I could tell her about you."

"Telling your mother about me?" I said teasingly, pinching his stomach. "That sounds pretty serious."

"Well, that's how serious I am about you," Lucas said, and there was no teasing in his voice at all. It made my heart ache. My heart was really getting a workout today.

Lucas rolled onto his side and I adjusted my head so his arm cushioned it and we were lying face to face.

"That's why it's so hard for me to see what I did last night and not want to jump into action. I care so much about you,

Katie. If someone's trying to hurt you—"

"Nobody's trying to hurt me," I said quickly, the lie turning sour on my lips as I said it. He'd been so incredibly honest with me, so vulnerable. This was the moment when I had to decide if I was going to be just as honest back.

"But you know who broke into your apartment. That's why you didn't want to call the cops," Lucas said. His eyes were fastened on my face. I could tell he'd been holding in these questions all morning, though he'd been dying to ask them. I wished he would look away, just for a moment, so I could think straight, compose my thoughts.

Compose my thoughts, I wondered, *or compose my lies?*

"I-I think it's…an old boyfriend," I forced out.

"Does he go to Queen's?" Lucas asked.

"No…" I said. "I'm not even sure if he's the one who broke in. It might have been one of his friends. He's been…contacting me lately. Texting me. He might be sort of…stalking me."

All at once Lucas sat up, pulling me up with him. His eyes were wide and serious, his expression tense. He pulled out his cell.

"I'm calling the cops," he said.

"No, don't," I said, covering the screen with my hand before he could dial. "It's not as bad as you think!"

"Katie, you're telling me an old boyfriend is stalking you, that he broke into your apartment, and you expect me just to do nothing? I'm not going to let this guy hurt you!"

"But I'm not hurt," I protested. "He hasn't done anything to me except rip up a couple of my paintings. Please, if you call the cops it'll do more damage to me than to him." If the police got involved the whole story would come out, I knew it. And then everyone would know I was a liar, Lucas included. I pictured myself being led away in handcuffs. I pictured the look on my mother's face, on Emily's face.

All of a sudden I couldn't catch my breath. I pressed my palm to my chest as I struggled to get in some air. Lucas's face was narrowing to a pinpoint.

"Okay, we won't call the cops," Lucas said, dropping his phone in his lap as he put an arm around my shoulders. "Just breathe, Katie. It's okay. I won't let anyone hurt you." I pressed my cheek into Lucas's chest as my heartbeat slowed and air came rushing into my lungs.

"I'm sorry," I mumbled into his shirt. "It's just that everything that's happened between Brandon and me...the story is long and complicated. I just—"

"You don't have to tell me everything," Lucas said, smoothing a hand over my hair. "Just promise me if you're ever in trouble you'll come to me. If you see him anywhere, if you hear from him, if you just think you see him, or if you feel scared, I'm the guy you call, got it?"

"Yeah," I said weakly, trying to imagine what that would be like. If I really did as Lucas asked, I'd probably be on the phone with him twenty-four seven.

We stayed a little while longer, snuggled in each other's arms, watching the clouds rushing by as the wind picked up. Then Lucas helped me up off the ground and we started walking back to his car. It had only been about an hour, but I felt like days had passed since our drive into Christie. This morning was a distant memory. My mind was full of everything I knew now, and everything he didn't know, my brain working so hard to keep it all straight I was starting to get a headache.

"So his name's Brandon?" Lucas said as he unlocked the passenger's side door for me.

I nodded.

"Will it freak you out if I say I wish I could find Brandon and pummel him in the face?" Lucas said. "I won't, I promise. But I really, really want to."

I smiled weakly as we got into the car, but the truth was his words did freak me out. Now that Lucas was involved in my life, I worried that he'd also get involved in my past. I didn't want to pull him into that mess. I didn't want him to defend me. I didn't want to make those same old mistakes again.

Lucas had said he wanted to be with me, only me. I tried to cheer myself up with this thought as he drove us back to

Kingston, but the lies I'd told him kept popping up in my mind, dampening my mood. Well, I hadn't lied exactly. Every word I'd said to him was true. I just hadn't told him the whole story.

That's right, Katie, said the familiar voice inside my head. *That's how you lie without lying. That's how you make sure he never, ever knows the real you. Because when he does, he won't want you anymore, you can count on that.*

"What does he think you lied to him about?" Lucas asked as we approached campus. "I saw what he wrote on your wall."

Keep lying, girl, the voice said.

"Just something that happened a long time ago," I said.

Once upon a time I'd thought of the truth was my enemy. I'd lied without question, without even thinking about it, the lies ready and waiting on my tongue, prepared ahead of time for easy use. Now, as I butchered the truth to suit my purposes, I found that lies, even lies of omission, were starting to take their toll.

I'd didn't want to lie to Lucas ever again.

I just wasn't sure I was ready to face the truth.

17

"So are you guys doing it or what?" Mariella said.

"Shut up!" I hissed at her, raising a spatula threateningly and shooting a glance down the hall at the closed bathroom door. I could hear the shower running, so I was pretty sure Lucas hadn't heard her. "We just fell asleep on the couch watching movies, that's all."

"Seems like you've been watching a lot of *movies* lately," Mariella said, her implication plain. She snatched a piece of bacon out of the pan as I moved them onto a plate.

"We've just been hanging out," I said, "and making out." I gave my friend a sly grin and she bumped her hip with mine, smiling broadly.

"That's what I'm talking about!" she said. "I told you he'd come around."

Lucas had actually been coming around a lot lately. Since the day we'd gone out to Christie we'd spent at least part of every day together. The thing he'd said about my calling him whenever I felt like I was in danger seemed pretty amusing now, since he was almost always with me.

As the school year wound to a close we'd gone to our separate classes each day and then almost always met up for lunch before art class. Now that exams were on, we often studied together at my place or at the library or worked on our final portfolios in the studio. I'd even hung out at The Limo with him during his shift, sitting behind the bar on a little stool, listening with delight as Brit imitated the irritating customers and watching the overdressed girls drool over Lucas—which might have bothered me if he hadn't made a point of kissing me dramatically whenever he got tired of them. That didn't bother me one bit. We'd definitely been doing a lot of kissing and touching—maybe it was more like groping—but we hadn't advanced any further than that. I wasn't really sure why, because I certainly wasn't the one hitting the brakes. I kept wanting to ask him why he was hesitating, but at the same time I didn't want to spoil a good thing. Just making out with Lucas was still plenty exciting.

"And now you're making him breakfast like the perfect little girlfriend," Mariella went on, pressing her hand to her chest. "I think I smell love in the air."

I swatted her hand with the spatula as she tried to steal another piece of bacon. "Nobody's said anything about love," I chastised her. "And don't you have a child to parent or something?"

Mariella leaned toward the open door as I grabbed the eggs out of the fridge and cracked them over the pan. "Are you alive, child of mine?" she called into the hallway where Ethan was playing with his toy cars.

"Still alive!" Ethan called back, and I heard one of his cars hit the wall beside my door.

"Great parenting technique," I said as the eggs sizzled. "I guess what I was really trying to say is stop prying into my personal life."

Mariella smiled broadly at my irritation. "I guess what I'm really trying to say is when are you guys going to start screwing like bunnies, 'cause I know you're dying to."

Before the words were even out of her mouth, I heard the

bathroom door swing open and Lucas's footsteps on the floor. My eyes flew wide open and Mariella pressed a hand to her mouth as Lucas stepped into the kitchen wearing nothing but a towel—one of mine. It had yellow daisies all over it. "Did I hear something about bunnies?" Lucas asked with mock curiosity, his dimples showing.

Openly staring at Lucas's smooth and muscular bare chest, Mariella dropped her hand to display her mouth hanging wide open.

"Mariella was just leaving," I said to my friend, shooting daggers at her with my eyes.

"Right, right," she said, finally pulling her gaze away as Lucas retreated down the hall, chuckling. "Gotta get the offspring to school, a mother's time is never her own and all that..."

As soon as she heard my bedroom door close, she leaned in toward me and whispered, "Oh my *God*. Have sex with that as soon and as often as you can, girl. I mean, do it right here on the kitchen counter if you have to!"

As I rolled my eyes, unable to stop myself from smiling, Lucas piped up from my room, almost as though he'd heard every word, "Goodbye, Mariella!"

"Bye!" she called with the widest grin imaginable, and scampered out the door.

Still shaking my head, I turned back to the eggs, which were burned into a solid yellow and brown mass. I could hardly focus enough to turn down the burner. Just imagining Lucas changing in the next room was making me dizzy. The image of his bare chest, which I'd never seen before—at least not all of it—kept floating into my mind as I tried cracking a new egg into the pan. It ended up on the floor.

"I'm pretty sure the five second rule doesn't apply here," Lucas said into my ear as he put his arms around me from behind. "But I promise to eat the egg off the floor if we can keep on discussing that bunny thing Mariella was talking about."

"I have no idea what you're referring to," I said smoothly,

turning around so I was facing him. He'd put on a t-shirt, which was slightly disappointing, but he was still wearing the towel. "And for your information, the egg on the floor was always going to be yours. I don't believe in waste."

"Really? Because it seems like we're wasting tons of space right here," Lucas said, grabbing me by the waist and pressing my body to his, our hips aligning almost automatically now. Immediately I felt him pressing against my leg, through his towel and my apron. He reached up and plucked my glasses from my face, putting them down on the counter. I closed my eyes and let a long breath escape from my mouth as he nuzzled my neck with his lips. Then our mouths connected and I felt his hands behind my back undoing the knot of my apron. The burner clicked off.

"I see your multitasking skills are improving," I said breathlessly between kisses.

"I've been practicing," he replied with a proud smile.

Picking me up by the waist, Lucas slid me onto the kitchen counter and then moved forward, pushing his hands into my hair as he continued to kiss me. Mariella's earlier comment about the kitchen counter came to mind as I dropped the spatula and cupped his face with my hands. His groin was now pressing between my legs and my thin pajama bottoms offered almost no barrier. I gasped as I felt his fingers running up my back, under my tank top, though I wished he would move them around to the front. He'd still never touched my bare breasts and I was dying for him to. The feelings building up in the burning hot centre of me were beginning to drive me wild and I made a noise, a combination of a groan and a growl, as I wrapped my legs around his hips.

"Katie..." Lucas said. I could feel him stilling his hands, pulling back. He was putting on the brakes again. "I don't want to do anything that reminds you of... I don't know why you're so afraid of him, but you said he was violent. Did he ever try to—"

"He didn't force himself on me," I answered quickly.

"Oh, good," he said, heaving a sigh of relief. "I wasn't sure.

I didn't want to do anything that would make you think of him or make you feel—"

"You don't remind me of Brandon," I said, interrupting him. And as I said the words I knew they were true. Maybe I had thought of Brandon the first time we kissed, but that was far behind me now. This was undiscovered territory, and being here with Lucas was the best thing I could imagine. "Besides, he never hurt me, not in the way you're thinking. What he did…it has nothing to do with what's happening right now. So can we stop talking about him, please? I'd much rather get back to this." I tightened my legs around him.

"Forget breakfast," Lucas mumbled, pulling me to the ground. Our lips hardly losing contact, we stumbled down the hall toward my bedroom. I walked through the door first and in that moment made the sudden decision to let Lucas know exactly how much I meant what I'd said. I pulled off my tank top and dropped it on the floor, then turned to face him.

His eyes dropped from my face to my chest and then he walked into the bed and fell onto it face first.

I let out an open-mouthed laugh and climbed onto the bed as he turned onto his side, looking foolish. "Is it my imagination, or is Lucas Matthews blushing?" I said teasingly as he pulled me toward him. Just the feeling of his hands against my bare skin, the most skin I'd ever shown him, was enough to shut me up.

"I do not blush," Lucas said as he stared into my eyes. Before I could offer up a contradiction, he went on. "But I do trip all over myself every time I look at you. Do you have any idea how stunning you are?"

"I'm not—" I began, but then his hands began to move against my bare skin and I had to bite my bottom lip to stop myself from screaming with anticipation. The back of his hands brushed against the bottom of my breasts and I sucked in a breath, bracing myself against Lucas's body.

In one fluid motion Lucas pulled his shirt off and I found myself exploring the curves of his chest while he explored mine. There was something so intimate about being in bed with him, our bare skin pressed together, that I felt a little lightheaded. Then his thumbs slid across my nipples and I wasn't just lightheaded anymore. I was mindless. The tension inside of me began to build in a way I'd never felt before and a tingling took over my limbs as I found his lips, his hands still caressing my breasts with such delicacy, as though I were a precious thing. The room spun around me and I knew nothing at all except the feeling of his hands on me. Then he broke our kiss and lowered his face to the skin of my breasts. Just one touch of his lips and the world exploded into tiny little pieces that did not fall around us but drifted down, slowly, like snowflakes.

When I came back to my senses I was lying with my cheek against Lucas's chest, the bed sheet draped lightly over us, and my entire body seemed to be singing. Lucas trailed his hand along my back and it was as though a musical note erupted everywhere he touched.

"Well, that was new," I whispered. I was trying not to feel be embarrassed and failing miserably.

In response Lucas shifted me upwards and placed a kiss against my warm cheek. "That was amazing," he said, brushing my hair away from my face.

"Really?" I said. It bothered me that he hadn't felt all the same things that I had. Wasn't it my turn now? Wasn't that how this worked? "Do you want me to…"

I reached downward, wanting to feel him, but then I hesitated. I had no idea where the towel was at this point and touching him there without any barrier…that wasn't something I'd ever done before.

Taking my hand in his, he brought it to his lips and kissed it. "I definitely want you to," Lucas said, "but there is the matter of the exam I'm supposed to be taking in about an hour."

Glancing at the clock on my bedside table, I saw that he was right.

"All right," I said. "But don't forget, it's your turn next. Fair's fair."

"Oh, I won't forget. Trust me," Lucas replied, running an idle hand down the front of my body and planting a kiss on my lips before swinging his legs to the floor. "I'm pretty sure I'll be not forgetting all through my statistics exam, too."

As he got out of bed my suspicions about the towel were confirmed. He was entirely naked. As he pulled on his boxers and wandered down the hall in search of food, I pressed my face into the pillow and giggled like an idiot. For about five straight minutes.

"Will you stop picturing me naked and get in here?" Lucas said, poking his head back into the room. And this time I wasn't too embarrassed to show him my beaming grin.

We wolfed down our meal of cold bacon and toast, which had never tasted so good, and got dressed. He let me chastely put on my clothes in the bathroom, as I'd been doing every time he came over in the morning. I might have just been topless in front of him, but there was something about putting on clothes that struck me as decidedly unsexy. I wasn't quite ready for him to see me struggling to button my jeans as he displayed his rock-hard abs.

As we walked toward campus, Lucas took my hand in his. This was another new thing we were doing, that I was trying to get used to. It drew a lot of attention, which I tried to bear without too much squirming. It helped that he kissed me every chance he got. Nothing made my mind go blank like Lucas's lips on mine.

"So you and...Brandon," Lucas said. He always had trouble saying his name. "You never did anything like that?" I guessed his meaning: Had Brandon and I ever come close to having sex?

I struggled not to groan. Over the last little while it had become glaringly obvious that whenever he wasn't occupied appreciating my body Lucas's mind drifted to my stalker and the few details I'd told him about the situation. I wasn't sure how much longer the story I told him was going to hold up, which left me in a cold sweat.

"No," I said stiffly, hoping he'd sense my wariness of the subject and back off, but he kept glancing my way, waiting for more. "I was younger. We never got to that step."

Because I was in middle school, was what I didn't say.

"So you broke it off?" Lucas persisted.

Actually, no. When I woke up covered in blood he was already gone.

"I guess you could say it was a mutual decision," I replied.

He didn't look too happy with me when I was testifying that I'd never seen him before in my life.

"I'm getting the impression that you don't really want to talk about this," Lucas said, putting an arm around my shoulder. I leaned into him, letting the past fade to black as he held me close, feeling the safety of his arms. "I know you probably think I'm obsessing. I just can't stand the thought of him hurting you again."

"How could he," I said, forcing a smile, "with you standing guard?"

We went into our favourite coffee shop, the same one where we'd shared that molten brownie months ago, and my eyes lingered on the table we'd sat at that day. It seemed ages ago, before I knew Lucas, before I trusted him.

Before I put him in danger.

"Oh, I almost forgot. I wanted to show you something," Lucas said. He handed me a pamphlet as he stepped up to the counter and ordered our drinks—a hot chocolate for me, extra whip, and a coffee with sugar for him. There were photos of kids playing various sports on the cover—soccer, volleyball, basketball—but every time I tried to read the words across the top they blurred.

I had the oddest feeling, as though I should scream, but I couldn't think why. Outside the windows of the coffee shop the day was sunny. The leaves were beginning to grow in on the trees. The cafe was busy and buzzing with conversation. Lucas stood over by the counter, waiting for our drinks, winking at me. And yet it felt as though the world had suddenly tilted off its axis.

Something's wrong, I thought to myself. *What is it? What* is it? My phone buzzed and I took it out.

Em: So how's Hottie McLover who makes you ignore your own TWIN?

I let out a breath I didn't know I'd been holding and searched for a clever response.

Me: Divine. Best McLover I ever had.
Em: I'm glad you're happy, sis. You deserve it. But so do I, so he'd better have some hot friends.
Me: Like you've ever needed help finding a guy.
Em: Not in the Matthews league. You're moving up and you're taking me with you.
Me: You got it, sister.

I was still smiling at my phone when Lucas sat down at the table with our drinks.

"God, I'm going to need this to get through my exam," he said, taking a sip. "Who're you chatting with?"

"Just Em," I said, pocketing the phone quickly. I'd been careful to keep my phone away from Lucas ever since I'd told him Brandon had been texting me. His nasty messages had been coming in steadily for the past few days, and they were just as curse-ridden as ever. If Lucas saw the true extent of those texts I was pretty sure he'd go mad and drag me to the police station kicking and screaming.

"So what do you think?" he said, looking at me expectantly.

"What?" I said in confusion, and then looked down at the table in front of me. "Oh, the pamphlet!" I saw now that it was a brochure for a local kids' sports day camp.

Lucas said, "They need a basketball coach for this summer. I was thinking of applying."

My mouth fell open a little as I looked from Lucas to the pamphlet. It stayed that way until he leaned forward and gave me a peck on my open lips.

"I guess your look of utter shock means you think it's a good idea?" Lucas joked, but I could tell he really wanted to hear my opinion.

"I'm so glad," I said, poring over the glossy photos of the recreation centre that would be used for the camp. "I never thought you'd get here so fast. I thought it might take you months, even years to learn to love basketball again."

"Well, I don't love it yet," Lucas admitted. "But I thought maybe helping some kids learn to love playing might help me remember the good times I had with my dad. And it's a paid position, too, so maybe I won't have to work quite so hard next year."

"You'll be a natural," I said. "Though, I warn you, all the little girls will be falling in love with you."

"Too bad I'm head over heels for my girlfriend," he said, and my heart skipped a beat.

Girlfriend.

I leaned forward and hugged him, breathing deeply of that intoxicating Lucas scent. "I'm so proud of you," I said into his ear. "If only your old party pals could see you now. I bet they wouldn't believe their eyes, Lucas Matthews out there doing his bit for the community."

Lucas waved at someone over my shoulder. "Well, I guess we can ask one of them. There's Oleg," he said.

I froze in my seat, gripping my drink with both hands at the sound of the name. Oleg was the friend Lucas had called to clean up my apartment while we were in Christie the day after the break-in. He'd finagled Mariella into letting him in. He's done an amazing job, too, even cleaning all the red paint off my walls and buying me a new pillow so that when we returned the place looked exactly as it had been before. It was such a relief to have the mess gone that I didn't have the heart to scold Lucas for letting one of his friends into my nightmare. He wouldn't have understood, anyway. The secret Lucas held was painful, but if someone found out it wouldn't break him. He didn't live in fear of the world finding out the truth about him.

Lucas didn't know what it was like to live in shame.

"He's waving me outside," Lucas said as he got to his feet.

"Come say hi."

"No, you go. I want to read over my essay one last time before I hand it in," I fibbed. "Tell him thank you for me again."

"He was doing me a favour," Lucas said, shaking his head at me. "And I already thanked him for you, twice."

"Thank him again anyway," I said as I rifled through my bag looking for my essay. "That's a good friend you've got there."

Any friend who would come clean up a mess like that with no explanation at a moment's notice was as good as gold in my opinion. As I watched Oleg give Lucas a big bear hug— apparently he gave these out freely, drunk or not—I found myself hoping that Lucas would tell him about his father. I had the feeling Oleg would be more understanding than he knew.

When I pulled out the binder that held my essay, a small, balled-up piece of paper rolled out of my bag. Still half-gazing out the window at the guys, I wasn't even paying attention as I straightened it out. I was so distracted that my hands started to tremble before the meaning of the words really penetrated my brain.

Enjoying that hot chocolate? Hope so, because it might be your last. Ditch your handsome friend if you know what's good for you.

Crumpling the note in my hand, I subtly scanned the room around me. The strange feeling I'd had before suddenly made perfect sense. Brandon had been here, in the room, watching me. He'd been close enough to put the note in my bag. And this time he hadn't sent a friend to do his dirty work—I was sure of it. No, I was more than sure. I *knew* it. The feeling in my gut that something was terribly wrong—I'd only felt that way once before, the day he'd leaned toward me, knife in hand, and whispered murderous words in my ear.

A wave of nausea threatened to overcome me and my heart began to pound. My eyes darted around the room, but I couldn't find him. Maybe he'd already left? Didn't seem likely. This moment, the moment I read the note he'd placed so perfectly, was his prize. He wanted to see me shake. He wanted to make me cry with fear.

Suddenly I realized that unlike every time I'd received a text from him, unlike the day of the break-in, I didn't feel the urge to burst into tears or to hide. Instead, I felt an all-encompassing rage. My fingers gripped my drink so tightly the cup collapsed, sending scalding chocolate over my hand, though I hardly felt it.

He thought he could threaten Lucas and get away with it? We'd see about that.

By the time Lucas returned I'd composed myself enough to look normal. I figured if he noticed I was on edge he'd think it was about my paper. As I stood up to meet him, I turned over the napkin I'd left behind on the table.

"I was thinking of driving up to see my mom," Lucas said as we crossed the campus. "I figure it's about time, and I don't have any exams for a few days. I could tell her about the job."

I grasped his hand tightly. "Sounds like a great idea," I said.

And it did, considering the note I'd left for Brandon on my napkin back at the coffee shop.

I'll be waiting

18

But he didn't come.

I knew Lucas wouldn't make it easy for me. Since he couldn't be there to babysit me while he was visiting his mom, he brought in reinforcements. That very night, just minutes after I'd waved Lucas off on his drive to Christie, Em showed up with a pile of rom coms for a movie night. She claimed we'd planned it weeks ago, but I knew better. Who planned a movie night in the middle of exams? By the way she kept glancing at me as Julia Roberts laughed her big-teeth laugh, I could also tell that Lucas hadn't given her all the details about why I needed watching. He probably thought she already knew the whole story, and Em, who thought we told each other everything, would never have asked. Her expectation of a big tearful revelation—I could feel her readying herself whenever the movie went quiet enough for us to talk—made me fidgety. I ended up eating more than my half of the bowl of extra butter popcorn. Okay, I basically ate the whole bowl.

Then I realized I'd just ingested all those empty calories for nothing. If Em didn't know why she had to stay, I could easily make up a lie to get rid of her.

It only took about ten minutes to convince my sister that: One, I knew Lucas had asked her to come over. Two, Lucas was just being way overprotective. And three, she didn't really have to stay over because I wasn't in any danger. I used my master lying skills to make up a story that Mariella had seen a creepy guy lurking around the building and Lucas had overreacted. But I was pretty sure it was just the super's son, Gregory; I knew Em would buy this, because she also thought Gregory was creepy. I finished off with some sappy comments about how much I liked Lucas and how I was pretty sure we were falling in love—not even really a lie, at least on my part—and wasn't it sweet of him to be so worried about me?

Emily ate it up.

By nine o'clock she was out the door and I went into defence mode. I pulled my baseball bat out from under my bed and put it on the couch. But one weapon didn't seem like enough. What if he wrested it out of my hands? Then I'd have nothing. I prowled around my apartment looking for anything I could use as a weapon. At the end of thirty minutes I had two butcher knives, the lamp from my bedside table—it had a heavy base—a cast iron pan, and a roll of duct tape. I figured if I got him on the ground I'd need something to tie him up with before I ran for my life.

I assembled my collection on the coffee table—except for the bat, which never left my hands—and then I was back in my ideal spot on the couch, watching and waiting.

I had plenty of time to freak out as my eyes flicked from the window to the door to the other window to the hall, but I felt surprisingly calm. I was glad I'd invited Brandon to come and find me, glad to be waiting instead of always wondering. I was ready for this to be over. Even though I had no idea what I was going to say to him, I was ready to face him.

But he didn't come.

As the hours passed my body began to protest. I'd been sitting with my muscles tensed for so long that when I put the bat down in my lap my fingers stayed curled. I needed water, but I didn't want to move, sure that he was waiting somewhere nearby and the sound of my footsteps would alert him to my presence. But then, wasn't that what I wanted?

My initial calm began to dissipate and a low-lying paranoia took its place as the night wore into the wee hours of morning. Every creak of the building, every tiny sound made me jump and grip my bat. At one point I nearly swung at Turner as he crept across the carpet. After that he smartly kept out of my way. I started furiously planning how I would handle each of my weapons, the best way to grip the lamp, how I would lunge, with the knife in one hand or both. These fantasies got more and more elaborate as I began to incorporate all the different ways Brandon might attack me. He'd probably learned all kinds of new techniques in jail, even if it was a youth jail. He was probably like an assassin now. I began to picture him wearing all black and a ski mask so he would blend in with the shadows. After that, even the shadows started to alarm me and I added them to my rounds of the room: window, shadow, door, shadow, shadow, window, shadow, hall.

Sometime around four a.m. I started to nod off from exhaustion. It was then, when my defences were down, that the memories fell over me like a suffocating blanket. This time there was no hope of turning my thoughts away. The memories were too many and too strong and I was too weak. I could do nothing but submit to them. I could do nothing but clench my jaw against the screams and endure.

I saw the blade of Brandon's knife against a background of green grass.

I saw little Tommy's back as he ran ahead of me— *"Race you to the train tracks, Katie!"*—his white t-shirt bright against the dark trees.

I saw the look of horror on the old woman's face as she took in the sight of me.

I saw the paramedic vomiting behind a tree.

I saw the caved in place where Tommy's face should have been, the bloody hole that had once been his smile.

I saw blood, I saw blood, I saw blood, I saw blood, I saw

blood…

Fingers gripped my own and somebody was speaking to me tensely, but I couldn't understand the words. My hands hurt for a moment and then they were empty. But I still had my bat. I needed my bat so I could face Brandon. Because he was coming for me. He was coming anytime now.

A glass was pushed against my lips but I shoved it away. The person kept blocking the door and I didn't like it. I needed to keep my eye on the door and the window and the other window. I needed to stay vigilant. I think I opened my mouth and said things, screamed things, but I wasn't sure what the words were. Whatever they were, they had the desired effect. The person cleared out and I was alone again. It was better that way, anyway. Brandon wouldn't come unless I was alone. And he was coming, I was sure of it. I'd told him to come. He would come. Any minute now.

A while later—I had no idea how long—I found myself staring down at my throbbing hands. They were red, raw, and shaking. They wouldn't stop shaking. Someone had put a blanket over my shoulders, but I shook it off. I'd lost track of my bat but it didn't matter. If I got the knife out of his hand I could get him before he got Tommy. I could stop him. He wasn't that much bigger than me. It was just a knife. I could do it. I could save him.

I heard a voice that sounded like my own, crying. Was I crying? I touched my cheeks but they were dry. My tongue was dry. I wanted so much to lie down, but I knew I couldn't. I had to save Tommy. People moved around me. Someone held my hand. I asked for my bat. I asked for my knives. I had to stay awake.

I saw Tommy running.

I saw the train tracks coming up to meet me.

I saw the knife in Brandon's hand.

"Girl, you're bleeding! What happened to you? What happened?"

"Race you to the train tracks, Katie!"

"Oh my God, call the police!"

"You heard him, Katie Kat. You'd better hurry now. If I get there

first, who knows what might happen."

   "Did you see what happened? Did you see who it was?"

   "Today's the day we take care of business."

   "Get her cleaned up. They found something. They found a body."

   "Just like you said."

   "Oh dear God. Oh holy Jesus."

   "Just like you asked."

   "Who was it? Who did this?"

   Tell me this isn't happening.

   "She's in shock."

   Tell me it isn't my fault.

   "She knows something. Let her speak."

   It wasn't me.

   "What did she say? Did she say a name?"

   It wasn't me.

   "Stupid bitch."

   It wasn't me.

   It wasn't me.

   It wasn't me.

When he came into the room at last I had nothing left. The others scattered as he approached the couch and I started to whimper. He picked me up and carried me into the bedroom. I guessed that was where he wanted to do it. Right on the pillow he'd pierced with his knife. He always did like to cut the same place twice.

He was whispering to me, but it was as though my ears were filled with cotton.

"I always knew you'd come for me," I said as he laid me on the bed.

There was some discussion in the other room, maybe an argument. I hoped he wasn't killing them. They didn't seem so bad. I hoped I hadn't brought this on them, too.

Then he was back, looming over me, touching my face. I swatted his hand away. "Are you going to kill me now?" I demanded. All this waiting around was beginning to seem awfully unfair. If he was going to do it, I wanted him to do it.

Get it over with. Unless he was waiting for something. Like my permission.

"It's okay," I mumbled. My mouth sort of felt like it was full of cotton now, too. My eyes felt so heavy. "I know I deserve it."

I heard a clicking sound and saw a dim light beside my head. Then he said two words, which I heard loud and clear: "Goddammit, Katie."

And then there was nothing.

19

I woke up in Brandon's grip. He was everywhere, his voice in my ears, his spiteful face reflected on the insides of my closed eyelids, his deeds running through my mind on a never-ending loop. He'd been my companion throughout my fitful sleep and for the tiniest moment when I opened my eyes at last I thought I was waking up in my hospital bed six years ago. It was as though Tommy had just died yesterday.

The pain that hit me in that moment nearly tore me apart.

My eyes focused on Emily lying in the bed beside me. One of her hands was wrapped tightly around my wrist. I knew precisely why: I'd tried to hit her in my sleep.

As I very carefully extricated my arm from her grip, a few stray memories of the night before floated through my mind. I tried to piece together what had actually happened, but it wasn't easy. Nothing made sense. I'd let the memories in. I'd let the fear in and it had overcome me. How many hours had I spent sitting there, obsessing over Brandon, waiting for him? I must have gone a little mad.

One thing was obvious: Brandon had not come, though my

brain told me without a doubt that he had. I flexed my aching fingers and felt my heart begin to race as I realized how much I'd given away. Emily definitely knew something was wrong now. I remembered screaming at someone. But maybe what I'd said had been unintelligible. Maybe I was still safe in my bubble of lies. Except...

Someone I'd thought to be Brandon had carried me to my bed. And I'd asked him if he was going to kill me. And I'd told him I deserved it. But if that hadn't been Brandon, then it could only be one person.

I started gagging and scrambled out of bed just in time. The popcorn from last night came up the second I gripped the toilet bowl. And then the burger I'd had for dinner with Lucas. And the yesterday's lunch and breakfast and on and on until there was nothing left, but still I kept on gagging. Eventually I slumped against the bathtub, pressing my cheek into the cold porcelain. I was back to feeling old feelings again, the paranoia of walking high school hallways and feeling their eyes on me, of being so sure they could see through me, that they'd found me out.

He knows.

Sipping from a cup that normally held my toothbrush, I tried to look at the situation with a clear head.

Yes, Lucas knew something, but he didn't know everything. And if Brandon had actually come to find me, wouldn't Lucas have found out everything anyway? Just because Brandon hadn't come last night didn't mean he wasn't still coming. My time was running out. My time to tell Lucas everything, in my way, on my terms.

As I pulled on some clothes I found in the bathroom hamper, I realized I wanted to tell Lucas the truth, even if it meant I would lose him. As he'd said, I wanted to get it out of me. But more than that, I wanted him to know me, all of me, the real me. It had been so long since anybody had. Even if I only got to hold him for a moment as myself, that was what I wanted.

I wanted to set Katie Archer free.

Much as it pained me to leave Emily without a word, knowing how worried she must have been about me all night, I knew waking her up would mean long hours of explaining everything. I had to talk to Lucas first. So I left a note for her on my pillow that I hoped said enough but not too much and tiptoed out of my bedroom. By the clock on the microwave I saw that it was already four o'clock in the afternoon. Already most of a day gone, with Brandon circling and Lucas thinking God knows what about me. I felt my feet itching to go and find him, but made myself choke down some dry toast first. Then I flipped through the school directory until I found what I was looking for and I left.

I walked the whole way there. I really should have taken a bus—it was drizzling, and wasn't there a murderer on my tail?—but it didn't occur to me. I just bowed my head and walked, one foot in front of the other, all the way through campus. I was hoping the words would come to me, that by the time I found my way there I would know exactly how to say what I'd never been able to say. But as I stood staring at the doors of Victoria Hall, I realized I'd spent the entire walk picturing the look I would see on Lucas's face when I began to speak.

Great. It looked like I'd be winging it.

By some miracle I managed to follow a lone student into the building and get directions from him to Lucas's room, which seemed odd for a moment, until I remembered he was Lucas Matthews. Of course everyone knew where his room was. The halls echoed with silence. Term was ending. It felt like everything was ending. It seemed fitting; the end of school, the end of Lucas and me, the end of my charade…the end of me?

The door to his room was partly open and I didn't let myself stop and think. If I gave this any thought at all I'd been running for it in seconds. I pushed it the rest of the way open and let it hit the wall with a *thump*. The room wasn't tiny, but it was overcrowded considering there were three beds and desks and wardrobes squished into the space. One mattress was bare and another was covered in half-packed bags and piles of books and hockey equipment. On the third bed, which faced the window, sat Lucas.

He turned to look at me and our eyes locked. His faced seemed lifeless. It was almost as though he didn't recognize me. That expression almost had me making a break for it, but I braced my legs instead, staying put. He walked over to me, his shoulders slumped. With one hand he cupped my cheek, barely touching my skin, and I looked up into his eyes searching for a sign, some indication that he still cared, that I wasn't about to bare my soul for nothing. His eyes were still the colour of liquid gold and they burned straight into my heart, but in their depths I could only see one thing: sadness. After a moment he dropped his hand and turned away.

He didn't want to have anything to do with me.

"Can I have my phone back?" I said, my voice harder than I'd meant it to be. But what did it matter anyway? If he was done with me, there was nothing to ruin. It was already ruined. I'd ruined it.

Lucas hesitated a moment before reaching into the pocket of his jeans and pulling the phone out. He placed it on the bare mattress without looking at me. When I turned it on, it opened to the texts I'd received from Brandon.

"How many did you read?" I asked.

"We were panicked," he said. "You were practically catatonic. You'd mentioned Brandon had been texting you. I thought maybe if I could see what he'd said to upset you so much…"

I scanned through the texts, page after page. I hadn't realized how many there had actually been. I'd just started ignoring them after a while.

"How many?" I asked again.

"All of them," Lucas said, his voice rough, as though he'd spent the night yelling.

My heart sank into my shoes. All of them. Every disgusting name and degrading threat, every shaming, hateful, spiteful one of them. It wasn't the fact that Lucas knew that someone else thought these things of me that made me want to curl up and die. It was the fact that I thought them, too, and maybe now so did he.

"Well, I guess now you know—" I began.

"That you *lied* to me?" Lucas said loudly, spinning around. His eyes weren't liquid gold now. They were on fire.

"You think I should have shown these to you?" I said shakily, holding up my phone. "You would have called the cops in a second."

"Oh yeah, wouldn't want to get your *boyfriend* into trouble," Lucas said bitterly.

As I tried to figure out what the hell that meant, Lucas cast around the room, looking for something. Then he picked a basketball up off the floor. I thought he might throw it at me, but instead he pressed it between his hands, as though he planned to pop it like a balloon.

"You're still in love with him," Lucas said. "That's obvious."

I let out a short, loud laugh and his eyes snapped to my face, incredulous. "You think I'm in love with Brandon?" I said, unable to stop myself from grinning. It was just so ridiculous. "I haven't seen him in five years!"

Lucas stared at me, breathing hard, then began to pace in front of his bed, still gripping the ball. "You don't protect someone from the cops unless you love them," he said. "You don't let them say things like *that* to you and then say it's no big deal. He threatened to kill you, Katie! Not just once but again and again."

He was furious now, though I couldn't really tell with whom. Brandon? Me? Himself? He threw the ball hard against the brick wall and then caught it as it flew back. He did this several times more, knocking things off his desk, and hitting a clock that fell of the wall and broke. Then he started yelling.

"You've been having some kind of twisted love affair with him this whole time and making me...and telling me...!" He didn't finish, just continued slamming the ball around the room.

I stood frozen in place, paralyzed with fear of this anger that poured out of him as he kept throwing, the ball bouncing precariously close to the window. Then, as he reached back to fling it one last time, aiming for the glass, my hands flew forward and grabbed the ball out of his grip.

The fight went out of him right away. Without his ball, he just looked like a lost boy who'd run out of things to break, his arms hanging heavily at his sides. His feverish eyes found my face and searched it, full of questions. I knew I owed it to him to answer them.

I rolled the ball under one of the beds and then folded my hands. "I am not in love with Brandon Tomko," I said firmly. "I'm in love with you."

It was the first time I'd said the words out loud. Something flickered behind Lucas's eyes, but otherwise he didn't react. I could understand that. He thought I was a liar. I was a liar.

"And because I love you, I'm going to tell you the whole story," I said, my voice cracking on the last words. "I'm going to tell you the truth."

I moved to his bed and sat down on the worn flannel cover, pulling my legs up underneath me. Lucas stood staring at me for a moment before following suit. He sat down gingerly, almost warily. In that moment, watching him, I really felt as though I'd already lost him completely. I wasn't sure if it would make it easier or harder for me to tell him everything, but I knew it didn't really matter. There was no going back now.

I cleared my throat and waited until he was really looking at me to begin. This was the kind of conversation that needed everyone's full attention.

"Have you ever heard of the Kindergarten Killer?" I asked.

Lucas frowned slightly. "Sure, everyone has," he said. "The kid who murdered Tommy Wesley. The most horrific homicide in recent history, if you believe the papers. It's been all over the news, because he just got out. Why are you—" I held up my hand to stop the question I knew he would ask. We'd never get anywhere if we did it this way. I just had to tell the story and let him hear it.

"I was thirteen when that happened," I said. "He lived in my neighbourhood. The media frenzy was unbelievable. Even when they don't publish your name they find you anyway—nobody ever mentions that. His parents barricaded themselves inside their house. The parents of the dead boy, the Wesleys, were crying in the papers, on the news, on their lawn. They lived on my street.

"Emily didn't understand why I reacted the way I did. Why I changed into this sullen, silent creature that roamed the house at night because I couldn't sleep and stopped caring about anything, stopped living. I couldn't face the Wesleys, even though they wanted to see me, to comfort me. They thought I was on their side, but I knew better. I knew more about Tommy Wesley's death than anyone."

"What do you mean?" Lucas said, his face clouded with confusion now instead of anger. "How could you know more than them about their own son's death?"

I raised my chin. "Because it was my idea," I said.

20

"I met Brandon at the park," I went on, looking out the window now. I couldn't look at Lucas anymore. "That's important. We didn't go to the same school. The park near my house was this huge, wild tangle of nature, with a forest and hiking trails. I used to go into the woods to sketch on these huge boulders. That's where I met him. He liked to smoke there and I thought he was cool because he smoked for real. You know, not like a kid pretending to smoke. He smoked like he knew what he was doing, like a grown up. Remembering it now it seems absurd, but I was so impressed with him at first, even though he was a year younger than me. He never said much, which was so different from all the boys at my school. He had these intense dark eyes. And he was cute. He called me Katie Kat. We met up every day for a week and a half and I called him my boyfriend, in my head anyway. A week and a half. That's all it took.

"I didn't tell Emily about him, which I was really glad about later. It was the first thing I'd ever kept from her." My mind reeled as I said this, because I'd lied to her so constantly every day since. "I didn't know it until…after, but Brandon never told anyone, either. If what happened next hadn't happened, Brandon Tomko would probably be erased from my memory by now. There wasn't much to our relationship, really. We never even kissed. But what happened did happen, so Brandon and those days we spent together in the woods are now and forever a major event in my life that I can't ever escape."

My voice quavered and I felt Lucas's hand cover mine. His thumb smoothed the skin on the back of my hand and I knew that I'd been wrong. Whatever might happen in the next little while, I hadn't lost him yet. He was still here with me. It gave me the strength to go on.

"Tommy Wesley was five and Ricky Wesley was nine. I was their babysitter. It was my first babysitting job. I'd watch them two or three times a week after school while their mother was taking a class. Copywriting, I think. I wasn't a very good babysitter. Mostly I'd just let them watch TV for three hours straight, which was completely against the rules. Tommy would sometimes talk me into playing trains with him. He adored trains. If he hooked up all the toy trains he had—which he did once—it made one gigantic train that stretched all the way from the kitchen to his bedroom door. He was a cute kid, very cuddly. He still had that baby sweetness. It was Ricky that was the problem."

"I don't remember ever reading about a brother," Lucas said, frowning, pulling me out of my story for a moment.

"Yes, you do," I replied, my eyes on the sycamore across the street. "At the funeral he tried to climb into the coffin to be with his brother and an uncle had to drag him away, screaming."

The papers had printed that detail over and over the week of the funeral. I knew Lucas would remember it. Everyone did. The dead child, the inconsolable brother, the sobbing parents, the nation in mourning.

The tears that I had wrought.

"Oh, right," Lucas said grimly, remembering. "Keep going." He squeezed my hand.

"Ricky hated me," I said. "He didn't want a babysitter. He thought he was old enough to stay on his own. Remember, I was only four years older than him. He would spend the afternoons doing anything he could to get rid of me. He broke a vase and said I did it. He played too rough with his brother, and when I pulled him off he accused me of abusing him. He poured soup into my backpack. Basically he acted like a total brat. By the time I'd been their sitter for a month, I hated him, too."

"On the day I regret the most, the day that started it all, I met Brandon in the park when I was done babysitting. It was already getting dark, but I knew he would be there. I was excited to see him, because usually I could never think of what to say to him. I didn't know how to talk to boys. But on that day I had plenty to say. And I remember word for word how I started. I said, 'I want to kill Ricky Wesley.' Then Brandon put out his cigarette and said, 'Tell me.'"

I felt the tears building behind my eyes, threatening to fall, but it was way too early to start crying. There was so much more to go. I sucked in a shuddering breath and felt Lucas's hand on my back, his legs pressing against mine. When I'd started the story he'd been sitting all the way on the other side of the bed, but now he was right in front of me. I wanted to lean into him, but I didn't. I needed to hold myself up as I told this story. I needed to be strong.

"I ranted for a long time. About how much I hated Ricky, what a brat he was, how mean he was for no reason. That day he'd slammed a door and my finger had gotten caught. I was sure he'd done it on purpose. I used all the most vicious words I could think of to describe him, mostly because I thought Brandon would be impressed if I cursed. I never even mentioned Tommy. I figured Brandon wouldn't want to hear about the sweet five year old I liked to hang out with after school. The evil one was a lot more interesting. But this omission would turn out to be the biggest mistake of my life. It meant that in Brandon's mind I only babysat one kid. One kid I wanted dead.

"After about an hour of cursing Ricky I started to lose steam, and that was when Brandon took over. He wanted to know how I would kill him. Would I set him on fire? Hang him in the closet? Chop off his head? In retrospect the excitement in his eyes should have set off warning bells, but...I was the one who'd brought it up. I thought he was excited by my hatred, my passion. I thought he was interested in me, when really..." I bit my lip.

When really it was the kill that turned him on.

"Brandon thought sawing off his fingers one by one would be fitting, followed by his arms and legs and head. But I disagreed. I said—" I choked on the words. My head fell into my hands as the first tears begin to fall and I knew I'd never be able to stop them now. I felt Lucas trying to pull me toward him, but I pushed his arms away and turned to face him. He deserved to look me in the face when I said this. "I said I'd use a knife if I had a choice. I'd cut him right down the middle, gut him like a fish, so I could see the evil lurking inside."

I saw the look of recognition on Luca's face as he recalled the phrase "gutted like a fish." The papers hadn't spared the details for the Wesleys' sake. That exact phrase had been used in every article about the murder as though the gruesome nature of the crime would convince the world of something, as though describing every bloody detail had some purpose beyond torturing me. Though if it did, I could never figure out what it was.

Vaguely I heard Lucas saying something about how I'd been just a kid. Kids said all kinds of horrible things. I hadn't really meant it. But I wasn't listening. The rest of the story tumbled out of me in a monotone, as though I were reading from the script of a horror movie in which I was the star.

"The next afternoon I was getting Tommy ready to go to the playground when Brandon showed up at the back door with the knife in his hand. It was a switchblade, still folded closed. I remember wanting to hold it because I'd never seen one before and I wanted to see how it opened. I didn't understand what was happening yet. He told Tommy he'd push him on the swings, which was enough to make the kid fall in love with him. Then he leaned in and said in my ear, 'Today's the day we take care of business,' and I knew something wasn't quite right.

"That's when I should have grabbed Tommy and run. I should have screamed my head off. But I just couldn't comprehend what he meant. Take care of what business? The murdering business? Ricky wasn't even there that day—he was sleeping over at a friend's house. I assumed Brandon was kidding and that we'd just take Tommy to the park and watch him play. I assumed it was a joke because he was my boyfriend and that meant he knew me. He knew I didn't really want to kill Ricky, didn't he?

"But then, when we reached the woods, Brandon started describing to me, step by step, how he was going to do it. He kept pointing at Tommy, who had run ahead of us. Because he thought Tommy was Ricky. He thought Tommy was the bratty one, the horrible one, the one I wanted dead. He whispered his plan into my ear, and it was exactly as I'd described it the night before. He was going to do it, just like I'd said. Just like I asked. He was going to do it for me."

Lucas's eyes were riveted to my face now, his shock evident, though he was trying to hide it. I was rewriting a story that had been told thousands of times, unraveling the mystery that had gripped a nation. The Kindergarten Killer never had a discernible motive. His entire defence had hinged upon that fact. And all the time I'd had the answer.

His motive was me.

Just as Brandon had led Tommy and I into the woods six years before, I followed him in now. I continued to recount the story to Lucas, while in my mind I lived it: the darkness of the trees descending around us; the clearing appearing ahead, divided by the long-unused train tracks; and the sky still bright with the dying day, the sky I could not escape, the sky he died under.

Is this really happening?

The question runs through my mind on a continual loop as we walk through the trees, looking for all the world like three kids with nothing to do on a Thursday afternoon. Three kids taking a shortcut to the park through the woods. Three innocent kids.

Except Brandon is whispering bloody things in my ear. And the voice in my head is rising to a scream. And one of us might soon be dead.

"Race you to the train tracks, Katie!" Tommy cries, because trains are his favourite things in the world, because he has no idea my boyfriend plans to butcher him.

I want to tell him to keep running, to run for his life, but I'm shaking with fear and the words stick in my throat.

"You heard him, Katie Kat," Brandon says. "You'd better hurry now. If I get there first, who knows what might happen." He's only pretending to taunt me, posing his arms as though he's about to start jogging ahead, but not actually going through with it. He thinks I'm on his side.

"I'm coming!" I call to Tommy, who shrieks as though he's being chased even though I haven't moved a muscle.

Then I turn to Brandon and my voice falls to a whisper. "This isn't funny, okay? Pretending you're going to kill a five year old isn't funny." Because this is a joke, it just has to be. Twelve-year-old boys don't murder kindergarteners. Brandon isn't a killer...is he?

"Who's trying to be funny?" Brandon says, his voice flat, all the mirth from a moment ago completely gone.

"Just give me the knife and we can forget this ever happened," I say reasonably. "I won't even be mad." I hold out a shaking hand.

"Mad about what?" Brandon replies. He seems genuinely confused. That's when I know he isn't joking or playing a trick. This isn't a game to Brandon.

This is really happening.

In desperation I try to snatch the blade out of his hand, but he's too quick. He shoves me away roughly and I nearly trip and fall.

"You're not really going to do this," I say frantically. "You know I was just joking around last night. You know I don't really want you to kill anyone. He's not even—"

"I heard what you said," Brandon replies. "I heard it loud and clear. I'm going to take care of it for you. You'll thank me when it's done, trust

me."

"You're right, that is what I said. I do want him dead," I say, switching tacks. Maybe if he thinks I want this too, maybe if I convince him, maybe, maybe, maybe… "But this kid isn't the one I hate. It's his brother I want dead. You don't want to kill the wrong kid, do you? You don't want to make that mistake."

He gives me a look of disgust. He thinks I'm lying, I can see it in his eyes.

"Having a change of heart?" he says. "Don't worry, I'm not like you. I won't lose my nerve. I never do."

"Brandon, please—"

He takes my hand and twists it behind my back, pinning it painfully. I let out a gasp of shock and pain. When he speaks, his voice is hard. "Don't even think of getting in my way. This is what you want. You've forgotten, but you'll remember when it's done. You'll see how good it feels. When he's dead, you'll understand. You'll love me for it."

I can't see him now because he's standing behind me, but I can see his free hand as he flips open the knife. The knife he will use to kill Tommy, and probably me, too.

I begin to breathe quickly, too quickly, and the forest path tilts in front of me. I will myself not to pass out. Because if I do, what will happen to Tommy? I find out what it means to piss yourself with fear when I feel the warmth spreading over the crotch of my jeans.

"Say you love me," Brandon says as he presses me forward, toward the clearing.

"I love you," I gasp, because it's what he wants to hear, because love conquers all, doesn't it? Maybe love can conquer Brandon's bloodlust. Maybe love can save us. "I love you, Brandon. I really do. I'll do whatever you want. Just leave the kid alone. You can tie me up. You can cut me as much as you want."

"Why would I want to cut you up?" Brandon says. He seems almost hurt by my words. "I love you. I'm doing this for you."

I try to struggle against his grip, but he only yanks my arm harder, eliciting a small scream from my lips. "Keep quiet," Brandon says immediately, clamping a hand over my mouth. "Don't say a word, or I'll kill him slowly."

Hearing my scream, Tommy appears up ahead of us on the path and my eyes fill with tears. My voice has called him back when I wanted him to run.

"Katie, hurry up!" Tommy calls, then frowns as he takes in the scene of me and Brandon and his knife.

I want to beat Brandon to the ground, but I'm too weak. I want to go back to the minute before I told him about Ricky and still my lips, but I know I can't. I want to whisk Tommy to safety, but I'm trapped. I'm useless. And it's all my fault.

So I do the only thing I can think of. I bite down on Brandon's hand hard, tasting blood. My eyes find Tommy again and I scream, "Run!"

Brandon swears and lets me out of his grip, shocked by the wound, and suddenly I'm running down the path after Tommy, who has disappeared from view. I don't look back, though I can hear Brandon's clumsy footsteps behind me. For five seconds I imagine that we might get out of this. As I reach the clearing, the trees open up to reveal the sky, full of fading light. I still have hope until the moment I see Tommy standing there, waiting for me, his eyes enormous with fright.

"No!" I cry as Brandon shoves me from behind and I fall forward, the metal railroad tie coming up to meet my eyes.

"Stupid bitch," Brandon says.

The last thing I hear is Tommy's scream.

Lucas held me in his arms, rocking me as my entire body was racked with sobs. The only word I said for a long while was "Tommy," and each time I did he stroked my head and told me everything would be okay. But it didn't feel okay. Reliving that moment felt almost exactly like Hell, and I didn't want to be in Lucas's arms now. I didn't want to drag him down to Hell with me. But he wouldn't let me go.

Eventually, once my tears had slowed to a trickle, Lucas loosened his hold, allowing me to pull away. Immediately I turned my back as I wiped at my face.

"Katie…" Lucas said, reaching for me, but I flinched at his touch.

"Don't touch me," I warned. "You don't want to hold me. You don't want to hold a killer."

"You're not a killer," Lucas said steadily, and I snorted. "Brandon is the Kindergarten Killer, not you."

I twisted around to face him, suddenly furious. "It was my idea!" I cried. "Tommy's murder started in my head, not Brandon's. Sure it was Ricky I wanted dead, not poor Tommy, but what's the difference? Brandon cut him down the torso, just like I asked. Split him almost in half. You know, you read all about it. Everyone did. And he did it for me!"

"That doesn't mean it was what you wanted," Lucas protested. "That doesn't mean you would have done it yourself. You were a pissed off kid and you said you wanted someone dead. That's not the same as going through with it. Brandon is the murderer, Katie."

"Yeah," I said, "and I'm just the girl who drove him to it."

He was about to retort, but instead Lucas's face stilled as he took in my words. "Is that why you were so afraid when I knocked down Buck? You thought I'd turned into Brandon?"

"It's what I'm good at," I said bitterly. "I drive guys to madness, to violence. It's my talent."

Lucas sighed and took me by the shoulders, forcing me to face him. Reluctantly, I raised my eyes to meet his. "I know a little bit about the Kindergarten Killer," he said. "I read every article about it when I was in high school. We even followed the case in class. The teacher thought it would be better than gossiping about it in the halls. Brandon's father used to beat him with tools from his workshop. When they arrested him he had broken ribs from being beaten. He'd been killing animals in those woods for months, mutilating their bodies. Practicing. His teachers admitted they thought he was off. I think his mother said he tried to kill his little sister once. He was a killer long before he met you."

"Fine, he's the killer," I conceded. "He murdered Tommy, not me. But it's still my fault!" My tears were running again, blurring my vision.

"Tell me why," Lucas said, tightening his grip on my shoulders as I tried to pull away.

"B-because," I spluttered. "Because, I-I—"

"Because you were his babysitter? Because you once said you hated his brother so much you wanted to kill him and a psychopath decided it was a good idea?"

"Because if not for me, he'd still be alive."

"That's crazy logic, Katie," Lucas said, his kind eyes boring into mine, trying to fill me with his compassion. But my heart was too full of self-loathing to let him in. "You didn't want either Tommy or Ricky to die, not really. I know you, maybe better than anyone now. You're not to blame."

Reaching up swiftly, I yanked hard on Lucas's arms, dislodging them from my shoulders, and shot to my feet. "You know me?" I said, angrily wiping at my wet cheeks. "Haven't you been listening? Everything I've ever told you is a lie. I'm not the shy artist who likes brownies and rescues kittens. I'm a liar and a phony. I'm a fugitive. I lied to the police and I lied in court. I belong in jail!"

I began twisting my fingers, falling into that same old habit. I remembered then the reason I'd started doing it in the first place. In the ambulance, after Tommy died, I'd twisted my fingers just like this, trying to get the blood off. I imagined I could still see it there even months later, even after a hundred washings. Tommy's blood would always be on my hands.

"You were just trying to protect yourself," Lucas went on in that same sympathetic tone, and suddenly I wanted to hit him. "You were thirteen. Do you know how many lies I told when I was thirteen?"

I'm guessing you weren't under oath at the time," I said. "I'm guessing you drew a line somewhere. You'd lie to your mom, but not your best friend. You'd lie about getting detention, but not about stabbing someone to death. Do you know how many lies I've told, who I've lied to? I'll tell you who: everyone. I lied to the press about that day. To my friends. To my parents. To my sister. To you. I've been lying so long I don't even recognize the truth anymore. Is that the kind of person you want to be with? A pathological liar who'll say anything to save her skin?"

"Would it have made that much difference if you'd told the

truth?" Lucas countered. "Being a liar isn't the same as being a killer."

"I claimed I didn't even know Brandon," I spat. "I said I'd never seen him before in my life, and they all believed me because I was the sweet girl from the nice family and he was trash. I washed my hands of Tommy's death and let Brandon take the fall." My head began to pound and I gripped it with my hands.

"You didn't *let* him take the fall. He's the one who committed the crime. He got what he deserved," Lucas said.

"I was a coward," I whispered between my fingers.

"Oh, Hero," Lucas said, getting to his feet and moving toward me.

"Don't call me that," I snapped, my face contorted with fury at the sound of the word. "Don't *ever* call me that again."

Turning away, my arms wrapped around my stomach, I felt the warmth of Lucas's body behind me before he put his arms around me. I wanted to struggle away, but I was just too tired. Tired of trying to make him see the truth. Tired of thinking about that day. Tired of trying to push him away.

In that moment, all I wanted to do was sink into his warmth and forget.

"You'll always be my hero, Katie," Lucas said as he fitted my body against his like a puzzle piece clicking into place, his lips against my hair. "You're the girl who saved me from the darkness of grief, and from a panic attack, and from a lifetime of meaningless hookups. You made me feel something amazing when I thought I'd never feel anything good again. You might not have been able to save Tommy, but you saved me. You made me love you."

I felt him turning me around to face him and let him do it. Within the cocoon of his arms, I pressed my hands to his chest as he pressed his forehead against mine.

"I love you, Katie," he repeated.

I looked up at him, shaking my head. "But how?" I asked, my lips trembling.

"Like this," he said, pressing his lips gently to mine.

I wanted to melt into his kiss, but my reeling mind wouldn't let me. I knew this couldn't be real. When tomorrow came, when he'd had a chance to think about it, he would change his mind. He would see that I wasn't worthy of love, not after what I'd done. He would see that being with me would change him into a monster, just like Brandon. He would see the truth.

"Stop doubting me, Katie," Lucas said, cupping my cheeks. "I know what I'm saying."

I closed my eyes, an entire lifetime of wanting drawing me toward him. He lifted me off my feet, settling my legs around his waist, wrapping me around him. "But what if—" I said, but he pressed a kiss to my lips again to silence me.

He sat down on the bed without letting go of me. "Nothing you've done or will do could ever make me stop loving you," he said. "Nothing you say about yourself will ever convince me that you aren't the incredible girl I've known for the past two months. I'm not going to change my mind about this. You're stuck with me, so you'd better get used to it."

I rested my cheek against his chest, so overwhelmed with emotion, love for Lucas and hatred for myself swirling inside me, mixed with fear and hope, despair and gladness, sorrow and joy. Could a single person really feel so many things at once? I guessed so, because I was.

Lucas ran his hands up and down my back. He said, "Promise me you'll try to believe me."

"I need you to promise me something first," I said, drawing away so I could look him in the face.

"Anything," he said.

"When you change your mind, I need you to tell me right away," I said.

He brushed a piece of hair behind my ear. "I'm not going to change my mind," he said.

"Then it's an easy promise to make," I answered. I really needed this. I didn't want to be the fool who went on thinking he loved me when he didn't. And I knew the day would come when he didn't, and soon.

"Fine," Lucas said. "If you'll promise to let me love you, I'll promise to let you know when that love ends."

I nodded numbly.

"Even though it never will," Lucas finished, kissing my cheek. "Because I plan on loving you for the rest of my life, Katie Archer."

You don't know what you're saying, I thought. *You don't know who I really am.*

But as his lips met mine again and I surrendered to his embrace, I heard a new voice inside my head, a jubilant voice that had something very different to say.

You know me. You know me. You know me. You know me. You know me, the voice said, and for the moment, I let myself believe it.

Locked in Lucas's arms, my chin on his shoulder, my legs and arms around him just as his arms were around me, I told him the rest of my story. As I spoke, I felt little pieces of the pain I'd been wearing like a cloak falling away. I wondered if when I was done telling I'd be able to take the cloak off, or maybe it would have disappeared all on its own. I hoped so.

The story that started after that day in the woods was even longer than what came before. I told Lucas about waking up covered in my own blood from my head wound and then stumbling over something in the dark, the horror of touching the pulpy flesh and realizing it was what was left of Tommy. Then there were my screams ping-ponging around inside my head and the wild run through the woods and being found by the lady walking her dog—the look on her face when she saw me covered in blood—the discovery of Tommy's body and the lies I told the police, and my parents, and Emily—oh God, Emily. I had a concussion and a broken arm and had to stay in the hospital overnight as the horror of Tommy Wesley's death played out on the TV attached to the wall. My statement is what led to Brandon's arrest, the first arrest of a twelve-year-old boy for murder the province had ever seen.

Then there was the media hounding my family every time we left the house, and the wrenching guilt as friends and neighbours poured out their sympathy, encircling me with a concern and affection I felt I did not deserve. Tommy's funeral, which I attended under protest. A school year done and a summer of living under self-imposed house arrest. Then a new year began and I had to face high school as this new, darker version of myself, to withstand the looks that followed me everywhere I went. But they weren't looks of accusation, only pity, only disgust at the mess I'd made of myself.

A year passed before the trial began and I had to relive that day in the woods all over again. Brandon's lawyer tried to pin the murder on me, but I was too good of a liar by then. Too practiced. Too sympathetic. Brandon eyed me with silent hatred whenever I was in the courtroom, and I kept my gaze lowered, destroying my hands, praying I would get away with it. In the end he got the maximum sentence possible in youth court: six years in custody and four years' community supervision. The papers railed against the fact that he couldn't be tried as an adult, but he was too young, He was only twelve. Ten years was the best they could do. By the time he turned eighteen he would be back out in the world. I prayed that day would never come, that something terrible would happen to him in that place. Because I knew he would come for me when he got out and I would have to answer for my lies.

"But the day did come," I said. "It was that day I called you over to help me watch Ethan."

Lucas leaned his cheek against mine. "I remember reading the headlines. If only I'd known… Your freak-out over Ethan makes a lot more sense now."

"He's the same age Tommy was," I said sadly. Though Ethan would grow older, Tommy would always be five years old. Tommy would never grow up.

Because of me, I thought, then corrected myself. *No, Katie, because of Brandon.*

I described my need to escape the Vancouver suburb, my home, which had, over six years, become a stifling prison. I needed to be somewhere no one knew I'd been a victim of the Kindergarten Killer. So I'd applied to art programs out east and picked Queen's on a whim, moving across the country with my sister in tow to escape my past.

"Except it caught up with me," I said.

Then came the hardest part: telling Lucas the whole truth of Brandon's assault on me over the last two months, from the first Facebook message to the texts he'd already read to the break-in. Though it pained and frightened me to see his anger, I had to let him pace and rage as I recounted the worst of it. I had to let him express his frustration, his desire to rip Brandon apart, and believe he never would. It was almost harder than telling him about the murder itself. Watching Lucas's muscular arms ripple with tension brought out a terror in me that was all too familiar.

He's not Brandon, I reminded myself. *Lucas is on my side.*

But this truth was harder to swallow, because hadn't Brandon been on my side, too?

When I told Lucas about the crumpled message in my bag and explained that he must have been in the coffee shop with us, his face went blank—with anger or fear, I couldn't be sure—and he was silent for a long time. We sat together in this quiet, leaning on each other, holding each other. Even though he didn't say a word, those moments of silence meant so much to me—almost more than any profession of love. I'd been sitting in the dark for so long. I'd never realized how much I'd been yearning for someone to sit there with me and hold my hand and let me feel his heart beating insistently under my palm, telling me I wasn't in this alone.

"I won't let him hurt you," Lucas mumbled into my neck as we lay down together on his bed. "I'll stay with you always. He won't be able to find you behind me."

He put his arms around me protectively, holding me tightly even as he drifted off to sleep. There was comfort there, but also dismay. Lucas thought he could hide me from Brandon, but I knew the truth.

Eventually he would find me.

21

When I woke up the next morning, Lucas was gone. I stared at the empty space beside me in the bed for a long minute, trying not to blame him for running. If anyone understood the urge to run, it was me. I sat up in bed with a heavy sigh.

"Morning, Hero," Lucas said. "I got you a hot chocolate."

Snatching my glasses off the nightstand, I turned my head to find a fully dressed Lucas sitting on the bare mattress on the other side of the room, a newspaper spread out in front of him. Not only was he awake before me, but his hair was wet so it even looked like he'd showered.

Smiling so widely my cheeks hurt, I padded across the room and kissed him on the side of the head before accepting my drink.

"Didn't think I left you here, did you?" he said teasingly. Apparently my sigh hadn't gone unnoticed.

"Not at all," I said mildly. "I was just regretting the idea of sleeping over here in your pygmy-sized bed. The crick in my neck regrets it, too."

"Agreed," Lucas said with a laugh. "All future sleepovers will be conducted at your apartment where there is not only a double bed but also no roommates. Luckily for us, Danny is trying to spend all his free time with his girlfriend before she leaves for her internship."

My brain snagged on the words "future sleepovers" and didn't even take in the rest. My heart did a little flip at the idea that Lucas was still thinking of a future with me despite everything I'd told him. Then I remembered how many times he'd told me he loved me the night before and my heart did a double flip.

His attention drawn back to the newspaper, he held out a paper take-out bag from the coffee shop. "I got you a cruller," he said as he took a bite of a raspberry danish.

I peered into the bag suspiciously. "No chocolate icing?" I complained.

Raising his eyebrows at me, Lucas grabbed me by the waist and pulled me down onto the bed in front of him, tickling me mercilessly. "Not even a, 'Thank you, Boyfriend, for going out in the rain to get me a tasty breakfast?'" he said as I squealed and squirmed, crushing the newspaper underneath me. Then he leaned forward and gave me a kiss so deep that suddenly I didn't feel much like laughing at all. "How can you stand that much chocolate so early in the morning, anyway?"

I gave him a look that was equal to the alarming nature of his question. "How much you have to learn," I said, shaking my head.

As I hoisted myself up off the bed, I pressed my hand down on the newspaper, crushing it further. "Careful, I'm reading that," Lucas said. As he straightened out the page, I looked down to see the front page headline.

Kindergarten On The Run?

I spun around, holding my stomach as it clenched painfully. Telling Lucas had not stopped the automatic reaction I had whenever I caught wind of a news story about Brandon.

Lucas took my hand and pulled me back around while simultaneously folding the newspaper over with his other hand. "There, it's gone," he said. Getting to his feet, he took me in his arms. I breathed in his scent and breathed out the bad memories. After about a minute of breathing like this and feeling his arms around me, my stomach had unclenched.

Like I said, magic arms.

"That's why you ran away from Tim and me that day on campus, isn't it?" Lucas said, putting it together. "I remember there was a news report blaring out of his ear buds. That idiot always plays his music too loud."

"You remember that?" I said.

"Of course I remember it," Lucas said. "About five seconds later you slipped and fell on your ass. How could I forget that?"

I pressed my hand against his cheek as his dimples popped. "That's not what I remember," I said. "I remember you picking me up."

"I'll always pick you up," Lucas said. "I'll always be there for you, Katie." I closed my eyes at the sound of his lovely words and wondered if I would ever believe them completely without wondering why. "I promise I'll throw the paper out right after I finish reading this article."

"Deal," I said, giving him my best half-smile.

Lucas shook his head, still looking down at me. "I still can't really believe you're 'the babysitter.' I must have read dozens of articles about you over the years. I think I even saw a picture of you once, but your head was turned away from the camera."

I remembered that picture, too, and the way my father had torn it out of every newspaper he could get his hands on. He'd walked down the block ripping the front page off the newspaper on every front stoop until my mother screamed at him to get a hold of himself.

"Yeah, that was me. Being the sole surviving victim of a notorious child murderer sure can do wonders for your celebrity status," I joked. I was trying to lighten the mood, but Lucas didn't laugh. I think he could tell I didn't really think it was funny, either.

"I'm sorry," Lucas said, shaking his head. "I hide the paper and then a second later I bring it up all over again. I shouldn't be talking about my amazement like it's important. It's just a lot to get my mind around. But we don't have to talk about any of it if you don't want to. Not if it hurts you."

I shrugged. "It's a good hurt. I've been holding that day inside of me for six years. I have to get used to talking about it. Making the subject off-limits would just be more hiding."

"So they know he left Vancouver?" I asked tentatively as Lucas picked up the folded paper. Though I didn't want to read any details about the crime, which always surfaced in any article about Brandon, I definitely did want to be aware of a possible manhunt.

"His probation officer reported him missing when he didn't show up for an appointment," Lucas replied cautiously, watching my face for distress. "The cops are on it—if he left the province, it's a violation of his community supervision—but they don't seem to be aware that he's in Kingston."

I nodded, unsure how to feel about this news.

"Although," Lucas went on, "they could know where he is if I anonymously tipped them off."

Grabbing the cruller, I stuffed a piece of it in my mouth to stem my rising anxiety. Sugar beat panic, right?

"They'll put together in about two seconds that I go to school here, Lucas," I said as I chewed. "They'll realize he's after me and start asking why."

"They'll probably assume he's just still blaming you for the whole thing," Lucas said. "His lawyers did try to pin it on you. They'll probably issue a restraining order to protect you."

I swallowed the last bite of doughnut before answering. "I'm pretty sure staying away from me is already part of his sentence. 'Stay away from the victims.' I remember hearing it during sentencing. The only living victim right now is me."

As those words sunk in, Lucas placed a hand under my chin, gently urging me to raise it instead of hanging my head in shame as I had been. "All the more reason to call in the tip,"

Lucas insisted. "He's already breaking two of the rules of his parole. They'll have to take him back into custody."

"Not before the press gets wind of it," I said. "If they start digging even a little… It always amazed me that nobody ever saw the two of us together at the park. Six years is a long time for a witness to sit around wondering if they really saw what they did, to stew in their guilt. The right question from a journalist and the case could blow wide open again."

"You don't even know if this witness exists," Lucas said patiently.

"I lied on the stand, Lucas," I replied. "I lied with the whole country watching. We can't take any chances right now."

"You mean like the chances you're taking with your life?" Lucas said, and I pulled out of his arms in frustration. I was beginning to realize that telling the truth came with some unforeseen consequences. Like Lucas's opinions about everything.

Facing the mirror above the nightstand, I eyed my frizzy hair and tried to remember the last time I'd washed it. I couldn't. Instead of having pointless discussions about turning Brandon in, what I really needed to do was get home and take a shower. "Do you have a comb?" I said, not even bothering to cover up the hostility in my voice. If Lucas wanted to be with me, he was going to get all of me.

Unzipping a canvas bag sitting on the floor, Lucas took out a plastic comb. "You know I'm right," he said as he handed it to me.

I let out a groan of frustration, both at Lucas's persistence and because my hair was so knotted I could barely move the comb an inch. As I glared down at the nightstand, I noticed it was oddly bare, as were the shelves of Lucas's wardrobe. I knew he didn't have to clear out of the Res for another few days—he still had two exams this week—and Lucas might have been many things, but he didn't strike me as the pack-five-days-ahead type.

"What's with the suitcase?" I asked, pointing at it with the comb.

"Well, I figured since I have to be out of here soon anyway," Lucas explained, "and since we've already established you have that awesome double bed, I thought I'd just…move in."

"To my apartment?" I squeaked, taking in the larger suitcase by the door. In addition to showering and picking up breakfast while I'd been snoozing this morning, he'd apparently also been packing.

I tried not to hyperventilate at the thought of Lucas living full-time in my apartment, with my hair clogging the drain and my dirty underwear and my enormous jar of Nutella.

"Did you really think I was going to let you out of my sight?" Lucas said into my ear. "I need to be there every second so we can continue this argument ad nauseum."

"Can't wait," I said, giving him a spiteful look as he began to strip the sheets off his bed. But as he finished his packing, I thought about how nice it would be to have him there, to lean on, to snuggle up with, and to do other things with in my double bed.

I turned my head so he wouldn't see my smile. After all, I was still mad at him.

Can't wait, I thought.

Lucas and I spent the next few of days getting to know each other all over again. I'd been so hesitant to tell him anything about my past that he realized he knew almost nothing about my life back in Vancouver. His curiosity piqued, he started quizzing me about my history, asking some silly questions, like what board games I'd hated as a kid and what kind of apples I'd liked packed in my lunch, and other less silly questions, like what it felt like when they put me on anti-depressants.

It was hard for me to answer without being evasive. My years of avoiding ever talking about my past had me tensing my shoulders and bracing for the worst, my lips clamping shut, my eyes searching for the exit. One day, when we were both supposed to be studying but instead he was asking about my mother's reaction during the trial, I felt tears running down my cheeks before I even realized I'd started to cry. Lucas caught each tear with his fingertips and wiped my face dry, but the next day he was back at it. I never asked him to stop. He said he wanted to know everything about me, that he couldn't help it, and truthfully that was what I wanted, too. I wanted Lucas to know me through and through. The questions felt like a different kind of exam, a test of my courage. Once every detail of me was laid out for Lucas to see, as nobody else ever had, I knew I would feel better than if I'd aced a test. It was like a cleanse.

His love was washing me clean.

There were other lessons, too. I learned that Lucas was a lot neater than me, folding his clothes at the end of the day instead of leaving them in a pile on the floor for him to trip over like me. I learned that Turner far preferred Lucas to me. Turner's little ears perked up every time he heard Lucas's voice and he spent all his time tangling himself around Lucas's legs, purring like a lawn mower, which didn't make me jealous in the least. I also learned that Lucas did *not* know how to cook—he managed to botch boiling pasta—and since neither could I, we ordered in a lot. Because leaving the house was definitely not on the menu. My flight back to Vancouver was booked for Saturday morning, and until then Lucas had appointed himself my personal bodyguard. With Brandon still on the loose, he ruled that we should stay inside at all times except for exams. Granted, when he said this his hand was on my ass, and when I agreed I was slipping my tongue into his mouth, but the seriousness of the situation wasn't lost on us.

Though he tried to do it when I wasn't looking—a hard thing to do in an apartment with only two rooms—Lucas was still reading the paper obsessively, trying to track Brandon's movements by the police reports. They still didn't know he was in the area. There were no new threats stabbed through the door, and no texts, either. I tried not to wonder what that meant. Lucas thought it was a good sign—maybe Brandon was losing interest—but I knew better. If six years hadn't worn him out, six days of watching me shacked up with my boyfriend wasn't going to do the trick.

Letting myself think of Lucas as my boyfriend—that was another lesson.

Our argument over calling the police continued without much progress. Finally realizing I was never going to budge on the issue, Lucas stipulated instead that once I was safely installed in my parents' home he would go ahead and make the call to the cops. I countered that calling the police once I was gone didn't solve the problem. Kingston was still the town where I went to school. Brandon's presence there would still be linked to me. Lucas then agreed that he would wait until Brandon had followed me back home, as we knew he would, before calling in a bogus tip about this whereabouts. But how would that help? How could we know exactly where Brandon was at that point? What kind of tip could Lucas give then except to tell the police what they already knew, that he'd violated his parole by missing an appointment with his P.O. Then Lucas inevitably circled back to calling the cops right away and the argument started all over again.

One thing he wouldn't give up on was that if Brandon hadn't been picked up by the time I got home, I had to tell my parents the truth. He was a little fanatical about it. I think the idea that he wouldn't be there to protect me was making him a little mad, and he wanted to be sure that my parents understood the threat Brandon posed. I was also pretty sure he knew that when they heard the truth they'd be on the phone to the cops themselves in a blink. I never agreed to tell them—I didn't want to lie—but I never flat out disagreed, either. I was being Switzerland on that one, and Lucas knew it.

One cloud hanging over us—besides the homicidal ex, that is—was the thought of being apart all summer. Now that I had Lucas, I found I couldn't bear to lose him, and the very thought of all those days without being able to look at his breathtaking dimples was enough to drive me to distraction. Even his half-naked body in my bed couldn't keep my attention, as we both learned one night when one moment we were kissing and the next I was picturing my lonely bedroom back home and making lists of all the movies I could watch to pass the time over the summer. When I shook myself out of my reverie and looked up at Lucas, he said, "What kind of alarm system do your parents have in their house?"

I guess we were both a little distracted.

But not so much that when my hand brushed over his boxers a few minutes later I didn't feel his now-familiar arousal.

"Thinking about alarm systems, eh?" I said, and he turned on his side so we were spooning. In this position, I could feel him even more.

I could hear the grin in his voice as he whispered, "I told you, anytime you're near me…"

For the next twenty minutes, before our minds wandered again, I learned about some of the other perks of having a live-in boyfriend.

One lazy afternoon, as the sun streamed through the windows onto the couch, I lay with my head in Lucas's lap trying to keep the names of the Pre-Raphaelites straight in my head. (I kept forgetting the second Rossetti.) Turner had reluctantly given up his place on Lucas's lap to me, opting instead to lie on the floor by his feet. Every once in a while he swiped at Lucas's shoelaces.

Lucas's questions that day had been getting more and more esoteric. Did I think of my father as strong? What was my friendliest memory? Then one of his questions struck a chord.

"What are you most afraid of?" he said. He felt my body react and immediately his hands went around me, tugging me closer, if that were possible. I felt his fingers digging into my shoulders, trying to loosen the muscles.

"I'm afraid of losing," I replied softly. "That's always been my biggest fear. Of telling the truth and losing the people I love. Losing you. Losing my parents. Losing Emily. When they know the truth about me, I'm afraid I'll lose their love."

Lucas sighed and smoothed his fingers over my hair. "You

lived so many years thinking such awful things about yourself, Hero," he said, "without anybody having the chance to contradict you. You've thought these horrible things for so long that you've convinced yourself they're true. But they aren't true. You told me everything and I still love you. There's nothing awful about you at all. You aren't going to lose anyone."

I clung to his arms like they were a buoy as fear pumped through my veins, spurred by something I couldn't explain. The idea of his love. And the idea of losing it. The idea of telling the truth to more and more people. And the idea of lying instead.

"Think of it this way," Lucas said, gazing down into my eyes, "if you do lose your family over this, then what?"

My body actually spasmed at the very thought. I dug my fingers into Lucas's skin. "Don't," I whimpered.

He shook his head. "You won't, but let's say the world turns on its head and you do. You have to know you'll be okay. Look at how strong you are. You've lived with this secret eating away at you for six years and you're still standing. I can't say I could have done the same. You moved away and made a life for yourself. You make beautiful art. You're in school, doing what you love. You made it, Katie. You survived. You can survive anything. You're so much stronger than you think."

"I'm not," I protested, tears stinging my eyes, but I blinked them back angrily. "I-I'm not strong. I'm weak."

"Being afraid isn't the same as being weak. You're brave," Lucas said.

"I'm a liar," I said.

"You're a survivor."

"Coward."

"Smart."

"Manipulative."

"Cunning."

"Selfish."

"Human."

"Cold-hearted."

"Warm-blooded."

"Ugly."

"I'm not even going to dignify that with a response," Lucas said, prying my hands away from my face. I was trying to hide again.

I looked up at him, his golden eyes, his kind face, and a new word came to my mind, one I never could have said before I met him: "Hopeful."

Lucas nodded. "And remember," he said, "even if everything goes wrong, and you find yourself feeling weak, there's one thing you'll always have, one thing you'll never lose no matter what."

"What?" I asked. If he said something like "your self-worth" I was going to puke, but of course he didn't. He said the perfect thing instead.

"Me," he said softly, and brushed my lips with his. "Forever."

On the day of Lucas's last exam we treated ourselves to Chinese food. Up until then we'd been going cheap and splitting every bill because I knew Lucas didn't have a lot of extra cash. I didn't even know how much money he was losing by not showing up to his shifts at the club all week, though he said it was no big deal. This philosophy exam, however, was one he'd been studying hard for, and, as it was an evening exam, I felt he needed a big dinner to get through it. Besides, my credit card, which my parents paid for, was happy to take the hit.

We were sitting on the stools at the kitchen counter, eating spring rolls and leaving sticky fingerprints all over each other when I heard the muffled sound of my phone ringing. I'd misplaced it the day before and had forgotten all about it.

"Check who it is first," Lucas warned as I jumped off the stool, wiping my hands on a napkin.

"Okay, Dad," I sassed as I searched for the source of the

ringing.

It turned out my phone was underneath the rug in front of the couch—God knew how it had gotten there. Pulling it out and dusting it off, I saw that there were at least a dozen texts from Emily, and her name flashed across the screen as the phone continued to ring.

Crap.

I answered the call with a timid, "Hello?"

"I *cannot* believe you!" Em said. She was someplace loud. Over her yelling I was able to make out a voice asking passengers to report to the gate, final call.

Oh big, big crap.

"Oh, no. Did I—"

"Did you forget to help me pack up all my stuff?" Emily interrupted. "Did you forget your only sister was flying back to Vancouver today? Did you forget she's terrified of flying *alone?*"

Due to our conflicting exam schedules, Emily was flying home three days earlier than me, though if I'd known my anthropology exam had been moved up, we could have flown together—a fact she'd been holding against me.

"I'm so, so sorry," I said, eyeing Lucas miserably. He mouthed the word, "Uh-oh."

"I lost my phone and I totally forgot and—"

"That's not even what I'm mad about. Did you even look at any of my texts?"

I'd only scanned them. I wanted to read through all of them right that second, but that would have meant taking my ear away from the phone. "No," I answered lamely.

"We haven't even spoken since you left me that stupid note on your pillow," Emily said, her voice shrill. She always sounded like that when she was trying to scream instead of cry. "Mariella called me that night, hysterical, saying you were screaming at her. By the time I got to your apartment you were catatonic. It was terrifying. Katie, what the hell is going on?"

I sat down on the arm of the couch and realized that amid all of Lucas's questions I hadn't asked any of my own. Like what exactly had happened the night I'd waited for Brandon to come and find me. I hadn't even known that Mariella had been involved at all, though that did explain the chicken stir-fry she'd left at my door with a note saying she hoped I felt better and to call her, which I hadn't done.

"Oh, Em," I said, my heart filling with regret.

"Obviously the story you told about the creepy guy in the building was a lie," she went on. "Lucas totally freaked out at me for leaving you alone." My glance darted back to Lucas. "I was so busy with packing and studying for that insane exam for my accounting class that I had no time to come by your place and scream at you."

I closed my eyes. I didn't even bother replying. She needed to have her say.

"You're keeping something from me," she said. "I know you are. Something big. And you've been keeping it from me for a while."

My heart broke a little as she said this, knowing hers must have been doing the same. The one thing Emily prized more than anything else was her belief that we told each other everything.

She said, "I just want to know one thing."

"Okay," I managed to say.

"Are you all right?" she said.

Lucas was sitting with his hands folded, his eyes riveted on me. "I will be," I said, and then I continued, shocking even myself, "and I'm going to tell you everything. I promise."

"Good," Emily said before hanging up.

I slunk back to my chair and nibbled at my food half-heartedly as Lucas rubbed my back. "Be strong," he said.

I guessed I was going to have to be.

An hour later I was in no mood to accompany Lucas to his exam, not after the calamity of that conversation with Em, but Lucas insisted. Even an offer to stay over at Mariella's place wouldn't sway him.

"If I could I'd take you into the exam room with me and make you sit right in front of me. That way you'd be in my line of sight at all times," Lucas said as we walked through the windy evening toward campus, sauntering at Lucas's usual pace. Apparently not even a final exam could make Lucas hurry up.

"I know what you're after, Matthews," I teased. "You're only saying that because the top I'm wearing is kind of see-through." It really was. I pulled the zipper on my jacket higher just in case.

"It's what he's after that I'm worried about," he replied, his manner tense. I squeezed his hand. For the first time it occurred to me to wonder how he was dealing with the atomic bomb I'd dropped on him when I'd told him the truth. The thought of Lucas losing himself to the paranoia I often fell prey to made my stomach twist into knots. I didn't want that for him. Nobody deserved that.

Not even me.

By a stroke of luck, Lucas's exam had been moved to the fine arts building because of a water leak in Watson Hall. As part of their final grade, the fourth year art students had to turn all of Ontario Hall into a gallery with their own art on the walls, and I was eager to see the paintings of the advanced students. Walking down the hall toward the classroom we passed lots of students from our painting class, many of who knew us both by name, but for once Lucas and I weren't the centre of attention. We barely even merited a glance. Their eyes were glued to the art on the walls as they stood in clumps, evaluating aloud like it was crit day, debating which drawing or painting had the most merit. I couldn't help but feel glad none of my work was on display. It wasn't that I didn't think my paintings would measure up. But I did feel my paintings that year had closed me in, locking me to the past, and I knew I wanted to tackle new subjects now, paint new things. I was ready to look ahead.

The crowded hallway seemed to reassure Lucas as we reached the door to his exam room. I knew he thought I couldn't be in danger when I was surrounded by people. Of course, he wasn't the girl who'd found a note threatening her boyfriend's life in the middle of a busy coffee shop. But I didn't point that out right then.

"Don't go anywhere," Lucas said, pressing a kiss to my lips that started out soft, but deepened as the moments passed. The hallway faded to nothing around us as his arms pulled me closer, his hands roaming dangerously close to my ass.

"I think you're getting a little bit off topic," I said, struggling out of his arms. The students filing into the exam room were either smirking or giving us dirty looks. We were sort of blocking the door.

"Can you blame me?" Lucas murmured. He tried to kiss me again, but I pushed him toward the door.

"Go!" I said. "Exam now. Kisses later." I would have said something a lot dirtier than "kisses," but there was a hallway full of people listening. But Lucas apparently had no such qualms.

"Oh, I plan to do a lot more than kiss you later, trust me," Lucas said, giving me a smoldering look before flashing his dimples and strolling into the classroom, leaving me blushing with desire and embarrassment.

After that, I did get some attention, or as much as a group of preoccupied art nerds could muster. Naomi called me over to examine a black and white photograph of a crowded restaurant. For a short minute everyone wanted my opinion, as if by virtue of being Lucas's girlfriend my thoughts held more weight, but when they found my take on the photo's composition differed from theirs they quickly turned on me and my moment of notoriety was over.

As I wandered away from the fray, my mind drifted back to my call with Emily and I felt the weight of what was coming. Telling my family the truth would be even harder than telling Lucas, not because they were more important to me, but because they were there. They got the call that I was in the hospital and ran to my bedside. They shielded me from the reporters and stood by me through the trial. They were the ones I'd tested my lies on first.

Staring at a charcoal drawing of a swing set in a back

garden, I felt myself growing angry, and for once my anger wasn't aimed at myself. I was angry at the lies themselves and all the chaos they'd caused. I was angry that I'd wasted so much time hating myself. I was angry that now I had to face the prospect of hurting my family again. If Lucas was right and what happened really wasn't my fault, then the only person to blame was the same one I was hiding from. And I was angry about that, too. I was furious with Brandon Tomko for the mess he'd made of all our lives: mine, Tommy's, the Wesleys', his parents', my parents', Emily's, the whole country's.

The door to the art studio at the very end of the hall stood open. Wandering inside, I found my final painting sitting on the easel where I'd left it. In the painting I held Tommy by the hand and the train tracks ran beneath our feet. Tommy was smiling. It was a painting of what might have been, or almost. But there was still that sky above us, filled with threatening clouds to the east, and the figure lurking behind, dressed in black, waiting for just the right moment to spring.

"You did this," I said, my eyes narrowing on that black form, almost melting away to nothing in the trees.

"Keep telling yourself that, Katie Kat," a voice said, and I spun around, flattening myself against the wall so hard I smacked the back of my head. It began to bleat with pain, or maybe that was my internal alarm telling me to run, run, run.

There was nobody there. The studio was empty, and when I stepped out into the hall I saw the other students were still congregated far down at the other end, out of earshot. Nobody was close enough to tell me if they'd heard it, too. Pressing a hand to the back of my head, I backed away from the doorway to the studio, still unsure if I'd imagined it or if Brandon was going to leap out of a shadow. When I hit the opposite wall with my back I staggered. I was having trouble breathing. Air, I needed air.

Pushing through the door to the stairwell, I scrambled down the two flights of stairs and fell out into the night. The wind was blowing harder now, a gale beginning to build, and the air forced its way into my lungs, leaving me gasping. I looked up at the stars as my breathing returned to normal and thought that no matter how many times I painted it I could never really capture the immensity of that sky, or the horror of it. That sky had watched as Brandon had killed Tommy. It had been the only witness. That sky knew the truth.

Truth or lies—that was what it always came down to. My lies or Brandon's truth—neither really covered what happened that day. Maybe no article or painting or piece of testimony ever could. Maybe trying to make right something that was so wrong to begin with was the real problem. No truth I told would ever bring Tommy back. No lie would fill the gaping hole in his mother's heart. Maybe the trick to moving on with your life was saying goodbye.

I closed my eyes and painted myself into the clearing. The train tracks ran ahead of me and behind. The sky was blue and clear. And I was not running or bleeding or crying. I was still. The woods were peaceful, just like I hoped he was. Just like I hoped I would someday be.

"Goodbye, Tommy," I whispered. As I opened my eyes again, a star winked brightly, exactly above my head. I knew it wasn't Tommy, but it made me smile.

"Alone at last," a voice said, and I knew it was him. I would have known that voice anywhere. I'd been hearing it in my dreams for six long years.

Brandon Tomko had found me.

22

My first thought was that he was shorter than he was in my nightmares. We'd been the same height once, and he was taller now, but not by much. I estimated about two inches. That random thought echoed in my brain—*Two inches isn't much*—as he took a step toward me and I could see his face more clearly. Then all the air was sucked out of my lungs and I couldn't breathe. It was as though the world went still—no movement, no sound. There was just Brandon and me and the moment I'd been dreading every day since Tommy Wesley died.

"I've been looking for you everywhere, Katie Kat," Brandon said. His voice was the same, but with a rough quality to it that I associated with worn-out old men. Men who tiredly stalked the woods at night looking for their next victim. Men you didn't want to run into in the dark—oops, too late.

"Really? Seems to me you found me last week," I replied, surprised to find that my voice wasn't shaking, though my hands were. "At least that's the impression I got from the knife you stabbed through my pillow. I'm not the one who's been hiding, Brandon."

He flinched when I said his name, almost as though I'd insulted him. "Well, aren't you lucky," he sneered. "You're free to grab hot chocolate and kiss your boyfriend and take naps in the park and go to class. You don't have to hide. What a great life your lies have bought you."

Take naps in the park? Did he mean the day Lucas and I had visited the basketball court in Christie? Had he followed us there, too?

I tried to stem my panic by wrapping my arms around my stomach tightly, clamping down. It didn't work.

"I lied because I had to," I said.

He chuckled humourlessly. "You had to. How convenient. I guess the fact that your lies threw me to the wolves was just a happy coincidence, then. None of your doing, really. Since you *had* to."

His words sounded so familiar, filled with blame, with reproach. *It's all your fault, Katie*, they hissed. *You're a liar, a coward, a hypocrite, Katie.* All these years I'd thought it was my own voice haunting my thoughts. Now I realized it was Brandon's voice I'd been hearing all along.

"Now who's lying?" I said. "I'm not the reason you were locked away, Brandon. I didn't kill Tommy Wesley, you did."

His eyes burned into me, fixed on my face. His entire demeanour changed, becoming somehow menacing simply by the shifting of his weight, the movement of his shoulders. In that moment, as he stared at me, I began to regret coming out the back door of the building. Though there were campus paths leading off in every direction, all the streets were out of sight. The halls inside the building might have been filled with people, but outside it was quiet, the campus nearly deserted. Nobody could see us right now. I was all alone with him.

"I killed that kid because you asked me to," Brandon said, his voice dead calm.

That did it. Those words. It was the first time I'd heard him admit to it out loud and it woke something up in me.

This was Tommy's killer. I was face-to-face with him. There was nobody around.

He's going to kill me, I thought, amazed that it had taken me this long for the thought to enter my frantic mind. *Unless…*

"Oh, cut the crap, Brandon," I snapped. "We both know that's not true." Those burning eyes flared again and I took a step to the left. I needed to get away from the wall of the building and onto the path. I needed to be as clever as Lucas said I was. I needed a plan.

"You're telling me to cut the crap?" Brandon said. He smiled, and this time it seemed genuine—until I saw the knife in his hand. One look at that knife and any plan I'd been putting together went right out the window. "Why don't you say it again?"

I ran.

Right away I knew I'd taken the wrong path. If I'd turned left around the side of Ontario Hall I would have reached the street in a minute, but instead I went straight on the path that went behind the library. I was aiming for Union Street where I could see a car pulled over and several people getting in. I should have screamed right away, but all I could see was red and all I could think was, *Run.* I could hear the thudding of his boots as he came running after me, both of us pushing against the wind that seemed to want to hold us back. *Run, run, run!* By the time I opened my mouth, the car doors were already slamming shut and I was still ten feet away.

"Wait, I—" I called out before he clamped his hand over my mouth, the rest of my words drowned out by my high-pitched scream.

He pulled me tight against him, yanking me backwards until we were hidden behind one of the building's ornamental buttresses.

He panted into my ear, his breath and body giving off a smell of dirt. It was as though he'd literally just slithered out of a hole in the ground.

His other arm was locked around my middle and I struggled hard against it. Then he raised his hand and the knife glinted in the light from the streetlamp and I fell still, my eyes following the blade. It wasn't the same knife. I knew it couldn't be. But it looked just like it, right down to the colour of the wooden handle. For a moment I imagined I saw a smear of blood across the blade and wondered if it was Tommy's.

"Tell me, Katie," Brandon rasped into my ear, "what was it like waking up to find Tommy's body? I've always wanted to know. I couldn't watch, of course. I had to disappear. But I wish I could have been there to see you discover my present."

I closed my eyes in disgust. The smell of dirt got stronger, filling my nose and mouth, pressing into my throat. Then I realized it wasn't dirt I was smelling at all. It was the smell of the woods.

I open my eyes to the fireflies. They swim across my vision, their blinking lights making me think of flashlights bobbing through the trees, of rescue. But there is no one coming.

Pushing myself up on my knees, I feel warm wetness running down my face and wipe it away. It's too dark for me to see my own blood. I can't see anything at all except the fireflies. I can't hear anything but my own hectic breathing, and that's how I know I'm alone.

I need to find Tommy.

Swaying on my feet and stumbling repeatedly, I walk down the tracks in the direction I think will take me to the street. I'll get some help and come back. I'll bring the police and those huge spotlights. I'll bring dogs and helicopters. I'll find Tommy. I'll find him in time.

I throw up once, then again. I'm off balance and my right arm feels weirdly heavy, but I ignore all this. I know I have to keep moving. I have to get help.

Then I slip in something slick and fall on my knees, gasping loudly. A rail cuts into my shin. I move my hand and it sinks into something I cannot describe. Something wet and a little gooey. Something that was warm a little while ago. Something I don't understand until my fingers run over the long, soft fur and I realize it's not fur at all. It's his hair.

As I run I scream his name.

I whimpered and kicked at Brandon with my feet, wrenching against his grip even as he pressed the blade to my cheek. I needed to get away from him and his smell. I needed to get away from that night more than anything.

"What was it like going to school and walking the halls, everyone feeling sorry for you, when you knew you were to blame? And on TV, watching me get labelled the Kindergarten Killer when you knew, you knew…"

He pressed the tip of the knife into my cheek, twisting it ever so slightly, and I felt it break the skin. His hand smothered my screams.

"What was it like to get away with it, Katie Kat? Tell me, because I'll never know. Did it feel like this?" He moved the knife to the other cheek and again I felt the blade twisting, cutting. My blood was running down my neck. I could smell it.

"Or like this?" The knife disappeared and instead I felt his clumsy fingers groping at my breast, a hard and cruel jab that felt nothing like Lucas's gentle hands. The revulsion that wracked my body snapped me back into the present, and the same instinct that had taken over that day so long ago took over once more: animal fear.

I sank my teeth into his hand.

He howled and released my mouth, but unlike that fateful day six years ago, he didn't let me go. I guessed that was a lesson he didn't need to learn twice. His right arm held me around my ribs with a brutal strength that terrified me more than the knife. If he could hold a full-grown woman with just one arm, what could he do with two?

"Hel—" I cried, but again my plea was cut off when he grabbed my entire face with the hand I'd just bitten, smearing his blood across my nose and mouth. He pressed his palm so hard into my face that for a moment I couldn't breathe.

Then he said a single word into my ear before shoving me roughly to the side, releasing his hold on me. My hair whipped around my head as I backed away from him on wobbly legs, uncomprehending. His burning eyes bored into me as he repeated the word, louder this time, commanding me: "Run!" And this time I did as I was told.

He wasn't letting me go. I knew this as I ran down the path with more speed than I'd ever imagined my body could muster.

This was what he'd done to Tommy. He hadn't killed him right away, that wasn't his style. He'd made his first cut and then he'd made him run. He'd even given him a head start. He'd made Tommy run for his life and now he was doing the same to me, knowing he would catch me, knowing he was faster. But that wasn't the point. The running was the point.

Because Brandon loved the chase.

Think, I urged myself, *think of a plan. Lucas says you're clever, so think. You're smarter than he is. You can do this. Think!*

Already I could hear him coming after me, though he was grunting and his steps were uneven. Maybe I'd injured one of his legs when I'd kicked him.

Get to people, I thought frantically. *Get to safety. Call for help!*

I ran up the stone steps onto the landing behind the library and threw myself at the wooden doors, but they were locked. Going back down the stairs would have brought me back toward Brandon, so instead I climbed over the balustrade and leaped the four feet to the ground. In front of me was the side of Ontario Hall, the light falling through the windows of the corner classroom where Lucas was taking his exam on the second floor. *Lucas*. But I remembered now that those back doors locked when they closed, too. I'd have to go around the front.

Adrenaline pumped through my veins as I shot toward the street. I couldn't hear Brandon behind me, but I wasn't stupid enough to think that I'd lost him this quickly. He was stalking me. He was watching. As I rounded the side of the building I looked up and down University Avenue, desperately searching for someone, anyone who could help me, but the street was empty and silent as the grave. Where was campus security when you needed them? Then I remembered—my phone!

Luckily, I hadn't dropped my bag because it was strapped across my body. As I continued toward the stairs leading into Ontario Hall, I reached into my bag and rustled through my junk, searching for my cell phone. I could call campus security myself. They'd be here in minutes. And Lucas was right upstairs. I wasn't going to die. Not today. Not now.

But where was it? Panting as I reached the bottom of the stairs, I plunged both hands into my messenger bag, emptying my wallet, an umbrella, paintbrushes, and my sketchbook onto the ground, but I couldn't find my phone anywhere. Had Lucas taken it when we'd left the apartment? Had I left it behind?

"You've sure gotten an awful lot of texts from an unknown number," Brandon said.

My head snapped up as he rounded the low wrought-iron fence and stepped toward me, my cell phone in his hand. He must have slipped it out of my bag when he was holding me. He paged through the messages, his face contorted with mock concern.

"Some of these are absolutely appalling! You really should be careful who you give your number out to," Brandon warned. "There are all kinds of crazies out there."

"You don't say," I shot back then turned and began to run up the stairs. I thought I could make it. The beckoning light of the front doors was only a few feet away, but he was on me before I'd even made it to the top. In a blink I was dragged backwards down the steps and thrown down onto the cement. I landed hard onto of my bag, momentarily glad I'd just emptied it. Then he yanked my head up by my hair and I screeched as pain seared through my hairline.

"I have to say I expected more from you, Katie," Brandon said, his lips against my ear. "Is this all the fight you have in you? Haven't you been anticipating this moment for the past six years? Is this really the best you can do?"

You can do this, Katie. You're strong. You're smart. Don't let him do this to you twice. You can think your way out of this.

"Isn't that how you like them?" I said. "Weak and small? Just like Tommy. I'm just trying to give you what you want."

Baiting him had seemed like a good idea until he yanked on my hair with a growl and I regretted it with every fibre of my being. Grabbing me by my collar with his other hand, he pulled me up to my feet then kicked me in the back, causing me to fall forward onto my knees again. In desperation I began to crawl forward and I heard him chuckling at me. He thought I was easy prey, a weak and cowardly girl he could stalk and torture and kill, taking my life just as he'd taken Tommy's, without much hassle, without even breaking a sweat. Listening to him laughing at my fear, I decided I had to get back at him for what he'd done to me. Even if he was going to kill me, he would pay first. I'd make him pay even if it was the last thing I did. I had to do this. For the little girl I had been, now lost forever. For all the people whose lives he'd ruined.

For Tommy.

Scrambling to my feet, I spun around to face him. The knife was in his hand again. He was getting ready to finish things off. To finish me.

"You killed Tommy for me, huh?" I said, backing toward the line of trees that separated the buildings.

"You know I did," Brandon answered. I could see the creases lining his forehead as he scowled at me. This was no twelve-year-old boy. He was a full-grown man now. A full-grown monster. But even monsters had their weaknesses.

"Pretty romantic," I said. "What was it like sitting in that cell, knowing the girl you loved enough to kill for didn't love you back? I mean, I denied even knowing you. I testified that I'd never seen you before in my life. That's gotta sting."

Brandon shook his head. "You think I've been pining for you all these years, just waiting to get out so we could be together again? Don't make me laugh. Any feelings I had ran out long ago, Katie Kat. I spent those years planning out this moment. I've been dreaming about watching you die ever since I made the mistake of letting you go that day. I never make the same mistake twice."

We reached the trees and I backed under them. Brandon's face fell into shadow as he continued to advance on me, his eyes little pinpoints of light in the dark.

"Kind of seems like a waste of time, though, doesn't it?" I said, tripping over one of the cement borders that circled the trees, but righting myself before he could reach me. "All those years of your life spent locked away, all for nothing."

"Oh, I wouldn't call it nothing," Brandon said. "Killing can be its own reward."

As the horror of that statement sank in, he began to advance more quickly and I struggled to keep ahead of him. There was a large field coming up behind me and I was counting on his not wanting to attack me out in the open. It seemed like a major murderer no-no, but Brandon didn't really seem like the type to follow the rules.

I wished I had my bat. Risking a glance behind, I looked around wildly for anything I could use as a weapon. The wind was really picking up now, tearing petals off the crocuses and sending stray plastic bags and twigs flying around our heads. I began to hope for a lightning strike.

"Killing me will make as little sense as killing Tommy," I said quickly as we stepped into the field. "Nobody will understand why you did it. They'll all still think you're the Kindergarten Killer. Is that what you want to be known for, murder with no motive? They'll call you deranged. They'll put you in the psych ward again."

"You're right. I guess I'll have to leave a note explaining things," Brandon said. He lunged forward all of a sudden and I shrieked as he grabbed my arm. "Should I carve it into your arm? Or maybe your stomach—bigger canvas."

Suddenly the sky opened up and the rain came down in a sheet, drenching us both in seconds. At the same moment Brandon leaped toward me and I found myself on my back on the slick grass as thunder rolled. My glasses were thrown off and though I felt around on the ground, I couldn't find them. It was almost better this way. Now he was nothing but a dark figure looming over me, the figure from my painting, the villain of my story brandishing his knife.

This is how Tommy died, I thought.

"Are you looking forward to being cut open?" Brandon taunted. He pressed a knee into my sternum, securing me in place as he trailed the tip of his knife down my neck. His other hand pressed me into the ground at the shoulder, heavy as a brick. "It seems fitting, doesn't it? Since it was your idea."

I tried to scratch his face, but it was just inches out of reach. Reaching helplessly, I began to realize that this was it. This was the moment. This was my last chance. I was going to die here in the mud. Unless…unless…unless…

A wave of unbelievable sorrow threatened to pull me down as I thought of Lucas finding me here, just as I'd found Tommy. I thought of my mother getting another horrifying phone call. I thought of my sister lost without her twin. I thought of all the paintings I would never paint, the things I would never do, the life I would never lead with Lucas.

Be strong. Be clever. Make him pay. Think of something. Think!

Brandon cut open my jacket, the knife blade slashing easily through the material. I felt the rain pattering against my bare upper chest.

"Now, where to start…" he muttered.

"I loved you once," I blurted out, gripping the hand that held the knife with both of my own, trying to stop its progress. "The little girl you met in the woods is still inside me, just like that boy is still inside you. I loved you and you killed Tommy and it ruined everything!"

"I killed him for you!" Brandon yelled, his mouth inches from my face. "I killed him to make you happy. I killed him to make you love me!"

He jammed the knife into the grass right beside my head.

"You're the one who changed your mind," Brandon went on, gripping my face with both hands. "You're the one who ruined it. I did my part!"

There was a terrible *crack* as a tree branch buckled in the gale and slammed to the ground to my right. When I swung my eyes back to Brandon he had the knife in his hand again, and though I couldn't see his expression I knew it was filled with hate.

Last chance.

"But you killed the wrong boy!" I screamed. I watched the hand that held the knife falter, his grip on my shoulder shifting. "It was Ricky I hated, Ricky I complained about. But you went and killed Tommy. I loved Tommy. He was sweet and he was only five years old and he didn't deserve to die. I told you. I told you it was the wrong boy but you went ahead and killed him anyway!"

He didn't know. For all these years he hadn't had any idea. Even though I'd told him that day that Tommy wasn't Ricky, my words hadn't gotten through to him, or he'd really believed I was lying, or maybe he'd blocked them out. Whatever the reason, I'd shocked him. I heard him breathing hard above me as he tried to work it out and I turned my heard slightly, eyeing that fallen branch.

If he would only move his knee...

He said, "But you—"

"You want to know why I turned on you, Brandon?" I interrupted. "You want to know why I told the court all those lies?"

He seemed to have forgotten what he'd been about to do. The knife dangled in his fingers as he stared down at me. I couldn't exactly see, but I thought his mouth was hanging open.

"I said what I did because when you killed Tommy Wesley you broke my heart," I cried.

I would never know if Brandon Tomko had ever really loved me, or if he'd just thought he did. But I knew in that moment that the idea of killing for me, like some deranged chivalrous knight, was the thing he cherished most of all. I knew this because it was the reason Tommy Wesley died. And it was also the thing that saved me.

As Brandon's body sagged under the weight of my confession, he fell back, lifting his weight off of me. I saw my chance. Scrambling out from underneath him, I sprang forward and dug my thumbs into his eye sockets, making him scream. I was screaming, too. He tried to swipe at me with his arms, but I darted out of his reach and ran for the broken tree branch.

"You're lying," Brandon cried, slashing the air with his knife. His eyes were running with blood, but he rose up onto his knees, getting ready to come after me. "You stupid, lying bitch! I don't believe a word of it. You're a liar!"

"No, I'm not," I said, and I swung the tree branch, just like a bat, right into his head.

There weren't many people left in the hallway, but they all parted to let me pass. Their gasps swept around me as I spotted Lucas standing with a group of other students from his class. I watched him turn, his curious expression changing to shock as he took in the sight of me, soaking wet, dripping blood.

"K-Katie," Lucas choked out as I reached him. His hands moved automatically to the bloody mess of my face, but he hesitated, seemingly unsure of how to touch me without hurting me.

I gazed up into those beautiful, honey-coloured eyes I'd thought I would never see again.

Lucas.

"It's over," I said, and I could see all the questions crowding his mind.

There would be time for them later. Right now there was only one thing I wanted. "Kiss me," I said, raising my face to his.

I knew he really loved me when, even though I was covered in blood, he didn't hesitate to press his lips to mine.

23

After the sirens and the ambulance and the police with all their questions, after the paramedics checking me over and dodging the reporters and telling the whole story to Lucas, after showering away the blood and crying in Lucas's arms and sitting for an hour numbly staring at nothing, I picked up the phone to call my parents. It was a short conversation. I told them I was fine, that Brandon was back in custody and would likely be facing time in prison. And I told them we needed to talk.

"What is it, Kaitlyn?" my dad said, his voice taking on a particular timbre that implied this was a moment he'd been expecting. That was a surprise.

My mother, on the other hand, seemed only to inflate with accusatory alarm. "Talk about what? What else could there possibly be to talk about? What did you do?" she demanded. Mom could always be counted upon to be consistent.

"I'll see you guys tomorrow," I said, my eyes lifting to Lucas's face. He was sitting right next to me, holding my hand. Without him there I might not have been able to get out the rest. "I'll explain everything."

I ended the call and stared down at the phone in my hand. Why was it that even though I'd faced Brandon, even though I'd fought for my life and won, I still felt like the worst was yet to come?

"After you do this, it'll be finished," Lucas said. "You'll be able to put it all behind you." He ran a finger across my jaw, careful to avoid the bandage covering my cheek, and tipped up my chin. "You can do this, Katie."

"I know I can," I answered, "because you're coming with me."

We left Kingston at ten a.m. and, due to the time change, even though we'd flown seven hours total with a connection in Toronto, it was still early afternoon when we walked up the winding driveway to my parents' house. I pretended not to notice Lucas's gaping stare as we walked up the front steps—it was a big house. Not mansion big, but pretty grand nonetheless. It was one detail that hadn't come up in any of our conversations about my past. Being a little rich girl wasn't something I liked to gush about.

As we stood in front of the enormous wooden double doors I noticed that Lucas looked a little green and stopped myself from ringing the bell.

"Are you going to puke?" I asked him. I sort of wanted him to say yes because I was feeling pretty pukey myself. Misery loves company.

Lucas swallowed, steadying himself against the wall of the house. "No," he said. Then, with less confidence: "Maybe."

He leaned over with his hands on his knees and I ran my hand over his hair, happy to be comforting someone else for a change. I had the feeling I would be getting a whole lot of sympathy in the coming weeks. Just the idea of it upped my pukey quotient by half.

"Is this a 'first time flying in a plane' thing, or a 'meeting the parents' thing?" I asked as Lucas stood up again. His face seemed to be returning to its natural colour, but even green he was still startlingly gorgeous. I tried not to hold it against him.

"Flying," he answered. "Although, now that you mention it, I'm not feeling too good about the other thing, either." He stared at the doors with a worried look on his face, which was pretty adorable.

"They're going to love you," I told him. "Or they'll be so busy screaming at me they'll barely notice you. Either way, I think you're good."

"If I can sit drinking a Diet Coke while travelling at eight hundred kilometers per hour, ten thousand meters above the ground—which I'd just like to point out again is against nature—you can do this."

"I told you not to read the airline magazine."

"I thought it was a good alternative to crying like a baby," Lucas replied.

I sighed. Now I was the one staring at the doors. "I keep trying to think of the right way to tell them, like if I pick the right words everything will turn out okay. But there are no right words to explain this. Then I start trying to think of the best route back to the airport." I gave him a sheepish look then averted my gaze. I knew I sounded like a coward.

"You're scared," Lucas said, looping his arms around my waist, "and flying makes me want to pee my pants. So let's not try to pretend otherwise. Let's just be scared together."

I pressed my face into his chest and closed my eyes. "So if I burst into tears you're saying you'll cry along with me?"

"Uh, sure," Lucas said uncertainly. Then he whispered in my ear, "But could we try to avoid that? I'm trying to make a good impression here."

I grinned up at him and gave him a chaste kiss on the lips. I wanted more—when it came to Lucas I always wanted more—but getting caught making out on my parents' front porch wasn't the way I wanted to start this particular visit.

"Are my bandages okay?" I said, touching my cheeks with both hands. I hadn't warned my family about the injuries to my face, and I knew they'd be getting a lot of attention. We'd tried to cut the gauze as small as possible that morning, but there was no hiding the fact that I would have scars. I also had some bruising around my nose and mouth in the places where Brandon had held my face. Basically, I looked like someone had tried to kill me, and given the conversation I was about to have I figured there was no point in trying to cover it up with makeup. Today was a day for the brutal truth.

Lucas fingered the medical tape on my cheek gingerly. "You look beautiful," he said, but there was sadness in his voice.

It was going to take some time before Lucas stopped blaming himself for leaving me alone while he took his exam. We were all going to need some time to heal.

"Well, it's now or never, I guess," I said. He gave my hand a quick squeeze and I was about to ring the doorbell when I realized I had my keys and unlocked the door myself instead. "Remember," I whispered quickly to Lucas, "my dad doesn't know anything about sports and if my mother terrifies you, that's normal."

"Got it," Lucas whispered back a second before the door separating the front hall from the house burst open and Emily threw herself into my arms.

"Oh my God!" she cried when she saw the bandages on my face. Then she burst into tears. Lucas and I exchanged a look. "I can't believe this happened! Did he really try to kill you, like actually kill you? Anita said there were cops all over campus. Did he really try to chop off your head with an *axe*?" She screeched the last word.

As we walked toward the kitchen, my sister recounted several other stories she'd read about my run-in with Brandon. The journalists were already getting everything wrong, as usual. I was surprised they weren't camped out on the front lawn, though Em did mention they'd been calling the house non-stop since the break of dawn. My father had unplugged the phones by breakfast time.

I took Em by the shoulders, looking her in the eye. I said, "There was no axe, no noose dangling from a tree, no array of

knives to torture me with. My life is not a horror movie."
Actually, it kind of was, but this wasn't the moment to bring it
up.

"But he tried to cut your face in half?" Emily said, reaching
up to touch my bandages but shying away at the last moment,
he finger left hanging in the air.

"Tried and failed," Lucas piped up, and Em spun around,
startled. He gave her a winning smile.

"Oh, Lucas. You're here," she said then looked back at me.
"You sure you want to bring him into the mix *today*?" she said
in a typical Emily not-quite-a-whisper voice.

"I'm sure," I said, threading my fingers with his. I felt
reassured just having his tall body standing next to me.

Emily eyed our linked hands and our faces then gave me an
unreadable look. Our conversation on the phone came back to
me. It was a distant memory to me, since the whole life-in-
danger episode had happened between then and now, but it
occurred to me that it was the last time we'd spoken, and it had
been just yesterday evening. I wondered when time would start
to make sense again.

"You knew this was going to happen, didn't you?" Em said,
her tone hard as stone. "That night when you freaked
out…you knew Brandon was coming for you."

It was so hard to look her in the eye, but I did it. "There's a
lot I didn't tell you. I know that's hard to hear—"

"Mom and Dad are on the deck," she said abruptly, then
walked quickly through the kitchen and out the door to the
backyard, letting it slam closed behind her.

I sighed hard and turned away from the bank of windows
that took up most of the back wall of the kitchen. I could just
make out my mother sitting in a patio chair. How was I going
to face her?

Lucas put an arm around me and I leaned into his side.
"Weak," I said.

"Strong," he said.

"Liar," I said.

"Survivor," he said.

"Unforgiveable," I said.

"Loved," he said, and kissed me on the top of the head.

It was like the break in a boxing match. With Lucas in my corner, I felt ready to face round two.

The scene on the back deck was exactly what I'd expected: my mother at the patio table under the umbrella, surrounded by case folders, cartons of documents piled beside her chair; my father lying in a reclining lawn chair in full sun beside her, a biography of Sherman sitting open on his stomach. It was still a little early in the season to be lounging on the deck—they were both wearing thick sweaters and holding steaming cups of coffee—but small concerns like the weather never stopped the Archers. The only difference from the usual scene was the fact that my father was gazing morosely at the yellow blooms of a forsythia bush instead of sleeping, and instead of taking diligent notes my mother's pen was still capped. There was also Emily leaning tensely against the deck railing looking furious. Hanging out on the deck with Mom and Dad wasn't exactly Emily's style. I actually couldn't remember the last time we'd all sat and had a conversation together, any kind of conversation. Well, our first try sure was going to be a doozy.

"Hi, Mom," I said as we stepped onto the deck. My mother just stared at me. It was my father who leaped to his feet and gently cupped my cheeks, his long-fingered hands engulfing my face just as they had when I was little.

"No," he said, and in that one word I heard his heart breaking. "No, no, no. Not your lovely face."

"I'm okay, Dad," I said, giving him a hug. Lucas's arms were magic, but nothing could compare to a hug from my dad. "I got away."

"Of course you did, my smart girl," he said, holding me at arm's length. His eyes were watery, but I was impressed to see he was holding back the tears. "We Archers are tough. We know how to fight." This was amusing, given the fact that I didn't think my bookish father had ever been in a fight in his life.

"Come let me see," my mother commanded in her no-nonsense voice. I sat down in the chair next to hers and let her peel off the bandages and assess the wounds.

She didn't speak for several moments and she didn't try to hold me, but I could see her concern in the way she sighed and bit her lip and re-taped the gauze so carefully. Her dark eyes explored every inch of my face as though trying to reassure herself that there were no other wounds I was hiding. I wasn't looking forward to breaking the news that my worst wounds weren't on my face.

"You should take the bandages off completely when it's scabbed over," she said with the confidence of a mother. "Daddy can take you to see his plastic surgeon friend in the city in a few weeks about the scarring."

I nodded to show I understood, but I wasn't so sure about it. Sometimes scars were a good reminder of what you'd been through and what you would never do again.

They wanted to know all the details of Brandon's attack and my escape and his arrest and I filled them in as best I could, much as it pained me. My father kept saying the words, "But he's locked up now," as if to reassure me—or himself—that the danger had passed, that I'd survived. Again. My mother listened very closely to my every word and I could see her lawyer's brain going through the next steps, envisioning the upcoming court dates. I left it to her. Personally, I didn't want to think about it, not until I had to.

Though I could see Emily trying not to cry when I described the moment when Brandon pulled out his knife, otherwise she didn't react at all.

I'd almost forgotten Lucas was there when my mother suddenly said, "And who's this young man who wandered outside with you? Did you hire yourself a bodyguard?"

"Not a bad idea," I heard my father mutter. He didn't seem to be kidding.

Lucas was leaning against the railing next to my sister, looking like he felt incredibly out of place. I shot out of my chair and took his arm, shooting him an apologetic look.

"Mom, Dad, this is Lucas," I said, "my…boyfriend." As Lucas shook their hands, calling them Mr. and Mrs. Archer, which really seemed to impress my father, I glanced at Emily, trying to gauge her reaction. But she was staring steadily out at the covered pool.

"Well, Lucas *Matthews*," my mother began, emphasizing the last name she'd pried out of me weeks before on the phone, "where on earth were you when all this was happening?" She gestured at my face.

"Mom!" I cried. Five seconds. After meeting someone for the first time, my mother always gave them at least five full seconds before pouncing. She was considerate that way. "What are you talking about? That doesn't even make sense."

Lucas went very still as I looked to my father for help. Not that he was ever any help when my mother was concerned. He shrugged and pointed at her, as if to say, *What can I do?*

"She has every right to ask," Lucas said to me. "I was taking an exam when Katie was attacked. I'll never forgive myself for not being there."

"This isn't your fault. Not even a little. Not in any way," I protested. "It's not your responsibility to keep me safe."

"Yes it is!" Lucas said loudly enough to make us all stare. "That's what it means to love someone. You keep them safe. You take care of them. Always."

I could see my mother's raised eyebrows at his use of the word "love," and then I saw her gaze moving over to me.

"Well, I won't have it," I said. "I'm not going to let Brandon Tomko hurt anyone else that I care about. I'm not going to let him take anyone else away from me."

"Who's he taken from you, darling?" my mother asked.

"Tommy," my father answered.

"Yeah, Tommy," I said, "and, in a way, he took me, too." Their puzzled looks said it all. The time had come to fill in the blanks. I was ready to put my days of lying behind me. I was ready to tell. "There's something I need to tell you guys, something I should have told you a long time ago. It's big."

"How big?" Emily said.

So big I don't know how to start. So big I'm afraid it will change everything. So big I can't hold it in anymore.

"Six years big," I answered.

Lucas and I sat down at the table with Mom, and then Dad and Emily joined us. It was nice to see all the people I loved in one place like that. Too bad it had to happen now, right before I gave them the news that would tear us apart.

I was glad to have told the same story to Lucas just a few days before, to have those words to guide me, because without them I would have been lost. I started again with Ricky and Tommy and the babysitting job I wished I'd never had, then went on from there. I was proudest of the fact that I didn't cry when I came to the moment when I found Tommy's mangled body—probably because I'd cried so much the night before—though the looks on my parents' faces almost pushed me over the edge. Then came the trial and my many, many lies, and the fallout that took me through high school. My mother kept flinching as I described my terrible depression. My father held his head in his hands.

I watched their horror grow when I began to describe Brandon's harassment during the lead-up to his release. Only when I explained it did I realize I'd never found out from him who had made that first post and sent all those texts. I decided then and there to let that mystery die. I didn't want to spend the rest of my life looking over my shoulder, searching for Brandon's accomplices.

Once I reached the events of the night before, my father was weeping. Even Lucas had closed his eyes. Only my mother was still staring at me, following every word. But there were no more words. I'd said it all.

I took a few deep breaths, staring through the glass tabletop at my feet, before meeting their eyes. Under the table, Lucas put his hand on my leg and squeezed.

"Why didn't you tell us?" Dad said, his eyes bloodshot. In his tone I heard a combination of despair and outrage, as though he wanted to scream at me but didn't have the heart.

"Didn't you trust me? I could've... I would've..." He trailed off, his thoughts caught up in all the things he could have and would have done, if he'd known.

"I was afraid," I said. A tear rolled down my cheek. "I couldn't face it. I was only thirteen. I thought I was to blame because I'd said all those terrible things about Ricky. Even if Brandon killed the wrong boy, it still felt as though it was my fault. And then once I'd told all those lies—"

"But it wasn't your fault," my mother said forcefully, cutting me off. "No, you were just a girl. *I* was the mother. *I* should have seen the truth..."

"No, Mom, don't—" I implored, but there was no stopping her now.

"I knew," she said, nodding her head. "I knew something was the matter. You changed so suddenly and you had this look in your eyes all the time. A mother knows." She was wringing her hands. "I didn't want to see it. I wanted you to be stronger than it, to beat it. But you were just a girl and I should have been there for you. To think of what you went through while I was off in court, fighting for other people's daughters. I should have been fighting for you!" My father was talking to her in low tones, trying to reason with her, but she was beyond reason now. "No, *you* told me," she said to my father. "You saw it, too. But Dr. Lepore...he was nothing. We should have taken her to the best therapist in the city. We should have tried harder. I should have made her tell me!"

She began to weep. My steadfast, indomitable mother who never cried, ever. I'd broken her.

"I'm sorry, darling," she sobbed. "I'm sorry!"

Her face was buried in my father's shoulder, but she reached blindly for my hand and I caught it, too shocked to do anything else. I looked at Lucas, my mouth hanging open. I'd imagined this conversation a thousand times in my head. I'd expected screams, accusations, even contempt. I'd expected her to be outraged at my perjury on the stand. Never once had I imagined this.

"You're *sorry?*" Emily cried, jumping to her feet so quickly her chair fell over behind her. Her eyes were rimmed with red, her cheeks pink with emotion.

Oh no, Em, I thought. *Not you. You're the one who's always on my side. You're the one who loves me no matter what.*

Her lips quivered as she stared down at me. "You've been lying to me about this for *six years*? What happened to 'twins tell each other everything?' How could you keep this from me?"

I looked at her beseechingly. "I-I wanted to tell you, but—"

"Brandon was your boyfriend? Brandon's been stalking you? Brandon killed Tommy because you told him to? Who *are* you? You are not my sister. That is not my sister's life!" She smacked her hand down on the table so hard the umbrella shook above us.

"Emmy," Dad said, a warning tone in his voice, "you have to think of what she went through. Think of it from her point of view."

"I *am* her point of view!" Emily shrieked. I don't think anyone at the table understood what she meant, but I did. We were sisters, twins. She'd followed me to Queen's without a second thought. I texted her every day. Her friends became my friends. We defended each other, pulled for each other. When we were little we believed we had the same thoughts. She was mine and I was hers, but I'd betrayed that. It was an epic breach of trust.

I could say nothing in my own defence.

"It tore her apart to lie to you about it," Lucas said, "you more than anyone else."

"You don't know anything about it," Em said, holding up her hand as if to block him out entirely. "You've been in her life for, what? The past five seconds? I've been hers since birth!"

"But I saw it right away when she told me," Lucas persisted. "You were the one—"

"You told *him* before *me*?" Em said, and this time I had to meet her eyes, to see the tears coursing down her cheeks. She was slipping out of my grasp. I couldn't take the coward's way out and shut my eyes as I lost my only sister. "I will never forgive you for this," she said. Then she turned and ran into the house. We could all hear her crying loudly through the open door as she made her way up to her room.

"You know how she is," my mother said as she wiped at her smeared mascara. "She'll cry it out and then she'll come around."

"I'll talk to her," Dad said. "It'll be fine."

But I wasn't so sure. Neither of them knew Em the way I did. I'd seen her hold a grudge for years over a suspected stolen hairbrush. It had seemed funny then; we'd laughed about it together, back when we were always on the same side.

My parents wanted me to stay the night in my old room. They offered to make up the guest room for Lucas. But I couldn't stand the thought of spending the night listening to my sister bawling in the next room, or to be separated from Lucas by an entire hallway. When I told them Lucas would be getting a motel room and I'd be going with him, my father cleared his throat and wandered off into the dining room. Shockingly, it was my mother who seemed to understand that I needed Lucas that night. Maybe it was the way Dad had held her as she'd cried that made her see that sometimes closeness is something you need more than anything else.

"You go, darling," she said, pressing a wad of bills into my hands. "Go with him, as long as you promise to come back."

"I'll always come back, Mom," I said. "Thank you...for surprising me."

"Thank you for giving me the chance," she said.

We left them with promises to talk more, share more, tell more. I knew telling the story was just the beginning, that their anger toward me might still be waiting in the wings. The road to the truth would be a long one, but we were on it now. I'd put us on it.

As the cab pulled away from my parents' house, I saw Emily peering out at me from her bedroom window. She didn't wave.

I was right. Telling the truth was exactly like setting off a bomb. We'd all survived, all except Em, who would struggle through the night on life support as we all waited, as I waited, to see if she would come back to me.

24

We checked into the most expensive hotel I could think of. In her emotional state, I think my mother had pressed a few more bills than she intended into my hand, but I had no qualms about spending them. *I* was spent. I wanted to sleep the night in two-hundred-dollar sheets and order way overpriced room service and bathe in a tub so big I could swim in it. I wanted to indulge my every whim. So that's what we did.

Lucas kept talking about the size of my parents' house. I hadn't really told him how wealthy they were, mainly due to my mother's practice. He acted impressed, but I think he really just wanted to take my mind off of Emily.

"How many bathrooms are there, again?" he asked as we dug into our room service meal. He'd ordered a fancy burger and I'd ordered filet mignon, which came with a baked potato that was carved in the shape of a rose and carrot slivers woven into a basket.

"Four," I replied, "one for each of us. And of course they each have their own attendant. Mine is named Pierre."

Lucas swallowed and wiped his mouth. "Don't ever tell your parents I share a bathroom with twenty other guys, okay?" he said.

"I was kidding about the attendants," I said, though I was pretty sure he already knew it. "My parents aren't snobs. Em and I used to say..."

I stared down at my food, my appetite disappearing. This has happened several times already. Just the thought of Emily brought the conversation to a screeching halt.

Lucas set the metal cover on top of my plate. "Let's watch some TV," he said gently, taking me by the hand and leading me over to the gigantic bed.

We snuggled up together, leaning back against the pillows and switched on the flat screen, which took up the better part of the wall. Lucas began swiftly clicking through the channels, but, naturally, every station was showing the same thing. Of course, I should have known. I was the one who'd been through all of this before. The country had been waiting six years for a new story about the Kindergarten Killer. My life would be the top story for months to come.

"I'll turn it off," Lucas said, but I stilled his hand.

"No, leave it," I said. I'd been hiding from the news for so long, averting my eyes from the headlines, depriving myself of music to avoid hearing the top story update at the end of the hour on the radio. It was a stupid way to live, and I'd resolved to stop letting Brandon's actions make me do stupid things. "It's about me, isn't it? We might as well hear what they're saying."

There she was, Leslie Wong, looking exactly the same as she had when I was thirteen, her shoulder-length hair perfectly coiffed, the teeth perfectly straight. To me, the sound of her voice was like nails being dragged down a chalkboard, but I tried to remind myself that it wasn't Leslie's fault that she'd joined the news team the year my life went to hell. As the camera zoomed out I realized Leslie was standing on University Avenue, the fluttering yellow police tape behind her cordoning off the pathway between Ontario and Grant Halls.

"Isn't that your apartment building?" Lucas said. We both leaned toward the TV as Leslie's voice-over played against footage of my building.

"This apartment complex is where victim Katie Archer had been living a quiet life at school until the Kindergarten Killer, now known as Brandon Tomko, came back into her life and tried to take it a second time. Though Katie and her family have been following their 'no comment' rule established six years ago, her friends were quick to comment about the character of the girl we all knew as 'the babysitter.'"

The face of Pompous Guy from my art class filled the screen and I quickly reached forward and muted the TV before we could hear whatever nonsense he was telling the world about me. I'd never had a conversation with him in my life.

Lucas was still gaping at the television like he couldn't believe his eyes. I remembered that feeling. As a seasoned victim of the media, I shot right into action. Grabbing my phone—which I now saw had thirty-seven recorded voicemails—I left a quick message on Mariella's machine apologizing for disappearing without filling her in and telling her I was fine and not to talk to any reporters. I sent similar texts to Em's friends, though I was pretty sure they'd all gone home by now. It was lucky the semester was over. The journalists would be hard-pressed to find someone to give them a sound bite about me, which explained how they'd landed on Pompous Guy.

"You should call any friends who you know are still on campus," I said to Lucas as I scanned through my insanely long list of missed calls. Where exactly had the journalists gotten my number? "If they're talking to random people from our class, they know we're together. I hope you're ready for the spotlight."

"Don't think that," Lucas said, pulling the phone out of my hand and tossing it across the bed.

"Hey!" I cried. "What? Think what?"

He turned off the TV and then tugged me onto his lap. I hooked my legs around his waist and laid my head against his chest, marveling at how perfectly we fit together in this position. Though my head was full of racing thoughts, I wasn't too preoccupied to notice that certain very sensitive parts of our bodies were touching, causing a little flame to ignite in my centre, its heat rolling through my body.

"You're thinking that I'm probably having second thoughts about you now that our relationship is going to be broadcast to the world," he said into my ear. That was pretty much what I had been thinking, though now my thoughts had wandered to other things. "But don't think that. I don't care about any of it. I just want to be with you. Okay?"

"Okay," I said weakly. He ran his hands up and down my back. He was trying to be comforting, I knew. I was sure he had no idea the reaction my body was having to his touch. It was as though a growling animal had been awakened inside of me, and she wanted to be fed.

"Why don't I run you a bath," Lucas said, delicately kissing my cheeks and pulling out of my arms.

I flung myself back on the bed as I heard him turn on the water in the bathroom. Maybe a bath would do me good, help me clear my head and focus on what was important instead of the sex-crazed thoughts that had invaded my mind as if from nowhere. Or maybe all that hot, sudsy water would only inflame my burgeoning libido. I groaned softly to myself as I pulled my hair up into a bun.

Get control of yourself, Archer, I commanded. *You are not a sex monster.*

Except this was a whole new world and a whole new Katie Archer, wasn't it? Who the hell knew what I was.

Lucas gave me another one of those frustratingly chaste kisses before leaving me alone in the bathroom to undress. I wanted to ask him to stay with me, to get into the bath with me, to do ungodly things to me with his insanely chiseled body, but instead I let him go. I had to get a grip on myself. Getting my freak on on the same day I broke my sister's heart was way inappropriate. Besides, my body had just been through a terrible ordeal. I needed time to recover, no matter what my loins were telling me.

I took of my clothes and stood in front of the mirror as I peeled the bandages off of my face. Mom was right; they were starting to scab. I could probably leave the bandages off tomorrow.

As I gazed at my ravaged face, the blue-green bruises on my upper lip and chin, the dark red wounds in the centre of either cheek, I realized that this face was mine alone now. I would never look exactly like my sister again. Brandon had taken my twin from me forever.

With this sobering thought circling my brain, I stepped into the bathtub and lowered myself into the steaming water. I was right—the tub was almost big enough to swim in. Closing my eyes, I let my thoughts run over everything that had happened yesterday and today, but it was as though I were watching a movie about someone else's life. Maybe in time I'd fully understand what had happened to me and what was left of me now that it was done, but tonight it seemed easier to let my mind go blank. Everything I had to worry about could wait until tomorrow. Tonight I just had to let it all go.

Just around the time the water was beginning to cool, Lucas knocked on the door. "I was thinking of taking a shower," he said.

There was a stand-up shower in the bathroom next to the tub. I noticed with appreciation that its walls were made entirely of glass. When the door to the bathroom didn't open, I realized he was waiting for me to say something.

"Go ahead," I answered casually, biting at my bottom lip.

Lucas came into the room in his boxers looking mildly bashful, which was amusing since he'd been sleeping next to me in just his boxers all week. But there was a difference between seeing Lucas in his boxers in a dim bedroom and seeing Lucas in his boxers in a bright bathroom, knowing he was about to take those boxers off. I tried not to drool at the thought.

He looked over at me and I didn't miss the way his eyes lingered on the water in the place where my breasts were submerged. The bubbles were mostly gone now, but the tub was so deep that I was still completely covered. I noticed him shake his head abruptly, as though trying to banish something from his thoughts. Then he grabbed a towel from the back of the door.

"All right, no peeking, Hero," he said as he placed his thumb on the elastic waistband of his boxers, giving me an admonishing look.

"As you wish," I said. With a smirk, I closed my eyes. It was only fair, since he'd let me get undressed in private. But it was also pretty ridiculous, given that the shower stall was *transparent*.

When I heard the shower turn on and the door click closed, I figured it was safe to risk a peek and tentatively opened one eye. Then I snapped both eyes wide open and stared, my body flushing so completely and so quickly I was surprised the water in the tub didn't start to boil.

Lucas was standing in the stall with his back to me, letting the water pour over his body. And what a body it was. True, I'd seen him naked before, for about a split-second that day in my apartment. I'd never before had the chance to really look at his body and admire the tight muscles, the broad shoulders, the tight, sculpted ass. I kept blinking, sure what I was seeing couldn't be real.

How does he do it? I wondered to myself. *He doesn't even go to the gym!*

Then he took the soap in his hand and started rubbing it over his torso, and suddenly the bathwater was sloshing onto the floor as I got to my feet in a rush.

To hell with letting myself recover. Lucas couldn't possibly be expected to wash that whole body all by himself, and the shower stall was more than big enough for two.

With a wicked grin I stepped out of the bathtub, nearly slipping on the waterlogged tiles, and pulled open the shower stall door.

Blinking in the spray, it took Lucas a second or two to take me in, standing utterly nude before him. Then I watched his eyes turn dark as they wandered down my body. I was surprised to find I didn't feel afraid or even nervous. I knew what I wanted, and he was right in front of me. As I smiled and stepped into the shower, Lucas dropped the soap. It clattered around our feet as I closed the distance between us and pressed my skin against his.

"I bet you thought this was my plan all along," he said as I ran my hands over his chest, and then farther down to that place I'd never touched.

"Nope," I replied, my lips against his cheek, "I'm pretty sure this idea is all mine. But it's a good one, don't you think?" My fingers closed over him, making him gasp and grip me against him.

"Oh God, yes," he said, and then his lips met mine.

His skin was gloriously slippery and after a few minutes under the spray mine was, too. I luxuriated in the feeling of my breasts slipping against his chest and his hands running through my hair and over my back, then dipping downward to cup my ass, pressing me into him in delightful ways. Snatching up the bar of soap, I started lathering his chest, but quickly lost the bar to Lucas.

"I don't think that bath got you clean enough," he teased as he lathered up his hands then let them slide over my breasts. I arched into him automatically, crushing his lips with mine, my tongue probing into his warm mouth suggestively. "I see we're in agreement," he said against my lips.

"Oh, I agree, I agree, I agree," I said as his sudsy hands made their way across my stomach and then farther down, causing me to let out a low moan of pleasure.

When I copied his gesture, letting both my hands slip along the length of him, he pressed me back against the wall, his every muscle tensed. He groaned loudly as I did the same thing again, more slowly this time. He began to lavish his appreciation on my neck in such a way that for a second I was literally seeing stars.

"Maybe we should take this to the bed," I gasped, and Lucas nodded mutely before picking me up right then and there and stepping out onto the tile.

I giggled. "But maybe we should rinse off all the soap first," I reminded him.

"Oh, right," he said with a laugh, setting me back on my feet and shaking his head. "I can't think straight when you're naked," he said into my ear as we let the water wash over us. "I think you'll have to be in charge of all major decisions for the rest of the night."

"Does that mean I get to decide where you put your hands?" I said, taking both of his palms and pressing them to my butt. "Or your mouth?"

I gently pressed down on his shoulders until he was crouching slightly in front of me, his lips grazing my nipple. It wasn't a position he could hold for long, so as soon as we were properly rinsed of soap we stepped out of the shower stall and he lifted me onto the counter, which placed me at just the right height. He continued nuzzling my hypersensitive skin for an eternity before finally taking my nipple in his mouth, and I actually screamed at the sudden release of tension. Slapping a hand over my mouth, I stared down at him, my cheeks burning with embarrassment, but the sound of my scream only seemed to invigorate him. His hands gripped my hips as he continued what he was doing, turning now to the other breast. Water dripped off of us both, creating a pool beneath us as I gripped his shoulders and leaned my head back, my body trembling under his touch.

Eventually I began to shiver, even in the steamy bathroom, so Lucas wrapped a towel around us both and we tripped out of the bathroom, aiming for the bed. I thought maybe we should dry off properly so we wouldn't make the bed all wet, but Lucas had other ideas. Flinging himself onto the mattress, he tugged me on top of him so that I was upright straddling his waist, my knees pressing into the mattress on either side of his hips. This wasn't something we'd ever tried before and I felt suddenly self-conscious with my breasts on full display while he was mostly covered up. I let my hair fall forward, covering my nipples, but he pushed it out of the way. I frowned at him and made an unhappy sound, folding my arms to hide myself instead.

"You're beautiful, Katie," he said, gently pulling my arms away and then brushing his thumbs over my breasts, sending flutters of feeling through my body. "Don't cover yourself, not in front of me."

"Beautiful…" I said, my hands moving to the wounds on my cheeks. It was so easy to forget about them. After all, I wasn't the one who had to see them, unless I was looking in a mirror. But Lucas would have to see my ruined face whenever he looked at me. Did he see me differently now? Was it just my body he wanted, or was it all of me? Was I a disappointment and he just didn't want to say so?

I found I couldn't remove my hands from my cheeks, but Lucas didn't make me. Hoisting himself up into a sitting position with me still straddling his lap, he placed delicate kisses over my fingers and my lips until my hands fell away of their own accord. He kept on kissing, one kiss for every single cut and bruise. "I don't even see it," he whispered. "Nothing that happens to your body could ever make you less beautiful to me. Nothing."

I wrapped my arms around this surprising and thoughtful and romantic and amazing, amazing boy and wondered how on earth I'd managed to find one as perfect as him, almost by accident.

"Maybe so, but there are still too many lights on," I said shyly, and he got up to turn off most of the lamps, giving me another chance to ogle his lovely body.

Still, my limbs protested as soon as he let me go, my arms aching for him. Only when our heads were side by side on the pillow and his arms were around me once again did I feel right. That's what it was. This felt right. It felt good. It had been so long since I'd felt right in my own body and mind that I almost didn't recognize the feeling.

His hand was running up and down my hip lazily, his eyes roaming over my face. Every few seconds he leaned forward and kissed my lips. I felt so relaxed I was worried I might fall asleep, and that was definitely not what I wanted. Not tonight.

"I want you, Lucas," I said, keeping my eyes on his.

"Mmmhmm," he said. "Me, too."

Yeah, he clearly wasn't getting what I meant.

"No," I said, easing myself against him so that we were hip to hip. "I mean I want you, right now." His sleepy eyes flew open and his hand stilled on my hip, his fingers digging into the fleshy skin. I leaned in and took his mouth with mine, claiming every inch of it, my tongue slipping against his as he pressed me back against the pillows, making a tortured sound deep in his throat.

"You're making it impossible to resist you," Lucas panted. "I mean, I'm in physical pain here. It's unkind, what you're doing."

"I beg to differ," I said. He was leaning on his side and I looped my leg over his hip, drawing even closer. Feeling exploded in my groin as I felt him brush against me there. "I think I'm being very kind."

"Katie," he said, his breath ragged as I let my mouth explore his chest, while my hands took on a mind of their own. "Kat...oh my God," he moaned, gritting his teeth as I let my lips creep lower and lower and lower. In the end, he had to pull me up and bind me in a mammoth hug, his arms pinning me still to get my attention. "Are you sure about this?" he said. "Do you really want your memories of our first time to be all mixed up with... I don't want you to regret this. Having sex just because you want to forget, it's not—"

Dislodging my arm, I reached up and pressed my hand to his lips.

"I want to do this now because you held my hand while I broke the news to my parents," I said. "Because you defended me to my sister. Because you moved in to my apartment to keep me safe. Because you poured me a bubble bath. Because you're more concerned about my first time than I am." His dimples popped and I ran my fingers over them. "I'm not trying to escape, or to lose myself, or to prove anything. I just want you, Lucas. I just love you so much that all the rest of it doesn't even register. Not when I'm with you."

I had to catch my breath after I was done. That was a lot of feelings and a lot of words for me. It had to be some kind of record. But it was worth it, because I'd never seen Lucas look so enamored of me before. When he kissed me then, softly at first, teasing open my lips with his tongue, and then gradually deeper and with such intensity, I thought to myself, *This is what it feels like to be loved completely.* I wanted to wrap myself up in that feeling. I wanted to wrap myself up in him, so I did.

When the moment came at last and he hovered above me, his chest against mine, I felt a shiver of fear, remembering how hard I had fought to avoid this kind of intimacy. I would never be more vulnerable than this, more naked, more open. And I could never take it back.

He brushed his lips against mine. "Are you ready?" he whispered, and I knew. I would never really be ready. Not totally. Not one hundred percent. There would always be a part of me that would want to push the world away, to hide myself, to guard against anything good, assuming it would turn bad. But I could still choose who I wanted to be, and I wanted to be with Lucas, even if he was bad news, out of my league, and one hundred percent trouble. I was ready to take this leap, as long as he was taking it with me.

"Yes," I said, and our eyes locked as he rocked into me, filling me, tipping me over into a new place I'd never been to before. A place where I could be seen without shaking. A place where I could be held without breaking. A place where we could put me back together.

25

Lucas pulled the car into the school parking lot and we both looked out at the playing field on the other side of the fence. There was a group of boys playing a game of touch football while other kids sat in clumps on the bleachers. Three girls sitting on a bench on the sidelines seemed particularly interested in the game, though they were pretending not to be. The one in the middle reminded me so much of Emily at that age that it made my heart ache.

"There he is," I said, pointing at a boy with light hair wearing a blue t-shirt.

"Are you sure about this?" Lucas said. He placed a hand on my arm and it was as though an electric current was running through my body. It had been like this since the moment I'd woken up in his arms, our bare skin glued together, our bodies ready and eager before we were even fully awake. We'd made love before breakfast and then again in the shower before we checked out of the hotel, and now every time he touched me it was like he was flicking a switch. I swear, if we hadn't been parked in the middle of a schoolyard, I would have taken him then and there.

I might have been embarrassed except that the silly grin on Lucas's face told me he was feeling the exact same way. He pulled me into a kiss that became hotter than I think it was intended to be, his fingers smoothing my skin at that place where my shirt met the waist of my jeans, my hands running through his hair.

"Because you don't have to," Lucas said as we broke apart, both of us a little short of breath.

"Don't have to what?" I said. My head was a little hazy, swimming in Lucas's scent, but then I shook it briskly and came back to my senses. "Oh, right. This. No, I'm sure. I want to." I put my hand on the door handle, readying to get out.

Lucas frowned, making me pause. I hated to see even the tiniest bit of distress on that gorgeous face. "It just seems like you're punishing yourself, Katie. And you know you don't have to do that."

Cupping his cheek with my palm, I gave him a reassuring look. "It's okay," I said. "I just want to talk to him. It's something I should have done a long time ago. Not because I owe him but just because...because I need to, I guess."

I looked back out at the field, feeling a little less sure myself now.

"Because you feel guilty?" Lucas asked, brushing a lock of hair behind my ear.

"No," I answered. "Because the two of us started it all, in a way, and I guess I want to end it with him, too."

Lucas didn't look the least bit satisfied with that answer, but he let me go anyway, staying in the car as I'd asked him to. It was my mother's car. She'd let us borrow it after our mad dash to the taxi stand through the hordes of reporters surrounding our hotel, only to find a similar contingent besieging my parents' house. Luckily, Lucas had surprisingly creative driving skills—considering he didn't have a car of his own—and we'd lost the couple of journalists who were tailing us pretty quickly. Looking back, I waved at him, marveling at how natural it felt to see Lucas behind the wheel of my mother's Volvo.

I stood by the fence watching the boys play, and waiting. Sure enough, after a few minutes he noticed me. He stood stock still among the grappling boys for a full minute before walking toward me. Even though it had been six years, I knew he would recognize me. I'd recognized him, hadn't I? But it was more than that. We were woven into each other's lives by what had happened in such a way that we would never forget each other for as long as we lived.

As he came closer and I could see his face more clearly, a feeling of intense nostalgia overcame me. There he was. Ricky Wesley. The boy who, for one afternoon when I was thirteen, I'd hated so much I'd wanted to kill him.

We looked at each other through the fence.

"What are you doing here?" he said. There was no hostility in his voice, and also little surprise. He seemed mainly just curious.

"I had to see you," I answered. He was staring intently at my face, which unnerved me until I realized he was looking at my scabs. "I guess you must have read in the papers about…" I gestured at my face.

"Are you all right?" he said. Something about the way he said it made me immensely sad. His voice was full of real concern, as though he'd been worrying about me, and I had to admit that until this day I'd never once worried about him. "I mean, I can't believe that bastard—"

"I'm fine," I said before he could get too worked up. "I got away." I didn't add anything more, but I knew what he was thinking, because I was thinking it too:

I got away from Tommy's killer a second time. I was big enough and strong enough to get away. I got away, and Tommy did not.

He looked back at his friends. The game had pretty much disintegrated and they were chatting up the three girls, wrestling with each other, and showing off. I looked him over while his head was turned. He was all grown up—fifteen years old now—and quite good-looking, with his blue eyes and blondish hair. He was almost a man. I noticed with a start that though he was slouching, he was taller than me. It was stupid, but in my mind he'd stayed forever nine years old, when in reality he'd left childhood behind years ago. Ricky wasn't Tommy. Ricky had had the chance to grow up.

"I heard you hit him with a tree trunk," he said, looking back at me.

I smiled. "More like a branch," I corrected.

"But you hit him," he persisted, his eyes zeroing in on mine.

"Yeah, Ricky, I hit him really hard," I said, and he nodded once, as though that was all he needed to hear.

He looked away again and I began to worry he might go before I said what I needed to. "I wanted to come see you because there's something... I just wanted to talk to you, and tell you... I never explained... Well, really, I lied, and I always thought—"

"Thought you should tell me that I was the reason Tommy died?" Ricky said. His tone was so matter-of-fact that it stopped me dead, and I could only stare at him. The right side of his face was streaked with mud and he scratched at it absently.

"W-what?" I stammered finally. "No, you aren't the reason! Brandon is the reason Tommy died. But how did you—?"

"I know," Ricky interrupted. "I know it was supposed to be me, but he got Tommy instead."

I gaped at him. He started walking slowly along the fence and I followed him.

"How do you know?" I said a little too loudly. I couldn't believe what I was hearing. How on earth could he know this?

Ricky looked around, but the other kids were clearing off the field. There was no one close enough to hear.

"I was in the woods, too, that day," he said. My mouth actually fell open. "I saw Brandon kill Tommy and I didn't save him. I let my little brother die."

We came to a gate in the fence and I walked through it. We sat down on a yellow bench at the side of the field and I wrapped my arms around my middle, taking deep breaths.

"You were *there*?" I said finally, my eyes blurring with tears, though I wasn't sure why. As I watched him nod, I had the sudden urge to throw my arms around him. A terrible kinship grew up between us in that moment, born of cowardice and fear and regret. I could see it all over his face. We both felt that we'd failed Tommy. We both blamed ourselves. For so long I'd thought I was all alone in my shame, when just three blocks away I'd had a partner in agony, and I'd never even known it.

Ricky licked his lips. "I wasn't over at Steven Lipinski's house. Steve wasn't even my friend. That's just what I said because I didn't want to be at the house with you and Tommy," he said. "I followed you guys to the woods. I saw him shove you down, and then..."

He clenched his jaw. He'd shown very little emotion until now, but I could tell he was trying desperately to hold back tears.

"He talked the whole time he did it. He kept going on about how much you hated Tommy, and describing the horrible things Tommy had done to you. But they were all things I'd done. That's how I knew."

"Ricky," I said, gripping him by the shoulder, "you have to know that wasn't what I wanted. I didn't want either of you to die. Brandon was—"

"A total psycho," he finished. "I know. I know you're not a killer, Katie. Whatever you said just got all twisted up in his head. I know that."

I nodded, amazed that a fifteen-year-old kid had put this together when I never could.

"So you saw everything?" I asked slowly. The horror of it was beyond imagining.

Ricky shook his head. "It was kind of dark, and there were all these bushes in the way. I didn't dare go any closer. But I heard it all." I clenched my eyes shut as Ricky's tears finally came. "I heard Tommy whimpering and screaming and crying until...until he stopped. I sat there listening and I did nothing."

I put my arm around him as he wept. I told him all the things Lucas had been telling me, that it wasn't his fault, he'd been just a scared little kid, that it hadn't been his job to stop a killer. I knew just how true those words were, and just how easy they were to dismiss. Ricky wiped at his face with his dirty hands and I saw that there was still some kid left in him, and I was glad. Maybe by the time he was my age he could put all this behind him. Maybe he could do what I couldn't when I was thirteen or fifteen or eighteen. Maybe he could forgive himself.

"You're not going to come clean, are you?" he said suddenly.

"Well, I already told my parents, and yours," I said.

My call to the Wesleys that morning had been much easier than I'd expected. At first I'd thought they hadn't understood what I was saying. As soon as I'd mentioned Tommy's name Mrs. Wesley had dropped the phone, and Mr. Wesley had just kept saying, "That's okay, dear," as if I were confessing to having accidentally shredded one of their bushes with the mower.

"They seemed surprisingly unconcerned," I said.

"Yeah," Ricky said knowingly. "They've been like that ever since Tommy died, like nothing can ever shock them again. I got a tattoo when I was twelve and they didn't care. I crashed their car. It's better now that I'm not living with them."

The Wesleys had moved to Alberta a few years back, but Mr. Wesley had explained to me on the phone that Ricky had insisted on staying behind. He lived with a friend's family during the school year. He'd also told me his son liked to play football during lunchtime.

"Why didn't you go with them?" I asked.

Ricky shrugged. "I told them I wanted to stay with my friends. But really, I couldn't stand to leave Tommy. He's buried here. I couldn't leave him alone." He kicked at a tuft of grass with his sneaker. "But what I mean is, I know you lied on the stand. You pretended you didn't know Brandon at all. And maybe you're thinking of telling the truth to the world now, but…I lied, too, you know? I lied to everyone for so long and I felt like crap about it, until one day I realized that the lie was good. The lie put the blame where it had to go—on Brandon.

The rest of it should just stay buried, with Tommy."

I sighed. I hadn't really thought about this part—telling the truth to anyone beyond my little circle. I also knew it wasn't entirely in my control. Brandon knew about my lie, too, and he could bring it all back up again if he wanted to, not that anyone had listened to him the first time.

A part of me did want to tell the world the truth. It seemed like the perfect way to finally free myself of the past. But another more sensible—and yes, fearful—part of me was afraid of the consequences that would follow. There was always the possibility that if I did tell Brandon might go free, and Ricky was right: the blame was his. He was the one who had to be punished, not Ricky, and not me.

"I don't know what I'm going to do," I said honestly, "but I'll leave your name out of it, Ricky. I'm not going to tell the media that your brother died because you were such a brat. I wouldn't do that to you."

He gave me a small half-smile. "I had a crush on you, you know?" he said. "That's why I was always such a jerk to you."

I snorted. "Yeah, right. You hated me."

"No," he replied. "I could see you liked Tommy better and I was jealous. You were so pretty and I wanted you to like me, but you just saw me as this little kid."

I blinked at him in surprise.

"You're even prettier now," he said shyly, and I had to look away so he wouldn't see me smile. I wasn't laughing at him. This was just the most surreal conversation I'd ever had. "Is that your boyfriend?" he said, pointing over at Lucas, who was leaning on the front of the car, sipping the coffee my dad had given him.

"Yeah, it is," I said. Looking at Lucas grounded me back in the moment. I felt the dark forest which had been surrounding both Ricky and me begin to recede.

"It figures," Ricky mumbled.

The school bell rang and we all turned to look at the drab high school building. I'd spent four years of my life wandering those halls, lost in a haze of pain and self-loathing. I was glad

I'd come to find Ricky, but I was even gladder I hadn't had to go inside the school to do it. I didn't want to step foot inside that building again, ever.

"I'm going to be late," Ricky said as he got to his feet.

He turned to me, licking his lips again, and I knew this would be the last time we would see each other. There was so much I wanted to say to him. I wanted to warn him not to believe his own lies. I wanted to tell him that I never hated him. I wanted to say goodbye and that I was sorry and that I didn't blame him. I wanted to tell him how glad I was he'd turned out to be such a nice guy. I wanted to thank him for not hating me.

But he was already walking away.

"Ricky," I called, and he turned back to look at me. "I hope you have a good life."

He smiled and the sun caught the gold in his hair. "You, too, Katie," he said.

As he ran across the field, I followed the fence back to the car and let Lucas engulf me in his arms. The tingles started up in me again, though they were a little muted now.

"How was it?" Lucas asked, and I could tell that even from a distance he'd seen Ricky crying.

"It was awful," I said, "but it was good. We both had things to say and now that we've said them...I don't know. I thought I needed to give him something, some truth that he deserved, but he already had it. I think he gave me more than I gave him."

"His forgiveness?" Lucas asked.

"No," I said. In the end I'd realized I didn't need Ricky's forgiveness. The only forgiveness I really needed was my own. "Just the truth, and goodbye."

"You were brave today," Lucas said. "I'm proud of you." He kissed me sweetly on the nose.

"You make me brave," I replied, kissing him back. "And now I think I just want to put my mind on something else."

Lucas opened the car door for me and I got in.

"I'm in full agreement with that," he said, putting both

hands on the wheel. "So, where to? My flight back isn't for a few hours."

"Oh, we need to drop the car off at my parents' house," I said. "I need to pick up a few things, too." I gave him a mischievous look.

"Pick up some things?" Lucas said. "I'm the one who's leaving."

I gave him my best shocked look. "You didn't think I was going to leave you to face the media hounds without me, did you?" I said as he eased the car out into traffic.

His dimples slowly emerged on his cheeks. "What about your subletter?" he asked.

The plan had been that Lucas would return to Kingston, pack up the few things I wanted for the summer and ship them to me, then hand the keys off to the subletter who would be living in my apartment for the next few months. He also had to pick up Turner.

"I called Mr. Subletter this morning to tell him the bad news. When he realized who I was, I think he was kind of relieved. Who wants to be mobbed by reporters every time you step out of your building?"

"Are you serious about this?" Lucas said, looking from me to the road. "What did your parents say? What about—"

Leaning over quickly, I pressed my fingers to his mouth to stifle his words. Then I moved in close, my lips just next to his ear. "Did you really think I was going to let you go after you made me scream in the shower this morning?" I breathed, feeling his body tense. "I plan on spending the summer making you scream, too, over and over and over…" I let my hand trail down the front of his shirt.

"Jesus, Katie!" Lucas cried as the car swerved and I giggled against his neck. "You're in for it now," he growled, making me shriek with laughter.

I knew I should let go and let him drive, but I couldn't. I didn't want to let go of Lucas ever, and I wasn't going to. We had the whole summer ahead of us, and who knew what else, and I planned on spending as much of it with him as I could.

Being with Lucas was so much better than anything else I'd ever tried. Better than painting. Better than chocolate. Better than ice cream. Actually, Lucas *was* my new ice cream, and I planned on enjoying every single lick.

EPILOGUE

Setting down my paintbrush, I take a step back to look at my painting. I've been working on it for two weeks in secret because I know that if Lucas catches wind of the fact that I'm painting again he won't be able to stop himself from sneaking a peek, and I don't want that. I frown and bite my lip as I gaze at the interplay of light and dark, the texture of the trees just visible in the background, and the figures, one on each end of the canvas. The snow was the hardest to paint by far, and Lucas's face the easiest. I'll never forget the look in his eyes as our lips parted that night, or the way the furiously falling snow obscured him from view almost immediately as I walked away from him.

In the painting I've captured a moment that never happened but should have. Lucas is watching me walk away, and instead of ignoring my heart and leaving him standing there I'm turning back, my head turned toward him as though I know he's still there on the other side of the wall of snow.

It's a good effort, considering it's the first thing I've painted in over three months. What I like best is that there's no sky, just a sea of white. Not a dark cloud in sight.

Leaning forward, I use my smallest brush to paint the title in the bottom-right corner. I'm calling it *Firsts*.

My phone rings as I'm walking to the kitchen to wash my hands, and I glance at the clock on the microwave.

Shit.

I answer the phone without checking to see who it is,

sticking it awkwardly between my shoulder and ear as I soap my hands.

"Where are you?" Mariella says. I can hear a hubbub of noise in the background. "Tell me you already left the house."

"Of course I did," I lie, jogging into my room to find a top that isn't paint-spattered. It's harder than it sounds. "I'm almost there. It didn't start yet, did it?"

"No, but it's about to," she answers. I wiggle out of my cut-off shorts and into a pink cotton dress I bought last week. I throw the shorts on top of Turner, who is splayed out on my bed. He meows plaintively. "They just came out, and damn your boy is looking *fine* today. Was he always this fine? Because my oh my—"

"Keep it in your pants," I interrupt. "Besides, I thought you swore off all white boys." I check my face in the mirror beside the front door, scratching at a patch of black paint on my chin before grabbing my bag and locking the door behind me.

"I'm an addict, what can I say?" Mariella answers, and I chuckle as I walk through the lobby. "Just hurry up, okay?"

"I'll see you in five minutes," I say, and hang up the phone just as I reach the front door of the building. I take a deep breath before I open the door and scan the street to the left and right, but there's no one there. I grin at the sun-dappled sidewalk as I half-walk, half-run down the block.

It's been a solid month since the flurry of renewed interest in me due to Brandon's plea of not guilty at his arraignment. For a while the reporters were camping out on the front stoop again, just like they were in April, and Lucas and I woke up every morning to the sound of Mariella's curses as she shoved her way to the sidewalk. Luckily they quickly lost interest in my boring existence of summer classes and trips to the recreation centre, even if my basketball coach boyfriend was a total dreamboat. My story wasn't particularly riveting. I wasn't suicidal or popping pills or on my way to the nuthouse. I was just a student trying to get on with her life. So, after a while, they seemed to decide as a group to leave me alone, though I'm still a little surprised not to find one or two of them tailing me everywhere I go.

It's a little strange, not having to look over my shoulder all the time, but I'm getting used to it.

As the park comes into view I feel my bag vibrating, letting me know I just got a text. I plunge my hand in, feeling around for my cell. It feels a little strange in my hand as I pick it up, but I don't think much of it as I turn the phone over and see who messaged me. I beam.

> **Em:** Ugh. Did I mention I hate flying?
> **Me:** Repeatedly.
> **Em:** I still don't get why you couldn't fly home just to fly back to Kingston with me.
> **Me:** Maybe because that's insane?
> **Em:** Sanity is overrated. Bring on the madness, I say!
> **Me:** Are we still on for tonight? Chinese?
> **Em:** I want to immerse myself in General Tso's chicken. Only breaded chicken can save this awful day of cross-country travel.
> **Me:** I'm glad you're back, Em.
> **Em:** Me, too.

I heave a sigh of both relief and happiness as I stare down at the screen, falling still for a second. Things between my sister and I have been a lot better lately. I don't think we'll ever be the same as we were, but I'm also always reminding myself that I don't want us to be. I'm completely honest with her now, and she is with me, too. At the beginning of the summer every conversation we had was just one long fight as she dug up every lie I'd ever told her and threw it in my face, and I struggled not to scream at her for being so oblivious to my pain. Eventually we started talking about everything I'd never told her, how I'd felt then and how I felt now and how she felt about everything. There were a lot of feelings flying around for a while there. Slowly she started trusting me again, and as August approached she took back her threat to transfer to another school and booked her flight to Kingston. When she told me I cried, because I knew then that I hadn't lost my sister after all.

Starting up the path through the trees, I turn the phone

over and my heart skips a beat as I see the sticky note on the back of it. I let my eyes run over the words written on it, then stuff it back in my bag and charge the rest of the way to the court at the centre of the park.

The grass slopes upward away from the cement and there are people sitting in clumps on all sides. I spot Mariella right away, sitting with Sally and Anita. I'm guessing Melissa is running late again, which is sort of gratifying. I can always count on Melissa to be later than me.

"Finally!" Mariella exclaims as I join them on the grass.

"I just got a text from Em," I announce as I dump my bag on the ground next to them. "Her plane just landed."

"Yay!" Anita says, clapping her hands, but Sally is too busy craning her neck to check out the group of boys sitting to our left.

"Look at that one," she says. Following her gaze, I notice the boys are all wearing bright red camp t-shirts, which means they're definitely too young for Sally. They look to be about fifteen, if that.

"Ew, Sally," I say. "Can you say jailbait?" She gives me a confused look.

"What?" she says. "There's no harm in looking, is there?" Anita and I exchange a glance as Sally and Mariella giggle together, pointing at a different guy sitting at the front of the crowd. As I watch Sally whisper something in Mariella's ear, I shake my head and wonder if introducing them was a bad idea. Sally is a handful all by herself. Add in Mariella and we've got trouble on our hands.

"Did you finish it?" Anita says in a low voice, and I grin, giving her a little nod. She squeezes my arm.

"I'm going to go say hi," I say as I get to my feet. "Keep them away from the underage boys." I jut my chin at the terrible twosome.

"I'm all over it," Anita says with a wink.

I pick my way through the crowd to the front where there are more campers sitting in rows. The day camp officially ended last week since school is about to start up again, but they're all wearing their camp t-shirts for the occasion. Since the campers were the ones playing sports all summer while the counsellors coached and taught, the kids made them promise to play one exposition game for them at the end of the summer, which is what today is all about. First up is basketball.

Gazing out at the court, I watch Lucas do a perfect layup, to the delight of the crowd. My stomach hitches just looking at him, not because he's so *fine*, as Mariella would say, although he is looking pretty hot in a form-fitting grey t-shirt and black basketball shorts, but because he looks so at ease. This will be his first time playing a real game since last fall, and I was worried about how he would react to being out on the court again, actually playing instead of watching his campers play, but I see now that all my worry was for nothing. He's in his element with the ball in his hands. As I watch him faking left, then right before shooting for the basket, it's impossible not to see that he's having a great time and making it all look so easy, which I'm sure is terrific fun for the other team.

Someone tugs on my dress and I turn around to find Ethan looking up at me, wearing his oversized bright yellow camp shirt. At his sides are two other boys about his age. I think the blond one's name is Davey.

"Do you think Lucas's team will win?" Ethan asks, and I see the other two staring up at me eagerly. I spent so much time at the rec centre over the summer that all the campers know I'm Lucas's girlfriend.

I crouch down beside them. "Well, I don't know," I say. "He's been missing his free throws lately."

Davey shakes his head scornfully, looking out at the game. Ethan's eyes are wide with worry. "Oh," he says, his shoulders slumping.

"But look at those other guys," I say, nodding at the court. "They're shrimps! Lucas is at least a head taller than every one of them, and you know he's got the moves."

Ethan nods his head enthusiastically at my change of tone.

I put my arm around him. "He's got it in the bag," I say and I can't help but laugh as I watch the three of them shoot back to their spots on the grass, reporting my assessment to the other kids like I'm some kind of oracle.

The game breaks up for what I've learned to identify in recent weeks as halftime, and I step through the last of the campers and linger by the edge of the court. Lucas spots me almost right away and flashes those unbelievable dimples. He wipes his face off with a towel then jogs over to me, and my breath catches, just a little, as I watch him. Even now I sometimes can't believe he's all mine.

"You're late," he says, his warm hands grasping me by the waist, contradicting his scolding tone.

"Nothing important ever happens in the first half anyway," I say flippantly, and Lucas chuckles. A whole summer of watching sports has taught me a thing or two, though I still usually spend most of the time sketching, except when Lucas has the ball in his hands. Because nothing is more mesmerizing than watching him play.

"Are you working for the other team?" he says. "Because that dress is pretty distracting." He likes this dress because it's sleeveless and shorter than any other dress I've ever owned. I like it because it makes him look at me the way he is right now.

"What, this old thing?" I say, and then I lean in to whisper in his ear. "If you win the game I'll let you take it off me."

I feel him exhale against my cheek, his fingers squeezing my hips, and I know we're both thinking the same thing. This game cannot end soon enough.

"You know I never would have gotten here without you," Lucas says, pressing his forehead to mine. "You really are my hero, Katie." Distantly, I hear his teammates calling him back to the game, but they seem very far away.

"Right back at ya," I reply as he pulls away, readying to dive back into the action.

"Hold on a sec," I say, calling him back. "I was told I'd be rewarded if I made it here by halftime." I hold up the sticky note and Lucas grins as he steps toward me again.

"Found that, did you?" he says, taking me in his arms. My body tingles as his chest presses against mine.

"So where is it?" I demand, looking up at him. "Am I getting the pony I always wanted?"

"Nope, just this," he says. His lips meet mine, sweeping me up into a kiss that's so much better than any present he could have bought me. I lean into it, taking his face in my hands.

"Ooooooohhh," the campers chorus before collapsing into giggles all around us. A high-pitched whistle directs my attention to Oleg, who waves at us from his spot in the crowd, sitting between Brit and Eric. As we wave back, I realize all eyes are on us. I am kissing Lucas Matthews, after all, former Golden Gaels MVP and all-around stud. Half the campers have raging crushes on him, and most of the female counsellors, as well. I know I should be blushing at the spectacle we've made of ourselves, but I can't really bring myself to care. Reaching up, I plant one more generous kiss on him before smiling into his lips.

"Knock 'em dead, or break a leg, or whatever the proper term would be," I say.

"Thanks," he says, kissing me again, and again, until all the counsellors are calling his name and he really has to go. "Watch closely, Hero," he says just before he lets me go, "because the next basket is for you." I smile like a lovesick idiot as he walks back to his team and the game starts up again.

When we were little, Emily and I liked to imagine what it would be like if we switched lives. It wouldn't have been very hard, we thought—after all, we were identical—but we always lost interest when she realized she didn't like the way my crayons stained her hands and I didn't want to wear any of her frilly clothes. After Tommy died, when I was in high school, I used to spend whole days dreaming of the lives I could have if I was someone else, someone who wasn't miserable all the time, someone who could stand to look at herself in the mirror, someone who'd never known Tommy or Brandon, or hurt, or lies.

Now, as I watch Lucas make a spectacular slam dunk—just for me—I realize how much things have changed. For the first time in what seems like forever I don't want to be someone else. I like the life I've painted for myself, full of rough edges and bright colours, dazzling sunshine and dark shadows, a life filled with pain, but also love. These days, when I look at myself in the mirror, I see a girl who's not quite in focus, a girl in transition, with wild hair and fingers spattered with paint, haunted eyes and a big smile. I'm looking forward to the day when that girl will be glued back together, when she'll stand tall, when she'll be whole again.

I think it's coming soon.

ACKNOWLEDGMENTS

First and always I'd like to thank my husband for putting up with my first draft moods and my final draft excitement without once telling me to *calm down*. I love you more than ice cream (even if you don't have dimples).

To Arijana, thanks for creating a cover I can proudly display to the world.

To Claire Grady-Smith and Veronica Monture, thanks for putting up with all my nagging questions about art school and helping me get the details all (pretty much) right.

To my beta readers Maia Sepp, Cathryn Baker, and Terri Corriveau, you guys are the awesome! Thanks for all your feedback, kind words, encouragement and for being willing to find the story behind the spelling mistakes.

To Google Street View, thanks for all the details.

To all the authors who inspire me, thanks for being brave enough to write and publish and fill me up with bravery, too.

To any reader who took a chance on my book, thank you from the bottom of my heart. I wish you lots of love (even if you don't think you deserve it), lots of desserts (even if you don't think you should eat them), and lots and lots of amazing books to fill your days and nights. Even if they're not my books. Though I hope they will be.

ABOUT THE AUTHOR

I'm Lola Rooney, romance writer and part-time hula-hooper.
For a long time I was a lonely girl who didn't believe in love.
Now I like to write about lonely girls and the boys who make
them believe in love. I enjoy cupcakes, dimples, hula hoops
(obviously), writing in my tree house and flirting with sexy men
(who have dimples). When I'm not yachting the Mediterranean
I call Montreal home.

Lola Rooney is the pen name of Shayna Krishnasamy.

Also by Lola Rooney:

Watch Me Fall Apart (Scars Run Deep 2)

Also by Shayna Krishnasamy:

Come When I Call You (The Violent and Dead 1)
We're All Mad Here (The Violent and Dead 2)
Macabre Montreal — Ghostly Tales, Ghastly Events, and Gruesome
True Stories
Home
The Sickroom
Regan

Visit me at:
Facebook: www.facebook.com/shaynakrishnasamyauthor
Goodreads: www.goodreads.com/shaynakrish

If you enjoyed reading this book, I'd be so grateful if you
would Like it, review it on the site where you purchased it, or
recommend it to a friend.